Killing Time: The Story of Projekt Töten Zeit

A Novel

Michael Patrick O'Hara

KÖNIG PRESS
North Carolina, USA

DEDICATION

Unlike this fictional account, there are no do-overs, no chances to go back and fix the mistakes of the past. This story is for all those family and friends who accompany us on our brief journey through time. They help us make the most of that one chance we get at what becomes our life's story.

CONTENTS

ACKNOWLEDGMENTS

It was those early television pioneers of Science Fiction in the 50's and 60's that inspired my writing. I was fascinated by the vision and creativity that they brought to life and into our homes each week. They include Rod Serling of The Twilight Zone, Joseph Stefano and Leslie Stevens of The Outer Limits, and Gene Roddenberry of Star Trek. Those pioneers, along with the imaginative writings of Arthur C. Clarke, Isaac Asimov, and Ray Bradbury, created new worlds for us to explore. Not to be forgotten, the early dreamers of Science Fiction like Jules Verne and H.G. Wells, they opened the door, and the minds of so many others to think and dream of what might lie in the strange realm of our imagination.

A special acknowledgement to the creators and producers of the classic sci-fi movie "The Final Countdown", my all-time favorite, and to Herman Wouk, author of "The Winds of War" and "War and Remembrance". Both works provided inspiration for this story.

PREFACE TO THE STORY

The novel, "*Killing Time: The Story of Projekt Töten Zeit*" and the accompanying short story, "*The Assassination of Franklin Delano Roosevelt*" are fictional works created in the imagination of the author. The main characters, including Jake Kelly, Beth Milano, the Kelly family, the Milano family, Thomas "Mac" McCarthy, Jennifer Davis (and aliases), Charlie Carter, Viktor Polechenko, Dr. Josef Scheel, and Rick Wilson are all fictional constructs of the author's imagination, and any resemblance to persons living or deceased is purely coincidental.

This "alternate history" does contain real-life figures, locations, and some actual events from history interspersed with fictional characters and events. The dialogue, actions, and portrayal of these historical figures are not in any way intended to represent their true words, beliefs, and deeds. It is necessary in this fictional, "reimagined history", to merge what occurred with an inspired, albeit, a fictional retelling of events in history.

PROLOGUE

The fiercest and most violent creature the earth has ever produced is not the lion or the tiger, not the shark or the crocodile, but man. Man is an animal who has learned to tame, but not eliminate that which evolution has given him. He is an instinctual predator who preys on the weak to fulfill his hunger and strives to outsmart the strong with his deception and cunning.

Throughout time, mankind could not resist the lure of the weapons of war. A man would turn against his brother if a place at the throne of domination could be secured. As man evolved, so did his craft of waging war. He has honed his ingenuity and skill to create more and more frightening tools of the trade. For as long as man will walk the earth, he will always seek a way to tilt the balance of power over his fellow members of the human race.

Peace is a hollow term, an unnatural concept for such a primitive creature. However, man has a natural enemy, one more powerful and one that until now could not be tamed. That enemy is time. Man barters his soul for a brief existence in time and space. In exchange, he is granted a free reign to live in peace or kill on the fields of war. Ultimately, time is the God that gives and takes at will and commands the limits of man's reign.

This is the story of one such heinous weapon born from the imagination of man and used by those who would seek to use time to wage war under the auspices of peace at any price.

As the path of an eclipse casts a shadow on the continents is crosses, so too did time and destiny intersect on my life and brought the forces of darkness where once there was light.

In life, a minor delay of minutes at a stoplight has the power to cascade and eternally shape the course our life follows. The effects are sometimes noticeable, but others imperceptible, or so we think. Do we know or understand the events that have transpired to get the world to right here, right now? Turning back the clock not by minutes, but by hours, years, and decades can reshape a destiny we thought had already been written. Now, let me tell you that story.

Summer was coming to coastal Maine. I watched as the sun rose over the vast distance of ocean and space. I have seen it many times before and still watch it with awe. There are far more sunsets behind me then there are sunrises ahead. While this late spring day was unusually warm, the cold dark ocean would not let go. The morning breeze had a chill that ran through me. I shivered. Time had caught up with me as I neared the finish line of my life. My youth had long faded.

As the years went by, I sensed the fragility that we humans all encounter. It is that period in our lives when the march of time stages a comeback and the vitality we enjoyed in our younger years can no longer hold its ground. We begin to slowly lose the battle we have fought so hard and for so long.

On this day, different from others, I sense the end is closing in on me. The ocean, the dark shadowy clouds at sunrise, and the cold air reaching into my bones as if to grasp me away. I took it as a sign that fate was dealing me its last hand. It is only now, in these waning days, that I have finally decided to take the time to put thoughts to paper and recall my life's experiences.

I have stood the test of time, and now my words must do the same. I am doing what I have always done, standing my ground like the rocks below me in the sand, beaten relentlessly by the waves, but still weathering the storm.

In many ways, it seems like just yesterday this long journey began but has lasted a lifetime. It was about doing what was right for a higher cause, a greater purpose where the wants and desires of one are not as important as the needs of the many. In my moments of reflection, I cannot resolve in my mind if what I have done was right, or if I should have made other choices along the way. All of that now is in the past. There can be no second-guessing, what is done is done. It is, as they say, history. All of that now is far too many sacrifices ago to remember or taunt myself with the "what ifs" or "what could have been" thoughts. I hope they will say of me when I depart this world that he left it a better place than he found it. I hope that would be true.

I am, or should I say that I was, Jake Kelly, a captain in the United States Air Force, and today is May 20th of the year 2009. My long life began not on a December day in 1986 when I first came into this world but, in the month of November seven years from now. No, you are not mistaken. I am writing about events that will happen and did happen. It is a paradox. It was on a day in November 2016 that a meeting took place in a situation room deep inside the Pentagon. Unbeknownst to me, it was a meeting that would change my life and the lives of so many others. In attendance was the who's who of the American defense and intelligence community. The often-heated discussion, I would later come to learn, was about a "black project," a title reserved for "off the books" classified initiatives with a high emphasis on national security.

Black projects ranged from the ridiculous to the hypothetical to the potential game changers. When money is not an issue, then even the most far-fetched idea may find an interested agency willing to write a check. This particular black project had been in progress for over forty years and had the backing of every President since Lyndon Johnson. Many a President had gone to his grave with the secret of this effort. I wasn't there in the room at the time history was being made. Maybe it was more appropriate to say that history was being re-made or rewritten.

Oblivious to those events, I was going about my routine business in the Air Force. I was en route to Andrews Air Force Base in Maryland, just outside of Washington. Soon, though, I would get all the information I would ever need to know about what had transpired that day.

As I sit here getting ready to the write the next chapter, I can't help but wonder if this story will ever be told. There are forces that would stop at nothing to silence these words.

The events of what I am about to say are classified and will likely remain so for all eternity, and of that I am sure. I write partly as therapy for myself, and mainly because it helps me bring closure to the events of my life that I've kept secret for so long. Now, as the sun rises higher and chases away the dark clouds, there is a quick lift in my melancholy mood. Still, I can't help but recognize that the twilight of my life has arrived. Time, the ultimate victor and ruler of man, is ready to take one more prisoner.

Throughout my life, I've studied with great interest the events of World War II. I had hoped to teach strategy at one of the military's war colleges after my stint as a pilot was complete. Irish ancestry on my father's side and German on my mother's. Those grandparents had emigrated from Germany after the war in 1947. My grandfather served in the Wehrmacht, the German Army. As a soldier, he saw action on the Eastern Front and was one of the few to have survived the brutal conditions and several brushes with death. Cheating death provided him with a different future and the opportunity to start a new life in America.

While the war did not take his life on the battlefield, it still haunted him years later. A piece of shrapnel that had lodged in his leg formed a clot that eventually broke loose and made its way to his heart. He was a casualty of war, like the millions who died in that conflict fighting for causes they believed in on each side. Death from war had found him twenty years after the last shot was fired. I had never met him, but I would have liked to hear his stories. He was a young man, handed a rifle, and sent to fight where the odds were against him succeeding. I would have listened with great interest and intense fascination to his eyewitness account. I wanted to know what it what like to be there and what was going through his mind as faced death and fought for his country. I can still feel the blood of my ancestors with that Irish temperament and German ingenuity coursing through my veins. That mix has caused an internal conflict within me at times, but overall, the legacy of my ancestors is one that has served me well; honor, integrity, hard work, loyalty, and sacrifice.

I grew up exposed to a mostly German and broken English environment. My mother was born here in America, but my grandmother never entirely mastered the language. That was the beginning of my lessons in speaking German. Through high school and college, I continued to perfect my command of the language. As a result, I speak and read fluent German as well as any native. During my time stationed in Germany, I had no problem passing as a local and was often mistaken for one. To this day, I still have distant relatives in the town of Barssel, near the Dutch border, where my great-grandfather was a Burgermeister. It has never escaped my fascination how such a small country nearly dominated the world through determination and ingenuity. From their pioneering work with submarines, the use of rocketry and jet aircraft, and the work to build nuclear capabilities, this small country used innovation to overcome an enormous disadvantage in size and numbers. They almost pulled it off. What was it about these people? Was it will? Was it the circumstances of World War I that forced them to use their intelligence? It could be that it was just a matter of survival to find new ways to do things or perish at the hands of their foes.

Ironically, my interests and curiosity about the past and that meeting in the Pentagon have a lot in common. On that day, the United States Military achieved an enormous capability, one that would change the world, change history, and change my life forever, but first, a little background.

Back in the early 1940s, Adolf Hitler realized his good fortune was not to last. Several apparently strategic military blunders worked in his favor, and several others did not. Hitler was a firm believer in the occult, and the Nazi philosophy had its roots in mythology and the supernatural. The symbol of the Nazi party, the swastika, was widely used by Far Eastern religions long before it became a symbol of hatred and destruction. Adolf Hitler and Henrich Himmler were the architects of this philosophy, and in turn, dictated the course of a nation based on how its fate could be tied to the stars and to the ancient Aryan mythology of a German master race. However, he also believed that sheer military might and the engineering prowess of the German people was his greatest asset.

Throughout the war, Germany never ceased to undertake projects that were advanced and out of the mainstream thinking. If it is, as they say, "necessity is the mother of invention," then out of necessity for survival, the Germans had to find an advantage any way they could. They were bold in their thinking and put their ideas into action. Getting the most attention at the time was the effort to build a "super bomb," what we call today the atomic bomb. The high-ranking members of the Third Reich thought Germany's fate lay in developing and using this super bomb to wipe entire countries off the map. Hitler and Himmler were unconvinced, and the mystical mythology they largely fabricated had become a real and powerful force driving Nazi strategies. In turn, they opted for what seemed to be less practical and increasingly "magical" options.

It was Hitler who came upon an idea that every military commander dreamed they would have at their disposal. The answer he arrived at to winning the war was as simple as having the ability to fix all the mistakes of the past. Success would come from knowing all the enemy's moves before the enemy positioned a single tank or unit. How? That would be the question. Taking scarce financial and physical resources from other critical war projects, he immediately put the best engineers and physicists to work on finding a way to send a message back in time. Even a delusional Hitler thought that was too unrealistic and unachievable to have a person traverse time. If he could send a signal or message that would tell him what decisions to make and avoid the ones that would cost Germany defeat, he could dominate the world.

Hitler had figured that if a lowly Italian, Guglielmo Marconi, figured out how to send wireless messages through the air based on the work of the German scientist Heinrich Hertz, then surely Germany's best and brightest could leverage Marconi's work. They would need to refine it and send the message farther back through time. So convinced he was that it would work, he began looking for signs in everything that was going on around him and started second-guessing events in the past. Had it already worked? Was this the past? Were there messages or signals he had missed. His increasing addiction to medication and deteriorating mental state continued to feed his paranoia. It became an obsession, and his military staff could only watch their Führer's continued descent into madness. To Hitler, it all seemed feasible and realistic given what had already been accomplished. If he succeeded, then instantly, time would be altered, and his rule would extend over half the world. The "Thousand-Year Reich" would fulfill its destiny. The project received the codename: "Operation Killing Time" or in German, "Projekt Töten Zeit."

Convinced that this was the way to winning the war, he diverted more and more financial, human, and technical resources to the project. Fourteen months after the project began, late in the summer of 1943, the war was taking a turn for the worse. Reports to Hitler on the project were not optimistic. The team had several working theories and formulas on how such a feat would be accomplished. Their most significant obstacle was that they were operating in an era of limited technical means, and that left them far from ready to build any real capability. Working at a fast pace, they had made little progress in finding out if messaging back in time was even a possibility, but they had yet to rule it out either. Hitler pressed on. As the war outlook began to look more desperate, it became apparent this was Germany's only hope.

With the fall of Berlin in April 1945, the war was over. No mysticism or military ingenuity was able to save Germany. On April 30th, Adolf Hitler committed suicide in his fortified Führer bunker below the Chancellery to the sounds of Russian artillery shelling the city above. In his last moments, he knew that it was only a matter of hours before Stalin's troops would find him. The defense of Berlin was in the hands of untrained young boys and old men. They were the last of Germany's once mighty army. Recruited to defend the city, they fought bravely to the end. Their fierce loyalty had bought Hitler only days to continue to hope for a miracle. Before his death, he ordered the destruction of all of Germany, including all secret and sensitive projects and military installations. This last order was to be an extension of his "scorched earth" policy. He wanted Germany to be in ruins rather than be in enemy hands. He exclaimed, "that if German's didn't have the will to fulfill his prophecy and win the war, then they didn't deserve to live." The decimated Wehrmacht did not follow Hitler's orders. The German army had nothing left to give, including the will to destroy what little remained of their once proud Fatherland.

After hundreds of thousands of shots exchanged during the war and the death of tens of millions, it was a single shot finding its mark and the death of a lone man, that brought the war to an end. The Fuhrer was dead. Hitler's remains, along with his newlywed wife Eva Braun's body, were carried by his remaining loyal staff to a garden outside the Chancellery building. There would be no time for a long goodbye to their fallen leader. The thick smoke from a city in ruins hung like dense fog but provided little cover. In the air, the endless sounds of nearby rifle fire and the rumbling of the ground from Russian tanks rolling through the streets of Berlin served notice that the enemy was approaching the front door of the Chancellery. Following his wishes, the bodies of Hitler and Braun were placed in a hastily dug shallow grave, doused with gasoline, and set ablaze. Hitler feared that his body would be put on public exhibit by Stalin and hung in the streets for all to see. He denied Stalin his wish. As the body burned, and with their work done, the staff scattered for shelter to wait out the remaining days of the war.

In May of '45, with victory in Europe achieved, the Americans and Russians began the process of taking and dividing the human and intellectual capital of the Third Reich, as well as other military documents and evidence. The race was on to secure the papers and the minds of Germany's top scientists. In one such raid, the Americans and the Russians stumbled upon the works of "Operation Killing Time" at the German fortification known as "Mittelwerk." The site was located near a small town named Nordhausen in central Germany. Nordhausen was the heavily fortified site carved out of a mountain where the V-2 manufacturing facility was housed to protect it from Allied bombing. In its cavernous halls, the works of Projekt Töten Zeit would lie. The significance of the work initially was dismissed as Nazi propaganda. The Americans were ready to abandon the work to the Russians, placing little value on it. Eventually, the secrets of the facility were indiscriminately split between the two countries. At the last minute, the Americans, while moving as much V-2 technology as they could, also collected information about the remaining "Wunder Weapons" underway in the complex. In the end, there was too much to logistically move in such a short period of time. Tons of equipment and hardware, box after box of diagrams, papers, plans, and other artifacts were moved to safety. What remained was left to the Russians.

The end of the war came none too quickly for Mittelwerk, for in this fortification lay much of the horror, and the genius, of Germany. The complex used slave labor to build its weapons of war. The weak and the sick were discarded like trash in a crematorium that sat atop a hill overlooking the worker's barracks. Lining the tunnels inside the mountain were explosives designed to destroy the entire complex, including the people who worked inside. It was part of an effort to keep from the world's eyes the vast store of technology that Germany had achieved and the atrocities it committed. Had the explosives been successfully detonated, the mountain would have collapsed on itself, hiding its secrets forever, but as the war advanced quickly, the site was abandoned and left intact.

The Americans first discovered the Dora-Mittelbau labor camp and then quickly descended upon the Mittelwerk complex. In one of the most extensive logistical efforts of the war, American forces mobilized to move as much material as they could from the complex. They were hampered by railroads that were out of commission and Russian troops that would lay claim to Nordhausen as part of a postwar settlement. Time was of the essence, and as days passed, it became more and more apparent that some of the secrets of Nordhausen would undoubtedly fall into the hands of our then ally and soon to be future adversary.

In the files and vaults of the complex lay the collected works from the years of research of project Töten Zeit—most of it useless brainstorming of ideas and dead-end theories. From all accounts, it appeared that about forty-percent of the Töten Zeit work eventually fell into the hands of the Americans, and the remaining sixty-percent went to the Russians. No one was sure what the total body of work looked like to know for certain who had the advantage. It encompassed years and years of work from perhaps a hundred or more of the Third Reich's top physicists and engineers. Not known at the time was the fact that even though the Americans received less of the work, what they did get contained the heart of the most promising theories under consideration at the time. Germany, it seemed, may have been on to something after all, and lacked only the sophisticated technology of today to make a far-fetched idea a reality.

One of the documents captured was incomplete. It was missing a critical volume. Nonetheless, it proved immensely valuable. It was the author of the material who would eventually lead an American team on a chase through history. The project, as it would turn out, was not the result of a Nazi propaganda campaign to shake the Allies, but the work of Germany's brightest scientists striving to achieve the unthinkable. The ability to send a message back through time was a military weapon that would change the world. Once the documents were inventoried after the war, the works of Project Killing Time sat in archives for more than twenty years. Eventually, they were found in the early sixties, when German scientists who were at Nordhausen and were now working on the Apollo lunar project mentioned it. In a casual discussion with high-ranking military officials, they asked whatever became of the project. While not directly involved in the project, they knew of the work. They told the American command that while the Mittelwerk complex was secret to the world, inside its walls, there were few secrets among engineers and scientists. That prompted an investigation into the work and the feasibility of the project.

The works were located and reviewed. It seemed impractical, but a project was authorized in an attempt to fill the missing gaps in the documentation. Their goal was to see if, indeed, what began as a desperate measure to save a country from destruction could provide an advantage to an already potent nation, America. There was a fear that those missing gaps lay in the hands of the Russians, and that they may have already started on their project. No effort could be more critical to a nation, or more dangerous, than the ability to continually change itself or its enemies by altering the course of history. After 40 years of work, more than one hundred billion dollars buried in black project budgets, millions of man-hours, and thousands of tests, "Project Killing Time" was reported to the President as operational. It had become the newest weapon in the U.S. arsenal.

The meeting at the Pentagon on that cold November day was to determine how and when this "weapon" would be used. They wanted to know how such a power could be used to go back and "right" the all the "wrongs" in history. The biggest difference between the original "Töten Zeit" and the new "Killing Time" project was that sending a message was no longer the objective. Sending an object or human back was now feasible, and we stood ready to use it to change history and change the world. In the wrongs hands, it was as dangerous a weapon that has ever existed. Enabling this technology for the betterment of society was not likely how it would be used. Instead, the potential to send back advanced aircraft, weapons, bombs, technical knowledge, and even a history book could give the weak power to level the playing field.

Here is where my story first begins. During that November meeting, it was decided that the first "use" or "test" of this new capability with humans would be to send two American military personnel back in time to just before the fall of Germany in 1945. The objective would be to secure a critical missing component of the "Killing Time" project documentation, leave any remaining work or prototypes that weren't retrievable intact to preserve history, and ensure delivery of the retrieved document to the U.S. Allied Command in England.

Securing the document meant that the Russians would never have the necessary information or detailed knowledge about the project to leapfrog the United States; there would be no head start. If the Russians were to develop such a capability, they would have to do it on their own. No one knew how far the Russians were or if they ever started work on a project of their own, or if it had languished in obscurity in a World War II archive, still waiting to be re-discovered. It didn't matter. All that mattered was that we had it, and this was the first objective.

There were numerous debates and discussions about how the capability would be used, or if it should ever be used. Only after this one crucial mission, given all the risks and ramifications of altering time, should it become just a weapon of last resort. Tampering with history and the downstream implications of even the most minor, seemingly innocent events seemed fraught with risks. From the moment someone from today arrived in the past, history in the present would already be altered and changed. No one knew what would happen. It could have made the past better or the future worse.

My role and involvement in the most significant peacetime project the United States had ever undertaken are documented in these notes. I decided to keep a mental journal of my thoughts and experiences throughout the project. I could not keep a written log, but sensing a pivotal point in history, I etched into my memory the events of what transpired from my point of view. At this point, I was one of only two people on the planet whose destiny did not lay in the future, but whose future would lay in the past. I am confident that they must have screened every possible candidate in the armed forces and in civilian life. Someone had to be picked, and it was just my lucky number. I had several factors weighing in my favor: youth, experience, fluency in German, being a top student, and having no immediate surviving family members. To put it bluntly, I wouldn't be missed should something go wrong. That last one may have been the most essential qualification.

As I would learn, the only drawback to Operation Killing Time was that it was a one-way ticket. The two people selected would take the trip of a lifetime, but there was no way ever to return. Through all the work and research over the past few decades, it was determined that sending a person or person back in time would be the reality, and returning them would always remain the work not of scientists, but of science fiction writers.

NEW ORDERS

I just turned twenty-nine at the time my new orders had arrived, out of the academy five years, top of my graduating class at Colorado Springs. From there it was off to Randolph Air Force Base in Texas for early flight training, again finished at the top, then off to Nellis Air Force Base in Nevada for F-15 training. I had been training to be a fighter pilot all of my life. I had started young, taking flying lessons at 14 and becoming a private pilot at 15. Day after day, night after night, I flew more combat missions on my computer than most real pilots probably flew in their career. It is what I always wanted to do, and I turned out to be pretty good at it. I spent a few years in Europe based in Ramstein, Germany and did some tours at Eglin Air Force Base in Florida and the Air War College at Maxwell Air Force Base in Montgomery, Alabama.

Now, I had a sudden change in orders. I received word to report to Andrews Air Force Base in Maryland. As far as I knew, my assignment to report to the Test Pilot Program at Edwards was still valid. My trip would take a slight detour through Washington, as I was to report to Andrews and await further instruction from the base commander. The request was a bit unusual and had a "cloak and dagger" feel to it. It had come from a unit that wasn't listed as being stationed at Andrews or the Pentagon, and that only served to heighten my curiosity.

One fact, though, was inescapable. After five years away, the detour afforded me an opportunity to be back at home. I had no relatives here, but it was the one area where I had put down the most roots. Being here meant a lot to me, places of my childhood and friends lost long ago. One of those lost friends was very important to me. A first love, her name was Beth, and this was my chance to reconnect and fix my own mistakes of the past. Beth and I were a childhood item, as childhood items go. Call it a puppy love that never grew. She was the typical girl next door; only instead of being next door, she lived a few blocks away. But the distance was never measured in the miles between us; we were always close.

There was an eerie sixth sense connection between us. During that brief moment in our lives where our paths crossed, we did everything together. We said we were in love, but neither of us really knew what it meant back then. So young, we thought it would go on forever. We thought we would be married and live happily ever after, but every young boy believes that about his first childhood sweetheart. But soon, flying caught my eye and I started dreaming of what I wanted to be when I grew up. It took more and more of my time, and Beth took less. Her parents had decided to move to another nearby town about twenty-five miles away, but at that age, might as well have been a thousand miles. With my eyes set on a career in the military, I decided this was a good breaking point. I let her go.

It wasn't long after that I realized how much she had meant to me. I kept tabs on her over the years, running into her once or twice and calling her a few times. After a while, the simmering embers of love had started to go cold. I thought too much time had passed between us. As is usually the case, as people grow up, they often grow apart. I knew I had changed, and I knew she must have too. I hadn't found anyone else, but I wasn't actively looking. School and flying had kept me pretty busy over the years. In my heart, I knew she was irreplaceable.

Being stationed on foreign soil for the last five years made the time away pass by quickly. It was so easy to lose touch with friends and even family as days run and years run together. It often became hard to distinguish weeks from months and months from years. I had little need to track time on a calendar. It all went by so very fast.

Here, back in my homeland after so long, I thought there was a slim chance she'd be interested in seeing me again. For all I knew, she could be married and have kids. I would be happy if she found a good life. She was a little younger than I was, but not by much. In the pedestal I had put her on, she was a catch. It was highly likely that she would be married with kids. Even so, I wanted to find her, if nothing else to tell her I never forgot her and how over the years, and I thought about her all the time.

When you are active duty in the military, someone you know is always getting new orders. It was a way of life, and now it was my turn. A change was in store. My application to the Air Force Test Pilot program was accepted. Being a test pilot was my first step towards a long-time goal of landing in the space program, either via a direct assignment or as a civilian. The transfer to Edwards would be my last tour of duty.

When I received my orders, I caught a Space-A flight on a Military Airlift Command C-130 back to Seymour Johnson Air Force Base in Eastern North

Carolina. Seymour Johnson was as close as I could get hopping a free ride across the Atlantic, but that would be okay for me. Being single and living abroad for months and sometimes years at a time, home came to be defined as wherever your feet are planted at any given moment. There is no need to accumulate personal items. I had learned that the story of your life could often fit into a backpack. For me, it was the few things I had with me: clothing, photos, my favorite books and movies, and my laptop. The remaining stuff, a few small pieces of furniture and other souvenirs from my time away, were being shipped to Edwards. It would be weeks before they would make their way to me. If they made it at all.

As I stepped off the transport onto the tarmac, I realized I had left behind another temporary home, and I was now back here in the United States, for good, I hoped. I don't know why, but I reached down and touched the ground. Slowly, I dragged my fingers across the asphalt. I wanted to know I was back and back safely. So many others could not do the same. Life in Europe as a pilot had a special meaning to me. I stood on the ground that my grandfather fought to protect as a member of a service we fought against; I flew in the skies from where many brave pilots fell back to earth. It was a place where the two major wars of our lifetime were fought and where the sacrifices of many were buried in that hallowed ground. I will miss being there and being a part of the history of that region. I felt a strange affinity to that land and an era that long since passed.

The winds of change had blown into my life, and perhaps they were sending me a signal that it was time to settle down. My next assignment wasn't the type that was conducive to a stable family life. It was dangerous and risky, and no wife or child should have to know that on any given day, if their spouse or parent walks out the door to work, that it could be their last. Such is life in the military. There are no guarantees. Every day a man or woman puts on their uniform of the armed forces, they also put their life on the line. Settling down could still be too far in the distance for me to see.

Coming back stateside and traveling light left me without the basic necessities. I didn't have a car here. I had sold mine years ago before I left. My orders for Andrews, while a mystery, were hopefully only a slight detour on the way out to Edwards. I could have quickly hopped a flight up to Washington from here at the base. Renting a car and slowing things down a bit was in order. I wanted to take my time and enjoy the beauty of America. I had been away from for so long.

At first, I thought about driving up the coast and spending a few days at the beach in Ocean City. After some thought, I decided it was probably better to just get to the base and get settled. There would be time to do all the things I had been missing somewhere down the road. I opted to take the scenic route up through Virginia into Maryland. On this late fall day, the air was crisp, and the leaves were well past their peak, but still falling and dotting the landscape with various hues of red, yellow, and green. Just after crossing the state line in Maryland, I drove through the town of Lexington Park, a place at the heart of a bygone era. The area was becoming a victim of ever-increasing suburban sprawl. Marinas and large houses were dominating the landscape.

Positioned right where the Patuxent River meets the Chesapeake Bay, the location of the town holds the Navy's Test Pilot School. The Patuxent Naval Air Station is a pilot and sailor's dream. Between flying and sailing, the least amount of time they spend is on land. This town seemed on the fringes of life itself—a place frozen in time and a throwback to when the world was different. I could almost visualize what it must have been like over sixty years ago when the base was in its heyday. I can feel the spirit of all those who passed through here. There is a strange romanticism about the place and the time to which it belonged. Now it seemed the world had discovered it, but no urban sprawl could take the charm and mystique from it.

The base itself is old and has survived many attempts to close it. Like most military installations, it stands as part memorial to the past and part sentinel standing guard on the future. Over the years, it has been upgraded and refurbished in places, but the core infrastructure of the base is still from the early forties—a result of the rise in America's military might during World War II. I was thinking not just about the impressive list of pilots who trained and tested high-performance aircraft here, but of all the men and women who came through here on the way to fates unknown. Some went on to the space program, like Alan Shepard, John Glenn, and Jim Lovell, others to higher commands in the Navy, some to success in the business world, and a few became elected officials. It was the path I was hoping to take, with the only difference that I would go through the Air Force's Academy and Test Pilot Program. Those two accomplishments on your resume were like getting another hole punched on the golden ticket of your career. It could only mean better things ahead.

But even on this chilly day, it couldn't have looked more inviting. As I passed by, I thought about the men and women stationed there, doing what I hoped to be doing out in the California desert. I drove on watching that part of history fade in my rear view mirror as I edged closer and closer to Andrews. I was ready to put my feet on the ground for a short while. My new life back in the U.S. offered me so many opportunities, and after five years of my world being at military bases in foreign lands, I was ready for a new chapter. To add to that, for the next few days I was home—well, at least in my home state.

How quickly the hours passed since I left Seymour Johnson. As I crossed the Woodrow Wilson Bridge, I could see our nation's capital in the distance just to the west. I wasn't on the Capital Beltway in Maryland very long before I spotted a massive water tower with the words "AIR FORCE" and the Air Force logo emblazoned the side of the tank. It was an unmistakable landmark, and I was here. Since Andrews is the home of Air Force One, the airfield itself is well hidden from public view. I had been here numerous times in my youth to watch the Air Show held each year on Armed Forces Day in mid-May. Maryland looked different to me now. More crowded and more congested, I could see what were once sleepy towns had now become bustling hubs. How quickly things change when you are gone. Long ago when I would make the trip here to watch the Thunderbirds or Blue Angels perform, I had dreamed that my return here might be as a part of that show, and although it wasn't, it still felt good to be here.

My instructions were to check in to the base hotel, the Gateway Inn. There was nothing unusual about that; the base hotel was standard accommodation for those who didn't have base housing ready or for officers like me who were passing through on their way to another duty station. Upon arrival, I checked in and got a room assignment. The room was comfortable, nothing extravagant by any means. The jet lag and the drive left me tired. I arrived early and still had a few days off coming to me before I needed to report here on Monday for a briefing. Hopefully, by mid-week, I'll be on my way to my new assignment as a test pilot out at Edwards. There, my job would be flying modified and prototype Air Force aircraft, pushing them to the limit and beyond. A dangerous job, but I was happy to be doing what I loved and pushing my plane and me to the extreme was precisely what I wanted to do. I had no idea why I was here at Andrews or that my fate and my future were being decided just a few miles away in Washington. There were two things on my mind. Getting out to Edwards and starting my assignment and visiting my old friend. After a short respite and now with a second wind, I took my time off and headed up the road north of Baltimore to see if I could find Beth.

I didn't know where exactly to start looking. I would take the few days and make it a mission. I was uncertain what the outcome would be, but by the end of the weekend, I knew I would have at least found her. My information had become outdated over the years, and I didn't have any reliable contact information on her. I checked the Internet. Stationed overseas, the web was an indispensable resource, but she wasn't listed. Her parents were unlisted too, and I knew that from when she had moved the first time. We hadn't stayed in touch the last few years, so I had no idea where she was or what she was doing. Her childhood home would be as good a place as any to begin my search.

I got in the car and started the roughly hour-and-a-half drive from the base up to Westminster. There was a cold rain falling as I got north of Baltimore to the last address I knew for her parent's house. It was a Thursday night; a dark, ominous sky foretold a coming storm. I was a bit nervous as I approached her door. I expected and was hoping she would be the one to answer, but I knew odds were against it. I wasn't even sure that her parents were living anymore or still in this same house. She'd be 27 now, and living at home was a very remote possibility. It was not likely I would strike gold the first time out. Flying high-performance aircraft and expecting uncertainty every time I climb into the cockpit, you'd think seeing someone I knew wouldn't make me nervous, but I was shaking. Maybe it was just the cold, damp night air, but I had my doubts. It was something more.

How many times I had made this drive to this house when I was younger only to drive by and never knock on the door. I had always feared that something as important to me as us would be lost in a moment of disappointment. It was one of those paradoxes in life. Don't knock and never be rejected, and of course, never know the outcome, or do knock and risk it all. For many years, I chose not to knock and only touch base from afar, and even then, never let her know my true feelings never stopped. Here I stood again at another crossroads.

After a few knocks and after ringing the doorbell, it didn't appear anyone was home, or if they were, they had chosen not to answer. I felt a little relieved. The nervousness started to subside as I walked back towards the car. I was a couple of feet from the vehicle when the front porch light came on, and the door opened. Someone asked if they could help me. It was Beth's mother. I went to the door and introduced myself. It wasn't necessary, as she recognized me as soon I stepped into the light on the front step. I asked if Beth was around. She said Beth moved out when she went to college and was living and working in Towson, approximately 45 minutes away. She asked me in, and we talked for a while about what I had been doing and about what Beth had been up to over the years.

The warmth from the gas fireplace took me back to my own house growing up. The sterile base environment I had been exposed to over the years had numbed me to what it was like to be in a real home. For the moment, this feeling was as close as I had been in years to family life. As we talked, she brought out a few photo albums; we looked at pictures of Beth's high school and college graduation. She appeared as beautiful as I remembered. Her mother offered to call Beth and tell her I was here. I thanked her for the offer but said I wanted to surprise her, and that even though the hour grew late, I might try to make it over there tonight. I took the address and phone number clutching it tightly in my hand.

As I left, the once cold rain was now turning into a substantial snowstorm. I was debating whether or not I would try to make it over to Beth's apartment or find a local hotel for the night and track her down in the morning. I was pretty familiar with the area where she lived. I knew the general vicinity but was unfamiliar with the exact apartment building. My phone was not yet activated. I would have to use recall and dead reckoning to find it. I didn't want to wait another day to see her. My leave and this detour would be up soon, so each minute that passed would be a wasted opportunity. Well, it was decided, despite the weather, this mission would have to be a go. Life was too short to waste even a day.

I began the trek from the far northern edges of this Baltimore suburb over towards Towson. In my time away, the area had become significantly more built up than I remembered, parts of it were unrecognizable to me. As I made my way through the back roads to her apartment, the snow was beginning to stick on the deserted country roads. Nonetheless, I was determined now. There would be no turning back.

It was approaching nine-thirty in the evening when I found the apartment complex. In my discussions with Beth's mom, the subject never came up whether she was married or attached. It didn't occur to me to ask since her mom had offered to call. I guess I thought she wasn't involved with anyone. Now here I was second-guessing myself again. It appeared that she had always had that strange effect on me.

It would be a terrible embarrassment to show up unannounced this late and find her with someone else. I started thinking, "What am I here for anyway?" It'd been eight years since I saw her last, and a good twelve years since we were an item. We were just kids. I let her go the first time, and now I was standing wondering what she was doing. Was she seeing someone? There would be no long hello. I had another assignment waiting, and soon, I would be across the country.

Answers to all my questions came quickly; of course, she must be involved. By now I'm a distant memory for her, having long ago faded from sight. But as I stood there, I was thinking how much I wanted to see her and how good those times were that we shared. I had nothing to lose. I wanted to see her. Even if it was only to talk to her one more time.

Apartment 1002. I listened for a minute as I approached the door. There was that strange stillness in the air that always seems to happen when snow is falling. There were no sounds from the apartment, no sounds from a radio or television - only silence. I knocked again. I stood in the cold, watching the snow falling harder. Even this close to the city, the streets and grass were covered. No answer. It was looking like I might strike out and not be lucky enough to catch her tonight.

I began to think that it might be prudent to get back to the base. The roads had gotten quite slippery, and it might be worse in the morning. Maybe I could find a hotel nearby and stay there. I could call Beth early in the morning before she left for work. Perhaps meet for coffee or breakfast. My mind was in a daze pondering the possibilities when suddenly, the door opened. Those eight years were erased in a mere moment. She didn't say a word - just hugged me. Her mom had called earlier and told her I had stopped by; she said she hoped I would come to see her tonight. It had been too long.

She was beautiful; her warm smile melted my heart. It was so good to see her. I stepped inside out of the cold and took my coat off, and we hugged again. It sure seemed like we stood there for hours, but it was just a few minutes. Sometimes you just know a "good to see you hug" from something else, something more. This was something more. I could feel it. While we were standing there, I heard a cell phone ring. The natural reaction, I reached and grabbed for mine, but it was Beth's. She grabbed it off the table near where we were standing, glanced for a second at the caller ID, paused, and took the call. She gestured to me with her hand indicating this would only be a moment.

I heard her say, "Hi Jim, what's up?" then she mentioned that "the weather was too bad, and it was late, but maybe some other time." She closed with "I'll call you later, bye."

Putting the phone back down she looked at me and said with a smile, "Hi, now where were we?"

Before I answered, I asked her, "Was that your boyfriend?"

"No," she replied. "Just a friend anticipating a snow day tomorrow and who wanted to grab a pizza, come over, and watch the snow fall."

Well, it sounded a little odd this late at night and on a work night for just any friend to call. I thought there was more to the story, but I figured I'd deal with it later on. I had only been here a few minutes, and already I was feeling jealous, but for right now, it was just the two of us.

We spent the next few hours talking about old times. The hours passed like minutes as we talked about things we had done and things we missed. Not much surprised me about what she had done. Her life was as I pictured it, one of success and accomplishment. As we sat there and talked on and on, I felt so comfortable. It felt as if I belonged here. Being around her always seemed so natural. I sat on the sofa with my arm around her; she rested her head on my shoulder. This time, it was much better than the old days when we were kids.

There was always something about her that made me feel so good whenever we were together, and I knew she felt the same. You know how people say they feel as if they are one with another person? That is how I felt. In the few hours we talked, I realized how much I had missed her and how much I needed her in my life. As she spoke, I listened and thought how my whole life was now in question. The most important things I thought about and worked for just didn't seem quite as important as they had before. Call it a moment of weakness or an overactive libido, but such was the power she had over me that my dreams were worth putting by the wayside to be with her. I felt not like an Airman, but a sailor on shore leave with my emotions running high.

I glanced at the time, and it was already three o'clock in the morning. Where had the past few hours gone? It seemed she had the cure for my jet lag. I was still energized, riding an adrenaline high, but I could that she was getting tired. She asked if I had to be back tomorrow. I told her I had a few days off. She wanted to take the day off and spend Friday and the weekend together, just hanging. It sounded like a great plan. I wanted to be so close to her and selfishly wanted to get my bearings on where this was heading.

I told her I would find a hotel for the night and be back tomorrow. She insisted I stay there at the apartment; I started to get comfortable on the sofa. As she walked to her room, she stopped at her door, turned, and said, "How about you sleep in here and hold me tonight?" I spent the rest of the night lying next to her, holding her close to me. After all this time, I was here with her. This moment was what I had always wanted. We finally had come around to finish what we had started so long ago.

Morning arrived. I hadn't slept much, but how could I? It had just been a few hours, if that, of sleep, but the best few hours. A few inches of snow had fallen overnight, coating everything in a blanket of white. I wanted to run out and grab some coffee, hot chocolate, and bagels for her while she was still sleeping. I didn't know where the nearest one was, and the snow probably meant they weren't open anyway. She was asleep when I heard a cell phone ring. This time it was mine. Talk about bad timing. The cell phone carrier had to pick this time to activate it? It was an Assistant to the Base Commander at Andrews. He said something had come up. He said that he couldn't reach me at the base hotel and that I was to report back to the base immediately.

This command wasn't highly unusual, but it was out of the ordinary for me considering this wasn't my permanent duty station. My thoughts were that I was temporarily going to be re-deployed somewhere due to a crisis; maybe back to Europe or the Middle East. Even that didn't make much sense. This type of information typically came through regular channels. I wasn't sure what was going on, and he wasn't telling me over the phone. I said to him that I would be there as soon as possible depending on traffic and the weather. It sounded urgent, and he wanted me to report to the base commander upon my arrival.

I walked back into Beth's room and woke her. I broke the unfortunate news that our plans for the day and weekend had taken a slight detour. I would need a rain check. She looked so gentle and sweet with the sleep still in her eyes. I was torn between leaving her and staying. I had gone once before, and this time, I didn't want to go. She was still tired and said it was okay; we'd make it up soon. I gave her my information at the base and told her I didn't know what was up, but as soon as I could, I would call her, and we would get that time together.

I let her know that I likely would be on my way to Edwards before next weekend, but if I could get away before heading west, I would. Either way, I would call her no later than Friday, and probably sooner. Just a few hours ago I hadn't seen her in eight years. Now it felt like I was going away again.

Before I left, I wanted to show her something I had kept over the years. I reached for my wallet and pulled out an old picture of her she had given me back in the high school years. It looked worn and slightly tattered on the edges. On the back, she had drawn a little heart and written the words "I will always love you...Beth." I told her that I had hung on to this over the years and considered it my good luck charm. Through my training and every flight I ever made, it was with me. There was silence, and that particular look was on her face, an almost sad look; I could see her eyes welling up followed by tears running down her cheeks. She was surprised and touched by the fact that I had hung on to it. I could tell that she had no idea about how I had felt about her over the years.

Suddenly, her face lit up, and she exclaimed, "I can't believe you still have that after all this time! Wait, don't move!" She ran towards her desk and returned with a newer picture. "Here's one I took a few months ago. This one has extra luck attached!"

No sooner than she handed it to me did she all of a sudden snatched it back out of my hands. She walked over to the kitchen counter, picked up a pen, and wrote something on the picture. Then she took a letter envelope out of the drawer, put the photo in, and sealed it. Handing it back to me, she said, "Open this when you get back to the base and not before, do you promise?"

I was curious but agreed. The mystery of what she had written would bug me the whole way back, but I would keep my promise. We hugged for a while, and I kissed her goodbye. It was hard to let go.

AN APPOINTMENT AT THE PENTAGON

As I drove back to Andrews, she was on my mind. Whatever was up at the base would have to be pretty important to have pulled me away from her, I thought. An average commute back to the base would be forty-five minutes, but in the traffic and bad weather, I made it back in three hours. It was early afternoon; I stopped by the Gateway and changed into uniform. I pulled the envelope she had given me out of my pocket and opened it. It was a great picture, and she looked terrific. I turned over the picture to see what she had written. "Some things never change. I meant what I said the first time." It took me a minute to figure out that the message was referring to what she had written on the first picture. I think she was telling me that she still loved me. I wasn't sure. Is it possible I was that clueless? Next time we would talk about it in more detail, and I would find out exactly what she meant. I stood there thinking about it for a few minutes, then put the picture in my uniform pocket and proceeded to the Base Commander's office.

It was our first meeting. I had arrived at the base early, and we weren't formally scheduled to meet until Monday. He was pleasant but formal. The conversation was to the point and lacked specifics. He told me my orders were to report to the Pentagon at 0800 hours tomorrow morning. A chopper would be ready at 0700 hours to take me there. It wasn't a mutual exchange of information, and there was no opportunity for Q&A. I had my orders, and that was that. The military is full of secrets, but even for them, this was very unusual. Thinking through it, I was at a loss as to what this might be behind this sudden turn of events. Giving me orders to report to the Pentagon in the morning and a ride on a chopper to get there? I was a damn good pilot, but way too young to get any attention from the Pentagon. I was curious about what was going on. Maybe I was in some trouble for something, but I discounted that. No one got called to the Pentagon for that. I didn't know, but I had a few hours to think about it.

By now, the weather had cleared. I made my way over to flight operations to check out an available aircraft. I made a call to my old wing commander at Ramstein who was now stationed at the Pentagon, and I asked him to make a few calls to see if he could pull a few strings and get me something to fly. He said he'd be glad to do it and wanted to know if I had time to stop by and catch up. I told him I would be in his neighborhood tomorrow and would drop in if I had the chance but couldn't be sure of my schedule.

"I'd love to catch up if you get the chance – let me hop on this, and I'll call you back." About ten minutes later, he called back to let me know that an F-16 was available and the crew chief was getting it prepped for me as we spoke. He told me to head over to the hangar, and it would be ready by the time I got there. I thanked him for getting that worked out for me and told him I'd see him tomorrow. As a captain, even I couldn't stroll onto a base and check out an aircraft. I needed help on the order of a few more stripes and few pretty big strings being pulled to get that done, and he was able to make it happen for me.

When I got to the flight line, she was ready to go. I thanked the crew chief and his men for getting her ready to fly so quickly. I climbed aboard and began my taxi past the hangar for Air Force One and out to the end of the runway. My usual routine was to clip Beth's picture to the canopy rail in the plane. I slipped her new photo into a spot on the left of the instrument panel. She never knew it, but she made every flight with me. She was my good luck charm. As soon as I received clearance from the tower, I eased the throttle forward and began my acceleration, pulling back on the joystick and starting my climb. There was a lot of traffic in the area, and I was authorized to head due east for a run out over the Atlantic. It looked like I would be able to squeeze in a few hours of flying time.

There is something so peaceful about flying - the blue sky, the solitude; it was a chance to just put everything aside for a few hours. The weather at forty thousand feet was smooth. At this altitude, the sky on the horizon and above was a darker shade of blue. I was just a few miles above the ground, but closer to space than most everyone else on the planet. As I cleared the coast, I accelerated past Mach 1 and broke the sound barrier. It was always my dream to go a little higher, and a little faster and perhaps make it to space, but for now, this was a darn good substitute. After a nice ride that took me about as far as my fuel would allow, I turned and headed back to the base. I made it back to the base and touched down just as the sun was setting. When I got back to the room, I had a message from Beth on the cell. "Just wondering if you made it back okay."

I tried to call her back but didn't get an answer. On her voicemail, I said to her that I just came down from forty thousand feet, both literally and figuratively. I didn't know much else but shared what I knew and said that I would call her soon with an update. This night I really needed some rest to be refreshed for what could be another long day tomorrow. I had so much on my mind that sleep would be hard, but I would try anyway.

It's 0500 hours. I'm up and need to get ready. In the military, we are all about precision. George Washington was the first to instill that in his revolutionary war troops, and every member of the armed forces since has been trained to operate that way. Washington hired Baron Friedrich Wilhelm von Steuben, a former member of the Prussian Army, to teach his recruits. Baron Von Steuben implemented discipline and drill, march and precision. The work he developed and passed to each regiment created a unified capable force that could match the British army. That tradition lives on in each member of the military. I was to be present and to be prepared whenever and wherever I was needed, but prepared for what? My training involved expecting the unexpected at any time. So, I was ready for what lies ahead and did not think I would disappoint.

I looked down at my watch, 0700 hours. The chopper's warming up when I get to the pad. I'm dressed in my "blues," my officer's uniform. The pilots on board are kidding me about my expensive limo ride to the Pentagon. They said they were up late last night and that I may have to fly this thing if they can't keep their eyes open. I told them no luck, and that I was fixed wing only. We took off and made the short hop to the Pentagon. I didn't bring anything but myself, per orders. This short hop was a drop-off for the pilots, a "turn and burn" for them, and the base was so close that I could grab a taxi back if I couldn't find a ride. The idea of shuttling over to the Pentagon was embarrassing to me. It was a luxury I wasn't accustomed to having. Whatever this was about, I should know soon enough. I seemed to be getting the red carpet treatment, which was just one more piece of the puzzle that just didn't fit. If this was a trip to the woodshed, it was definitely overkill. It was an odd sequence of events and outside the normal procedure for Air Force personnel, but I was "true blue" and would do whatever was asked of me.

We landed on the Pentagon Helipad where a Lieutenant Commander serving as an assistant to an Admiral met me. The noise from the chopper's rotors and engine were deafening. It was impossible to speak or be heard. Keeping our heads down, we hurriedly left the pad and headed inside, where he briefed me on the day's events. Apparently, I was scheduled for a round of individual and panel interviews. It seemed as though they had some job in mind for me. In reviewing the itinerary, I thought that it must be a significant role, judging from who was interviewing me. I was told that I shouldn't make any arrangements for dinner that night and that per orders from the Secretary of Defense; I shouldn't make any outside calls or have any external contact until further notice.

I was intrigued by the escalating secrecy of all of this, but I didn't let the excitement of the moment get to me. I relaxed and didn't think too much more about it. I figured whatever I speculated would be wrong anyway. Besides, I would learn soon enough whatever they had in mind. With the word to hold dinner open, this almost had a congratulatory tone to it, with the interviews a mere formality rather than a test. By the time the sun would set on this day, I'd be through this and could get back to a regular schedule. If they had something special in mind and I didn't get it, well I had a pretty good job waiting for me at Edwards.

I started to think that if I got a job here in D.C., then I'd be close to Beth. Maybe I'd even live in Baltimore and take the train or drive down to Washington each morning. I'm a pilot, and a desk job to me is like water is to oil—a bad mix. Under normal circumstances, I would have no interest in working here at the Pentagon. While that may have been the goal of many an officer, it wasn't mine. I belonged in a cockpit traveling Mach 2 at forty or fifty thousand feet.

The feelings of last night came back strong, and maybe being here for a while wouldn't be so terrible after all. It may have been the settling moment I'd been looking for in my life. I was doing exactly what I said I wouldn't—speculating. I still didn't know what they wanted me for, but the drama was about to begin, and soon I would know the answer.

While I waited, I looked more closely at the schedule for the day. I was set to interview with high-ranking members of each of the branches of service. The last meeting was with the Secretary of Defense. Meeting with so much brass could only be something here at the Pentagon, and most likely something in line with serving as a top aide to the JCS (Joint Chiefs of Staff). As the day wore on, I met with each member. No details about the job, only questions about me, my background, what I would do in certain situations, challenges I've faced. It has been an interesting process, and in my Air Force career I hadn't quite seen or heard of anything like this before. There were lots of questions about history, military involvement in past conflicts, and strategic what ifs. There was specific focus on the military tactics in World War II, in particular by the Axis powers.

I loved engaging in dialogue on that subject. It was a significant area of interest for me, and I had studied it thoroughly. I might be bragging a bit, but if this was a history quiz, I am confident I passed. Anybody would be hard-pressed to match my knowledge of German tactics. Even with this focus on Germany, I doubt we were preparing to refight a war against one of our staunchest European allies. However, I had gotten the impression this was an important job they had in mind for me.

Now it sounded more like a strategic planning role. Perhaps there was an open position in a senior war planning capacity. That would be of great interest to me. It would be an impressive move so early in my career. The last interview of the day was on deck. It was now 1800 hours, six o'clock in the evening. The Secretary of Defense was behind schedule. I'd been here for an hour and a half, and he still hadn't arrived at his office.

Finally, at 1915 hours (7:15 PM), he arrived and apologized for the wait. He told me we had dinner plans at the White House tonight with the President. By this time, the whole thing had become somewhat hard to fathom. It was a fortuitous change in fortune for me. A choice between two excellent opportunities seemed imminent. I had my sure thing at Edwards and this possible opportunity, even though I still didn't know what the job was all about. He told me there were several attendees. We would all caravan over to the White House. He asked me to wait a moment as he got into his office. Moments later the Secretary came out and told his assistant to go home and that he would see her bright and early in the morning. We walked the long corridors of the Pentagon and exited where several black SUVs were waiting.

Getting into the vehicles were several of the brass I met with today, a few I didn't know and one other officer. From what I could tell, he was a Navy Lieutenant in his dress blues wearing a SEAL insignia. We made eye contact, and he looked a little puzzled, as was I. After all the interviews, either we both had a job or were about to get a final interview. I doubt I'd get a ride to see the President and have dinner at the White House to be told: "thank you for time today." This could be two big days in a row for me—first Beth, and now a new job. This had all the makings of an exciting night ahead.

As we drove through D.C., I could see both the Capitol and the Washington Monument brightly lit as I peered out the window. We pulled up to a security station on the side of the Executive Mansion. From this angle, I could only see a small part of the East Wing. All of this seemed to be a privilege reserved for special guests of the President. There were Secret Service agents stationed around the area, but I was surprised that there was no security check before we went in to see the President. We left the vehicles and were met by aides who escorted us inside the building. This time I knew I'd at least have a ride back.

For all the time I'd lived in Maryland, and all the times I'd been to D.C., this was the first time I'd ever been inside the White House. As we entered, I couldn't help but try to absorb as much as I could. It always appeared small to me when I drove by it. It seemed much larger as we walked down a long hall and entered the State Dining Room. There was a small card in front of each place setting. As I walked around the table, I noticed the card at the end read "President of the United States." I followed the lead of my superiors and took my place midway down the table. The mood was somewhat quiet as if no one wanted to talk about anything for fear that the question of what we were doing here would come up. The feeling I had was one of anticipation. That some big moment was about to occur and it would be the President who would let the rest of us in on what was going on. We were not sitting there long when the President arrived. We rose to attention and saluted our Commander in Chief.

"At ease," he said.

Before taking his place at the head of the table, he introduced himself to the Lieutenant and then to me. He asked us to sit and immediately began talking about a "grave" threat to American security, potentially more serious than anything we'd ever faced. It seemed that he was speaking in general terms, nothing specific. Then he reminded us why we'd joined the service—to protect and defend the Constitution and the citizens of the United States at all costs, even with the highest cost of all, our lives.

With his few words, the picture became clear to me. It was evident that this wasn't going to be a desk job. This mission would be high-risk. A million thoughts began racing through my head. I guessed this would involve flying the SEAL somewhere, and that the odds must have been long and stacked against us to get all this attention. I went from thinking that perhaps I wasn't so much one of the selected few, but one of the expendable many. I was wondering, of all the pilots in the armed services, how was it that I got to be this lucky? If the SEAL had to be deployed somewhere on a clandestine mission, why not use a Navy pilot?

The SEALs had teams for precisely this sort of thing. This type of operation occurred all the time, but never got this type of attention. Something much more significant was at play here. The President sat and asked the Chairman of the Joints Chiefs to offer some opening remarks. He starts by saying, "We have been carefully selected to complete a hazardous and risky mission. The odds are against us, but the country's fate and maybe that of humanity may hang in the balance". Of the millions of men and women in uniform, it appeared to come down to the two of us to protect the future freedom of America.

The fate of our country and humanity is hanging in the balance? The forcefulness in his words put this in a different perspective for me. I was in a moment of shock and disbelief. This was not at all what I had expected. The President asked us what our thoughts were. We still didn't know any details, but I told him that one thing that didn't cross my mind was failure. We would beat the odds and succeed. He smiled, and so did a few of the Air Force brass. They looked like proud papas. We were told that we had an option to decline the opportunity before this went any further and details were revealed. If we agreed, there was no turning back.

"I understand you are being asked to agree to something that you're totally in the dark about, and we all would understand if you declined," the

President told us. He then added, "I want to paint as clear a picture as I can - the chance of survival is zero." He clarified and said, "Truth be told, it's less than zero from the moment you accept you will have signed your death warrant. While the mission objectives may be achieved, it is a certainty that you won't survive. Until the mission is complete, it is important that no contact occurs with any personnel other than those who will be involved in the mission unless authorized."

At this point, I was excited about whatever the mission was going to be. I was not at all fazed by his insinuation that this was a suicide mission. This is what I was trained for, to be someplace where I could make a difference and to be there when it mattered. For me, this was it!

For a moment, the thoughts of last night and Beth left my mind. I was thinking about the mission. I would beat the odds and come back. I just knew I could do it. No one could make a statement that a mission would end with no chance of survival. We were trained and taught to be the victors and that we do not fail. My new partner, I knew, shared my sentiments, and neither of us was interested in dying. Mission success was the only option. I would have to get to know him pretty well during our prep; our lives may very well have depended on each other's skill and ability.

The rest of the evening passed quickly. We were served a feast of a dinner. I glanced up at a large mirror on the wall. Seeing us gathered around this large table reminded me of that famous painting, *The Last Supper*. It was a ghostly feeling that momentarily gave me a moment of pause. I wasn't expecting that reaction. The President was on the move throughout the evening, working his way around the table and engaging in personal conversation about friends and family. I told him about recently hooking up with an old friend; it seemed to catch the ear of one of the Admirals who interviewed me today. Whether he looked interested or disappointed, I was not sure, but it seemed to bother him. He said nothing about it. The friendly conversation went on and on, until finally at just after midnight we are done. The President grabbed my hand and said, "May God bless you and the United States of America" and added, "A grateful nation thanks you for your service and your sacrifice to our country." The words hit home, and there was a lump in my throat. The President's final comments were nearly the same as what is said at a military funeral. Unknowingly, he gave us an ominous farewell.

The long day and the dinner were over, and I had new orders. We were to fly out tonight to Minot Air Force Base in North Dakota. Minot was not a place where I would expect the red carpet treatment to continue. It was a remote base that housed strategic bombers and was near a strategic missile site. I had been a lot of places in my career, but never Minot. The weather would be cold there this time of year, and hardly the warmth of the southern California desert where I had hoped to be. The sound of a chopper could be heard outside. The President said that the least he could do was to order Marine One to take us take us back to Andrews. It would be there that a jet would be waiting to take us out to North Dakota tonight. Time was apparently of the essence, and everything we needed would be there waiting for us when arrived. It was fortunate that I had put Beth's picture in my jacket. There would be no stopping back at the room to pick anything up. We exited the White House and walked across the lawn to the chopper, which was already running and waiting for us.

It was an honor to walk the steps that so many leaders of our nation had done before us. On board, we took our seats as the engine revved, and the chopper lifted off and made a dash across the city below. In less than ten minutes, we would touch down at Andrews, and I could see the plane about a hundred feet from where we were. Its lights were on, the door was open, and it looked ready to go. It was an Air Force Gulfstream, comfortable and relaxing. This plane was the type used to ferry Generals around the country. Both the Air Force and Navy Chief flew back to Andrews with us and escorted us over to the waiting jet. As we got ready to board, I turned to salute.

"Good luck, gentlemen," said the Navy Chief.

I smiled and climbed up the ladder and into the passenger cabin; I felt the effects of the hectic past two days. It was late, and I was tired. On the long flight out, I was hoping to get some sleep, but my new partner and I hadn't exchanged words all night, and we'd need some time to talk. His name was Rick Wilson; he was slightly older than me at 31. A Naval Academy grad, he went through SEAL training right out of Annapolis. He finished near the top of his graduating class, a familiar trait we both shared. We talked about family and friends, things that we'd done, goals that we had. Our military training conditioned us to anticipate what lie ahead, but not speculate without the facts. We didn't talk much about what we thought the mission would entail. After all, it could be anything.

I had a sense we had both seen our share of fellow servicemen lost. This time, it would be different; it must be different. After sharing our lives for hours on the flight out to Minot, I got the feeling that I knew him as well as could be expected for such a short period of time. I knew we'd make a good team and that we could trust our lives to each other if necessary. We both had a fire and a desire to succeed. It seemed we had a lot in common, which explained why we both were here. The flight was long. We talked a while, and I reclined the seat and closed my eyes to catch what little time I had left to rest.

MINOT

It was the early hours of Sunday morning before sunrise when we touched down at Minot Air Force Base. It was dark, and the lights from the plane reflected on the area around the runway. The ground here was covered with a blanket of white snow. Here in this hostile environment, I stood in the wee hours of the morning near the Canadian border, wondering what I got myself tangled up in. The feeling I had was as cold as the air around me. We were greeted upon arriving by our commander for the mission, Colonel Tom "Mac" McCarthy. I saluted and introduced myself. He indicated that he'd read our files and that from here on out, we could refer to him as "Mac." "Mac" instructed us that we were to have no contact with anyone outside of the mission until the mission was complete and that from here on out, we were to communicate any issues, problems, concerns, or needs directly to him and him alone. We then had the rest of the day (Sunday) off to rest. Training and briefings began Monday morning.

The rest came at the right time. I was exhausted physically and emotionally and not sure what the training would involve, so rest was definitely in order. We were shown to our quarters where we'd reside at least for a short while. I slept into the late morning, a rare luxury in military life, and even more unusual for a pilot. I got dressed and took a stroll out on the base. The weather was inhospitable. It was bone-chilling cold with a wind that felt like razors cutting on your skin. A run in these conditions was out of the question. Since there were only bombers here, I wasn't sure if I would be flying out of here as part of the mission.

On the line in Europe, I flew every day with little downtime. It had been only a few days since I last flew, but after five years of non-stop flying, even

29

this short break was hard to get used to it. It wouldn't be long before I would be back in the cockpit. For now, I gave up on that idea and headed to the chow hall for lunch, then over to the BX, the Base Exchange. There, I picked up a book and returned to the warmth of my room to read. After a few hours, I put my book down to watch the Minnesota-Green Bay game. For all the high drama that surrounded me being here, it seemed a letdown to be sitting here in the freezing snow-covered plains of North Dakota watching a football game.

I was itching to get into the action, whatever it would be. Perhaps, I thought, this was the strategy. Dull my senses by sticking me here, and after a few days, I would agree to almost anything. It was not unlike a form of solitary confinement. It wouldn't take long here, and I would jump at anything. It wasn't my patience that was running thin, but my boredom was running long. After the game, I grabbed a quick snack, then read for a few more hours. This had been a lazy day with not much accomplished. I decided to call it an early night. The upside to this was that I was rapidly getting caught up on the sleep deprivation I'd had over these past few nights. Tomorrow was fast approaching, and I didn't know what the future would hold for me.

The sound of the alarm clock woke me. I turned and saw 0500 hours. It seemed to be a lucky number for me. Even with all this sleep, I was still unusually tired. The emotional drain was behind it. I wondered if they had done their proper psych workup on me. That alarm may have been going off for a few minutes before it managed to stir me from a deep sleep. The whirlwind of the past few days, the jumping of six or seven time zones in a short period, and the anticipation of what I would learn today had all caught up with me, and I had still not fully adjusted.

In the early moments of consciousness, it often seems like your mind is overwhelmed with the thoughts of what you have done in life and what you have left to do. It all becomes a twisting maze of things that mix and don't seem to make complete sense. Much like someone opened the floodgates and in comes rushing in so much information that it is impossible to control. And so, in my morning fog, I was trying to assemble where I was and where I was going. It took me a few minutes to realize that this indeed was happening to me. I hadn't dreamed it, and I wasn't delusional. This was as real as it got. I got up and could now feel the adrenaline starting to surge inside of me, as understanding all the details of what I would be doing was now just hours away.

I flipped on the early morning news and caught the weather forecast. As usual for North Dakota area in the middle of November, the temperature would be in the teens, and this was, as the weatherman said, "Unseasonably warm." The skies would be clear today, but more snow was in the forecast. If flying were on the schedule today, then it would be a perfect morning, but with deteriorating conditions later. Based on my skills, my pilot resume would have been what stood out. It only made sense that flying would be part of the mission, but this base was too remote and didn't support the assets I usually flew. If flying wasn't on the agenda, then they picked the wrong guy.

I had extra time this morning, so I spent a few more minutes than usual taking a relaxing, warm shower. It was the perfect recipe to calm the rush I was feeling. Few things felt better than warm water flowing over your body on a cold day. Dress for the day was flight suit attire. I had brought only my Air Force Dress Uniform that I wore to dinner and out on the plane. These guys were well prepared; my room was stocked with everything I needed, including a uniform with my name.

I opened the closet and grabbed the flight suit and laid it out on the bed. I noticed there was a mission patch on the sleeve. It was a black circle with a grim reaper figure holding a scythe in one hand and an hourglass in the other and the words "Projekt Töten Zeit" around the circle. I recognized that it was German and quickly did the translation to either "Project Dead Time" or "Project Killing Time." It has no significant meaning to me, and I hadn't heard the reference before today. In the military, we are all about using unique symbols and insignia to identify our teams and units, and this was just another one to me. It reminded me of the Navy's "Grim Reaper" squadron. I wondered if there was a connection.

As I understood, Minot would be home base from here on out, but the itinerary would include several locations. Judging from the way my room was stocked, it seemed that I wouldn't be here too long. It had everything I needed, but there was just one problem. It appeared to be for only one day. This morning's orders were to be at Hangar 4 at 0700 hours. Other than during the flight out, I'd hardly spoken to my new partner. I decided to knock on his door so that we could walk over to our rendezvous spot this morning. He was up and ready to go. He pulled his door closed turning the handle to make sure it locked and said, "Let's hit it." He seemed a quiet type, but by SEAL standards, our adventure so far may be tame. Rick was a man of few words, but I sensed that behind the silence resided a person of action. I hoped my sense about him was right.

We walked to the hangar in morning air so cold you could feel it freezing in your lungs. A new dusting of light snow that had fallen overnight covered the sidewalks. I had a flight jacket on that was providing some warmth, but the flight suit offered little protection for the rest of me. I couldn't help thinking that Minot must be the coldest place on Earth. The years in Europe had made me soft and used to more temperate conditions. Suddenly, the roar of jet engines broke the relative silence in the air as the base came to life. I couldn't see them, but the sound was unmistakable. A B-52 was thundering into the early morning sky. As the day wore on, many sorties would keep the sight and sounds of bombers in the airspace around the base. It was this place's reason for existence to form a vital leg of the American defense triad.

31

The 5th Bomb Wing and the 91st Missile Wing called this place home, and for an undetermined period, so would I.

As I walked closer to the hangar, I could see two black SUVs with the engines running. The government must have cornered the market on these black GM vehicles. They seemed to be everywhere. Mac was standing beside the lead SUV. Rick and I got up to Mac and saluted.

"You can drop the formality with me while you are here. Get in," he said. "We're going for a ride."

Mac climbed into the front passenger seat while Rick and I got into the back. The driver was possibly another officer I hadn't met before. He was dressed in a black SWAT-type outfit without rank or insignia. He didn't bother to turn and introduce himself and looked straight ahead, waiting for the order to move out. Before the car left, Mac turned to Rick and me and said, "Gentlemen, you have a decision to make in the next twenty minutes. When we arrive at our station today, there will be no turning back, no second guesses. You'll be committed. I want to be crystal clear about this. If for some reason after we reach our destination, you change your mind, you'll never see the light of day again. Once security is compromised, you can't go back. You understand what that means and what I would have to do. Think hard about it one more time."

Mac's words seemed a little harsh, but they didn't change anything. I was all in. There was no turning back. I couldn't help but think that if they were going to tell me something so top secret or show me something that was highly classified, and they would "kill us" to prevent us from re-entering the public with this knowledge, then what would they do after the mission? It was a fleeting thought, but the "no chance of survival" comment back at the White House came to mind. Perhaps if we survived the mission it would be death at their hands – maybe that is where the guarantee that the mission was a death sentence came originated. It mattered, but it didn't matter – I was in regardless of what the stakes turned out to be. Mac turned around and told the driver to head out.

The ride was quiet. There was a silence in the car—an awkward silence. It certainly wasn't a situation where you made idle chatter or small talk. Mac's remarks put a damper on things to a degree. It also didn't feel appropriate to ask where we were going. We would know soon enough.

I noticed on the drive that we didn't leave the base but merely headed out over the terrain, driving to what seemed like nowhere. After fifteen minutes or so, I could see a building up ahead. It looked like a standard military building, a small three-story office complex. There appeared to be nothing extraordinary about it. Located nearby was a hangar and a runway. It seemed to be an old abandoned airport without a control tower. I could see a paved road leading up to the building that must have led to a separate entrance. It appeared we took the more direct cross-country route.

There were a few cars in the lot, but nothing that would indicate a significant amount of activity. The building almost looked abandoned up close. The runway and hangar appeared new. There was also a massive set of concrete blocks on rails. It reminded me of a reinforced concrete hatch over a missile silo, but it was far too large for a missile silo. I could see a camouflage scheme in spots where the snow had melted. The rails didn't sit above ground, but were recessed and painted in a beige color. It was clearly intended as a tactic to prevent prying eyes above from spotting it. The size of the "hatch" or "cover" was about one hundred and fifty to two hundred square feet. It must have weighed hundreds of tons. We pulled up to the parking lot, and the driver shifted the car into park. Mac turned and asked, "What'll it be?"

I replied, "Count me in."

Rick took a second longer and said in a stoic demeanor, "I'm in."

"Good." Mac smiled and said, "Let's go."

As we got out of the car, it was apparent that the building was vacant. It was well kept, but there was no activity in sight. The blinds were drawn. Up close, something about it just didn't look right. We followed Mac up to the front door. Mac inserted his ID and let us into the building. The "lobby" was, small and the walls were plated with thick steel. We were inside, but not really inside. There was what looked like a steel revolving door with no glass. Mac stepped inside and said, "Follow me".

He put his hand on what looked like a scanner on the inside wall. The door let him through to the other side. I went next and put my hand on the scanner, and I was through. Rick followed, and he made it. It is the simple things that usually don't work, but surprisingly, this did. The driver and the team in the other vehicle didn't enter the building behind us. It was only the three of us for now. We walked down a hallway to another door. Mac inserted his badge, and the door opened. Inside, the room was clean and modern. There were elevator doors. Mac pushed the button, and the elevator opened. The elevator was modern. There was a camera system and a communication system inside. There were no floors listed and no buttons. The doors closed, and I sensed we were not going up, but down. The ride was short. It felt like two or three stories, but I couldn't be sure.

When the elevator stopped, the doors opened to a large, black room with several armed Military Police and a "reception area." Thick, bulletproof glass surrounded the MP behind the desk. He asked for identification. He then asked each of us to authenticate again using a hand scanner on his desk. After he cleared each of us, he said, "Welcome to Wolf's Lair." I knew immediately that "Wolf's Lair" was the name given to Adolf Hitler's headquarters in Poland on the Eastern Front. That complex was large and had numerous interconnected underground bunkers, its own power supply and life support system, and entertainment for those stationed there. It was a self-sustaining complex.

The choice of the name seemed more than a coincidence, and this would be the second time a German reference was used. First the words on the flight suit patch, and now the use of "Wolf's Lair." It could have been a coincidence, I supposed, but I doubted it.

The guard instructed us to maintain our IDs on our person at all time. The complex was highly secured, and he told us that we couldn't go anywhere without being required to insert our badge, and in ultra-sensitive areas, we would be required to use our ID and place our hand on the scanner. He directed us to another steel revolving door. Once through, there was another small room and an elevator. There was no question now that we were in a highly classified, highly secured facility. There had been redundant security at every step along the way. I wondered how much more before we would get to our destination. "The last one," Mac said as he inserted his badge to call the elevator. The doors opened, and we got in. Same setup, only this time, there were choices. The panel indicated Level M, Level 1, Level 2, and Level 3. Mac pushed Level 1, and we descended once again.

The ride was short again, but by now, I knew we must be several hundred feet below the ground. The elevator doors opened to what appeared to be a standard work area. The walls and ceiling were white, the floor tiled. It didn't feel like we were hundreds of feet below the ground. Where we stepped out of the elevator on the wall read "Wolf's Lair," and below it was a directory. The left-pointing arrow said "Operations" and the right-pointing arrow said "Complex Support."

"Well, gentlemen, you are here," Mac said.

"I know it seemed like an endless stream of security, but in a little while, you'll understand why. You'll be staying down on Level 2 when you are here at the complex. Your living quarters are there, and there's a commissary, a gym, and a media room for you to keep up with the outside world. Training sessions and briefings will take place there also. Level 3 is restricted, and you will be there at least twice for sure, today and the day you leave. Perhaps more if a test is being conducted. As impressive as I think you'll find it, there isn't much going on most of the time anyway. That you may find it impressive is a vast understatement. There will also be several occasions when you will leave the Wolf's Lair and Minot, and I will go over that will you today. There are no secrets anymore.

You are now in the inner circle, and you will know everything you need to know and everything about this place. Before you even ask, I know what you are thinking. What is this place? I can't give it away just yet. We'll do that when we get to Level 2. Let me tell you something about this floor. There are 18 airman and officers assigned to this floor. Their job is to maintain the computer operations, power, communications, security, and other infrastructure. They are hand-selected and live in quarters about a half-mile from here. There is a tunnel to their quarters that is secured. They do not know what this complex does or what its real purpose is. They come here each day to ensure that this place can operate 24/7. They are the best of the best, and they wear a similar Grim Reaper patch that you have on your flight suit. They are members of the elite Unit 5545. The use of that number is by design. If that unit number were a date, would you know what it meant?"

I thought for just a second and replied, "If you mean May 5, 1945, then yes, that was the day Germany surrendered to end the war in Europe." I added that it was hard to overlook the German words on my patch, the use of "Wolf's Lair," and now the date reference to Germany's surrender as a mere coincidence. There was a common theme pointing to events that took place more than sixty years ago.

Mac smiled and said, "I really didn't think you'd get the date. Let's go downstairs, and I'll tell you a little story that will clear things up."

MISSION BRIEFING

We made our way back to the elevator and headed down to Level 2. The layout was similar. The arrows pointing left to the "Accommodations," "Media Room," and "Commissary" and right to the "Training Center," "Medical Center," and "Gym".

Mac pointed to the right and said, "Let's go this way. Your living quarters are back there, and we'll get you settled in a little while."

We went down the hallway to one of the two training rooms. It was a small classroom with maps of Europe on the wall and volumes of charts and reference material. There was a large table in the room with a model of the topographical landscape of Germany. I took a look as I walked by it.

Mac told us to be seated. He then sat on the edge of the desk in the front of the room. "This is the moment in an officer's career when the chance to make a difference rests solely in his hands. What you are about to hear is not a tall tale, not science fiction, but a true story."

He stood, and his voice strengthened. "You are about to embark on a journey more significant than man's journey to the moon, no less challenging and infinitely more dangerous."

He began to tell the story of "Operation Killing Time".

"During World War II, the Germans were trying everything they could to win the war. Some of the ideas had merit but came too late, and others were way out there. The reason you are here is directly related to one of those efforts, a project called Töten Zeit, or as we call it, Killing Time. That effort was a German attempt to send a message back in time to correct the mistakes of the war."

He told us that the project was only a collection of notes and theories that never materialized. But we, the Americans, perfected it, and now would send two men back in time to World War II. While a lot was still unclear, I at least knew that the two men who would make the trip would be Rick and myself. It would be a trip into history, both figuratively and literally. He went on that the mission would be to place Rick and me near Nordhausen three months before the fall of Berlin in mid-February 1945. Our task would be to retrieve a volume of data that was considered vital to the successful development of the project.

Mac elaborated, "In the division of assets postwar, we found that we had Volume II of the most important notes of the project. We could have had this capability a long time ago if we had the entire collection of research papers."

"What happened to it?" Rick asked.

Mac replied. "It is a bit of a mystery. The genius behind the work was Dr. Josef Hans Scheel, a physicist, and one of Hitler's top scientists. Most of the other project documents that the U.S. and the Russians received were about what didn't work. Dr. Scheel's volumes contained the information about how it could work. We believe he fled the complex the night before we raided Nordhausen, taking with him Volume I and leaving Volume II hidden at the complex where we found it. The book was stained with blood. It may not have been his choice to leave it behind. Whatever happened that that night, either Scheel or someone else managed to remove the most important documentation from that complex. Volume I is the Rosetta Stone of his work, and we want to retrieve it."

"What happened to Scheel?" I asked.

"We don't know for sure. No trace of him ever turned up, but we have a few theories. Our leading one is that he defected, or was taken against his will to Russia. Scheel's son Karl was a Luftwaffe pilot and was shot down two years before the war ended and held prisoner by the Russians. Two months after the war ended, he was released and sent back to Berlin. It could have been that his father traded himself and the documentation for his son's release. It's possible he may have promised to work on it for the Russians as part of the exchange. Scheel's biggest bargaining chip was that the volume he was carrying was only half the information. Not having it all almost guaranteed his leverage and his survival. There are other possibilities. Scheel could have been captured and killed. He could have gone into hiding and hid the works. The last possibility, it could be that the Russians have already developed the same capability we have and have gone back to 1945 and retrieved the document. Their goal would have been the same as ours, preventing the other from getting it first, but if they did get it, then something went wrong because it hasn't stopped us. We will go over this down to the last minor detail before you ever take your trip, but I wanted to give you at least a high-level overview."

I sat stunned. The story was too far out there to be believable. It crossed my mind that this charade could be some elaborate test. That maybe this ruse was a psychological evaluation and a cover for something else. I looked over at Rick. He was stoic, but perhaps he too was shocked at the thought of what we had heard. Maybe I was a little more intellectually curious or a skeptic, but I wanted to know how it would work, and if it had been tested. What was the mission plan, and what training did we need? If this were to be the most important mission I would ever go on, I needed to know I had every chance of making it a success. I asked Mac about the classic time travel paradox. If we could go back and change something that prevented us from being here or speed the project up so that other candidates were selected, how would that play out?

"Well, the people in the know have explained that to me, and it makes sense. Let's say you go back and are successful, and let's say we develop this capability ten years earlier and use it in some other way with different officers. All that would mean is that you, Captain Kelly, and you, Lieutenant Wilson, would be doing what you thought would be doing. Test Pilot School for you, SEAL operations for you. Nothing could change the fact that in this play of time, you went back and changed something. The next play would be different, but it wouldn't affect the first. You would be walking around today not knowing the part you played in shaping history."

Mac continued to speak. Whatever he was saying, I wasn't listening. So many thoughts were racing through my mind. I sat still, surprised, wondering. The job, and the mission was not all I had expected. I thought I would pull it off and somehow make it back. I just didn't know how. If this turned out to be true, then I felt pride and confidence to have been selected. It was more than a defining moment for our country; it was a defining moment for me.

Just then, I heard him say, "Gentlemen, you must have a million questions about this. You'll get more detail over the next few weeks as you prep from the mission, but I'll answer as many as I can now."

I didn't know where to start. Before I could get a word out, Rick launched the first question. "When do we go?"

Mac replied that training over the next few weeks would be intense. "Make no mistake. You will be prepared."

The current mission target date was April 23rd. The 23rd meant we would have about five months and some change of preparation. He gave a rundown of what those weeks would entail, starting with our roles. I would assume command of the mission once it was underway. I would be responsible for decision-making and the overall success once we were back in 1945. Aircraft would figure prominently in the plan. Once there, we would fly our way to the target area and then escape by using a plane. I would be the pilot.

Throughout the mission, we would play the role of German Luftwaffe officers. Once on the ground, Rick's part would be to get us inside the target using the SEAL tactics he was an expert at and to destroy the site if necessary once the mission was accomplished. The next three weeks, we would train apart. I would be off to Coronado Beach to get specialized training and conditioning at the SEAL training base. Rick would be getting a crash course in basic German at Monterey to learn to enough to carry on and understand the most likely phrases he would need. After that, he would get a review of strategy and tactics of the German forces guarding Nordhausen. Finally, he would get the basics of flying a high-performance airplane.

The flight training would be done at the Navy training school at Lemoore NAS in California. We both knew why learning each other's skill sets were necessary. Just in case one of didn't make it, the other would have to guarantee mission success. It would be cross-training with the best, but it would also be cross-training at a high level. Time would be of the essence. The remaining weeks, Rick and I would train together. We would need this time to learn each other's thought processes so that we could work as one. I would practice flying a WWII aircraft and engage in dog fighting drills should the unforeseen happen. After all, I would be in enemy territory, but who would be the enemy? We would then head to Germany to my old base at Ramstein, where I would fly a course to Nordhausen, roughly 430km to the northeast in a high-performance propeller-driven plane as a practice run over and over. I would learn the topography and the route as it was now and try to place it as it was then. Even though much had changed in the sixty plus years since war's end, it was an area I knew well from all my years there.

Finally, the last part of our training would be on the ground in Germany, reviewing our land routes and the facilities in and around Nordhausen. Then after months of training, sometime on the morning of April 23rd, we would be ready to go. I wanted to pepper Mac with questions, so I started firing them off. "How does this work?" I asked.

Mac replied, "I'm going to take you downstairs and show you the way you'll get there after we're done here. It'll make more sense when you see it. Simply put, you will transit via a device we've created that won't necessarily transport you back to 1945 Germany in the sense that you might have seen in the movies. Rather, the device opens a window, and you will climb, or in this case fall, through that window into the past."

"How do you know it will work?"

"We found a clever way to test this. Contrary to what you've seen on television and the movies, the reality of time travel is a little different. We don't turn a dial and 'poof' you are back in 1945. That's the movie version. And while it is somewhat like that, I suppose, it is a tad more complicated. I'm not the scientist, but let me try to explain. This place is the second site we've built. The first was located in a remote part of Nevada. When we first tested this, it wasn't at all like we could turn a dial to February of 1945. We didn't have any idea where in time it led or if it even did open a window to the past. So we had to come up with some way to calibrate the device, and since we couldn't peer through that 'window' to see where we were, we needed a method to validate. One of the scientists suggested we drop 'markers' through the device. It had to be something that would be easily identifiable, something large that would attract interest when found, nothing that had technology that didn't exist at the time, and something worth documenting somewhere for us to find when we researched it. So we had these hundred-pound large cast iron balls with the words 'Altoona Iron Works' forged in the side, each with a unique number for tracking."

Mac couldn't resist a tempered laugh.

"I think that goes to show that even physicists who are working on the most complex of the complex have to sometimes resort to simple tactics to get things done. Of course, there was no 'Altoona Iron Works.' There couldn't be. We wanted this to be a well-documented mystery that would make it easy for us to track. We began by dropping the iron balls through the window or let's call it a portal for simplicity. We would then document the settings. And here's the simple part. We would do a search for any historical mention of "Altoona Iron Works." The theory was that someone would find it, document it, or report it, and publish an article in a newspaper about it. Since it happened in the past, we would know the instant we dropped it where it was and when it was found. The first eight attempts, nothing.

"We were concerned initially that these things might fall on a house, show up in someone's living room, appear in the middle of a downtown street, we didn't know what to expect. Looking to see what happened, we went from excitement to disappointment. No trace of the first ones showed up anywhere. We knew they were going somewhere, but we were baffled. It was possible that they were sitting in some remote area of the planet and had never been found. Then finally, on the ninth try, we got a hit.

"We found an article in an Oklahoma Newspaper dated September 1957 titled 'The Mystery of the Iron Ball.' A rancher had found it in a field with no explanation as to how it got there, who or where the 'Altoona Iron Works' was, or where it was located. The paper concluded it was a clever hoax. We also learned that it appeared its the condition that the ball hadn't just appeared in the field, but had fallen from a height of about a hundred feet. They still don't have that one figured out, and it could be an error.

"The leading cause is a difference in elevation between here and where it appeared. You should have heard the room that day. We were elated that it worked, and we couldn't help but laugh hysterically at the article. The approach accomplished what it set out to do, but after the celebration ended, we realized that we had our first marker. We kept the experiments up, and a pattern began to emerge.

"We had plenty more that disappeared, but we soon realized that those had likely fallen into the ocean never to be found. The hits we did get told us what we needed to know. We had ones that were seen in Turkey, Iran, Spain, Northern Texas, Arizona, and Nevada. It took us a while to figure out based on where and when they landed how the device worked. We then were able to place the 'experiments' with some level of precision, although I use that word loosely, within nine days of our target time and within two hundred miles give or take a few of where we wanted it to land. We also learned that the facility in Nevada wouldn't work for this trip.

"That pattern of where the experiments landed could be plotted in a band roughly equal to where we were in the Nevada desert. How they got there is that when we dropped the ball into the portal, it arrived at whatever ground was below in that spot due to the earth's rotation at that time. For us to drop one at the exact site of the experiment would mean that we would have to calibrate the machine to know that when the portal opened that Nevada was there, minutes later it would be in California, hours later the Pacific, China, etc. It was challenging to get that, but we figured it out and got close.

"When you get back to your room and have some downtime, look it up it up. Our experiment has already become a part of history. Those tests told us that we could send something back, that it would arrive intact, but that we didn't have exact control over placement, and that was a going to be a problem. Perhaps our biggest problem was that the device opened a portal along a line that followed our spot in Nevada around the globe. We couldn't place anything north of the 40th parallel or south of the 35th parallel.

"When it had been decided that Nordhausen was the target, we had to build another facility as close to the line that Nordhausen was on as we could. It turns out that Nordhausen is 51 degrees north, and had we stayed in Nevada, it would have meant that the closest we could have placed you would have been Spain or Greece. Italy was too small a target along that band, and with our margin of error, you would have likely ended up in or over the Mediterranean Sea. Minot was the farthest secure site we had, and that's why we're here. It will put you within your fuel range by plane, and if that doesn't work, within an easy distance for you to commandeer ground transportation."

"Why us?" Rick asked.

"You both came highly recommended. Rick, you are the best, a Navy SEAL. We need someone with your skills. Should the two of you encounter problems getting to the site, or trouble when you get there, it will come in handy. Wherever you both are, you will be vastly outnumbered. You'll need every advantage you can muster. As for you, well, your background had what we needed. It is a mix of qualities that matched one to one what we were looking for in our candidates. We needed a pilot, someone who could speak German like a native, someone who knew the land, and someone who knew

41

the history, but for both of you, we needed the drive, the intelligence, and the leadership skills that would make this a success.

"I know how incredibly fantastic this all sounds, but when you are back in 1945, you will be two people on your own who won't have a friendly face in any direction. You will be alone. It will be the limited equipment you will take with you, your training, and the knowledge you have inside your heads will make all the difference between success and failure. You're going to get more of this in the next few months. Why don't we go down and take a look at your ride?"

We walked back to the elevator and proceeded down to Level 3. When the doors opened, it didn't differ much in appearance from L2. The signs showed "Control" to the right and "Transit Preparation" to the left. We followed Mac to a room that resembled the space center's Mission Control in Houston. There was no one here at the moment.

Mac told us, "We don't need anyone here around the clock. This room is staffed when we are conducting tests, and of course, when you make your trip. Let me show you something."

We exited the room and headed for another secured door. When we entered, we were standing in an observation area overlooking a cavernous room down below. Other than a massive crane, the features in the room were unremarkable.

We headed over, and Mac said, "That concrete cover you probably saw on the ground was an elevator. It was used to take material out of this place as it was being built and to bring equipment in at each level. It will also bring down a World War II German plane when it is ready. You will get in the plane, and that crane will hoist the plane and move it. When the time comes, you and the plane will be positioned over those doors. When the transit device is activated, the floor below will open. When the device has reached the operational level desired for February of 1945, the crane will release you, and you will fall into the past."

"Mac, why did they pick this time to go back? Why not just go back and kill Hitler in 1933?" Rick asked.

"There are many terrible weapons in the world. his one could turn out to be the most terrifying of them all. That we have it is a blessing. We are using restraint, and it is a weapon of last resort. If we killed Hitler, then an entire course of history would change, and on the surface, I would say yes, for the better, but it could spawn a series of events that are worse. It is a case of better the devil, you know. To go back at this time minimizes the potential changes in history. Dr. Scheel is missing and was never found, and neither were the critical documents in that missing volume.

"All we want to change is to put that volume in our hands and prevent anyone else from having it. If you were to get to Nordhausen too early, it might alert the Germans to move, hide, or destroy information at the facility, and that would mean a change in history that would prevent us from having this capability. A day late, and it truly would be too late. The documents would be gone. You have to be there at the right window of time to preserve what you can of history. You've got just a taste of what this is all about, and you'll get plenty more over the next few weeks, but all in due course. For now, let's go back up to Level 2. I'll show you the living quarters."

As we walked, Mac started explaining the ground rules. "When you are back at Minot, you will be staying here at the complex. The temporary room you stayed in last night was just to give you time to catch your breath and relax, and of course, reflect on whether or not you really wanted to accept this mission. These past days have been a whirlwind, and we didn't want to overload you right away. You already had enough to digest. Yesterday, you knew little and could walk around the base much like it was a regular daily routine. Today, you know enough to be dangerous, and a threat should anything happen to you or should you have a change of heart.

"When you are off base for training, you will have at least one escort. Your quarters will be guarded for your protection and the project. You are restricted to base at all times. I don't want to make this seem like you're under arrest, but the project has to come first now. You are officers, bound by a sense of honor and of duty. I have made the same commitment you have. Gentlemen, I'm always here to help you whenever I can, but if you break the rules, I will do what I have to do to ensure the mission is not compromised. The world cannot know where you are or know anything about this project. The reality of what you've signed up for means that you don't exist anymore. I can't apologize for the way this has to be, just don't break the rules."

Mac's words were clear, and the thought hadn't really crossed my mind that I couldn't or wouldn't see the outside world for a while or even talk to a familiar face, but contrary to what Mac said, it did feel like I was in prison. I'd be watched as if I were a criminal when what we were being asked to do was all about trust. It seemed a contradiction, but Rick and I were playing by a different set of rules now, and we were both now in a game where we had little control over our fate.

"One more thing," Mac said. "Today, you'll undergo a small medical procedure. It's minor and shouldn't affect anything you need to do or have any lingering effects. We're going to insert a small RFID-type chip in your left arm. The chip won't be able to do anything for you, or for us in the short term. It is a small tracking device that emits a very narrow band frequency that wasn't used in 1945. The work you do in the past might affect the outcome of this project. It could be that Scheel's notes may allow us to perfect the portal beyond what we've done and maybe find a way to bring you back. If it does, then we would likely need a way to locate you. Even though we can't be sure it will work, it at least gives us something that we can track you down with."

My new quarters were spacious and comfortable. There was a bed, a chair, a desk, and shelves with reading material. I walked over to the books and glanced at the titles. All of the titles were about World War II. There was a day-by-day history, a photographic history of the war, a strategy book on how Germany could have won the war, and William Manchester's *Rise and Fall of the Third Reich.*

Mac remarked, "With what little free time you have when you're not training, you can look through those as a refresher. I've looked through the pictorial history before. You can't help but realize that any war is a terrible one, but this one was the most brutal. For us to have this capability could allow us to prevent this war, but the people above us have greater restraint than you or I, and we don't want to tempt fate any more than we already are."

I asked Mac what his thoughts were on the project, having been much closer to it then we were.

"I've not been in on the decision process," he said. "Mine is a role of execution, but if it were mine to make, I would have killed the son of a bitch, and that's why I'm here doing this and not making the decisions about how to use it."

"What will you do when this is over, Mac? Are there more of these planned?"

"I don't know about any more of these. I've not heard, and we don't have another team or another project in the wings. This is it."

I saw a different side of Rick. He began to get philosophical. "With this tool, we could go back and learn from the greats of history. You could meet Jesus, watch Michelangelo paint the Sistine Chapel, watch the birth of our country, stop the men who killed Lincoln, Kennedy, and King. The possibilities are endless."

Mac looked down at the floor for a moment. His face lacked any expression or emotion.

"Yes, there are a lot of opportunities and a lot of possibilities, but the dangers far outweigh the benefit. We also discovered a limitation in the system. So far, we've not been able to send anything back farther than seventy-seven years or sooner than seventeen years ago. We don't know why, but it is something that is a barrier to exploring those great periods in history. And all is well anyway. We are a world of explorers, and that exploration has often led to conquest. If we explored, the past we, too, may decide to re-conquer and do the very same thing Adolf Hitler tried to do, and that wouldn't make us any better than him. You know we could go on with this endlessly – the "what ifs" and the paradoxes. Do what you need to do when you get there and nothing more. Don't try to make it better and don't set it up to be worse. The time since 1945 has seen our country prosper and struggle, but we've still led the world and protected it. It's a fragile balance, but it is a balance. Let's keep it that way. Let's walk over the medical center and get this procedure done, and then at 1300 hours, you'll get a detailed briefing on where we go from here."

The small medical center was on Level 2 of the complex. Its purpose was to check up on us periodically and to give us the final medical okay to go when the time came, and of course to handle anything that may come up in the interim. Waiting in the room was a small team. There were two military doctors and two nurses getting the materials prepped. "Have a seat. This won't take too long," one of the nurses said. No sooner did we sit than the nurse asked each of us to roll up the sleeves on our right arm. She swabbed the area and told us she was going to give us a local anesthetic. One of the doctors remarked, "I'd like to do this with a local. No sense hauling out the big stuff for this."

The nurse injected me on the bottom of my forearm about midway between my wrist and elbow. Other than the momentary prick of the needle, I felt nothing. The doctor pulled up a stool next to the chair and asked me if I had any sensation as he pinched my arm. "Nothing," I said.

"That's good. Let me tell you what I'm going to do. You know how they microchip dogs? Well, I'm going to microchip you. I'm going to make a tiny incision right about here. Then, I'm going to insert this small item into your arm and then stitch you back up." He held up a small white square about the size of a pencil eraser. "The chip is inside of this package, and the coating will prevent any rejection by your body. I'm not anticipating that you'll notice anything except the stitches. You won't ever know it's there. Alright, I don't know if you're at all squeamish. I would be if I were sitting there getting my arm cut open. But feel free to turn your head if you'd like."

I was a lot more curious than I was squeamish. I wanted to watch what was being done. He picked up the scalpel from the tray and carefully made a one-inch incision. A trickle of blood ran from the cut before the nurse could swab it. The blood trickle dropped on the floor. Using a pair of tweezers, the doctor picked the chip up and tucked it inside my arm, pushing it gently in.

"A nice fit," he remarked. "A few stitches should do the trick. Bob, you want to go ahead and close him up while I start on the other one?"

He patted me on the shoulder as he moved over to Rick and said, "See, that didn't hurt your buddy over there a bit."

The other doctor started to stitch the incision up. I still couldn't feel a thing. While he was putting the finishing touches on me, I looked over and watched him do the same thing to Rick, same arm, and same spot. When they finished, they told us that it would heal in a few days.

"Keep a bandage on it and try to keep it clean. Other than that, no special care is required."

Mac asked us if it was starting to wear off yet. I told him not yet and that it was still quite numb. He walked over to the table and picked up a device with his left hand. The small orange box gave off a faint beep. Mac switched it to his right side and held it over my left arm. The device beeped as he moved it near the incision.

"Good work, Doc. Everything seems just fine."

Mac placed the device back on the counter. He turned to Rick and me. "You have a briefing in an hour, so go get some chow. The commissary is stocked with a variety of selections. There are microwaveable meals, sandwiches, and other snacks. Grab something and meet me in the training room at 1300. I've got a small office upstairs in operations. I'm going to go take care of a few things, and then I'll be back down later."

As Mac left, Rick and I made our way to get a bite. I wasn't hungry, and neither was Rick. There was so much going on that eating was way down on the list. I looked around the commissary. Mac wasn't kidding when he said this was well stocked. We had everything. "Look at this," I said to Rick. "I don't think there's one healthy piece of food in this place."

Rick replied, "When you don't have many meals left, you might as well make the most of it. They should be feeding us prime rib every night."

"So tell me what you think of this so far," I asked him.

"Well, it's a lot to take in. I always wanted to be a SEAL, and I knew that my first mission could be my last. I've been on quite a few, lots of close calls where I should be dead, but I'm alive. All of this time travel stuff and going back to fight in World War II is overwhelming for me to take in. Right now I just have the feeling that it won't work or what they have doesn't work. I'm not even thinking about what will happen when we get there. I'm just hoping we do get there."

I gave Rick my two cents and shared with him that this wasn't exactly what I had in mind. However, given what it was, there weren't any circumstances under which I would have turned it down or changed my mind. I told him that I had reconnected with someone before I left and that I would regret never having the opportunity to see what might have happened there. I told him what hurt the most for me was that I was the end of the line for my family. I always wanted to have a family, have a son, a daughter, and a few more for that matter. I wanted a legacy that could carry on what I knew and what I thought long after I was gone.

Rick had his own thoughts on a family. "My life has always been about the Navy, and that girl in every port stuff wasn't for me. Don't get me wrong, I've set sail more than my fair share of times, but a family was something so far down the road for me that I didn't think I'd live long enough to make it happen, and looks like I was right. In my line of work, I couldn't put kids through that."

"You were right enough for both of us," I said. "I had the tiniest thought that it might not work, but that Mac seemed reassuring. The testing method using the 'iron ball' to calibrate was clever. It would be quite a rouse to make that up. You know, let's go get online in the media room and check that out while we have a few minutes."

"It means nothing," he said.

Surprised, I asked, "What does that mean?"

"Can't you see they're controlling every aspect of our lives? They determine where we go, whom we talk to, what we see, and what we hear. For all we know, that information could be a setup. They want us to look, and it'll be there, but it could be a plant. They are probably watching and listening to us right now to see how we're reacting."

I was curious about his thoughts and wanted to probe deeper. This could give me insight into what he was thinking. "Rick, do you think this is some elaborate rouse? You think this is a test of some sort? For what?"

"I don't know. I just don't know. There aren't many people who would believe what we've been told. I think we're both entitled to our doubts."

Well, I wasn't nearly as suspicious as Rick. I didn't think he was paranoid. I wanted to give him the benefit of the doubt that it was his training. He had to be on the lookout for trouble all three hundred and sixty degrees around him. Maybe he was sensing something.

I had my own skepticism, but I didn't want to fall into the trap of not believing what I was being told. I hadn't questioned orders before, and I wouldn't start now. Just then, Mac popped his head inside. "Briefing time. See you in the training room in fifteen."

It would be a discussion item for later. For now, I had more interest in getting the show on the road, getting the training done, and just doing it. In the briefing room, it was only the three of us. "Let me go over your itinerary. When we're done here, we'll get in the car and head back to the base. Rick, you'll be off to Monterey for a few weeks of German language training. Then from there, you'll head to Lemoore for basic flight training. Jake, you're off to Miramar where you'll stay tonight, then head to Coronado Beach in the morning to begin conditioning and training in commando tactics. Then you'll head to Lemoore to practice in a Luftwaffe aircraft."

Rick leaned over to me and said in a lowered voice, "Been there, done that on the SEAL training. Good luck on that one."

I whispered back, "Viel Glück mit Versuch, Deutsch in drei Wochen zu lernen."

"What?" He exclaimed.

"Good luck learning German!" I told him.

Mac went on to say, "I'll join you at Lemoore in three weeks. We'll sync up there."

"What will you be doing between now and then?" Rick asked.

"There are a million details between now at the time we leave for Ramstein and a million more for when we get back. I'll be plenty busy. Go pack a few things and meet me up on Level M at 1800 hours."

Day one had turned out to be pretty eventful. There was the surprise of finding out what the mission was all about and the somewhat disbelief of what we'd be doing, and of course, we were quickly on the move again to another location. We were becoming tumbleweeds drifting from here to there. This was probably part of the idea baked into their training. Never let us get comfortable and keep us moving. At least I knew that I'd be in one place for the next few weeks, then after that, I'd be in the cockpit of a Luftwaffe plane getting familiar with it. It sounded bizarre saying that, even if only to myself. However, that was definitely something to look forward to. Tonight, when I got to Miramar, it would be a time to replay the day and time to get my head focused on the challenges I'd face tomorrow. I knew the SEAL training was intense, and it would be as physically demanding as it would be mentally demanding.

I went back to the room as Mac had instructed and started packing a few things into my backpack. I was sure they'd have what I needed at Miramar, so I packed light. It was quiet and my first chance to think things through. For the first time since Friday morning, I thought about Beth. My reasons to succeed in this mission were more critical than ever. I wanted to come home to see her again. All I could hope for was something Mac said earlier, that if we were successful, there was a chance it could change their knowledge of the process enough that they could bring Rick and me back. Perhaps we would change the future ever so slightly. Sufficient that Rick and I would never know what happened. If that were the case, I wouldn't have been called to Andrews and wouldn't have seen Beth. I only hoped that if it worked out that way, that I would realize how important she was to me, and that somewhere along the way, I would find her.

Those are the moments that define each of our individual histories. The chance meetings, chance events that accumulate and put us in a place down the road for something much more significant. The slim prospect of that and the small chip now in my arm were the only hope. With the communications blackout and the length of training, the trip back, and the promise of returning it could be months before I could contact her or ever see her again. There was a big "if" in there, coming back. As I was thinking about all of this, there was a knock on the door. It was Mac. He wanted to stop by and see if everything was okay and if I needed anything and get a pulse check on where we were after day one. I told him I had every intention of succeeding and making the mission a success. In a couple of months, if it all worked as planned, and if they could bring us back, I'd be buying him a beer at the Officer's Club.

He stared at the floor for a moment then said, "There are two reasons why the chance of survival on this mission is zero. First, we don't have a way to bring you back, and it's not likely we ever will. Never say never, but the best minds have been working on this for years, and this is the extent of what they have developed. I don't want to raise any false hopes. They don't think it is possible. The second is…" He hesitated.

"What?" I asked.

"You guys got a lot of information today. I didn't tell you everything because I didn't want to pile on to what you already had to process. When you're back there and the mission is done, it is too risky to let you go about your life in the '40s, '50s, '60s, and on and on. You know too much about the world and you can make a difference. The two of you alive during those years has the potential to disrupt time as much as we could with the device. If by some chance we can manage to bring you back, the window in which we would be able to locate you and find you would be narrow. It would only be a matter of days. When you've secured the document and returned to England, or if the mission fails and the Germans or the Russians capture you, there will be a cyanide capsule in your fight suit. No matter what the outcome, whether you are successful or unsuccessful, you cannot survive through time.

"After you complete the mission or when you are standing on the doorstep of defeat, you will have to put the capsule in your mouth and crack the casing. You will die in less than a minute, and the rest of history will be preserved. I know that's a hard one to take, but this is a one-way ticket you've purchased. Let me add one more thing. When I signed up for this mission, I got the same deal. This place goes into mothballs and my time will also expire. I am too great a risk to have out there walking around. I couldn't tell anybody how to build this thing, but I could tell someone everything else, and that is a risk no one wants to take. I don't like it any more than you do, but we have to do what we have to do. That old saying, 'The needs of the many outweigh the needs of the one,' or in this case, the three of us, and many others who worked on this project. Who knows? Maybe it will work out. I just wouldn't plan on it."

Suddenly, there was that lump in my throat and a pit in my stomach. Whatever ill feeling one could assemble. I didn't show it, but the energy had drained from me like someone flipped a switch. I wasn't sure if it was fear or something else, but my body knew what my head couldn't comprehend. The mission was tantamount to a death sentence for my life, as I knew it today.

With all that had been said by various people, the scope of it all hadn't sunk in until now. The thought of backing out hadn't crossed my mind. I knew this was important and a chance at history. I wanted to do this. But now I thought of people and places I would never see again. I thought back to never having a family and anyone to carry on, and I thought of Beth. It took me eight years to come around to know I wanted her to be a part of my life, and now I would leave without explanation. I dreamed of that moment of seeing her again, of holding her. What happened in Maryland, I knew this was what I was looking for in life. The wind had dissipated from my sails;

this dream would go on as just a dream. I asked Mac how our disappearance would be explained to anyone who may care to look.

"The standard practice applies. The military will tell any relatives or family that you were lost on a critical mission, and you died in the service of your country, that you died a hero. Your bodies will be listed as never having been recovered, but in Arlington, they will place a gravestone recognizing your sacrifice. Let's get you over to the base and get you on that flight. When you start the SEAL training, your mind will be off of this for a while. I know it'll never be off your mind entirely, but live every day you can while you're here. Those SEAL instructors are a crazy bunch, and they'll be waiting for you. An Air Force guy among deck swabbies, all I can say is that's going to be quite interesting, but you'll enjoy those guys. Give 'em hell.

"When you get to Lemoore, we will be into the thick of this. As a pilot, I know you will be chomping at the bit to fly that German plane. The one you'll take back is here, upstairs in the maintenance hangar, and will be brought down here soon. As a matter of fact, barring any problems, it'll be down on L3 when you get back. It'll be your baby. We don't have time to stop by the hangar today, but an identical one is at Lemoore, and you'll spend some time flying it. We'll do dogfight simulations, and you'll learn every inch of that plane and what it can do. There won't be anyone like you flying back then. Your training and knowledge make you the elite of the elite against any of the German, American, British, or Russians flyers. If they had you, we'd be in trouble. Before I forget, here's something I found in an old bookstore up in San Francisco."

Mac handed me a small, thin paperback book. It was an old German book. I looked at the cover. "*Fliegen Lernen!*" He explained that this was a book given to young men in Germany to get them interested in flying. The last 20 pages had pictures and descriptions of military aircraft of the Luftwaffe. The plane I would fly was on page 66, he said. "Carry it with you. It made through the war once. It might be good luck." When I flipped to the page, there was a picture of a Ju87d, a two-seat, dive-bomber. I smiled and said, "Thanks, Mac. I'll keep it with me."

I grabbed my backpack, then Mac, Rick and I took the elevator back upstairs, stopping at the main level to switch. For security purposes, no one elevator could go from the surface to the transit area. When we reached the outside, the vehicles we drove in were waiting for us. I asked Mac, "Who are those guys?"

"Your escorts," he replied. "I don't think they'll be too in your face, but I wouldn't mess with them. They've got the same orders I have."

We drove back the same way we came, and it was just as cold outside. The sun hadn't done much to warm the landscape. For a few weeks, I would be in sunny Southern California, not Edwards where I would have been reporting to this week, but California nonetheless. When we got to the base, the Gulfstreams were waiting. I saluted Rick and Mac and dashed for my plane. As I sat down, I could see out the window Rick boarding his. It would be several weeks before we saw each other. I hardly knew him. We barely had any meaningful dialogue, and yet we were going on the most dangerous adventure of our lives. The real tests, though, lay ahead. We would train together when it was most critical, on the ground in Germany.

The flight was smooth down to Miramar. We were chasing the sunset as we headed across the desert southwest. My two "escorts" didn't say a word, and I wasn't very interested anyway in talking to them. They were there to hover over me, and I wasn't at all pleased to have the company. Besides, they didn't at all seem the conversational type. I pulled out a book I grabbed off the shelf in my room back at the complex and began reading about Hitler's mistakes and how he could have won the war. There was a bit of irony in that. Hitler wanted to send a message back to himself to correct the mistakes of the war, and here I was holding in my hands the very answers he was looking for, and soon I would be there with that knowledge. It was a strange twist.

Upon landing at Miramar, I was greeted by a senior naval officer who took me to the Officer's Club for a late dinner. There was a distinct smell of the sea in the air. It was breezy and warm. A drastic change from where I came. The officer asked about the exchange program I was on and what I thought it would be like for an Air Force Officer to train with the SEALS. I told him I would have much rather been here to attend Top Gun training. When I finally got to the room, I felt tired but didn't feel like calling it an early night. The fatigue wasn't from doing too much. In the space of days, I crossed time zones from halfway around the world, stopping only a day or two before moving again. Those days included an emotional roller coaster that I still had not reconciled. I lay there on the bed just thinking about things. As the time grew late, I finally drifted off to sleep.

It was hard to sleep. I was catching forty-minute naps or so and then waking up. I wondered if Rick was having the same problem. My mind was racing with thoughts. I started thinking that maybe I could get a hold of Beth to tell her I hadn't forgotten our plans, just that I would be out of touch for a while. I wasn't sure how she felt about seeing me anyway. She seemed excited that night, then there was the note on the picture, but I didn't know if that was just her being her or whether she felt that spark. The spark inside of me was becoming more of a raging hormonal fire. I had to regain my focus, or this would drive me insane. I had these escorts glued to me for now, but somewhere I knew I could duck them and get a message off. That might help calm me down. Nobody would know if I called. I supposed it was all wishful thinking for now. I could think about it or dream about, but I was told no communications. I wouldn't break orders.

Whoever screened me did a good job; I was too loyal an officer ever to disobey a command. They knew it. Rick, I'm sure, was cut from the same mold. I wish I could have done something to talk to her, but it wasn't to be. Someday maybe the truth would come out, and she would know why I couldn't get back to her. I knew she would understand, but she would never know how I felt about her.

It was about 0200 hours Pacific time, and I was finally falling asleep at just about the time I needed to get up. I could get an extra hour's sleep if I skipped showering. That might be more of a necessity than an option. There were always more important things than looking good, and right now, sleep was one of them. I caught a quick power nap with what precious little time I had left. As the alarm went off, I cleared the fog from my brain. The next few weeks would be challenging. Perhaps, the toughest I've faced, and that was saying something. I quickly showered and shaved, then raced over the hangar to hop a ride over to Coronado Beach. Chopper rides seemed the norm of late. Lately, I was using them as taxis. It was out of the ordinary for me. The men at the field were also up early. One seaman on the pad handed me a helmet. It was the signal the pilot who was waiting for as the Navy Seahawk's engines started to whirr and the rotors slowly began to turn. The team here at Miramar must have gotten a heads up to keep the red carpet available. They had to suspect something that an Air Force captain would warrant such special treatment.

It was still dark as the helo lifted off and headed towards Coronado Beach. The side cargo door was left open, and a rush of air filled the cabin. There was no hint of sunrise to my rear, and only the even darker expanse of the Pacific Ocean lay ahead. It was strange, but with the noise and the sound of the wind as the helo picked up speed, it was peaceful. It was the thing I loved most about flying.

TRAINING WITH THE TEAMS

Morning always came too quickly for those of us in the military. It was dark when you went to sleep and still dark when you awoke. With this entire business of running around day after day, I was beginning to think I would never get used to being in a different place in a different time zone each night. I was thinking about what lay ahead. The past had to be the past for me; my remaining future was whatever the next few weeks and months held. I focused more and more on what it would be like when we left. For my immediate future, I would be getting personal instruction on tactics and training from the best of the best. There would be drills and tasks aimed at preparing me physically. I would do it all alongside a current group of trainees. The instructors here wouldn't know why I was here or singled out to get special treatment. They were professionals and took pride in making sure whoever came through this regimen was well trained for battle, and I wasn't going to be an exception.

SEAL training was probably the most stringent military training anywhere in the world. I knew and worked with some buddies who had been on the "teams." It took thousands of hours and roughly thirty months, give or take few, to train a Navy SEAL. I was getting the crash course. The next three weeks would be grueling, but I was looking forward to it in a way. I would need every advantage I could get, and this training might make all the difference in whether we would succeed or fail.

Rick's three weeks might be a little more relaxed of a regimen than I would go through, but he had already been through this very same training. They had no chance of making me a SEAL in three weeks, but they might get him to learn enough German to pull it off if questioned, and they had a better chance of getting him acclimated enough in a plane to know what to do in an emergency.

I started to think about that more, to be a pilot in the conditions we would likely face: dogfights, anti-aircraft fire, night flying, lousy weather, unfamiliar terrain, and host of other things that could go wrong. His skills would come in handy on the ground. Flying in an emergency under those conditions wasn't for the unskilled pilot, especially in a high-performance plane like the one we would be using. It would have to be in a limited set of circumstances for him to leverage what they were teaching him. The configuration of the JU-87 meant that the rear man was a gunner with his back to the pilot. It wasn't a trainer. There weren't dual controls, and if something happened to the pilot, it would mean both crewmen would be lost. There was nothing the gunner could do. When I saw him again, I would want to know what he learned and have him show me. I knew he would want the same. Now it wasn't about looking out for each other, even though that was critically important, this was about making sure that if something happened to one of us, the other could finish the mission alone.

I was sure he was bored having to sit and learn German at the Navy's language school in Monterey. I had the advantage of listening to my grandmother as I was growing up. I could understand it long before I could speak it. Strangely, it seemed to come naturally. An advantage when the time came to learn it formally.

The ride was short to Coronado. The ten-minute hop seemed longer. As the helo set down, there was a welcoming committee waiting for me. I could tell by the all-business demeanor that I was in for no special treatment.

"Welcome to Coronado Beach, lead wings" one of the instructors yelled. He tossed me a change of clothes and told me to change. "We're not like the Air Force around here. We're actually in a hurry to get things done," he barked.

SEAL training took months to complete and is broken into phases. The first phase was eight weeks and focused on conditioning. The third week was the infamous "Hell Week." During that week, a SEAL trainee was allowed a maximum of four hours sleep during the entire drill. It looked from my agenda like I'd miss all the fun of that adventure. Instead, I'd get to spend my first week with a new class of recruits already in their second week of training. They were being trained progressively harder each week to prep them for that week of hell.

It could have been worse. I was not coming at the easiest time, but I felt good that I could handle all that they would throw at me. My resolve was strong, and my desire to succeed stronger. I knew that they would run the other guys and me into the ground over the next seven days. I was always excited about getting in the game but was never a good practice player. I just wanted to get on with the mission; it was all I could think about now. This training was much like practice, though, a necessary evil.

As I joined the current recruits in training, it was explained that I was part of a group on a pilot exchange program with the Navy. I was there to get a taste of what the SEAL training was all about. During my four years at the academy for four years, daily conditioning was the norm. We left in great shape, and now I hoped I hadn't lost any of it.

The days were filled with calisthenics, obstacle courses, and long runs. Several times a day, I ran a four-mile trek in boots and gear. It was painful, and much more arduous than my current daily workout. As each night came, I was sore and aching and left wondering how I'd drag myself through another day of this. The good news was that I was starting with a body in pretty good shape, and by the time this week was done, and the next two weeks after that finished, I would be fine-tuned and ready.

The first week of training passed quickly. A harsh regimen, but the soreness soon faded as the week went on, and I now was beginning to feel good. I hadn't been through this physical rigor in a while, but I held up well. This week was meant to sharpen and fine-tune me physically. I felt that mission had been accomplished. Maybe this was giving me the extra edge I would need in whatever lay ahead on our journey.

During this first week, I met some new friends. I wondered if one of them would one day find their way into a situation like this one. After all, Rick did, and if they ever did, I would never know, for our paths would never cross again. Many of them would put their life on the line in many dangerous operations on behalf of the country. It was no different from what Rick and I were about to undertake. SEALs today had so many high-tech weapons and tools at their disposal. I wasn't going to get to use any of it.

There would be no 21st-century advantage in 1945. Too risky, should something go wrong and the technologies fall into the wrong hands. I would be trained, and it would be the old-fashioned way. I would learn the most critical commando tactics. I would need to parachute several times, which I had done many times before in pilot training. Perhaps most importantly, I would get the overview on the use of explosives. We would be carrying some back in the plane if we needed to use them. Aside from the teamwork, the most important lesson I learned in any of my training was that when faced with danger, you must kill before being killed. No hesitation. I trained on how to use all my weapons, how to assess and read a situation, and how to work closely as a team. It was the common sense stuff we often forgot.

The final two weeks, I would spend on San Clemente Island, a site used by the Navy for commando training of SEALS. I would spend the time learning what a SEAL could do to survive and be stealth-like. This time, I wouldn't be an observer joining another team. These resources were dedicated to me and me alone. It would be a crash course, intense and draining. I knew these guys had one goal, and that was to make sure I was as prepared for the unknown as anybody could be on such short notice.

My mind drifted for a moment as I thought about how much I would have to learn and in such a short amount of time. After all, I still had to fly a World War II German aircraft from God knows where to a destination in the middle of a war. A war where the very people I was impersonating were being swatted from the skies like flies and hunted on the ground by Americans and Russians. My training now was focused on us being there, and in the field, I was starting to think about just getting there, forgetting all the science of it and just navigating my way to a specific target. For the first time, I was feeling the weight of what we were being asked to do. I couldn't help but think that the magnitude of factors needed for this to be a success continued to mount. With only two of us, the margin for error was slim, and the odds are against us.

In battle, we used overwhelming force to capture an objective or defeat an enemy. Here, no overwhelming force was possible. We would have to rely on outsmarting the enemy and a healthy dose of luck. It made me wonder if my questioning and self-doubt were indications of weakness. Then I thought that anyone else in my shoes would be feeling the same. No one had ever faced what we were facing. It would be only natural to have some apprehension. I knew I would deal with it.

On San Clemente Island, I was partnered with a SEAL veteran, Jack "Black Jack" Foster. Jack and his team patiently walked through many scenarios as we conducted mock assaults and raids in conditions similar to what Rick and I could expect. Each situation was a little different. Each time the group we were trying to overtake was an expert group of commandos; there would be no holding back. To be the best, we had to face and defeat the best. I was a pilot by training, but also a leader, accustomed to making split-second life-or-death decisions. For today and tomorrow, that might be the most important skill I would ever need.

There was so much to absorb. These were just simulations, but they exposed my weaknesses, and as I was "killed over and over," the danger of all of this became apparent. A mistake here just meant we reviewed what went wrong and then did it again. A mistake there meant our lives. The odds seemed staggering. During one of the successful mock assaults, my partner and I successfully raided the compound and retrieved our target. However, getting there, getting the target was less than half of the mission. In my mission, I would have to escape undetected, get back to the airport, fly a German fighter plane across the English Channel into "enemy" territory, and hope I could get back and explain all of this before being shot down.

By the end of the second week of training on assault tactics and weaponry, I had gained new confidence in my abilities as a commando. Several short weeks of training does not a SEAL make, but the individual attention and focus had left me more prepared. During that time, I trained extensively with a handgun and knife and learned to use all my senses. In the cockpit of my plane, I would use weapons like missiles and rockets. The enemy was often faceless to me, but now, I was learning how to kill with my hands, and the enemy would have a face.

The weeks here in Southern California had gone by in the blink an eye. It seemed just yesterday I was in Washington finding out about the effort. Just weeks later, and another key milestone of the project was checked off. The last day of training had come and gone. I got the pleasure of going back to Coronado Beach on a small Navy specialized warfare vessel. It was about the size of an old World War II PT boat. As we disembarked, the whole team that worked with me was here for a last send off. We headed together over to the officer's club for a few drinks and a farewell. They didn't know the mission I would have to perform. They had no idea where I was going. All they knew was that this wasn't an exchange program, but something different. They respected that I would be putting my life on the line like they had done so many times and were prepared to do each mission they went on. The feeling was mutual.

I would be leaving with great admiration for those guys and the work they did. While we were talking and having a few relaxing moments, I got word that my ride was here to take me back to Miramar. I'd miss the camaraderie that I'd struck with these men in just a few short weeks. Like so many other things I thought of now, I knew this was the last time I would ever see them. As I was shaking hands and saying my goodbyes, Jack, my commando partner over the previous two weeks, took his SEAL insignia and pinned it on my flight suit.

He said, "This is for good luck. And besides, I've heard those Air Force Wings are made of lead. Navy gold is definitely a better color for you." Then he added, "But the most important thing this means is that wherever you are, we are there are with you. Look us up sometime when you get back. I know you will."

The sincerity and heart of this battle-hardened vet touched me deeply. I smiled and headed out the door. A jeep was waiting to take me to the chopper pad. On the short ride to the pad, I looked down at the SEAL pin and thought of my past three weeks. It had been a great experience. I knew I was better for it and that it gave me an edge I hadn't had before today. I thought about those last comments from Jack. We couldn't fail on this mission. We had to succeed. But no matter what we did, we'd never come back.

The Navy chopper saw me approaching and started the engines. I thanked my ride and ran to the chopper. I was handed a helmet as I climbed aboard for the last time. The engines revved, and we lifted off and accelerated across the field, slowly climbing out. As we swung around the base and began the trek toward the east, I looked down and could see new recruits working through the same routine I went through. Within minutes, it was out of sight and out of mind. My focus was now ahead to what was next back at Lemoore.

It had been just a little more than four weeks now since all of this started. I had begun to lose track of time. Christmas was approaching, but there was no stopping to celebrate. Even for one last holiday. We were moving fast and aggressively. The pace was picking up. So much more work to do to get prepared for that day in April. As each minute and each day passed, I was closer to my future and farther from my past.

The chopper was vibrating, and the sound was still loud, even with ear protection. I leaned back and closed my eyes for a minute and began thinking of Beth again. I was wondering what she thought since by now it had been a few weeks of no contact. I didn't know if she would guess I just wasn't interested since I didn't call, or what anybody would say if she tried me at Andrews or Edwards. Maybe there was a fairytale story of how she would find me before I left. I just wasn't sure. Through all the years we were apart, I had always felt somehow connected to her. I was feeling it now; I knew she was out there trying to reach me, but I knew that finding me wasn't going to happen. I would be in all the wrong places and never long enough at any of them.

ON TO LEMOORE

I would be catching a different ride up to Lemoore Naval Air Station. A Navy captain greeted me as I got off the helo. "You got gear?" he asked.

"Not much," I replied.

"Anything you can live without?"

"All of it."

"Well, I'm headed up to Lemoore, and they asked me to give you a ride. The Gulfstream you were supposed to fly out on has been delayed getting here, and they wanted to make sure you got up there tonight. That's my baby over there." He pointed to an FA-18 Super Hornet training model, a two-seater version of the typical single-seat fighter jet.

"When are we leaving?"

"How about now? If you need to grab something, let me know, but I have to tell you I don't have much space left in the trunk," he said as he laughed. "The other two with you will be catching another ride." We walked over to the plane, and he asked, "What are you flying? The 15, 16, or 22?" He was referring to the type of aircraft I flew.

"I fly the F-15E model, the two-seater version much like this one. I've done some work in the 16 and a little with the 22 and the F-35 JSF (Joint Strike Fighter)." I told him I was headed out to Edwards to do some work at the test facility out there but got sidetracked on a special assignment.

"That's too bad. I hope the detour doesn't take you too far out of the way. The TP program is where I'd like to be." He had no idea how far out I would be going.

The crew chief handed me a helmet, and before I climbed up, I asked, "'Fryer?'" referring to his call sign stenciled on the side of the plane.

"You know how these idiots are when you get tagged with a call sign. My last name is Tuck, and they started calling me 'Friar Tuck,' then they spelled it "Fryer" to be funny. I never even knew whom this Friar Tuck was to get the first joke, much less the second. What's yours?"

"I got tagged with 'The Baron,' but 'Baron' for short. At the academy, I was the World War II history buff, and I made the mistake of correcting a professor about his theory on German Luftwaffe tactics. He took some offense to it and announced to the class that 'Germany had the Red Baron and America now has the Red, White, and Blue Baron.' It stuck."

Before we climbed aboard, I took a good look at the plane and commented that I loved the design, how the wings blended into the body to the cockpit. It was always one of my favorite fighter planes. I climbed aboard and secured myself in. It had been a while since I'd been in the back seat and weeks since I'd been in a fighter. Unlike the two-seat version I typically flew with a weapons officer in the back, this was a trainer. As such, it had the full complement of controls. It felt good sitting back in the cockpit. This place was where I wanted to be.

"What's the flight time to Lemoore? I asked.

"They said they wanted you up there as soon as possible, but what would you like it to be?

"I'm all for the scenic route."

"We can fly out over the Pacific, and you can see how this puppy handles compared to what you've flown."

"I can honestly say that's the best idea I've heard in weeks. Let's do it."

He started the engines while the ground crew got into position to wave us out. I saluted the chief, and Tuck began our taxi. After you've flown a fighter, it's hard to drive anything else, and it's hard to be a passenger, but any time in the cockpit in any form is something that can't be beat. Tuck lined us up on runway 24 right. The word came over the radio that we were cleared. Tuck acknowledged with a "Roger" and pushed the throttle forward as the F-18 raced down the runway. He eased back into a steady climb and banked left. Within seconds, we were racing out over the Pacific. I spotted the Catalina Islands below as they passed off of our right.

"I'm going to take us out for a bit, then turn right and go up the coast. About forty-five minutes, give or take a few, to touchdown. I'm not carrying a full load of fuel, and this is one thirsty Hornet. No worries, though, I've got plenty to spare. This Hornet is a guzzler."

The time went by quickly; we flew north up the coast and out over the blue water with no land in sight for most of the trip.

"Want to take the controls and fly her for a bit? See how she handles compared to that eagle?"

I let Tuck know I had it and began testing the handling and performance of the aircraft.

"It feels lighter on the stick. A little snappier, but I probably have you beat on the top line."

After about twenty minutes, I turned it back over for our final approach to Lemoore. Tuck then turned the Hornet east and headed over land. We cruised over the California Mountains and began our descent into the San Joaquin Valley region, home to some of the most fertile soil in the country. "Cleared on runway 14 left" was the message from the tower. As I looked out over the landscape, the ground below was brown. Even in sunny California, midway between the southern and northern tiers of the state, winter had arrived. We glided in for a smooth landing on the airstrip.

For all the "fun" at Coronado, it felt good to be back in the air and at the controls of an aircraft. As we taxied over the hangar, I could see Mac waiting for my arrival. When the canopy opened, Mac yelled, "About time you got here!"

I climbed down, handed my helmet to the ground crew, and thanked Tuck for the lift. I then walked with Mac over to the jeep. "There's been a change in plans. We're accelerating the schedule. The brass are nervous. Ever since we figured this thing out, our satellites have watched the band in around fifty-one degrees north. We spotted activity south of Kursk. It's the right location, and it is a place where two crucial battles were fought in World War II, one German offensive against the Soviets and the second a Soviet offensive against the Germans. Between both of them, over one and a quarter million Soviet military and civilians lost their lives.

That spot fits the geography to build a transit complex, and it fits the history of why they would place something there. The Russians have a sense of history about things like that and a long memory. We were gathering additional intelligence and conducting satellite reconnaissance on the site. It could turn out to be a coincidence, but no one wants to take a chance. If it were true that they are still in the building phase, it would be a bad sign, but not the worst-case scenario. There was some school of thought that the Russians had done this and beat us there. If they are still working on it, then they didn't get operational, and we've got a fighting chance. Either way, we're not waiting to find out. Here's what we've got in mind."

As Mac was laying out the documents on the hood of the jeep, I asked him what the game plan was for Rick. "That was an area we compressed in the schedule. He was initially supposed to get some basic flight training in the aircraft. It could have come in handy, but realistically, the return on it was low. Even if we got him proficient at it to do what would need to be done, the potential of battling through American and Russian fighters would be suicide. It would doom the mission if it came down to that being the difference. If you and he can't make it by plane, then you'll do it on the ground, and he's already the expert at that. He's been back at Minot and will be coming in here tomorrow.

"Now I know you are a good pilot, but you're going to need a few days with an instructor in the plane to get used to it. After a few test runs, I want you and Rick in the aircraft together getting as familiar as you can with it. It isn't an F-15, and it isn't a private plane either. It's a high-performance plane from another era, and no matter how good you are at jets, you'll need some specialized training in this aircraft. You will need to practice the tactics of the day as it was in 1945. I can't emphasize that enough.

"We'll spend a week here doing that, and then back to Minot for a few days before we head on to Germany. You'll pick up flying a duplicate there. So you'll have plenty of time to practice. With the new schedule, we'll be back at Minot in a month, and so we'll be leaving a full month earlier than planned. I know this has all the earmarks of cutting time on training, which could bite us down the road, but we've got no choice."

It already felt as if this plan was going off the rails. Nothing was worse for a complex mission than shortcuts in training, and less time to fully prepare. Mac went on to paint a grimmer picture of the current state of thinking in Washington.

"They are so jittery about this that I've heard rumblings that an air strike is possible if they confirm the Kursk site is their equivalent of our Minot complex. Another option I've heard floated is to send a team in to sabotage the site. At least that would be less obvious, but would still cause a raucous.

"An air strike would mean all-out war, and unless cooler heads could settle it, most likely a tactical nuclear strike by the Russians on Europe or a comparable strike at Minot or the Nevada site. It makes what we're doing all the more important. If something terrible were to happen now, you and Rick going back and executing a successful mission would change that and undo that situation. It's a risk, but if that site were operational before we're ready, then there wouldn't be any good choices no matter how you look at it. Personally, I doubt they have it. It has all the makings of a deception on their part, but I'd hate to be wrong on this one. The odds that they would have something at about the same time are too large a coincidence. It would probably mean there is a mole in the project, but stranger things have happened, and we'd have to look hard at whether or not espionage was involved."

I was okay with the new schedule. I had always doubted that Rick's flight training would make sense, and for his mastery of the German language, it would have to be the basics anyway. I could cover for him. I was more concerned about on the ground in Germany. I was looking past this and looking ahead to being there. Just then, Mac asked, "You feel good? If it's alright with you, I want to get you started on training in the Stuka now."

I told him I was good and was anxious to get the preparation out of the way and get back to Minot. I was ready to get a look at the "Stuka," the nickname of the JU 87D model I'd be flying. "Hop in. Let's go over, and I'll give you the rundown on it."

When we got to the hangar, the doors were open. There was a sign outside for Carrier Air Wing Fourteen with their emblem and the words "Fortune Favors the Brave" below. As we walked inside, I took a pen from my flight suit and wrote the words down. I wanted to carry it with me, and if I found myself with all the odds against me, those words would be worth remembering. I wrote them on a small piece of paper and put it in my vest pocket next to Beth's picture.

It was quite a site to see two JU-87s positioned side by side and a P-51 Mustang also there. That they were relics from another era was unmistakable, and both were painted not in the Luftwaffe scheme of 1945, but a bright yellow—the same color used for trainers like T-6 Texans, the dominant America trainer of World War II. It was sleek, much like a P-51, and it bore U.S. markings. Despite its fast, streamlined appearance, I knew the Stuka wasn't a fighter, but a dive-bomber and ground attack aircraft. In a way, the venerable A-10 Warthog is a descendant of this type of battlefield capability. Despite its strengths against ground forces, it would be clearly outmatched in the air against the American P-51 or the British Spitfire. I asked Mac if this was an authentic Ju-87.

"There is nothing original about this plane. From nose to tail, it is brand new. We've done what we could to improve the performance of it without compromising the original design and without adding any technologies that are too far advanced for 1945. We built seven of these. There are two here, both of which are dual control trainers, two at Ramstein, and three at Minot. They are identical with the only exception that the ones in Minot bear the Luftwaffe markings."

Mac put his folder on the wing and began to walk around the plane, gliding his hand along the side. "It's beautiful, isn't it? A true piece of art."

It was a beauty, and so clean that it looked as if it had just rolled off the factory floor. The Germans built thousands and thousands of these, but as the Luftwaffe's domination of the skies dwindled, they became easy prey for Allied forces. As good as a plane as this was, it wasn't the first choice for dogfighting, and even though it had a fighter's lines, in the last days of the war, it couldn't match the superior Allied forces. Of all those Stukas that filled the skies over Europe, only three survived and were intact. Those three, and the wreck of a fourth were scattered in aviation museums across Europe.

As I walked around her, I was picturing another place in time. An era where machines like this filled the sky like mosquitoes on a hot summer day. It would be a place and time in the middle of which I would soon find myself trapped. Seeing this throwback to a bygone era made me feel one step closer to it. As I continued to look it over, Mac flipped through his notes. "She's aluminum with a carbon fiber skin. Wherever we could, we took weight out and improved its strength, whereas back then when they took out the weight it likely would have weakened the craft. When this plane is once again flying in the skies of its homeland, it will be the fastest of its type. It can outrun and outperform anything except the ME-262. There were so few of those jets in the air at the time, you will likely never see one. The engine is vastly improved, as is the time it can stay in the air without needing to refuel. We've nearly quadrupled the range to over eleven hundred miles. Some of those range gains came from efficiency improvements to the engine. Some of the weight reductions we offset by adding more fuel. There isn't any other modern technology in it. It would be far too risky.

"If all goes as planned, you'll climb back into this after you've retrieved Scheel's document and then hightail it across Europe. You shouldn't have to worry about fuel. The distance from Nordhausen to London is only 685 miles. You should be able to go across the channel and land in England easily. That gives you about 400 miles and some change to spare. Depending on how the tests go, we may pare the fuel back and give you a little more performance. Let's see, here are the stats on her. Original speed 373 miles per hour, this one 525 miles per hour, original range 311 miles, this one 1114 miles."

He looked up and me and said, "That 525 is not to exceed speed. Don't run her wide open like that for too long. The optimal cruising speed is 450. She may look just like the old Stukas, but based on pure performance, it would be a top-end fighter in anybody's air force back then."

Mac, glancing towards the hangar door opening, spotted the silhouette of a man walking towards us. "Hey there. Here comes your instructor now. He's one of the best I know. We'll talk about the rest when we're back at Minot. I'll be going over the mission from start to finish, so I'll cover more details at a later time."

As Mac finished, an older man came walking into the hangar dressed in flight gear. As he approached, Mac called out "Charlie Carter! How are you doing?" Mac introduced me to Lieutenant Colonel Carter, retired United States Air Force. Mac indicated he had hand-selected Charlie over a year ago to test the plane out based on his record and experience.

"Charlie's a seasoned vet when it comes to aircraft and dogfighting. This guy is one helluva of a pilot. He flew in 'Nam, and has over ten thousand hours at the stick. It is our good fortune and yours to have this ace on our side, then and now. Charlie's been flying warbirds since he retired. That's his

P-51 over there that he flew in on. He already had both of these birds up and has logged a few hours getting a feel for their performance and handling. Charlie, tell him what you think."

Charlie looked like a grizzled vet, and I felt like no less than Chuck Yeager himself was standing beside me. "It's the fastest thing with a prop on it I've ever been in, and it handles like a stunt plane. I've never seen anything like it. I'm just worried that whatever you've done to it to get this way is going to make it come apart while we're up there. That's why I'm keeping one hand on the chute's ripcord at all times!"

Charlie's jokes drew a laugh from Mac. I took it seriously, as I thought Charlie was. This aircraft had no history. The original Stukas had a long service history, and this wasn't that plane. This was plain and simple, a test plane. One built with composites and lightweight components. The reliability was unknown, and it hadn't been thoroughly tested. If in the heat of any battle when called on to overstress the aircraft, how would it hold up? If I had to outrun or outmaneuver the enemy or those in pursuit, it could very well come apart. For that matter, it could happen here and now while we were in training.

I was sure that the aeronautical engineers who worked on this and the people in the factory who fabricated it and assembled it did so with the utmost level of precision. Here, in a different part of California, I would be testing aircraft after all. I would get a chance to do what I would have been doing at Edwards. Actually, I would be more like a test pilot from that bygone era that I romanticized about so frequently. If I had to exploit its weaknesses or break it, let it be here. No question that if it could pass extreme maneuvers here in our controlled test environment, we would be okay. Without this initial shakedown, the first time it happened when it counted could be our last. I would have to keep my fingers crossed that she was as reliable as she looked.

"I'm going to leave you guys alone to go have some fun." As Mac walked off, Charlie started the pre-flight check. As he was checking the ailerons and rudder, he started giving me the lowdown on what I could expect.

"I worked with Mac a few times before over the years, and I never ask what it's about, I just do my job. But whatever your job is, you got one sweet bird to do it in. You're not going to need much instruction in this one. She handles with snap and precision and has a ceiling of about twenty-five thousand feet with oxygen masks. The controls are just as they would be in the Stuka. About the only thing we'll need to practice is that she's a taildragger that rolls like a runaway horse. Steering her on takeoffs and landings isn't difficult, just takes a little getting used to and some practice with the rudder. Because of the tailwheel flopping around back there, this will take much more rudder to steer her down the runway on takeoffs and landings than we normally would use.

"When we get her out there and start rolling, that damn thing will want to go every direction but straight. I've seen even the most experienced pilots get in these old warbirds and get frustrated with them. Two other things worth mentioning about these types of aircraft, and in particular this one - First, because of the taildragger design, she sits at a higher angle of attack. As she's rolling, we're going to need to get her tail off the ground for a bit, get some speed, and then lift off. The other is her slipstream. Because this thing is so light and is way overpowered, she wants to roll left as soon as you get her off the ground, so be prepared to give it a little bit of rudder right away. Other than those few things, when she's airborne, she'll feel about as responsive as your jet. So what do you say we hop in there and see what she can do? I've had fun flying this one, and I'm itching to get back up there."

We grabbed our chute packs and secured those to our back, put our helmets on, and were ready to get going. I took one last look at the aircraft. I couldn't help but admire it. Of the six Stukas built by Behrens Aviation for this project, this was the only one configured as a trainer. Other than that, it was identical to the other five in every way.

"Take the front. I'll steer from back here."

I climbed into the cockpit and began studying the gauges, instrumentation, and controls. It was all pretty familiar, much like getting into a Chevy versus a Ford. The arrangement may be different, but the same things were in both. It was still a plane like any other, and the principles and instruments needed to fly it were universal. This cockpit looked authentic to what it must have been like in the original Stuka. All the words were written in German, the gauges were metric, and there was no visible modern technology. Charlie leaned in the cockpit before climbing in the back and asked if I had any questions about the controls or if there was anything that I wasn't sure of before we started.

"Nothing. It looks familiar to me. Are we using the rudder pedals to steer her?"

"Yep, that's it. No tiller or brake steering in here. As soon as I hop in, get her started."

Charlie climbed in, and as soon as I heard his harness click, I started her up. I could feel the power in her engine as it started, then idled. I held her by keeping the pressure on the brakes. In World War II, pilots had communication equipment in the aircraft. Most missions were flown with a pre-planned target, and if they didn't have one, the Stuka pilots were free to attack whatever they felt of value. On these test runs, our equipment was state of the art. Our helmets had modern radio and excellent range. Charlie and I could talk back and forth through the training.

"Grab the steering wheel and ease off the brakes. Let's get her out of here and out on the runway."

I backed off the brakes, and she began to roll forward straight out the door. We must have been an eye-catcher as this shiny yellow bird gleamed in the sun. Using the rudder pedals, I steered the plane over to runway 14. So far, she was easy to handle on the ground. I stopped her short on the taxiway and grabbed the preflight. In the midst of the war, you would fire the engine up and go, but for all intents and purposes, we were in an experimental aircraft, and a prefight was required on each flight while we were still shaking this plane down. I ran through it step by step, and everything looked okay. I told Charlie that we were clear, and all systems checked out.

I called the tower and got the word to hold for a moment. I could see two F-18s in tandem on approach. I used the few extra minutes to go over the cockpit layout one more time. As I glanced up, the two F-18s soared by and touched down on the runway. The tower radioed that as soon as the F-18s exited the runways, we were cleared for takeoff. Charlie wanted to get this first one off.

"Keep your feet gently on the rudder pedals and stick. Get a feel for how much pressure I'm applying as we take her down."

Charlie took over and lined us up on 14 Left. He pushed the throttle forward as the sound of the engine became deafening. I could feel the pedals moving as he moved the rudder to keep it straight. We barely drifted off center. The tail picked up, and we were level, then Charlie pulled back on the stick, and we took off. I could feel the plane to try rollover and Charlie giving it a lot of right rudder as we left the ground.

"Go ahead and take it."

I took the stick and kept the climb steady. I adjusted the trim to take pressure off the rudder. The stick had a little vibration, but overall it seemed smooth. To me, it behaved more like a Lexus than a Chevy. It did not have the feel of the rugged workhorse of 1945 that I was expecting. We were heading to about eight thousand feet. The rising heat from below made the ride choppy as pockets of warmer air tried to buffet the plane, but I could feel both the power and precision she had. She was slicing through this air and seemed unaffected by the turbulence. I kept her straight on the climb out and headed once again for open water. As I leveled her off at eight thousand, Charlie called up.

"Do what you want with her. Push her a little, then a little more."

I started cautiously banking her about thirty degrees left, then coming back around right, doing an "S" maneuver to get a feel for how crisp the controls responded. Charlie was right; it handled much more like an aerobatic plane. The snap rolls were sharp. I pushed the throttle forward while starting another climb and banking thirty degrees. I momentarily leveled off, then pushed the stick forward and put her into a dive. That familiar whine of a dive-bomber could be heard as I held it in the dive until four thousand feet and then pulled the stick back skimming only hundreds of feet above the ocean.

"Gutsy move for a rookie, but a very nice one. Take her down to the deck and let's do some water skiing."

I took her down to about twenty feet above the water and flew her straight, fast, and low. It would be the tactic I would use to escape to England, flying as low and as fast as I could to avoid friendly and enemy fighters and to avoid the British RADAR installations on the coast. As we skimmed across the water, we were so close at times that I felt I could reach out and touch the tops of waves. I wanted to test her ability to climb, so I pushed the throttle all the way forward. The airspeed indicator jumped quickly to 425, 450, 475. As it hit 500 kilometers per hour, I pulled sharply back on the stick into a steep angle of attack about eighty degrees.

She climbed fast, racing past one thousand meters to two, then three thousand meters where I leveled off. I said to Charlie, "I could do this all day." I didn't have to look at him to know he was smiling ear to ear. I felt the thrill of it, and I knew had to be feeling it also. After a few hours of familiarizing myself with all the aspects of the Stuka's performance and handling, I had a pretty good read on this aircraft.

When we thought we had pushed her to the limit, Charlie said, "I think you got a handle on her. Let's head back and do a few touch-and-goes and a few takeoffs and landings. Let's get back to the field and bring her in. Remember, we don't have nose gear, so touch the wheels and throttle her back up. Get a feel for how she handles."

I brought her around in a gentle bank and headed for land. Once we got the clearance to touch and go, I got her lined up on 14L. As I came over the marker, I had her at just over a hundred miles per hour, right above her stall speed. I flew over the runway easing back on the throttle until the wheels gently touched, then I pushed the nose forward to keep her level, increased to full power, and she raced down the runway and up we went again. I did that a few times and then Charlie said, "Let's take her in."

I came around again, lined up, and floated her over the runway, touching the main landing gear, slowly bleeding off speed and letting the tail wheel touch down while I worked the rudder to keep her right smack down the middle of the runway, but it didn't fight me too much.

"You did good, kid. You didn't need much of my help."

I taxied over to the hangar where Mac was waiting. "Hey Charlie, how'd he do?" As Charlie ran his arm across his forehead to wipe off the sweat, he replied, "He's not going to need any more of my help, that's for sure. He ain't gonna have a problem with her."

I asked Mac if he wanted to go for a spin. He came back at me with, "I'd like to see you get a few more lessons first. While you're both still here, let's go over tomorrow's agenda. We're going to mix it up a little. I want Charlie in #1 tomorrow. Jake, you'll be in #2. I want you to practice dogfighting tactics with each other. I've got another P-51 on loan coming in that we can use too. I would like to get the heat on you and see how you do when you're outnumbered. It'll be another great test for the performance and give you a better feel for her handling under extreme circumstances. I want to see a couple more days of heavy flying in this baby. I need you to know her inside and out. You've got to be tired. There's a room in your name over at the base hotel, The Hornet Inn. It's about six blocks from here. I'm going to go over a few things with Charlie for tomorrow if you want to go on and head over."

I gave Charlie my thanks and said I'll see you tomorrow.

I didn't have any gear with me, so I'd be relying on the generosity of my hosts again. As I made my way over to the inn, I passed by the Base Exchange to pick up a few necessities. In every BX I'd ever been in, there were always a variety of little stores and shops, a barber, and a food court. This one was no different. As I went in to pick up a toothbrush, black t-shirts, and as these NAVY boys call it, a pair of skivvies, I noticed a kiosk advertising thirty minutes of internet access for five bucks. I walked over to it and sat down. I could send Beth a message; just a quick note to say all is OK nothing more. I was torn between mission orders and just jotting a quick note and not leave her hanging. I would never see her again and she would never find me. For all she knew I had just done a "hit and run." I pulled my wallet out and swiped my credit card.

The clock on the screen began counting off my thirty minutes. I sat there and stared at it for a few moments. I didn't think I could do it. I couldn't violate a direct order. I had never done that in my entire career. Why would I start now with the most critical of missions on the line? I thought this mission was a suicide mission and I was going to give it my all, but it wasn't right to not be able to say goodbye. If I were going to give my life for my country, this "goodbye" was all I was asking for in return. I realized that I had all of her contact information on the business card she gave me. I found it and clicked to bring up an empty message. I typed simply "Goodbye my love – I will always love you and carry you with me forever. I can't elaborate, mission thing, not looking good. Sorry I missed Thanksgiving. Love always, Jake."

I clicked OK and sent the message. I had just violated direct orders, but hopefully, no one would be the wiser. There was no way my little note could compromise the mission, and I had to let her know. I logged off and went into the BX to pick up my things and then headed over to the base hotel. I checked in and made my way to the room. The feeling of guilt was haunting me. Violating orders by sending the email was something I didn't want to do but needed to do. It crossed my mind that I should tell Mac and clear my conscious. He'd be disappointed, but better than him finding out. What if I did somehow compromise something? What was done was done. It was too late to undo any of my actions.

While still grasping with my guilt, there was a knock at the door. I opened the door, and Mac charged me and put his right hand across my throat pushing me against the wall. "You screwed up. I should kill you right now. You realize what you've done? Do you think for one minute that I wouldn't find out about the message? You think we don't know about her? You think you can outsmart us and that we aren't watching yours and her every move, every action? You broke a direct order, and my orders were clear. There are consequences to be paid when rules are broken. This shit drives me insane, I didn't think you of all people would do this, but you did. I can't trust you."

He took his hand off my throat, and I told him I screwed up. I knew it was wrong, but emotions are powerful. They drive us to do things we usually wouldn't do.

"Captain, you're not supposed to have emotions in this business. Maybe you weren't the right man for this job." He turned, put his hands on the back of his head, and walked towards the window. "You know, maybe in your shoes, I might have done the same thing. You're heading off, and you know you won't be coming back, and that makes a difference. You were wrong, make no mistake about it, but I understand it. If you screw up again, mission or no mission, I will do what needs to be done. Are we clear, Captain?"

Mac had always treated us with his version of respect. The incident exposed a different side of him, that part where his own frustrations lay. I had never asked him if he had his own family that he had left behind, and maybe that was a part of his reaction. Either way, he had cut me a break, but probably only because the mission timeline was growing more critical. If he had the luxury of time to get a replacement, I wondered what would have happened. It went without saying that I wouldn't violate orders again. I hoped this wouldn't affect our relationship or the mission's remaining weeks. There was still so much to do. We needed to have a good working relationship to ensure success. I started to speak when he said, "It's done. There will be no more discussion of it from you or me. Tomorrow's another day and another busy one. After we're done here, we're off to Germany. Get some rest, Captain."

There was no mistaking the lingering anger in Mac's words. It would be difficult for me to move past it entirely. It would be awkward, but as a professional, it wasn't a choice. I just had to move on and move on quickly. It didn't cross my mind that they had been watching her. It could only have meant that they were watching me from the time I got back on American soil or that they picked up on my comment at the White House dinner and did some checking. My words to Beth were non-specific. She couldn't use them to find me, and I didn't say where I was or where I was going. It is quite possible she could have interpreted it as that I was letting her go again. I hoped not, but she could read it and just say "the hell with me" and be done with it. It was possible my actions put her in harm's way. I didn't want to think that it could impact others outside of us, but given Mac's reaction, it might have. Hopefully, cooler would prevail, and that Mac took care of it.

There was a book on the desk in the room with a note for me to read through it if I had the chance. The book was "Stuka Pilot" by Hans-Ulrich Rudel. I had read the book before. Rudel was a controversial figure in Germany. He was the most decorated pilot of the war, and in his Ju-87, he accounted for the destruction of over two thousand targets, including ships, tanks, planes, and other selected high-value targets. The controversy around Rudel stemmed from being a Nazi supporter through and through. He would forever carry the battle scars for that allegiance when near the end of the war and lost a leg. Rudel left post-war Germany and lived in Argentina with a high public profile, as did many high-ranking Nazis, but he returned to West Germany and had a career as a successful businessman and politician. I would flip through the book again to refresh my memory on any points he made about the plane and its characteristics as well as the tactics that gave him the edge.

From what I knew, I wouldn't be engaging in any planned ground attack, but who knew what events might take place when we got there? Anything that got us better prepared for the expected and the unexpected was a plus. I started reading and tried to put the events of the last hour out of my mind. I had made a stupid mistake that would bear on my mind, and any screw-up from here on out could cost us our lives. I turned the lights off and laid there thinking about all that transpired until I finally fell asleep late.

The rising sun of a new day didn't do much to clear my mind. Rick would be coming in today, and it would be another day of "practice." That meant more takeoffs and landings, learning more about more aircraft of the era, and of course, the simulated dogfights up against Charlie. I was looking forward to getting up against an experienced combat veteran to see how I measured up. I had been lucky enough to be selected to participate in the advanced training in the U.S. Air Force Advanced Warfare's "Red Flag" exercises at Nellis Air Force Base in Nevada. It was the most head-to-head engagement up against other experienced pilots that I'd received. I had been on tours in Iraq and Afghanistan, but for the most part, those had been offensive attacks against ground targets, and my biggest threats came not from the air, but from the ground to air missiles. We dominated the skies, and no enemy was willing to challenge our air superiority. As I headed over to the hangar, I noticed that my "shadow escort" was making himself a little more visible this morning—a certain fallout from yesterday.

When I got to the hangar, Charlie was already there. "Good morning, Ace. You ready for some more flying?"

"I'm always ready for that, Charlie."

"Well, I talked to Mac yesterday, and we want to do some range testing this morning while we have time. They're both fueled, so we want to take them out for a few hours to make sure we've got the fuel estimates right and that we don't have any problems crop up from running them at a relatively high speed for a few hours. I'd like to take them say about five hundred miles east and then turn around and come back. We won't cut it too close, but let's get that out of the way. Besides, it gives you a few more hours of practice in it."

I told him that per what Mac said yesterday, I would take #2, the trainer, and he could fly lead in #1.

"No, no," he said. "I'll fly #2, and you take #1. When we get back, we can grab some chow and refuel our bodies and these planes. Then we'll spend the afternoon having some real fun—practicing the lost art of dogfighting."

I had finished the pre-flight inspection of the aircraft, paying close attention to look for anything structural on the plane, since we'd put a fair amount of stress on it yesterday. It all seemed good—nothing out of the ordinary. We were getting our gear ready when Mac walked in.

"You boys going sightseeing this morning?"

Charlie gave him the rundown.

"Try to get wheels down back here somewhere near 1200. I've got Rick coming in this morning, and I want to keep the afternoon schedule tight."

With that, Charlie and I climbed into our cockpits. I'd be flying her solo this morning with Charlie as my wingman. I started the engine and waited for Charlie to get his running and then began the slow taxi out. After our preflight run-up, we waited for clearance, once cleared we turned onto runway 14. I took the lead position with Charlie just behind me on the right. I pushed the throttle forward, and we rolled straight down the line. There was a slight crosswind, and she was fighting me a bit more this morning than yesterday, but she was heading straight and true. I pulled the stick back, and she eased off the ground. I radioed over to Charlie, "Let's turn to a heading of nine-zero, keep the speed at four hundred, heading for an altitude of eight thousand."

"Nine-zero heading, speed four hundred, altitude eight thousand, copy."

I kept her in a steady climb, and it decided to hold us over land today. Our course would take us over towards Death Valley. The sun was bright and the sky cloudless as we headed out. We had been in the air for about an hour. We had cleared the mountains, and the expanse of Death Valley could be seen up ahead. It appeared to stretch all the way out to the horizon. The air was a little more turbulent, the ride bumpier, but through it, the aircraft handled it well.

Charlie came over the radio. "You know, I've got some strange vibration over here. You feeling any?"

I didn't think it was anything at first. The rising heat from the desert below was creating pockets of turbulent air.

"It seems persistent, and it's getting worse. I've got a pretty shaky stick over here. Something's not right with this aircraft."

I radioed back, "No, it's smooth, but let's not chance it. We'll go ahead and turn back now and take her in."

I banked the aircraft and headed back on a course of two seven zero. Charlie followed and said, "This is really getting bad. We're pretty far out. Let's look for any airport I can set her down, or I may have to ditch on the desert floor below. Can you see anything unusual on the outside of her?"

I climbed above Charlie's plane and drifted to the right to give me a good look down at him when suddenly, the right wing tore from the fuselage and tumbled in the air. The left side dropped, and the aircraft went out of control in a rapid downward death spiral.

"Charlie! Get out of there, get out of there!" I barked over the radio. "Mayday, Mayday. Plane down. Location twenty miles south of Lone Pine." I started to circle and kept descending to keep an eye on the damaged plane and to make sure Charlie was able to get out and get his parachute deployed. I got back on the radio. "Get out, Charlie! Get out."

I watched helplessly as the plane plummeted into the rough terrain below. I radioed the location and told the tower that I would wait and keep circling until help arrived. The mortally wounded Stuka plummeted to the ground in what seemed like less than a minute. I didn't see a chute. Charlie hadn't made it out.

There was nothing else on my mind and nothing I could do. The thought of a minor problem leading to a tragedy is something we all face every day, but hope never happens. It is what a test pilot does each time they climb into a cockpit. The rapid and violent motion of the plane must have left him unable to get his latch undone and bailout. Charlie had survived the battles of war only to be taken out in clear, sunny skies while over the friendly ground of his homeland, not in enemy territory. The terrain would be tough to get to, and after circling for forty-five minutes, I saw a rescue chopper arrive. I could see the twisted wreckage, but I couldn't see Charlie. There was still a slim chance he had made it out. They had radioed to me that a ground crew was on the way. I gave them the exact position so they would set down as close as they could to the wreckage.

My fuel was starting to become a problem. I had plenty to keep circling but needed to fuel to get back. A transmission came over the radio that I was to return to base immediately. I took one last look below and set heading back to Lemoore. On the way back, I hoped that when I touched down, Mac would have good news – that Charlie had made it out. I also thought about something Charlie said about the plane. He jokingly said something about the wing coming off and keeping a hand on his ripcord. Coincidence? Already, one of seven planes had failed after just a little bit of stress. One of two we were actively testing. I didn't like those odds. I brought her in and taxied for the hangar where Rick and Mac were waiting. I brought the plane to a stop, shut down the engine and climbed out.

"Any word?"

"Yes, they reached the site. Charlie is dead. He was still strapped in the cockpit. Apparently, the buckle on his harness jammed. What happened up there?"

I knew it was the longest of long shots that he might have survived. I took a moment to absorb it and then told Mac and Rick, "Everything was fine. We were cruising, he started getting a vibration in the stick, it started getting worse, and we turned around to look for an airport to put her down. I went to his two o'clock to look down and see if I could spot anything and it broke apart right in front of me."

Mac paced a few steps away and turned. "Did Charlie do a preflight walk around this morning?"

I knew I had done one, but I wasn't sure I had to replay our conversation this morning. "I'm not sure. We were talking about who would fly lead and who would fly wingman. I offered to take #2 and let him lead. I can't be sure that he did. I don't recall."

Mac turned around looking out the front out the hangar with his back to the two of us. "There's a lesson here. Bad things happen to people when they don't follow procedures. That could just as easily been you this morning, Captain. It is the second screw-up in as many days."

Rick look somewhat puzzled by Mac's harsh comments.

"Which plane did I assign you to, Captain? You were fortunate today. You are walking a thin line. Take time to grab lunch. Afternoon exercises are still on. I'll fly the P-51 up against you two. Dismissed. Get out of here."

Rick and I walked out of the hangar. He looked over at me. "What the hell crawled up his ass?"

I told Rick what had transpired and that I would likely be on Mac's shit list for the rest of the mission, and it was best if he could somehow manage to stay off it.

"That could have been you. What the hell would we have done?"

The answer had always been quite apparent to me. "Well, there wouldn't be many choices. My guess, there either is a second team training, or the only other person that knows this mission inside and out and could step in my place is Mac. I almost was in that plane instead of Charlie. I was supposed to be flying it. By the way, welcome back to this mess. How was the German language training?"

He smiled. "Ich hätte viel lieber ist gewesen in SEAL Ausbildung."

I started laughing. "You ate seal sandwiches for lunch every day?"

He stopped in his tracks and grabbed my arm. "Is that what I said?"

I couldn't help but laugh. "No. You were pretty close to right on."

We walked over to the mess hall and sat down to eat. We talked about the new schedule, the issue that I had caused, and what we thought the next steps were going to be. Rick wanted to hear more about Beth. Was I having regrets now about the mission? I told him absolutely not. I would have much rather it turned out differently, but I knew coming in that one-way missions could be part of the deal on any given day.

We had a lot in front of us still to get through. I told him we just needed to focus and try to get this in the rearview mirror. This time yesterday I was glad to be at Lemoore, excited to be flying. Now, just twenty-four hours later, this place has been a magnet for trouble. I was looking forward to getting back to Germany, but not after a stop first in Minot. When we finished and started walking back, Rick asked me if I thought Mac was somehow involved in Charlie's death.

"He was pissed at you. He could have been sending you a message."

It had crossed my mind, but to Rick, I discounted it. "Nah, he wouldn't do that. It was probably a defect, or maybe it was overstressed in a flight that Charlie was on before we even got here. Hell, these things are new, untested, made of composites, glued together, and we're flying them like them like they're proven well-tested machines."

Inside, though, my doubts were more serious. Mac was a no-nonsense prick. Could he have somehow done this? Yeah, I think he is capable of it. Or at the least knew who was responsible.

I would need to be watching my tail for the duration. As we walked, Rick stopped and grabbed my arm. "It didn't matter which plane you got in this morning, and no matter what happened, it would have been a message for you. Maybe we should watch things more closely."

I agreed, and we walked to the hangar where Mac was prepping the P-51. I asked him about Charlie's family.

"Wife, kids, and grandkids. He had it all covered. I'm sure they've been notified. It's a tragedy. After the Navy has done their work at the site, the wreckage of his plane will be taken to the Behrens's Aviation plant in Palmdale, California, where it was manufactured. The engineers will comb through it to see what went wrong. I'm sure they're going to want to talk to you also, since you had the best view of what happened. I would imagine we'd see them around here tomorrow or the next day. The brass will likely squash this thing in its tracks. So there won't be any NTSB or Naval Investigation into this. We don't need the scrutiny. If anyone asks questions, you will tell them it was pilot error. Tell them Charlie was showboating and flying unsafe when the plane ripped apart."

"That's not what happened," I told him.

He replied. "I know what happened. A good man is dead. This project is an off-the-books operation that we are doing in plain sight. Deal with it. The less time they spend on it, the better."

I asked Mac about the decision to fly any of the remaining JU-87ds if there was a design or structural defect. He was angry.

"Those are Air Force wings you're wearing, not chicken wings. A test pilot knows the risks and knows how to handle it. The likelihood of a second failure again is remote. Lightning isn't going to strike twice. You flew one without a problem. If we're up there and you get a shaky stick, we won't chance it. You'll bail at the first hint of trouble. I don't want to risk your lives and jeopardize the project, but we have no choice. We must move forward."

The odds were that Mac was right. He would be especially right if he had sabotaged the plane and knew why it failed. If he wasn't responsible, a double failure seemed highly unlikely, and we would bail at the first sign of trouble. It was clear that his attitude was getting increasingly aggressive and angry. It was something I needed to watch up in the air today. I had a feeling we would be in for a schooling this afternoon, but I had plans to be teaching my own lesson.

Rick and I headed to the plane, and he climbed aboard. Since Rick didn't get the basic flight training, I gave him the overview of what would happen if we needed to eject. There were no ejection seats in aircraft of that era, so we had to be very careful to slide the canopy back, unbuckle ourselves, and push ourselves out of the plane. I was upfront with him. Unless we are in a controlled descent, bailing out was going to be difficult. In other words, don't count on it.

As I walked around the plane and did my preflight check, I was paying attention to every detail about the aircraft. I would not take any chances this time around. The plane checked out fine. There still could be something lurking inside that I couldn't see, but for now, it looked good to go. I climbed in the cockpit and clipped Beth's picture to the instrument panel. Having her fly with me in spirit was a comfort. As I started the engine, my anger was building, and I was ready to take to the skies against Mac – for Charlie.

THE FIRE IN THE SKY

The sound of these "vintage" aircraft taxiing out to the runway must have been a treat for the Navy regulars. The loud roar of the engines seemed as loud as, if not louder than, the jets that routinely rumbled down this runway. Mac called over the headset that we would roll together, head out 90 miles to the west as planned, and break for dogfight exercises. This game, I was excited to play. It was a chance to show why I was here and reestablish myself as the right guy for this mission.

As we prepped to roll, I momentarily turned the plane-to-plane communications off and radioed back to Rick. I told him to hang on tight and that I expected this to be a wild ride. He replied, "Go for it. Get that son of a bitch."

With that, we rolled down 14L and took to the skies. I followed Mac's P-51 in a tight formation. The polished wings and fuselage, the yellow and black markings made that Mustang a beautiful aircraft. It was sleek and streamlined and seemed to cut through the air effortlessly. Back in its day, the P-51 was the superior aircraft to the Stuka. In this modern day, we would find out which plane would rule the skies.

What we were headed for this time would be less about the machines and more about the men flying them. I knew what they had told me, and to hell with all that nonsense about being careful with the aircraft. In real life, when you are in combat or a test pilot, the manual doesn't matter. It is kill or be killed, and you push yourself and the machine as far as it needs to go. The plane Mac was flying and my aircraft had simulated guns. At least after yesterday, I hoped that was the case. It would keep track of our "hits" and "kills." By the end of the day, I wanted to see Mac go down in flames, if only by the count of the tracking computer.

As we approached 50 miles out, Mac called over and told us to keep straight on this heading. He was breaking off, and somewhere down the line; he would surprise us and re-engage. When we got back to the skies of World War II Germany, we wouldn't have the advantage of knowing we were about to be ambushed. I had instructed Rick to continually pan the skies right to left along the horizon and then back left to right in an arc above the horizon. He needed to do this consistently. As the rear gunner, he was most likely to see a threat to us first, and his gun might make the difference between us being shot down or giving me a chance to out-maneuver the enemy without having to fire a shot. After all, who would be the enemy when we went back in time? I certainly did not want to fire on American or British fighters. It might be the innocent lives lost that altered history in a different way. At that late stage of the war, it was more likely that we would encounter a friend, but to them, we would be the enemy.

Plane-to-plane communications were off when Rick barked "enemy at two o'clock". I throttled up to out-run him. This would be my first course of action to avoid a direct conflict if possible. The P-51 was fast, and I could keep ahead of him, but I couldn't lose him. I decided to engage. I banked hard at 40 degrees to the left. A real Stuka was built like a tank, but it didn't have the thrust to weight advantage I had in this version. It would be a shock to anyone in 1945 that would see this aircraft outrun and outmaneuver a Mustang.

As I tracked Mac, I could see him trying to run to get a better position to go head-to-head. I could outrun him, but he couldn't outrun me. It would be just a matter of minutes before I would be tested. I was closing fast and rethinking my strategy. This is what Mac wanted—to lure me in with emotions and take his best shot. Any engagement would put our mission at risk. We would most likely be the victors, but we could never be 100% sure. It was a test to see if I would bite. For the moment, I had, but I still had the element of surprise in my favor. I could tell Mac had slowed to let me catch-up. I used this to my advantage and pushed the throttle all the way forward and banked hard right. As we came out of the turn and headed straight, my speed was picking up. We were over 500 mph and still accelerating. I put us into a climb to head for the cover of a few puffy cumulus clouds. We were clear.

Mac's voice came over the radio. "Okay, I thought I had you, but you passed test one. Never chase and engage when the enemy is on the run. You are just asking for trouble. The enemy threat over there will be real, and I still want you to have head-to-head practice. Take a heading of 075 at 4000 feet, slow to 225 mph. I'll be there shortly. Let's have some fun."

Following his orders might leave us a sitting duck for him. In my enthusiasm for a win, I was overthinking his strategy and motives. I considered turning us around and heading back on a course heading of 150.

A direction that would put us on a head-to-head encounter. That he slowed us to 225 had me thinking he was going to get ahead of us or come at us head-to-head or anticipating we would turn around and he would get us from behind. I stayed the course. This wasn't about tricks and strategy. It was about pure piloting skill.

We were in cruise mode flying a straight line. I was panning the sky from the front and to my side for a speck in the distance when I spotted him. He was on an intercept course coming at us from my ten o'clock position. My hunch was right. He did try to get us from the front after all. It wasn't the move I would have made in this aircraft. Mac was thinking like a modern-day fighter pilot with modern weapons. It was his first mistake. The right move for 1945 would have been to get in my sun or below where he would be hard to spot. I turned to take him head on and throttled up.

The engine sound in the cockpit was deafening. I wasn't interested in playing a prolonged cat and mouse chase with him. I pushed the aircraft to the limit using the same tactics as if these were two jet fighters. That's the way he was playing it. I banked almost 90 degrees left, a knife-edge, and exposed more surface as a target to Mac than I would have liked. I was safe for the moment as he was in no position to fire. I needed the aggressive move to get back around to tail him. He was on the run. Mac and his P-51 were purely in an evasive mode. I knew I had him. He was at full throttle, not nearly enough to outrun me. He was bobbing and weaving but to no avail. I closed and took the shot. It was far easier than I thought. Maybe he wasn't such a hot shot after all, or perhaps this plane was something special. It certainly was going to be a match for anything in the 1945 skies.

Mac called over and said, "That's enough for today. My fuel is getting close to the margin to get us back. Let's head home."

The next few days would be more of the same. The mornings and afternoons consisted of head-to-head exercises and more victories for the Stuka. I would come to realize that this plane was indeed the edge I would need. It would be as superior a technology as would exist in its era. There was little risk I assumed in taking a plane based on light materials and a more powerful and efficient engine back to 1945. As the training wound down, I missed Charlie out here with us. He would have been the second enemy pilot and given us a test of what it would be like to be outnumbered. I had asked one more time about him. His body was taken back to Oklahoma City for burial. None of us could have attended, and I felt some responsibility for what had happened. I could picture the hurt and sorrow on the faces of the family for a man who gave so much for his country and died giving it one more time. I cannot say this sacrifice was for something any less than the battles he fought and survived. It might be that he gave his life helping in the most important cause our country faced. Ironically, only time would tell if that was true.

For now, the mission was accomplished. I had become familiar with a plane from a bygone era, which was soon to be my era. These past few weeks gave me singular focus on the mission at hand. It had done the same for Mac. The weeks of flying and the simulated dogfights had mellowed him out, or so it had seemed. The tension had eased, and while I would not say we were buddy-buddy, the tone remained professional. Perhaps the most difficult elements of our training were behind us – weeks of conditioning, tactics, language, and piloting were done. What remained would seemingly be the easy stuff. The final preparation was now in the home stretch. We were heading back to Minot for a brief few days to walk through the steps we would take to make our time in Germany productive. That included getting our first good look at how all this would work.

As usual, we were on the move with little time for packing or goodbyes. We grabbed what we had and boarded the Air Force Gulfstream that would take us to the next stop in our travels. The plane rolled down the runway and gave Rick and me the only moments of peace we desperately needed. Getting any substantial amount of rest was a precious commodity.

At times, these constant hops from place to place, plane to plane, gave me an eerie feeling. An ominous sensation that I would equate to someone who was dying or who knew death was near. As I would look around, I would come to realize that for each place I left, for each sight I saw, it was last time I would ever see it. There are many places we go in life to visit or see any never return, but this was different. I knew I would not be returning because indeed, the finish line was in sight. In fact, in a way, I was dying, but that is true of all us, the only difference being that we live each day believing there will always be a tomorrow and many days after that. We waste time because we think we have so much of it to spare. It gave me a lump in my throat that made this fantasy all too real. I had to shake this morbid, melancholy feeling that was periodically finding its way to me. It was something the mission planners may have overlooked. My impending date with mortality did not give me second thoughts about what I was doing, but it was making me reflect.

There was no question that the urgency in the project had taken on a whole new approach since the Russian activity had been spotted near Kursk. The fears that something was underway with the Russians coincidently at the same time we were initiating our effort brought tension and suspicion to the effort. It was becoming more likely and possible that someone in the know on the project was spying and aiding the Russians. Maybe it was a coincidence that we both appeared to be heading down the same path at the same time. No one knew for sure what was going on at the Russian site, and even if they had something similar, what was the capability? Could they send people back, or was it just the original concept of sending a message back to the past? Of course, there was always the possibility that the Russian activity was nothing at all.

The more I had thought about it, the more I wondered what I would do if I were in the position to possess such a capability. Would I use it to change history and keep fixing the mistakes of the past? Of course, there was the classic paradox that always came up with the thought of time travel, and it loomed as an ominous specter over what we were about to undertake. What if we went back and avoided World War I or killed Hitler before his rise to power? There would be no World War II. Or would there? If there were no World War II, there would be no machine to correct the mistakes of history. What if remedying one problem fixed that error in history, but inadvertently led to other more dire events? There would then be no machine ever devised to go back and keep correcting the mistakes. It was mind-boggling and frightening at the same time.

Messing with the past had the potential to save the lives of millions, but with it came the possibility of killing millions more in other unforeseen ways. It was why this project was taking every precaution. The plan was to focus on this one particular event and leave no trace of our activities or us. In the short time of my involvement with the project, I have become a tumbleweed with no roots. Rolling across the country from site to site, always on the move with usually nothing but what I was wearing or carrying. I was tired. The makeshift SEAL training and the day-after-day flying had begun to wear me down. The head-to-head practice was not the real fire in the sky I was expecting, but it did the job. It built my confidence in the aircraft and sharpened my skills. The sound of the engines inside the cabin of this Gulfstream had a soothing white noise effect. I reclined the seat and began drifting in and out of sleep. Perhaps I would awaken to find that it was all just a dream.

BACK TO MINOT

The thump and jolt as the plane touched down ended any chance that all of this was just a dream. I looked over at Rick and saw that same look on his face. We had gotten three hours of sleep, and it seemed like only minutes. I peered out the window as we taxied. It was late evening; the sun was low on the horizon with these sporadic thin bands of clouds—the type you see, and you know the air is going to be cold. Mac stood up and informed us that we had the night off. We would head to our quarters and put in a few hours of studying, and then a solid eight of sleep, a rarity as of late. He indicated that at least for this month, and hopefully up until we departed, that eight hours would be the minimum. We were just weeks out from the first attempt to go back and change history. We would need all the rest we could muster to be fresh and ready for what awaited us. Rick and I grabbed what little we had with us, left the plane, and walked across the hangar, and climbed into the SUV. Mac followed and drove us to the project headquarters, and to what was our temporary home, although we had spent very little time here so far.

The short drive to the remote section of the base was quiet. Both Rick and I had learned to keep dialogue to a minimum, especially in the presence of Mac. We were sure that aside from his watchful eye, there were additional eyes and ears on us at all times. Once we had gotten to the operations building and cleared security, we headed to our rooms. We had separate quarters by design—first, to avoid unnecessary dialogue and discussion that would distract from the specific studying we each had to do, and second, to ensure that we got the required rest. When I got to my room, I dropped my pack and fell face first on the bed. I could have fallen asleep right away. For now, just ten minutes would suffice, but I couldn't do it. Dinner was waiting, then

I would hit the books for a bit, and then the opportunity to catch those eight hours of rest would finally come.

I walked across the hall and knocked on Rick's door. We walked to the cafeteria and grabbed a hot meal. After dinner, on the way back to the room, Rick asked if I had seen the schedule for tomorrow. I hadn't, and I wondered if he had seen it. He replied that it was printed and left on the counter in the room. In my haste, I had not even noticed it.

"What did it say?" I asked.

Rick replied that it was a morning of administrative tasks. 0800 to 0930 was measured for uniforms and gear. 0930 to 1030 was photography. 1030 to 1130 was documentation. 1130 to 1300 was lunch. 1300 to 1700 was "walkthrough."

"Walkthrough?" I asked.

"That was all it said."

When we got back to the room, I put my hand on Rick's shoulder and said, "Get some sleep."

I went into the room, walked over to the counter, and picked up the agenda. It was identical to what Rick described. I put the schedule down and grabbed the study/reference manual for the mission. I sat in the chair and began to flip through it. It was an aggregation of various and miscellaneous items we would need to know. It had sections on German uniforms and ranks, aircraft recognition, and a day-by-day record of key events from January 1945 to the fall of Berlin. It contained other details like the location of Allied and German troops as well as maps of critical installations still in operation during that same period in 1945. It would be a lot of detail to take in, but we had thirty days more or less to do it.

The map section of the guide fascinated me. As a pilot, it would be critical that I knew the terrain and could quickly recognize where we were at and where we needed to go. In the initial fog of the first few meetings on the project, it had not crossed my mind to ask a fundamental question – when we got back to the past, would it be day or night? Did they even know? Narrowing the arrival window would be an advantage in our preparation. At night, during the closing days of the war, cities would be dark and silent. There would be no obvious way to navigate, and certainly no GPS. Radio beacons used to guide planes would be turned off for fear that the enemy would use them to guide bombers for night raids.

If it were daytime, we would have more options, but the German countryside was lush, green, and our target was in the vicinity of a hilly terrain that might obscure our ability to see detail at a distance. I was confident that in the day we would find suitable landmarks. Reviewing the maps, a shaded section with a light green bullseye stood out. The markings indicated to be the most likely area they expected us to arrive. Subsequent pages further refined and showed increasing detail the terrain with photos of visual landmarks. I also noticed on the manual a table of each lunar cycle from January through June and the position of the stars during each month. It would be something of a help to us. Based on the location of the stars and the phase of the moon, I would have a pretty fair guess as to the time of night, maybe even the month, but most importantly the direction. After a bit of cramming, I was ready to call it a night. There was much work to do, but seeing the detail, I could tell that nearly every contingency was planned to give us the best chance of success. For now, I needed to get that eight and start fresh in the morning.

0700 hours – The alarm goes off. It was late by the standards we had been following since this started. That was the best night's sleep I had gotten in quite a while. As I looked in the closet, I wondered jokingly to myself what the day's dress was. It was the other thing I hadn't noticed I was missing until now. I hadn't worn civilian clothes in months. It was always flight suit or fatigues. I had time before the first 0800 hours event of the itinerary. After a shower, I dressed in the flight suit that bore the now familiar Grim Reaper with the hourglass on its sleeve. I stared at it for a moment, rubbing my thumb over the patch. I had never asked the origin of the project name. Why did the Germans call it that? That was just my curiosity. Whatever their reasoning, the Grim Reaper and the term "Killing Time" meant something more ominous to me.

We were getting closer now to mission execution. I had no apprehension despite all that had happened and all that would change for me. In the non-stop flurry of activity and fatigue over the past weeks, I hadn't forgotten about Beth. I just had to do what pilots do—compartmentalize it to stay on track. I wondered, though, what she was doing and what she was thinking. A brief moment in time has seemed to change so much. In a way, it could be a sign of things to come. A chance intersection of lives, albeit briefly, can have a lasting impact. I wished today were the day we would be leaving. Then my focus would be singularly and on the mission. The rest, unfortunately, would have to go by the wayside. There would be nothing that I could change about my feelings or the path I had taken. Squeezed between the proverbial rock and a hard place and caught between the future and the past.

I knocked on Rick's door, and he wasn't quite ready yet. I told him I would get a head start, and he could catch up. When I got to the cafeteria, Mac was already eating breakfast. This guy must never sleep. He was like a machine, always ahead of us. We were never waiting for him. As the senior ranking officer, he relished playing the role of alpha dog of this pack, and he wanted us to know it.

"Where's Wilson?" he asked.

I let him know that he would be here shortly.

He barked, "This crap can't happen and shouldn't happen. You two should be tied at the hip. You learn to work in sync and get your timing. Even little shit like this gets you on the same page with each other."

It appeared to be another day where we were off on the wrong foot with Mac. We never knew from day to day what was setting him off. He could have been feeling the weight of the project, or maybe he was the real wizard behind the curtain pulling all the strings.

Moments after that exchange, Rick walked in while Mac sat silent. I looked at Rick and gave the slight side-to-side no motion. Hopefully, he got the message that Mac was a powder keg looking for that spark. It was awkward. The cafeteria was not that big, more like a break room. There was no opportunity or privacy to get him aside to clue him in on the exchange.

I had the reference guide with me and was continuing to study the chapters. There was so much to learn. I decided to take the approach of spending a bit of time on each and then moving to the next and the next and cycling back through. I felt this gave the best chance to lock it into memory and test my retention as I went back through it. I knew the maps, star alignment, and those moon phase dates were critical. I was a bit of an astronomy buff, so this wasn't new to me. I knew the lunar cycles and its phases very well. I just needed to study the key dates for a few, and I could calculate the approximate day and time.

As the point guy for us, I also knew I could not make a mistake identifying German rank insignia. A minor slip-up might raise suspicion and blow our cover. I didn't expect Rick to get all this. He hadn't become fluent enough in his crash course of German to be the one to engage in any dialogue if we were confronted or challenged.

It was 0855 hours, and with Mac's typical precision, he said, "Let's roll. We won't be late."

I grabbed the manual, and Rick and I headed to the day's first stop. Per the schedule, today looked to be somewhat of a "down day." The first half would be taken up by what looked to be administrative minutia, uniforms, photos, and documentation. We took the elevator down a floor to the "Operations Checkout" facility. The best way to describe this room was to compare it to something similar to where astronauts prepped for launch. The room was large and white with a sterile feel. There were just a few "technicians" in the room. I noticed the two racks of uniforms. They varied from pilot to field to dress and had the markings of the standard Luftwaffe insignia from World War II. Based on our current uniform measurements, they had selected and tailored this specifically for us. All they needed from us was to try each set on and ensure the fit was precise. My collection contained uniforms for a man named Hauptmann, a captain in the Luftwaffe. Rick's would be an enlisted officer, a Stabsfedwebel, the highest non-commissioned officer rank—the equivalent of a Master Sergeant.

The "dress up" exercise would serve a few purposes. First, we had to have our 1945 attire fitted and ensure that every detail was correct. The Germans were not sloppy with details, and they would spot imperfection or anything out of order a mile away. Second, they would be taking photographs, many photographs, of us in these various uniforms. The photos would be doctored using today's technology to show us in several "scenes" that would appear to reflect our wartime chronicles. It would not be unusual for a pilot flying from one base to another to have a camera and photo album to document his wartime experiences. It would be further proof if we were questioned or checked at a stop.

Lastly, we would need the proper paperwork. It was a requirement of military personnel to have official papers and orders on their person all times. The team here would produce authentic orders and documentation using the photos and adding other vital information. I dressed first in the formal officer uniform. The technicians checked every detail comparing the insignia, and the positioning against authentic Luftwaffe photos of pilots of similar rank.

When they were satisfied, it was Rick's turn to walk the runway. For the most part, it was a good fit. Only minor adjustments were needed. As I changed back from flight suit to more formal attire, I experienced an eerie feeling to see myself in something other than American military dress. I felt I was looking at a different person. Even though it was never the intent of the process today, I could feel myself "getting into character," thinking about how I would present myself, how I would act and feel when I would finally be in action. I had to catch myself from that momentary daydreaming. I had been picturing myself in the field—ten steps, more like a thousand steps ahead of where we were. My mind had discounted the most likely scenario—one where we would be killed in the process of going back.

The big assumption was that the first test of this with human subjects was going to work. The idea of hopping in a World War II replica plane and flying back to Germany in 1946 was about as far-fetched an idea if there ever was one. Seeing myself in the Luftwaffe flight gear gave me an inspired level of confidence. The team around me, the effort, the money, and the time would not be for something where the odds of it working were slim. I was anxious and ready, but we had more to do, and the sands of my time in the hourglass here in the present were quickly disappearing.

Now that dress was done, it was on to the next scheduled task—photography. Rick and I moved to an adjacent room with what I would describe at the typical "green screen" setup. A section of the room had the floor, ceiling, and walls covered with a light green. There was no mystery to why this was needed. Using today's technology and a little camera magic, they would create a photographic representation of various scenes of a typical Luftwaffe officer and airman. There were several cameras set up to capture us from different angles. Something else had occurred to me along the line of what I was thinking earlier. With all this expense and trouble with details for this project, were we the first? If we were the first, then it appeared that this complex and its investment maybe meant that we were not to be the first and the last, but just the first of many. Mac indicated early on this was a "one and done" effort and would be mothballed after our trip. I wondered.

During the process, they had moved us to a table away from the cameras and screen. They had provided a set of authentic Luftwaffe officer photo albums that had survived the war. In it, they had marked different photos in the old album to use it as a reference to build a replica version for us. Our job was simple. We would dress in the uniform like the officer in the photo, go to the green screen, and pose in a similarly. They would take several shots from differing angles. We repeated the steps over and over. When we got to a photo that required more formal dress attire, they used that opportunity to take our identification photo. It had taken hours of back and forth, changing, shooting just to get what seemed like a minor detail correct. When they were satisfied, the dress up and photo shoot ended. We were told to get into our flight uniforms and were released to get lunch. As we sat down to eat, Mac joined us.

"What do you think so far?"

I remarked that I thought it was thorough and detailed for a mission where two guys would infiltrate the past, and their goal was to remain somewhat obscure.

"That's just it," Mac replied. "You won't be two obscure guys. We could have tried sending an army back to storm the site, but we wanted a small team to integrate with the Germans, not invade or infiltrate. You have to do this with minimal disruption to current events."

It made sense but added a level of complexity to the mission. Mac went on to tell us how the rest of the week would play out. We would be conducting "fit tests" of equipment and procedures. The tests were scheduled to take up the remainder of the week. If by chance, we finished early, we would get on to the next and last phase that much quicker. We had accomplished quite a bit so far in our training. The big test coming up would be the first time that an exercise did not focus on skills we would need as much as the means that would get us there.

CHECK RIDE

On our very first trip here, we had viewed the "Transit Operations" room. It was an empty cavernous room with a giant overhead crane. It was a white, bright, spotless, and a sterile environment. There was a large set of steel sliding doors on the floor and another along the wall. They were thick and slid back on rails. In appearance, it looked very similar to a missile silo. There was also an observation window overlooking this area. It, too, had blast doors that could slide to protect it.

This time around it contained the Stuka plane we would board to fly back to World War II Germany. The training planes all carried a standard yellow paint scheme. What stood before me was not a trainer and not a museum display.

"It's a beauty, isn't it? It is your aircraft, Captain. The spare is in another room just in case, but this is the one you will use."

It was a beauty. Unlike the training aircraft we flew at Lemoore, this bore the Luftwaffe paint scheme and markings. It was quite the sight.

"These are slightly larger than the original version. It is insignificant, and I doubt anyone would notice. We built these with room for storage of tactical gear, supplies, uniforms, the weapons you may need, and to carry extra fuel. There are other differences between this and the trainer that we will look at later."

As Mac was talking, I couldn't help but be enamored with the plane. I walked around the aircraft gliding my hand down the fuselage. It wasn't my intention to do a pre-flight inspection, but I looked over every inch of it. Its appearance was as if had just left the Junkers factory near Bremen. The technical team that had outfitted our uniforms was here and adjusting our flight gear. It included a parachute, a pistol, and a knife, along with a few other emergency survival tools should we have to bail out in an emergency.

Rick and I climbed into the plane. The team made adjustments to the seats to ensure our comfort and flexibility. The cockpit was tight, but it had slightly more room than the trainer I had practiced on at Lemoore. I looked for where I would tack Beth's picture and found a spot on the left just above the clock and bank indicator. The Stuka did not have a "steering wheel" layout, but rather a large "joystick" format. I moved the stick and looked over the wings. The movement was easy and free. I repeated the process with the rudder pedals. Again, the action was smooth with no resistance. I asked Rick what it was like back there. As the gunner, he was facing backward and had room to maneuver the gun to hit attacking aircraft. For us, the intent would never be to shoot at an Allied aircraft. We would always resort to evasive tactics and our ability to outrun anything in the skies. The gun would be a last measure of defense only if we were in pursuit by Axis forces. The potential of an air-to-air dogfight against the Luftwaffe was all I could think about at the moment. It was exhilarating, and my heart was racing with adrenaline. It seemed an over simplification of the situation, but this plane and the hole in the floor would be how we would be on T-Day. Transit day.

Mac climbed up on the wing and knelt beside the cockpit window.

"There are a few things I want to go over. First, this is just one plane, and it is something special, but even it would not be a game changer if it fell into enemy hands at that late stage of the war. Aside from the composites and engine, we purposely did not add any advanced technology. It is basic stuff. Still, we don't want to take a chance, and we need to play it safe. Before you leave, there will be small, strategically placed explosives on the plane. Those devices are hidden from view in a compartment on the wing and in the engine. Down on the right, there is a box covering a toggle switch. If you have to bail out, then flip the switch. If you are on the ground and feel like the plane may fall into anyone's hands, friend or foe, flip the switch. There is a three-minute timer before the explosives detonate and destroy the aircraft. Three minutes. That is it. It is barely enough time to clear the area. So, don't try to salvage anything unless absolutely necessary. I want you to climb out, and I will show you something."

Rick and I climbed out and down the wing towards the rear of the plane. Just aft of the gunner there was another hidden compartment. They had done an excellent job of blending it into the fuselage. It would have been invisible to even someone familiar with the place unless they knew it was there. That storage area was not a feature of the authentic German Stuka, but an add-on for this mission. Mac opened it up. It was a good-size storage area that was empty for now.

"When you get ready to leave, we will pack this with additional gear. It will have a few heavy armaments, explosive devices if you need them, additional uniforms, maps, flashlights, and ammo. All the typical stuff you may need once on the ground." We walked over to those massive doors on rails, and Mac explained what would happen. "In the center of the canopy, you may have noticed a circular hole." He pointed to the overhead crane. Affixed to the crane was a long steel or titanium pole.

"Positioned over the Stuka, the crane will lower an extension through the canopy and be mated to the airframe. It is something we designed for this mission. Once secured and locked, you will be given the signal to start the engine on the Stuka and set it to idle. The crane will lift the Stuka and the both of you to a position over these doors. When we are ready, the doors will open and the time portal activated. The crane will lower the Stuka into the portal and release it precisely at the right time to get you to February of 1945. At that time, you will put the engine to full throttle and pull back on the stick. If all goes well, you will find yourself flying in the skies of World War II Germany. We have to run a few more tests with the two of you to check all of the systems. Go ahead and get back in the cockpit."

As Rick and I settled back into the cockpit and were secured, we put on a wireless headset communicator. Communication between the plane and the control room would only be used for these tests and would not be part of the final mission. The Stuka's onboard original Luftwaffe radio equipment was not practical to use for communication on these tests. The crane was on the move and was positioned directly over our heads. The technicians were on each wing ready to help guide the mating apparatus it into position. As the extension was lowered ever so slowly, I heard it click, and I felt the aircraft push down and bounce up. The technicians looked at the observation area and gave the thumbs up. Over the headset, I heard the call that the Stuka and crane were successfully mated. Over the comm, a technician described the next step. The crane would raise the Stuka a few inches off the ground and release to test the mechanism to drop us into the portal. The technicians were alongside the plane as the crane picked us up with ease. I was alerted that the drop would occur from a three count, three, two, one, drop. The arm released and we fell the few inches to the floor. It felt as if we had just touched down on a runway. The Stuka barely bounced.

The next test and the ones that followed were designed to be increasingly more strenuous on the equipment and the aircraft. Once again, the technicians reinstalled the extension into the Stuka. After confirmation that it was locked, I was instructed to fire up the engine and set it to idle. The Stuka fired up on command. The sound of the mighty engine even at idle echoed throughout the room. It was loud enough that I was having a hard time hearing through the headset. The crane raised the aircraft what looked to be about fifteen feet off the floor and moved us towards the center of the room. When we were directly above the portal doors, I was instructed to increase engine power and hold. The arm flexed slightly, maybe an inch or two at best. Without much strain, it seemed strong enough to contain the Stuka. Additional instructions came over to increase a bit more. At this level, the Stuka was hardly flexing its muscle, but the arm swayed a bit. This power setting for the engine looked to be about the safest level of stress for the crane's attachment arm.

"Remember that setting, Captain. Do not exceed it when we do this for real" someone said over the intercom. "You can throttle down and shut the engine off."

The crane began to move us back towards our original starting area. It set the Stuka down gently and released the arm. As we touched down again, I glanced at the watch. This series of tests had taken all afternoon. I slid the canopy back, and Mac climbed up the wing.

"I think that went well. I don't think we need another day of testing, which is good. We will get an extra day of study before we head to Germany for what is your final phase, gentleman. We'll meet at 0900 tomorrow, sharp, to review what Germany will entail and we will do some studying and recap."

Rick and I climbed out of the cockpit. I patted him on the back and told him, "It's getting real now."

I asked Rick if he wanted to get in a quick run before chow. He said, "Good idea. Let's head back the room and change and get a quick mile or two in."

I changed into running gear and met Rick by the elevator. We were leaving our quarters without an escort for the first time. At this point, they had likely figured we were not going anywhere. There wasn't an opportunity here for an incident like the one at Lemoore. Getting off the base would be impossible. Based on our performance and enthusiasm for the mission, we showed no sign of stress or anxiety that might have us thinking AWOL. We looked like a safe bet.

Throughout the weeks of the mission planning, and training we were not locked up in an underground bunker. We were on the move, and most of the time was outside. That was especially true for me. I was either flying or training at the beach with the SEALs, but getting out for a run in solitude felt different. It was one of the few times during this phase that I felt at peace with the decision and myself. As Rick and I jogged down the road to the complex, I asked him what he was thinking. Due to the friction with Mac and the sense that nothing we said between us was private, we had limited meaningful conversation. Out here in this desolate place, I finally felt we could talk without restriction. He told me he was still absorbing it all and that he wasn't sure it was going to succeed. I asked him if he thought we wouldn't be successful or that this whole time transport wouldn't work.

"I just hope they are right," he said.

Rick went on to say that he didn't think we would ever get the chance to be successful, he was a skeptic that the machine would work, and felt that we would die before we ever made it.

I was a bit surprised at his thoughts. He seemed so unfazed to train and die without ever having had a shot at success. I told him I was leaning more on the flipside. I thought we would make it back. However, it would be just the two of us against the German SS and the Wehrmacht at a stage in the war where desperation and mistrust were prevalent. Even if we passed for perfect German Luftwaffe airmen, it would be a challenge to get the mission done. Everything would have to go off without a hitch for it to work. Of course, there was the chance that even with success, we were not destined to survive. We were not supposed to live on past our useful purpose and have a chance at altering history in other ways. He asked me if I feared that part of the mission. I was honest and told him I wasn't sure how that would pan out. In all probability, it would end as they had instructed us, and I was getting there but wasn't all the way there yet. There was still that remote possibility that they could bring us back.

He changed subjects and asked me about Beth. I told him that the thought came and went occasionally. It was nothing that took my focus off the mission at hand. I had come to terms with the decision that I made and what we had to do. I knew that all of that was in the past or the future, but no longer in the present. Based on what we were doing, I wasn't sure what was true anymore. I found some small comfort knowing that if this worked and I was in the past that the future was still ahead.

Decades from the moment I landed in the past, some future me would have his shot again, and maybe that version of me would be smarter and do something different. We jogged on for a while tacking on an extra mile to keep the conversation ongoing and to talk about lives and loves lost. It also took our mind off the fact that we were freezing. The wide-open spaces of North Dakota invited a constant wind chill factor that subtracted 10 or more degrees from the air temperature. We finally headed back to base. I grabbed something light from the cafeteria and took it back to the room. A warm shower did its job to thaw me out. Afterward, I managed to get some pre-studying in for a few hours before the night was over.

THE CALM BEFORE THE STORM

It was to be the calm before the storm. I would consider this a "down day" if there were such a thing in the past few weeks. We met Mac at 0900 hours and reviewed what he described as our "battle plan" or playbook for when we arrived in back in Germany. Sprawled out on the table were large maps. The first of the European theater of action as it was in February of 1945 with the position and activity of Allied and German forces. The Allies were closing in on the site. The second had an enlarged section of the first with several shaded green concentric circles. Mac pointed to it.

"Somewhere inside this circle is our best guess of where you will emerge. There is growing confidence that we will get you somewhere inside this bullseye. That would put you just a hundred miles from the Nordhausen airfield, and in that bird flying at top speed, you could be just ten to fifteen minutes out. However, we have to plan for every contingency, including ones where you might be outside the target circles. You are going to have several challenges, which is why going over these maps in detail will be one of the most important things for this mission."

As I recall, our most significant obstacle might be less of the Germans on the ground and resistance at the factory and more of our own friendly forces. At the time we'd get there, Nordhausen would have been the target of eight months of relentless Allied bombing. American and British fighters had air superiority. The airfield was a mess, as was the underground factory that housed the V-2 assembly line, and where the documents we were likely stored. The Dora-Mittelbau concentration camp was nearby, and its prisoners used as slave labor at the factory. The camp was one of the most brutal. By early 1945, the site was in chaotic disarray. Hopes that German

93

forces could defend the place had long been abandoned. The task at hand for the personnel that remained was to evacuate by train the prisoners in the camp and kill or leave dying those unfit for transit.

In early April, American forces would be at the camp to liberate the sick and dying who were left. I asked Mac if it wouldn't have been simpler just to go there after the site was seized by American soldiers and take the documentation or relay the importance to get the documentation.

Mac stated that that approach was considered and dismissed. "We had to get there before our forces. Once American forces reached the site and saw the V-2 factory, it was all hands on deck to get as much of that equipment and technology out. If we sent you back, there would be no record of you if they checked or questioned your presence. Even if you managed to get or secure the documentation and got caught in the process, they would assume you were spies. The easiest way was to get in-between the Germans leaving, and the Americans coming, and then get out."

In a way, the illogical logic made sense. It was the lesser of two evils. The Luftwaffe airfield near the V-2 factory conveniently happened to be a place where the J-88 Stukas refurbishment occurred. It mattered none. The facility now likely lay abandoned or had very few forces to protect it. I asked Mac if he had photos of the airfield taken by any Allied bombers or by forces that seized the base. He had several pictures that showed the main runway intact with only minor damage, but there was significant damage surrounding the field. I studied the images for other options to land. A flat grassy area would be a better option. We would need to conceal the plane from ground forces that may want to use it to escape or bombers that might find it as a target from overhead.

There were numerous open fields close to the target. Our best bet was to assess the situation from the air. Depending on the German activity and Allied forces in the area, it may have been to our advantage to use the runway and hope that the bombing was mostly over. We would be threading the needle between both forces. If the timing were right, it just might work. It could make for a short hike to the target and a quick escape.

Mac explained that there were other challenges. Looking at the target placement area, it was west of Nordhausen, but the width of the placement area meant we might have to fly directly east or southeast. We would need landmarks to identify where we were and how to navigate to the target. The Stuka had a compass and instruments to help, but it all was dependent on where we were. Navigation would be more problematic at night. With a communications blackout, any lights from cities turned off to avoid bombing raids, and if any directional beacons were shut off, we would be virtually blind. Mac explained that this was a reason for the added fuel and range of our Stuka. We might have to cruise a while until daylight or until we spotted a landmark. During the day, it would be easier. However, it would also easier for Allied forces to detect us and pursue. I looked at the map and drew a line from the center of the bull's eye to the airfield at Nordhausen. If I flew a course of 160 degrees for 30 minutes at 200 mph, it would have us very close to where we needed to be, assuming we hit the bullseye.

We spent the rest of the day reviewing different scenarios and photographs. It was akin to a game of war planning. I liked this stuff and could have played through multiple options and strategies endlessly. We knew just about everything that happened during those months, but it would be different when we were in the thick of it. At this stage of the war, anything that served as a landmark was ordered destroyed. To avoid being spotted and used as guides for attacking forces, Luftwaffe planes had even shot off the steeples on churches. There would be very little to guide us except roads, cities, and natural landmarks. I would cross my fingers that we would have daylight on our side. Mac explained the itinerary for this final phase. We would go to Germany and see the site at Nordhausen and practice flying the route. Assuming all went well, we would be back here in a week, have a few days of nutrition and rest, and then be ready for the transit nearly a month ahead of schedule. Mac felt we had a good day and as prepared as we could have given the circumstances. He seemed even to mellow a bit more the past day. As the project was coming to fruition, Mac's involvement was also coming to its end.

At sunrise, we departed Minot and headed to Andrews Air Force Base. Andrews was where all this started, but we would not be there for long. As soon as we touched down, we walked to the terminal and boarded a military transport headed to Ramstein Air Force Base in Germany. It would be a long flight and one with which I was familiar. Along the way, I toggled between studying maps and brushing up on history and occasionally watching documentaries on the war or just listening to music. When we touched down at Ramstein, it was late in the evening. We had been working long days and nights, but today we spent so much time in transit doing nothing that it made this feel like the longest day of this project so far. That precious commodity of time seemed to move slower today.

Mac took another pulse check on how we were feeling. He wanted to know if we were okay getting started early tomorrow or needed some extra recovery time. I was up for it. He laid out the plan for the next day. "Let's get to the hotel. You two get a good night of rest. It will be a busy few days. I have to do some paperwork and see the base commander on our operations. Let's meet here at 0900 hours for a briefing, and we will plan for wheels up at 1000 hours."

As Mac walked away, there was that display again of a man who seemed tireless. Mac was someone I imagined General George Patton would have liked. He was a relic, a soldier from the past. Like Patton, this guy was a bull of a man who charged through those around. He stayed ahead of us and always kept the mission front and center. As we walked to the base hotel, I asked Rick if he were nervous to fly with me today after our fun dogfighting Mac in the California desert.

He replied, "That was the least of his worries." That managed to get a laugh out of me.

After we checked into the hotel, I told Rick that I wasn't much for hitting the books or studying tonight. I was going to get an early start on that eight and get a fresh start in the morning. "Let's meet down here in the lobby at 0730 hours – flight suit," I said to him.

I got to the room, tossed my gear on the floor, and took a quick shower. It had been a long day.

As the sun rose on a new day, I felt alert and energized. I was anxious to get up in the air. As I dressed, I noticed our "Töten Zeit" sleeve patch. It was probably nothing, but there was a good chance I might run into someone I knew, and it might catch his or her eye. They might not even notice or care. If that happened, I would explain it as part of a test pilot unit. I had a flight jacket that would cover it, but we should play it safe at this stage. I rang Rick's room and let him know that maybe heading out early wasn't such a good idea. We had a reprieve from our leash, and wandering around the base for a while before Mac was supposed to meet us could be asking for trouble. I explained to him that I could run into people I knew and they would ask what I was up to, or if the cover story of us killed on a mission made its way through the Air Force, those people would remember seeing me here. It was better to be careful. Maybe I was too cautious. He understood but was restless waiting around. We adjusted our time and moved it to 0830 hours. Just enough time to get breakfast and walk out.

While had time, I pulled out that Stuka pilot book I brought with me from Minot. Luftwaffe ace Hans-Ulrich Rudel must have been some pilot for his day. He flew 2500 missions and was shot down 24 times and managed to survive the war. It was a credit to great piloting or a great aircraft, or maybe a bit of both. There would be no chance our paths would cross on the ground or in the sky, but I would have liked to go head to head with him and see who would win. Would it be man or machine that made the difference? I was reading the sections of the book focused on his tactics and the performance of the aircraft. Ours was a different aircraft from a different era but based on the same design. The tactics they used and battled against might be the same we might face at some point. There was a knock at the door. It was Rick. "This waiting around is not for me. Let's get rolling."

It was well into February, and the temperatures were relatively mild but somewhat seasonal for the area. It was close to forty degrees but felt warmer. It was what we might expect since we would be in Germany in February of '45, but I suspected it might be colder. There would be one difference—we would have an advantage and not need a forecast. We would know what the weather conditions were. I told Rick we could be weather forecasters if we survived this adventure. All we had to do was take the seventy-plus years of weather data with us. He laughed at that. "With our luck, we'd still be wrong."

It was still two hours before we were to meet Mac. Rick and I walked at a slow pace to the mess hall. I shared with him that I never had second thoughts about the mission, but at times I was still in disbelief what was going to happen and how it managed to catch the two of us. Rick said as part of the SEALs he was prepared for death with each mission and faced the unknown of each operation. His heart would pound with adrenaline for the excitement of combat, but fear was a feeling he didn't know. Those qualities are likely what landed him on this project. I, on the hand, was less than perfect. I had doubts and fears but had learned to rise above them in crisis. Accomplishing this task would be the ultimate test of my character and will.

We had managed to pass the time and were ready to rendezvous with Mac. He was waiting in the terminal, sitting and jotting notes on maps. As we approached, he rose and said, "I had to work a few things out with the base commander and the Germans. Our flight plan today should have been taken care of before now, but there were some snags. The Germans were curious as to what we were doing on this training mission. It wasn't the typical request, but we're good now. I made a few calls, and we shouldn't have a problem. Let's head to the hangar."

On the walk, Mac repeated what he had told us back at Minot. Two of the seven replica Stukas custom built by Behrens Aerospace for this mission were shipped here to Ramstein for our training. They were identical to the ones we flew at Lemoore, which were slightly different from the two housed at Minot. These planes had more advanced communications and navigation. It jogged my memory about Charlie. I asked Mac if there was any news on what happened to Charlie's plane that caused the failure.

"Yeah, I did get some word on that. I meant to say something about that to you guys. There is some good news about the failure. It turns out it wasn't a defect from the manufacturing of the plane. There is nothing for us to be concerned with or worry about with it. Somehow, a mystery solvent of some type worked its way into the wing near the spar. It corroded the bolts that attached the wing to the fuselage. No one knows how it got into the wing. It could have been some cleaning fluid, an accidental spill, who knows. It seems it was a one-off freakish thing. They've closed the case on it."

That seemed a pretty open-ended mystery that warranted more than just some "strange solvent" and "case closed." I found it odd that no one wanted to inspect the other planes for the same problem. Top Secret or no Top Secret, a man had died, and a few others of us were hanging out there at potential risk. It seemed that Rick and I were getting a first-hand account of the inner workings of these secret projects. Accidents got whitewashed, and lives were expendable. I wasn't buying Mac's story one bit. He either made that up in an attempt to appease us, or it was just swept under the rug. I would never know the truth and neither would Charlie's family.

Today's focus was something different—flying. The hangar doors were closed as we approached. There was something different this time. MPs were guarding the hangar, likely because this was a joint NATO base, and we were closer to Russia. The chance of a breach in security was greater. We entered through a door that led to the main bay. There they were, the two Stukas in their bright yellow paint. Mac laid out the same map we had reviewed back at Minot on the wing of the Stuka.

"Here is the game plan. We will fly to the center of the bull's eye and then set a course using the GPS for Nordhausen. On this first run, I want both of you to pay particular attention to the natural landmarks, the view of the horizon, and the mountains. Rick, you will have a different perspective facing towards the back of the plane. It won't be the same since it is sixty plus years later, but some things in nature don't change. After the first run, we will head back to the bull's eye, turn the GPS off, and navigate to what was the airfield. We will do this a few times from various edges of the bull's eye to get a feel for the landmarks, distance, and speed. First run always with GPS, second run without it. We will get as much in today as fuel allows."

There would be no fun and games on this run, just surveying, and sightseeing. Mac folded up the map and handed me a card with the coordinates for the bull's eye center, north, west, and south along with the settings for Nordhausen. While Rick put his chute on and climbed into the cockpit, I walked around the plane and did my preflight check. I was ever so cautious to look over every inch of the surface, including where the wings joined the fuselage. It all seemed good. This bird was fully fueled and checked out fine. I put on my parachute and climbed in the cockpit, securing myself while making adjustments to the seat. I looked over to Mac, who had just jumped into his plane after opening the hangar doors. While he was getting settled, I pulled out my good luck charm and the coordinates Mac had provided. I clipped Beth's picture to the panel and then touched it with my fingers.

Over the radio, Mac said, "You boys ready? Let's fire them up."

With that, I started the Stuka's engine.

"Pull out of the hangar, and we will do an engine run-up here instead of out there on the taxiway. This place is busy, and I want to head to the runway and get off quickly once we have clearance."

I pulled the Stuka out of the hangar to the left rear of Mac's. With my feet pressing hard on the brakes, I pushed the throttle forward, and it roared to life. It was like a bull at a rodeo kicking behind a gate ready to cut loose and throw its rider. I switched to the backups, and all worked fine. I eased the throttle, and she settled down. Mac slowly started to move, and I followed him out on to the taxiway. Mac radioed the tower, and we were told to proceed to runway two-seven and hold for clearance. While we were waiting, I took the time to plot the coordinates in the navigation system. I could see a C-5 Galaxy inbound on runway two-six. It was a giant of a plane. As it touched down, a puff of smoke came from the wheels as it hit the runway. We would be like a flea on that elephant's back by comparison. As it slowed, we waited for it to taxi and cross out of our way. After it cleared our path, the tower gave us the "Training aircraft #1 and #2 cleared for tandem departure on runway two-seven".

With the "all clear," Mac pushed down the runway with my aircraft tailing and to the right. I opened the throttle, and it pushed me back in my seat as the powerful engine came to life. I followed Mac's cue, and we lifted off and climbed to 8000 feet. We banked right and headed north to the bull's eye. Mac radioed, "Increase airspeed to 400 knots. Let's push it a bit."

The airspeed of 400 knots was about 460 miles per hour, well within the design limit. It felt good to have this baby stretch her legs. At 460 miles per hour in this plane, the perspective felt like we were in a rocket. It only took twenty minutes to reach our starting point. We slowed to a little over 100 knots, about 125 miles an hour, and began a full circle. Mac wanted us to survey the area, and in this slight ten-degree left bank, we had a good view of below and along the horizon.

The area was densely forested with few discernable landmarks below. Rick was checking the map to see if we could visually align with anything below. I spotted a mountain in the distance that looked to be on the heading to Nordhausen. After circling and surveying, we plotted a course for Nordhausen using the GPS. We cruised slowly, and I watched the landmarks on the horizon. At least on this route, I had a good feel for our position. Traveling at this slow speed gave plenty of time focus on our bearings and our timing. After about forty-five minutes, we were at Nordhausen. The area was vastly different from its photos. From above, there appeared not to be much left of the original sprawling complex. The town was clearly visible, and as we dropped to a lower altitude, I could spot the remains of the Dora-Mittelbau concentration camp. What was left was now a memorial. We flew around the area and by the mountain that housed the V-2 factory. It was also the place that was our target to retrieve the plans for Projekt Töten Zeit.

We made several runs that day from different angles. Off in the distance, dark clouds and lightning were visible. We had done enough, and even with our extended range, the fuel was approaching our margin of safety. Banking away from the storm and to the south, we headed back to Ramstein. The flight was smooth and uneventful as we touched down and rolled back the hangar.

Mac went over tomorrow's schedule. "There is an open field with a grass runway at Nordhausen. We will take the Stukas up there in the late morning. Tour the V-2 facility and get a feel for the surroundings, and then get a few night flights in before heading back. If all goes well, we will assess where we are at the end of day tomorrow. Maybe we will use one more day after that of just flying the routes again before we head back to the States."

I loved flying, and I loved the feel of a jet fighter, but being up there in that dive-bomber, a simpler plane from an era long ago, I felt like a pilot.

Night had fallen by the time we stowed and secured the aircraft. The air was crisp and chiller than when we left this morning. Clouds had rolled in, and the front we had spotted in the distance had chased us down and brought with it a change in the air. We had a long twenty-four hours of flying from Minot to DC to Ramstein and then took our turn in the pilot's seat for more hours of time in the air. The cold air had an energetic effect. The arduous schedule, whether intended to test our stamina or just aggressive, had not done its job. I could feel we were nearing the end, and my second, third, and fourth wind had kicked in.

The next two days followed the plan Mac had outlined. We flew to Nordhausen and landed on a grassy airport field where a curious flying enthusiast from a local glider club marveled at the planes. The tour of the V-2 factory was fascinating, but it was also gut-wrenching to know that the means of genius were fueled by the slave labor that carved tunnels and caverns until they were broken and then discarded.

The factory was in a cavernous hollow shell of the mountain. I could feel the souls of those who dug all of this by hand still here. This site now stood as a memorial to the heights of ingenuity that humans could achieve and depths of evil and suffering they can inflict. All that was left was an unrecognizable place littered with debris and rubble from bombs that shook this mountain from above. The war had seen many atrocities, and we could stop that suffering, end the war and the millions of deaths, yet our mission would be to save ourselves and protect our country decades later. Standing in the cavernous factory with its rubble and what remained of damaged V-2 parts was difficult to reconcile. On a mid-February night in 1945, we might see such sights again.

As the days passed, we executed a few more test runs, including additional night passes over our target. The visit we made to the grounds at Nordhausen still haunted me. It made me think that this "great capability" we had achieved should be used for more than going back and getting a notebook of formulas and theories. We should right the wrongs of history. Maybe next time someone would make that trip.

Our time in Germany, at least in this era, had come to an end. The next time I flew a plane would be for real, and I would be back in the place I had just left behind.

THE STORM BREWS

A late winter blizzard had hit the Dakotas. Symbolically, maybe the storm we encountered in Germany had followed us back here to Minot. Little did we know that it might have been a foretelling sign of the days ahead. The whiteout conditions at the airfield delayed our return to the base. When we were finally on the ground, heading to the mission operations center became a challenge with blowing and drifting snow and frigid temperatures. As we drew nearer to the first attempt at transit, the stormy weather seemed to be weighing in on our prospects. The forecast was cloudy, dreary, and more storms ahead. Our departure date was now just a week or maybe days away. Were we prepared? With the unknown lurking ahead of us, how would we ever know?

Since we got back, Mac was nowhere in sight. The closing agenda items that remained on tap between now and our T-Day was a mystery. The ever-present micromanager had finally appeared to let go and loosen the strings in the waning days of the mission. Somehow, I doubted that a blizzard, earthquake, hurricane, or other calamities could stop us now. He was likely working out the final details.

It was an odd thing to have come this far on what was, or had to be, the most classified mission the United States had ever taken, and here Rick and I were filling out some final paperwork. It was not unlike the military to make you make sure your affairs were in order before embarking on a suicide mission. There was life insurance, payroll, and reams of documentation to cover our tracks. When we finished, we went back to our rooms and waited. The day had turned to night, and we had an off day with little activity. It had crossed my mind that maybe there was a problem, something not working, or some other development that might, or was, holding us up. We retired for the evening, and from the start of this project to now, it was the first day we were without a plan.

In our underground bunkers, the only way we knew morning had come was from the time on our watch. I had no idea if the storm that met us on our return was still churning outside. I dressed and met Rick in the cafeteria for breakfast. Mac was waiting. "Miss me, gentlemen?"

His tone was sarcastic, and he knew what we were thinking. Mac was the type that no matter how hard they tried to be someone different; their true self always came through. In Mac's case, that wasn't a good thing. We sat down, and he said, "I spent the day yesterday going over everything we have done and our preparation. I explained to the powers that be that I wasn't sure we were as ready as we could be, but that we were as ready as we needed to be. We went long into the night, but at the end of the go/no-go meeting, we got the green light. The earliest attempt is tomorrow morning at 0948 hours. It has to be 0948, and I don't know why, but that is what they are telling me. It is an "attempt," meaning if something doesn't go right or look right, we abort and aim for the next window. I think we are ready, but we have things to work on today. I had breakfast, but you two get something, then get into your flight gear, and we'll meet here in an hour."

The new timeline came as a surprise. More like a bombshell. We all wanted to know when we were leaving. Given the magnitude of what we were doing, a little more notice to get our heads in the right place would have helped. Since the start, training was at a fast pace, and here we were, down to the last hours before testing would become a reality.

We met Mac back in the Operations Checkout room, the place where we initially did our fitting for the authentic replicas of the various Luftwaffe officers' uniforms. This time, there were no uniforms, no technicians. The room was empty except for us. Mac led us to the transit room. The Stuka was in the transit room this time, with a few technicians on the left side of the plane. The backup aircraft had been moved to an area behind a blast door in case we needed to make a switch. On the floor next to the plane lay an assortment of gear. The storage bay behind the gunner on the tail of the Stuka was open and empty. Waving his hand in a sweeping motion from left to right, Mac stated, "This is what goes back with you. What you see here is it."

Neatly arranged were two canvas backpacks, handguns, a single rifle, ammo, flashlights, packets of C4 explosives, ropes, knives, uniforms, documents, rations, including water, and a collection of other survival type gear. "Take a good look, gentlemen. This stuff could come in handy and could make all the difference for you. We have no way of knowing what you'll face or what you will need, so you get a bit of everything. It will all get packed into the backpacks and stowed. Rick, your pack will have extra smaller explosive charges. The rest will be divided evenly."

Mac knelt down and picked up two leather-bound books that looked like a small, well-done scrapbook. Each bore the Luftwaffe emblem embossed on the cover. I opened the book, and to my amazement there, I was in my full Luftwaffe officer's dress. Flipping through the pages, I found photos of me standing next to a downed aircraft. The black-and-white images looked incredibly authentic.

That day spent in front of a green screen became an archive of our history in a war we were yet to fight. "This will get stowed with the gear. You will have identification papers on you if anyone questions you. It is just further proof if you need it." As we walked away, I looked back, and the technicians were packing the gear in the backpacks. For the first time, I felt a lump in my throat and a pit in my stomach. A quick shiver ran through my body head to toe like a wave crashing on a beach. A realization hit me that this was going to happen, and here I was about to live my last day, my last hours, in this time.

Mac hopped up on the wing to the cockpit and gestured for me to join him. He pointed to the "three-minute" self-destruct box. "It is live now. It was connected and armed this morning. That is your last resort. Not that it would make a huge difference if the plane were captured, but it would be an anomaly and fuel speculation of conspiracy theorists for decades to come. Those crazies who believe that aliens gave the Nazis advanced technology might just have their proof."

We got off the wing, and Mac said to Rick and me, "It's ready, and so are you. There isn't much left to say or do. It will work or it won't. We will know soon enough."

Well, my curiosity had the best of me, and I asked Mac how exactly he would know if we were successful? It would be one of those classic paradoxes of time. If we succeeded, there would be no reason to travel back, and this complex and this room would not exist. It would have in another time, but not in this one.

Mac said they had wondered the same thing. "No one knew exactly what to expect if you were successful. They thought that nothing would change in this timeline. You are here now and would be there in 1945, but you would write a different future. One thing everyone agreed on is that after you go back, if we were still here and we knew nothing changed, then we would know it didn't work, or you failed."

One could be driven crazy wondering what the possibilities were. A possible outcome might be that we were successful. In that scenario, Rick and I are never recruited, and somewhere is a future timeline when this day rolls around I am a test pilot, maybe with Beth never the wiser to what I had done. As if I didn't have enough motivation to make the mission a success, that would just put the icing on it for me.

With that, Mac gave the orders for what was next. "I want both of you to go over the maps, photos, protocols, escape route, and anything else you can cram. I want you to be well rested, so lights out no later than 0800 hours. You'll need to be up at 0200 hours. Take a shower and head to the Operations Checkout room no later than 0300 hours. You'll get a meal, there will be a briefing on the process, and then you'll get dressed. At 0600 hours, you will go to the transit room for additional instructions and do a preflight on the aircraft, including an engine start and instrument check. If anything is wrong, we will have time to roll the backup plane out and transfer the gear. If that goes well, you will go back the checkout room and wait while the team checks the portal and does a warm-up on the equipment. Finally, at 0915 hours, you two will climb into the Stuka and get secured. That will give you about thirty minutes to get yourself calm and mentally prepared for the trip of a lifetime."

If all went well this time tomorrow, Rick and I would be back in Germany in 1945. We both now had less than a day to live in this time period. There were lots of things going through my mind. It was much too much to absorb. In any conflict, you would typically have the intel on the enemy. Here we had almost every detail, yet the unknown was our biggest hurdle. I didn't want to, but couldn't help reflecting and dwelling on my past, not the past I was about to face. I was thinking about Beth, but hopeful in my vision of the future that a successful mission would change the course of our lives. I was lost in my own thoughts, oblivious to everything around me. Then in what sounded like a distant voice getting louder, I heard Rick say, "What are you thinking about?" He was walking next to me, but my mind had been a thousand miles away.

I parroted a line back to him that he said to me once before, I just hope it works. I told him, the past, the present, the future, wherever this takes us, we had to succeed. We spent the day reviewing and going over maps and locations. During the past weeks and months, we had trained for our specific role in the mission. Now, it all had to come together. We had to work as a team, and still, we hardly knew each other. Certainly not well enough to know what the other was thinking. The hour grew late, and we were tired and anxious. It was 0500 hours, and a technician came into the cafeteria and said we were wanted down in the Ops Checkout room. There was a doctor there whom we had seen periodically taking blood samples and running tests on us. He wanted to check vitals and offered us a mild sedative to help us rest. We both refused, thinking it might have some lingering effects on our reaction time. He insisted. We took the pill but never used it.

Later that evening, it was impossible to sleep. I wished that maybe I had taken the pill. It was the adrenaline coursing through my veins, racing my heart with anticipation. In this solitude, the remaining hours would seem like days and minutes like hours. As the night progressed, what little sleep I managed, dozing off and on, would not keep me refreshed. The sound of the alarm clock broke the still silence of the air. I took a few minutes before I got up to think about it all one more time. Here I was standing on the doorstep of history and a historical moment. It must have been what was going through Neil Armstrong's mind on the day of the moon launch in 1969. It was 0200 hours, and I needed time to shake the fog and haze from my head and get ready. In the early morning hours of March 17th, five weeks ahead of our original departure date, one life's journey would end, and another life's journey would begin.

We made our way to the operations checkout area only to find we had guests. A few top-ranking members of the military as well as some civilians, likely CIA, were there to meet us. They were talking to Mac when we stepped into the room. We saluted and shook hands with each one. Mac directed us back out to a large conference room where breakfast was waiting. "Grab something, and let's get started on the briefing," he said.

The Navy Admiral opened up by saying, "This is a historic moment in more ways than one." He went on to say, "No one knows what will happen today, and from what I am told, if you are successful, we may never know the sacrifice you made. Gentlemen, I wish I were going with you. A commander longs for a battle, and this was the mother of all wars. Whatever happens, I thank you, and I wish you all the luck on this mission. One more thing—if you find yourself back in 1945 and failure is on your doorstep, you cannot let the enemy take or gain access to the information you have been sent to retrieve or the knowledge you possess. That might create a future that none of us can endure."

There were two other individuals in the room. They introduced themselves as members of the team that worked on the technology. They wanted to walk through the process and what would happen. On the screen in the briefing room, they showed us a video of a previous drop.

"This is what you can expect today." It showed the crane with a large iron "marker ball" attached. The portal doors were open, and a light was pulsating.

"What you see here is the portal in warm-up mode. It is running, but without enough energy to open a space in time. We took numerous measurements, and the radiation is nominal. The light is the issue, in the portal with unprotected eyes, it will blind you. Let's watch the rest, and I will explain."

The crane moved the ball over the entrance and lowered it. The doors above the portal closed. There was no light coming through it. It was sealed. On the wall, a clock was counting down from t-minus eight minutes. When it hit zero and starting counting forward, there was nothing. At T plus five minutes, the portal doors opened. The lights were still pulsating, but much slower. As the crane was raised, the iron ball was gone. Mac stopped the video.

One of the scientists remarked, "That is pretty much how it works. Not too much on the surface, much more going on behind the scenes. That video was of a successful documented and verified drop in Germany, 1945.

"About the lights, you will wear protective goggles to shield your eyes, and we will place a shield over the canopy. It won't be secured. It should fall off when the airstream hits it. It is an extra measure of protection for your eyes."

For a fantastic achievement as this was, it seemed quite unremarkable. There was nothing spectacular to see, no sounds, no fireworks. I expected more to it, but the real action was on the other side. The briefing went on, and it was primarily a recap of what we had been studying. We reviewed the weather forecasts in an eighteen-day window—nine days before February 15th and nine days after. It was the level of precision they thought would be achieved. That period also had a stretch of cold but clear weather, a plus for the mission. Lastly, we received a final recap of what we would face and the escape plan.

Mac explained, "In February of 1945, the handwriting is on the wall for Germany. The Luftwaffe had all but ceased to exist, Allied bombers and fighters are conducting round-the-clock bombing raids on Berlin, and fifty thousand would perish in bombings on Dresden alone. The Wehrmacht has resorted to calling up women and soon schoolboys to fight. Your biggest threat is the desperation of the German army and the airpower of the Allies. On the ground, the Russians are already into German territory from the east, and the Americans are closing from the west. There will be trouble everywhere you look.

As for the escape plan, if all goes well, you will land at the airfield at Nordhausen. You may find resistance, but remember; they think you are one of them. Use it to your advantage. If the German regular army or Gestapo are protecting the site, tell them you are following the Führer's direct command to retrieve and protect the secrets of the Reich from the enemy. There will be no way to verify the orders. Communications to Berlin would be almost impossible. Then take the Stuka and set a course due west for the British coast. Stay as low as possible. It is less than 500 miles to London, and it should be well within the extended range of your aircraft. Allied fighters will be swarming, and you can't afford to outrun them or toy with them for too long. Conserve the fuel along the way as best you can. You might need it to circumvent Allied air traffic. Go as far as you can. Anywhere east of the Rhine and you will find friendly faces. Your first goal is to make it England. Get to Allied Command Headquarters and get the documents in the hands of Eisenhower. He may believe you, he may not believe you, but the Americans will have control of the secret papers. If he resists and refuses to take the document, use the code word 'Operation Unthinkable.' It will stop him in his tracks.

"Operation Unthinkable was a plan so secret it wasn't revealed until fifty years after the end of the war. It was the British and American plan to invade Russia. He will believe you then. If you have to put down short of London, try to put it down safely on land. You will find civilian clothes and American passports in the aircraft storage area. Detonate the plane using the self-destruct. Take the document and head to the nearest city where you can secure transportation to London. There is some currency of the era in the clothes.

"Lastly, if along the way the Russians or Germans have you cornered, it is better to get rid of the documents. Do not allow yourself to be taken alive. You know what you will need to do when, and I say when, you are successful, and the documents are in the secure hands of the Allies. Then you also know what needs to happen next. Your knowledge of future events is too tempting. You cannot continue to live in a world where you know the next steps. Even if you could use that knowledge to prevent tragedies."

It sounded so easy. Drop in, grab documents, fly out, and avoid detection. I had a feeling it wouldn't play out so simplistically. The briefing concluded on schedule, and the military brass saluted us and wished us the best of luck. They would stay and observe from the transit control center and wait for some sign that we were successful. In the checkout room, we dressed in our Luftwaffe flight gear. Per the first go around, we were fitted per the specifications of the era and then double-checked one last time against period photos. This time, they armed us. I had a knife strapped to my left leg and a sidearm. I put my hand over the flight suit's left breast pocket and could feel the small vial that contained the glass cyanide capsule we were to use.

At 0630 hours, now just three hours and eighteen minutes from transit attempt number one, Rick and I proceeded to the transit area for some pre-flight systems check. In the room, the Stuka was already attached to the crane using the mating apparatus, just as in test number one. Mac was there and waiting for us. He greeted us and said, "She has been checked out thoroughly over and over, but as a pilot, I know you would and should want to keep tradition and do your own preflight. This exercise is really about the engine start and run up, just to make sure all is well and ready."

There was no need for Rick to get in for the test run up. He and Mac stayed out of the way, and when given the signal, I started the engine and let it idle. I scanned the gauges. All seemed normal. I switched to the backup system, and all checked out. I was flagged to increase the engine power, and I did it to the max limit identified during the test. After three minutes, I got the signal to cut the engine. Mac waved for me to get out and come back down.

"All okay?" he asked.

"Perfect," I responded.

"They will load the guns and attach two small bombs on the wings. When that is done, they will top the fuel tanks off. Next time you are in it, it will be a lethal fighter-bomber."

Next time was fast approaching. By the time the preflight tests finished, we had killed two hours just waiting. Meanwhile, the engineering team and technicians prepared and conducted the final checks and loading. At 0900 hours, we were instructed to go to the transit room. There, Mac, the technicians, the scientists, and the top military brass were waiting. We saluted and stood beside the aircraft. A hastily organized group photo of the entire Projekt Töten Zeit was taken with the Stuka in the background.

The highest-ranking Air Force General stepped forward and saluted me. He then presented me with a promotion to colonel.

"This is effective immediately and will be reflected on your permanent record. A grateful nation thanks you for your service and sacrifice."

I saluted, and he returned. The highest-ranking Navy Admiral stepped forward and presented Rick with a promotion to Commander.

"This is effective immediately and will be reflected on your permanent record. A grateful nation thanks you for your service and sacrifice." They saluted, and he returned to the line.

Mac stepped forward for what would be the last time.

"Gentlemen, it has been a pleasure. Until we meet again, good luck."

The pomp and circumstance were over. Everyone had left to go to the observation area. We were slightly behind schedule, but there would be no adjustments. We had to go at 0948 hours. The technicians were left to help us in the aircraft and make sure we were secured. Mac went through the final steps. I synchronized my watch to the digital clock on the wall in the transit room. At 0935 hours, the crane would pick the Stuka up and begin to move it into position. At 0940 hours, I was to start the Stuka engine and set it to the max speed we used for testing. At 0944 hours, the blast doors over the portal would open, and we would be lowered inside. Finally, at 0948 hours, the Stuka would be released. After I felt the release, I was to count to three and go full throttle, nose up on the Stuka, quickly removing the protective goggles. The shielding over the canopy should fall off, and we should be in the skies over another era.

The tech shook my hand and closed the canopy. It was then the protective shield was installed covering the canopy. I had a few minutes. It was 0933 hours. Just fifteen minutes to go. It was pitch black inside the cockpit. I turned the small light on in the right corner of the panel. I pulled Beth's picture from my pocket and clipped it to the left side of the instrument panel. If it were good luck, I would need it now as she flew with me one last time.

A JOURNEY TO THE PAST

The Stuka jostled, and I could feel the crane lifting it. I turned my head back and asked Rick, "Are you ready?" He replied, "Let's go." We were moving slowly. I kept looking at my watch, and at 0940 hours, I fired up the Stuka. The sound was deafening within the closed transit room. I moved the throttle to the pre-set location. The aircraft was vibrating and rocking just a bit. Suddenly, it was quiet. I checked the gauges, and the engine RPM had not changed. It was running. I looked at the watch. It was 0945 hours. The portal doors should be open. The air was noticeably cooler and getting colder. Even with a flight jacket over my flight suit, it was uncomfortably cold. I switched the cockpit light off and put on my goggles. I waited for the jolt. It would be a long two minutes.

I was not a particularly religious man, but in these last two minutes, I closed my eyes and said a prayer. There it was — the jolt that we had disconnected from the crane. I felt like we were in free fall. There was a burning smell — something like charcoal. I felt a pain in my left shoulder and arm. I was gasping for breath, but there was no air. I held my breath and tried to bear the pain. It was something we didn't expect, and they probably didn't know about it. I counted to three and pushed the throttle forward to full power. My right arm was trembling, and I couldn't move my left arm from the pain. I had to take my hand off the stick to pull the throttle, and I could feel the plane bank and go over. Rick must have had the same experience. I could hear him wincing over the engine's whine.

Suddenly, the sound was back. The air was thicker, and I could breathe again. It was cold but not as bad as before. I quickly pulled the stick back and regained control. I held the stick with my knees while I pulled the goggles off. The canopy cover was gone. It appeared to be near sunset or sunrise. I glanced at the gauge; we were at 3400 feet and climbing. I did not quite have my bearing yet to know what time of day it might be. There was still that burning sensation in my arm. The pain was intense — like someone has sliced open my arm. As the minutes passed, I was able to start moving it again slowly. I leveled us off at 5000 feet and began to circle to get a look below and get a sense of where we might be.

I hollered back to Rick and asked if he was okay. He said something was wrong with his left arm, but it was getting better. He had the same thing happen to him that had happened to me. I told him to keep an eye out for any potential air traffic. It would most likely be above us since we were at a low altitude, and probably hostile. Since we both had suffered the same effect on our arm, there was something unforeseen in the transit that caused the problem. It was the same arm in which they had placed the small locator chip. The chip that was a long shot ever to bring us back had apparently malfunctioned. A reaction of some sort had occurred, and judging from the pain we both experienced, I suspected that the chip was no longer of any use. The long shot of getting back to our own time had just gotten longer.

As I circled the plane, I noticed several anomalies that I did not expect. There was chatter on the radio. Unmistakably German. I started to look down at the landscape. There were visible lights from towns and homes below, and traffic was moving. It was expected that we would encounter radio silence and a blackout of the cities to avoid detection or use by enemy aircraft on bombing runs. It started to come into my mind that we might be in the wrong place at the right time or the right place at the wrong time or maybe some other possibility altogether. I widened the circle I was flying in to get more time to scan the horizon. I did not see any air traffic, friend or foe, anywhere in sight.

On the left side of the cockpit, there was a pocket with maps and manuals for quick reference. However, the best course before exploring other options would be to tune in the homing beacon at the Nordhausen airport. After making the adjustment, to my surprise, it was transmitting a strong directional signal — a good indication that we were within 100 to 150 kilometers. Sure enough, as I came out of the bank, the beacon appeared to be to the southeast, just as had been predicted. It was a good sign that we were in the right area, but the real question was whether we were in the right time.

Something was definitely wrong. What, I did not know. From the open-air broadcast, the airport homing signal activated, and lights and traffic below this did not look like war-torn Germany in the final stages of the war. There was no reason to run the Stuka wide-open. There was no threat, and we were not even sure yet where we were or when. I had the throttle set to cruise up at 120 kilometers per hour, roughly 200 miles per hour. At that pace, we would be over the Nordhausen target in thirty minutes. I would occasionally depart from the flight path and fly another sweeping circle to check behind and around us. I asked Rick how he was doing.

"Okay," he replied.

"What do you think?"

"It worked. We are somewhere."

I told him that something didn't seem right, but that I didn't know just what, and that I was going ahead as planned to the target. We would reassess when we got there. As the sun was setting, I noticed a crescent moon above the horizon. If this were February of 1945 and the middle of the month, we would expect to see a thin crescent moon on the 14th. It was not a paper-thin crescent, and it was slightly higher above the horizon. If all calculations were correct, this could be February 16, 1945, or March 17th or 18th of 1945. It could also be another month in another year. We just didn't know yet.

Nordhausen was just ahead. The distinct landmark twin church steeples of the town were visible through my windshield. I let Rick know we were approaching the target. It was evident that the facility was operational. The airport runway lights were on, the town lit like a blazing torch, and the facility near the mountain completely illuminated. A lighted trail or road from what I presumed to be the Dora-Mittelbau camp was visible. By all accounts, this did not appear to be 1945, but much earlier, maybe 1940, '41, or possibly '42. There was no sign of war or conflict evident anywhere. We had to be in pre-war Germany. It was the only explanation. It was difficult to get my head around this with all that was going on. I started thinking about if it was the wrong date? Was there anything in the documentation that would be spotted and trip us up? Also, was the documentation we were sent to retrieve even here at that stage of the war? Had Hitler even directed a team to work on it yet? We could land and the information we were sent to retrieve might only exist in the mind of Josef Scheel and not yet documented in his notes.

We had two options at this point. The first, we try to put down outside the town and work our way in to investigate. The approach had its risks. It was getting darker by the minute. I could not with confidence put us down safely without potentially trapping us there, or worse, damaging the plane or us. The second option was to go to the airport, land, and get an assessment of the situation on the ground. We would certainly get questions, and we were unsure about the security given that we appeared to be ahead of our time. Through our journey to get here, I had not thought about it until this moment that the project had worked almost as planned. We were dropped into a portal and came out somewhere. Perhaps a bit too early, but it did, after all, work.

I would have preferred to land out of the immediate area and do reconnaissance, but it was dark with no moonlight to help identify a suitable landing area. Plus, the Nazis or townspeople might have spotted our landing and assumed a downed plane. I didn't think we had any other choice than to chance a landing at the airfield. I let Rick know to be prepared that we were going in. I made one more pass downwind of the landing strip to get one more look at the activity. It was definitely not Nordhausen in the modern day and did not look a lot like Nordhausen in the later stages of the war. It was far more extensive than what I had seen in photos, or when I saw the camp remains.

The field had what looked like all ME-262 jet fighters lined up on the tarmac. There appeared to be more aircraft hangars and aircraft here than there should have been at any time in the war. This complex had all the signs of a busy military airport. I let Rick know that we were going in and to get ready for anything. I was worried. It was where we were supposed to be, but not what we expected it to be. It would be best if he stayed in the aircraft while I spoke to the ground crew. I would figure out "what time" we were in and to see what other information I could find out. I would be hesitant to leave the plane, but if it all looked good, we could say we were headed to Berlin and needed quarters for the night. We would need to look at the situation carefully.

Based on the intelligence, we should encounter a mostly abandoned facility, but it was evidently a busy hub of activity. he communication between Nordhausen and Berlin was also thought to be non-existent in the futile closing days of the war. Yet, we did not see any signs of chaos or confusion. If communication lines were open, they could try to verify our identities. In a worst-case scenario, I would make something up on the fly, a story that I had to land to check out a problem. At the first sign of trouble, we would get out of there as fast as we could. Rick would be manning a machine gun, but that kind of trouble, I hoped we wouldn't find.

Here we go. We were putting the whole mission on the line right now. I banked and put the plane on final to line up with the runway. My heart was beating out of my chest. From here on out, I would be on stage with the performance of a lifetime. There couldn't be one slip up with my German or my attitude. These guys would catch it in a second. As I flew over the end of the runway, I cut the power to idle and glided to a touchdown. A million things were racing through my mind. An excellent German mechanic would almost assuredly question our Stuka as non-standard. A curious one might start poking at it a bit more. I taxied to a hangar where a crew was waving at us to come in. I told Rick to be on high alert and that I had a strange feeling about all of this. I had second thoughts of just heading back to the runway for a getaway. The Germans would likely think something was up and send a fighter or two after us. There was no way we could match these jets for speed. We might have been able to out-maneuver them if we were lucky, but they would be on alert from here on out. We didn't have any good options.

I pulled the plane up and cut the engine. I took a minute to unbuckle myself and check my weapon. The German soldier was looking curiously at our aircraft. I leaned back to Rick and said, "Cover me if this goes downhill."

I got out on the wing and jumped to the ground. The guard approached, and in German, asked for my identification. I reached into my pocket and handed him my information. He gestured to Rick to come out and present his ID. I wasn't sure what Rick would do. If he got out and shot the guard, it would cause a commotion. We would need to get in the aircraft and get rolling through a hail of gunfire and a ground pursuit before we could take off. I wasn't sure we would make it. Ever the pro, Rick got out and did not take extreme action, but came down and handed his identification while surveying the situation. The guard looked at both papers and suddenly yelled. "Achtung! Das sind die Amerikaner."

I knew right away we had been made. His words were "Danger! These are the Americans!" From the hangar and around the airfield, Gestapo stormed us. There was no chance to escape. I didn't know how they knew or what gave it away. It seemed as if they had expected us. We may have inadvertently walked into a trap set for someone else, and it was just our bad timing to be here.

I felt we had failed miserably, captured without a fight. I did not have a chance to activate the self-destruct on the plane. Our weapons were confiscated. Now, the aircraft and the two of us were in German hands. The leader of the Gestapo group commended the solider for capturing the American spies. He walked over towards us and looked us in the face and with a stern voice said, "Amerikanische Spione auf deutschem Boden ist ein Akt des Krieges, aber die Führer ist ein Mann des Friedens! Wenn man Glück hat, wird er Ihre Seelen erbarmen!"

It translated to "American spies on German soil is an act of war, but the Führer is a man of peace! If you are lucky, he will show mercy on your souls! Heil Hitler!" In German, I said we were loyal to the Fatherland and were not American spies, but members of the elite Luftwaffe.

As I said my last words, he grabbed the rifle of a soldier and took the butt of the rifle and punched my gut. I buckled and collapsed. He pointed the rifle and yelled, "Lügner! Halt die Klappe du amerikanische Schweine. Ich möchte Sie jetzt töten und lassen Sie Ihre stinkenden Leichnam den Geiern. Auch würden sie nicht berühren!"

We were in trouble and up against a dangerous Gestapo Major. His words were of anger and hatred toward us. His words were "Liar! Shut up, you American swine. I would kill you now and leave your stinking corpse to the vultures. Even they would not touch you!" He knew we were not Germans. How he knew was the mystery.

I was reeling in pain. I was thinking of his words "an act of war." We should have been at war. War was declared on America by Germany after the attack on Pearl Harbor in 1941. For Germany and America to not be at war meant we had to be here before 1941. If that were true, we would be lucky to survive the night. They would likely torture us until we talked or beat us until we were dead. I should have trusted my instincts. Something seemed wrong from the beginning, and I made the wrong choice. I began to assess our options to take advantage of a possible lapse in security or judgment by our captors. It seemed an unlikely scenario. Security was tight. If they moved us, perhaps we would have a chance. We had to play a waiting game and hope that an opportunity presented itself.

We were shackled at the hands and feet and placed in a holding cell. There was no need to separate Rick and me any longer. I told Rick my suspicions that something went wrong in the transit. We were here too early — way too early. Even if we came in undetected, our target, Dr. Hans Josef Scheel, may not also have been at Nordhausen yet. Our job had just gotten tougher. We would first have to escape and second scour Germany for a man whose location we did not know.

Rick, thinking of escape, gave me his plan. "It is unlikely that we will get too many chances to escape. We need to seize every opportunity regardless of how good or bad it looks. There is no honor in waiting for the right moment to die. If there are just one or two armed guards who come into the cell, we must attack quickly. If they are unarmed, it means armed guards are nearby. We will need to strike fast."

That sounded like suicide, I told him. The armada of guards who surrounded us at the plane knew we were coming. They wouldn't lapse security now because they had us. We would have to hope we would get a better opportunity than just to kill two unarmed guards and be shot by a thousand when we stepped outside of this cell.

"Would you rather die without a fight and be beaten to death? I would rather kill two and die than kill none and the two of us die."

He had a point. If we were going to die a slow death by torture, we might as well take two with us and go fast. I heard our cell door unlock. Rick looked at me and said, "If we have the chance, let's take it now."

It was a risk. We would have to get the chains binding our hands around the guards' necks and hope that after we killed them, they would have the keys to unlock us. If not, we would have taken an enormous gamble and would not get far with these chains.

The door opened, and the Gestapo Major stepped in with four armed guards. "Wenn einer von ihnen etwas versucht, töten sie beide."

"What did he say?" Rick asked.

There was little point in hiding that we were Americans. I told Rick he said, "If either of them tries anything, kill them both."

The Major threw the civilian clothes and American passports hidden in the Stuka. It meant they had gone over the plane and found our weapons and supplies. He instructed that we be unshackled and for us to get out of those Luftwaffe uniforms and get dressed. We would be taken to Berlin for further interrogation. For now, it appeared that we had the chance we were looking for — more time to plan an escape.

ENCOUNTER IN BERLIN

Following instructions, we changed into the civilian clothes and promptly shackled again. Then, led at gunpoint from the cell and across the compound. There was an overwhelming show of force lining the route we walked. The Germans took no chances with us. We were thrown face down in the rear of a truck with guards seated on each side of us. After a short ride, the vehicle stopped, and we got pulled from the back. There was an aircraft waiting. It appeared to be a Ju 52 or Ju 252, a Luftwaffe military transport. There was one difference—this was a jet. Neither the Germans nor the British or Americans had this capability yet. The Gestapo Major directed a group of SS officers to load us into the transport and ensure we were secured to our seats. These were not the regular German army, but what looked to be an elite Special Forces type of the SS.

They put us inside the empty plane and further secured the shackles. We were to go into the interior exposed rib of the aircraft. It was now Rick, me, and thirty armed SS watchdogs. They sat emotionless on benches lining the inside of the cargo bay, sitting, waiting to do their job.

As soon as the rear door was locked, an officer yelled forward to the cockpit, "Entwarnung!"

It was the "all clear," and the engines started. Our next stop was to be Berlin. Remembering our original mission instructions, if the objective were out of reach, we were expendable and not to try to do anything that could further change history. We had gone beyond that not by choice, and we were in the hands of people who might fulfill those instructions for us or force us to linger here in the past.

I asked the SS officer nearby, "Welches Datum ist heute?" or "What is today's date?"

He replied, "Das siebzehnte Februar." It was the seventeenth of February.

"Das Jahr, können Sie mir sagen, was Jahr es ist?" I asked him, "The year, can you tell me what year it is?"

He replied,"Neunzehnhundert fünfundvierzig."

Rick asked me what that exchange was all about? I told him that I asked him the date.

"What did he say?"

He said it was February 17, 1945. I had to absorb what he had said. The date was right, but the setup was wrong. This was not what 1945 Germany was supposed to be like. Our journey through might have had unintended consequences that the planners had not counted on. It could also have been that we had made it to February 1945, but maybe one in another dimension or timeline.

The rest of the flight there was nothing but silence. There was no heat; it was cold inside the aircraft. Even the SS soldiers were heads down and hands in their coats to stay warm. Only the loud engine noise filled the interior of the plane. The flight was short. It was perhaps an hour before we touched down at what we presumed was Berlin. While the aircraft was taxiing to the hangar, Rick leaned over and said to me, "You're the military history expert. Could this be Berlin?"

"Not in 1945," I replied. The city would have been subject to around-the-clock bombing from the Allies. We almost certainly would have encountered Allied aircraft, and the Germans would not have flown a transport without a fighter escort. Here on the ground, other than the hustle of workers outside the plane and the sound of other aircraft, there was nothing unusual. As the door to the transport opened, and we were taken outside, the air was cold, and the dark skies were grey, covered with clouds. A Wehrmacht General was waiting to meet us. I recognized from his collar insignia that he was a judicial general and not regular army staff. He asked one of the SS officers, who was there when we landed, if we were the American spies. The officer acknowledged that we had been caught flying a captured vintage German bomber. He added that we were disguised as German pilots trying to infiltrate the base at Nordhausen.

The General introduced himself at General Otto Mueller. He spoke only in German and asked if we understood the language. I acknowledged. He indicated that these were serious charges for a country with which Germany was not at war, but at peace. He then ordered the SS to remove the ankle shackles. He told us that we were, for now, prisoners of the Third Reich, but also temporary guests. Germany had done nothing to provoke an act of espionage from a friendly country, and perhaps this was just a misunderstanding. He moved closer to our faces and said the following.

"Ich bin sicher, dass Sie den Ernst der Zwangslage verstehen, in der Sie sich befinden. Ich möchte Sie recht hier behandelt werden, aber diese Männer werden nicht zögern, dich zu töten, wenn Sie etwas, um zu versuchen, zu entkommen zu tun. Ich wird klar, dies sich und erhalten Sie zurück zu unseren amerikanischen Freunden."

I translated for Rick. "I am sure you understand the seriousness of the predicament you are in at the moment. I want you to be treated fairly here, but these men will not hesitate to kill you if you do anything to try to escape. I will help clear this up and get you back to our American friends."

The General went on to say that we would be taken by car to meet the Director of Reich Security, Deputy Führer Reinhard Heydrich. He would determine how this matter would proceed.

We were bound only at our hands. A guard shoved us into the back of a truck. Several others joined him to stand watch over us. There was no lapse in security. The truck was escorted front and rear by a convoy of SS on motorcycles and SS in open military vehicles. Escape was impossible. I was trying to place Heydrich's name and where he was in the Nazi hierarchy. As I recalled, Heydrich was a relative unknown until 1941. After '41, he became a Hitler protégé and rose rapidly through the Nazi ranks. He was considered the true architect of the Holocaust.

Under Himmler, it was Heydrich's plans that put in place the mechanics for the mass extermination of the Jewish people. Heydrich was at one point the Director of the Gestapo under Himmler, and then was the Director of Reich Main Security. Later, Hitler appointed him to a position that was the Governor of German-occupied Czechoslovakia.

In our history, Heydrich was assassinated in 1942. He was not still alive in 1945. Rick asked what else I knew about him. I told him "fair" was not a word anyone would use to describe him. He had as much blood on his hands as, and maybe more than, anyone in the Nazi regime. Through an opening in the rear of the vehicle, I could see Nazi symbols and flags draped from buildings, with banners hung from street lamps. The sidewalks crowded with people and the streets filled with cars. There was no evidence of bombing, war, or panic. It seemed a bustling city, peaceful, and prosperous. It didn't make sense. I told Rick that we should try to figure out what went wrong, why history had changed. If the world was at peace, even with the Nazis in power, perhaps this was a better place. If the Holocaust was happening, maybe this time we could stop it.

I looked out the window and could see that we had arrived at the Reich Chancellery building. It was the headquarters of Hitler and his high command. The car pulled into a covered area that looked to be reserved to cover the coming and going of Hitler, and high-ranking cabinet and military visitors. We exited the car and found the SS guards stationed around the inside of the entrance. The general who met us at the airport, Mueller, indicated that I would come with him first to meet with Deputy Führer Heydrich. Rick would be taken and held to meet with him later.

Separated for the first time since the mission started, this would make any joint or coordinated escape plan difficult. I am sure Rick was thinking the same, but at this point, if either of us had an opportunity to escape, we needed to take it and not worry about the other. We would need to get out, gather intelligence, and see if the mission goal was still attainable. There was a change in Mueller's tone, and he directed Rick taken away and for me to move with him.

The interior of the Reich Chancellery was ornate, stunning in its architecture, but all built with slave labor. Its beauty tainted by the horror and treatment of those who worked on it. I was led up to the second floor and down a hallway to a room with large, ten-foot, wooden doors. Mueller told the guards to re-shackle my hands and feet. When they were done, Mueller opened the doors and pushed me through. I almost stumbled due to the irons on my feet, but recovered. There was a figure looking out the window with his back to us. He was in the black Gestapo uniform, but the light coming through the window obscured any details. Mueller announced, "Mein Stellvertreter des Führers. Das ist einer der amerikanischen Spione wir am Flughafen in Nordhausen erfasst."

He told him that I was one of the American spies captured at Nordhausen. The figure at the window raised his right hand to signal Mueller to stop talking. The figure gestured his hand as if swatting a fly for Muller to leave. Without question or hesitation, Mueller turned and left the room, closing the doors behind him. I was here in the presence of a murderous maniac who struck fear in his subordinates as well as those he oppressed. I walked towards the desk and stopped. The figure turned slowly. Facing me with the light from the window still obscuring his face, he said, "Captain Kelly, I have been expecting you."

As the figure stepped forward, I could see the face of the butcher behind the mass killings of the Holocaust. It was Mac. Mac was Deputy Führer Reinhard Heydrich.

"Mac?"

"Yes, Captain Kelly, it is I." He was laughing to himself as he said it.

"How?"

"Your mission failed, Captain. You failed, Captain. After you made the transit, we should have noticed something change. Nothing did. Our control was the document. We expected to see the complete set on the table. We didn't. Nothing changed. I convinced them to send me back, only earlier — a lot earlier. Your mission failed because it was too risky from the start. I would go to Germany before the war with America, and it would be easier to find Scheel, follow him until he made progress on his works, and then seize the documents. It would have worked. I flew the Stuka back and was to destroy it when I got here, but I didn't. I found Scheel quickly and could move about Germany in the open as an American.

"Then it dawned on me, Captain. I was a Grandmaster who knew all the right moves. I could rule the world with my knowledge. There is an irony here, Captain. Hitler wanted a message sent back to himself in the past. He never dreamed that a messenger from the future would deliver that message. Do you get it, Captain? I was the message he was seeking. I had all the answers to the mistakes he had made. I appeared here at this time, just as if God had granted their wish in the form of a divine prophecy, or should I say prophet? Germany is at peace with America and Russia England is begging for peace for fear the Führer will wipe them from existence with his military might. Over the past few years, I have consulted with him and his military leaders. I have changed history. I may yet rule this country someday."

"You are insane."

"No, Captain, I am quite sane. This is who I was meant to be. The crash that killed Charlie, it should have been you. I sabotaged the plane. You were supposed to be flying that plane as I ordered you to, but you didn't listen, and instead, a good man lost his life. Now, you will pay for Charlie's death."

"You sick bastard."

"Careful, Captain. I have very little patience for you. You are in a very dangerous predicament. Your attitude may make the difference between whether you die today or tomorrow."

"I don't know how you convinced the Nazis that you knew the future, but your luck won't last."

"I had no trouble convincing Hitler. The rest of the staff was dubious, but I had an ace in the hole. In the secret stowage area of the Stuka, I put a history book. They were convinced quickly enough. As if that wasn't enough, I told them when and where you would be coming, and there you were, just as I had predicted. For four years, I have worked my way up the hierarchy. Only your pending arrival has held me back from what I can achieve, and now that you are here, I can eliminate my last problem. Come to the window. I want to show you something."

I walked to the open window and looked down to the courtyard below. There were four SS men with pistols pointed at a man's head. He was shackled and blindfolded. Mac yelled to them below, "Vorgehen. That was your friend, Captain. One problem solved, one to go."

As soon as Mac's words echoed in the courtyard, shots rang out. The assassins fired point blank, and Rick collapsed to the ground. He was dead.

"You fucking psychopath. I will kill you. That is a promise."

He laughed to himself and said to me, "He was the lucky one. In a few days, maybe weeks, you will wish it was you in that courtyard. It certainly is payback time, Captain. I am sending your back to Nordhausen. You will work at the Dora-Mittelbau concentration camp. During the day, you will dig out the mountain for a new rocket facility along with the other garbage. If you are lucky, at night, the guards will let you clean the dog shit from their boots. It may be the best meal you will get there. In a few weeks, like the others, you will become useless and too weak to work. You will reach the bottom rung of the ladder, hauling the dead and dying to a pit for burial. Then lastly, you will be too weak to do that work, and you will get hauled to your death. I have taught them this brutality and disregard for the useless of society. They learned it well. One more thing Captain, don't get any ideas that you might still accomplish your mission. Scheel is not there and never will be there. History showed your mission failed."

I told him it was Colonel, not Captain, and that this would not be the last time we would meet. He signaled for the guards to take me away. As they pushed me towards the door, Mac yelled, "Halt!"

I turned just as he yelled across the room. "Captain, remember this. Never underestimate the brutality and hatred that human beings have for each other. It is what makes the killing easy to take."

DORA-MITTELBAU

In a callous and cowardly act, Mac had Rick killed. A cold-blooded murder by one of us, a member of the team put together to protect the past and the future. If it took my last dying breath, I would do everything I could to avenge Rick and settle the score. We had made mistakes along the way. Maybe we should have risked it all to escape back at the airport or in the car to the Reich Chancellery. If we were to have ended up dead anyway, what could have been worse?

Now, it was different. I could not be killed and let Mac create a future in his image. There was no reason not to take him at his word, but the hatred in his eyes, I had seen it before. It was the same look when he put his hands to my throat at Lemoore. He had that look—the look of a person restraining the evil inside. It was without a doubt, the look of a person who wanted to finish the job. He wanted my end to come slowly and painfully. It was likely that I was headed to my death very soon unless I changed my destiny.

Our conversation was over quickly. Mac ordered me to be taken and sent to Nordhausen on the next available transport. The SS guards did not know anything about me, just that I was an American spy getting a taste of German justice. I was playing in my mind what Mac's end game was going to be. It appeared that he helped Hitler avoid the critical mistakes of the war. It was he who advanced their already superior technology far enough to stand unchallenged. It could be in this time that the Japanese did not bomb Pearl Harbor and that Germany did not invade Russia, but it appeared that Germany was at war with England. The fight with England might have been the phony war. It may have just been a war of words to gain status and further appeasement. Austria, Czechoslovakia, Poland, and maybe France had fallen and were used as bargaining chips for peace while Germany continued to build its most fearsome weapons.

It would have been a pivotal historical development if Mac had convinced Hitler to move on the atomic bomb and other advanced weapons before war broke out. Without the threat of war or American intervention, the Nazis could quickly become the world's preeminent military power. It may have given the Nazi regime enough time for the German military, within a few years or sooner, to have the ability to wipe out armies, fleets, or countries out at will. It was a frightening thought.

That I was being sent to the Dora-Mittelbau concentration camp to work as a laborer building tunnels did not surprise me. If Mac wanted to teach me a lesson, that would be the place. Worker deaths were frequent; those unable to work were killed. There was a crematory at the camp, and most workers labored night and day in the tunnels battling poor air and dangerous conditions without ever seeing the light of day. Existence in this system was beyond the equivalent of prison life. It was brutal and inhumane.

What struck me as odd was that the work at Nordhausen to dig tunnels in the mountains was a direct attempt to hide the V-2 factory and other essential work from Allied bombing. That Mac, or Heydrich as he was now known, ordered the construction while Germany was supposedly at relative peace likely meant that the Nazi regime was planning for a broader, more imminent war. It might also have indicated that they were close to having the means to wage a nuclear war.

Mac would not have possessed the knowledge to advance the Nazi nuclear program, but he would have known who could have helped. In his position, it was within his control to have prevented the departure of Jewish scientists from the country. The Nazis were so far ahead with missile technology that an advanced V-2 could have been built to reach Russia, and likely America. I might have had a new mission at Nordhausen, to stop the Nazi war machine before it became unstoppable. If I could recruit fellow prisoners at the camp, I might have been able to sabotage the facility. No longer would this have anything to do with the original mission but more about fixing and undoing what Mac had done.

I had time to think. Wherever my first stop was, it seemed to be outside of Berlin. They could have been taking me somewhere to shoot me. Considering what they did to Rick, it didn't seem worth the effort to prolong the inevitable and go out of their way for another spy. It wasn't about expediency, but this was about Mac's twisted measure of revenge. In the back of the truck, I had no visibility to see where we were. I asked one of the guards, "Was ist unser Ziel?" or "What was our destination?"

He replied, "Sie gehen nach Sachshausen, um für die Verarbeitung." My next stop would be for processing at Sachsenhausen

Sachsenhausen was north of Berlin and was a camp for political prisoners. Over its life, it housed many notable prisoners with high public profiles, many of whom did not survive the war. I could hear the truck brakes as we slowed, then muffled voices. The driver was likely speaking to the sentries at the gate. The noise of the truck and their low tone made it difficult to understand the conversation. As the truck moved forward, I could only assume we had entered the site. When it stopped, guards from the camp pulled the canvas back. "Nur ein Gefangener?" "Just one prisoner?" the guards asked.

One of my sentries on the truck replied, "Er ist der amerikanische Spion, der von dem Befehl der Stellvertretenden Führers Heydrich verarbeitet und zum Lagerkommandanten gebracht wird." He told him that I was the American spy to be processed and taken to the camp commandant by order of Deputy Führer Heydrich.

The guards prodded me across the central open area of the camp through a triangular yard with towers that had machine guns, and searchlights pointed toward the grounds. The facility appeared clean and orderly, but the air had a stench of filth and decay. Like all camps, it was a place of death. We proceeded to an office where an SS officer was waiting. The officer was looking down writing when the guards pushed me forward to his desk. He was furious. "Wer ist dafür verantwortlich, diesen Müll in mein Büro zu bringen?" he asked. "Who is responsible for bringing this garbage into my office?"

His quick temper and loud ranting rattled the guards. "Amerikanischer Spion hier von dem Befehl der Stellvertreter Führers Heydrich." They told him I was the American spy here on orders of Deputy Führer Heydrich.

"Wir erwarten keine Sendung für eine weitere Stunde." "We are not expecting a shipment for another hour," he told them. He demanded my identification. I handed him the false identity I was to use when we had reached friendly territory. He took the information and completed a form, which he handed back to me and waved the guards on. Next stop, a place where a man shaved my head, and then finally, the standard de-lousing shower. It was surreal not to know whether these showers might dispense water or gas to unsuspecting newcomers. This time it was water.

There was no special treatment. Like so many others, the standard prison garb was my new uniform of the day. It was something I was familiar with from photos of the era. It was a faded light blue with dark-blue, vertical stripes. They were oversized to allow workers a slight bit of comfort to facilitate more productivity. The material was coarse like burlap, but nothing more than a low-grade fabric that was mass-produced for the camps. From there, I was taken to the camp commandant, all the while surveying the layout for opportunities to escape. Outside the office of Commandant Anton Kaindl, I waited until finally signaled to come inside.

His demeanor was stereotypical, almost like a character in a movie. He questioned who I was, and when told that I was an American, he reacted.

"What is to be the disposition of this spy? Does Deputy Führer Heydrich wish me to hang him and make an example of him?" he asked.

The guard replied, "The Deputy Führer wants the prisoner to suffer. He is to be shipped to Nordhausen and worked until the skin hung from his bones."

Kaindl replied, "At Sachsenhausen, At Sachsenhausen, we can accomplish the same objective." He then asked,

"What did I do to earn the wrath of Reinhard Heydrich?"

At this point, I had to tread carefully. I was in the hands of a man who could have me killed and tell Mac that I had tried to escape. I decided the truth was the best option. I said to him that I was an American spy from the future, and Heydrich was also from the future. I was sent to prevent Germany from conquering the world. As I had expected, he laughed and gave the guard orders.

"Stellvertretender Führer Heydrich hat mich gesandt, dieser wahnsinnigen und verrückten Amerikaner. Ich will nicht diese Geisteskranker hier. Senden Sie ihn auf den nächsten Zug nach Nordhausen. Lassen Sie sie mit ihm umzugehen."

He bought what I was selling; he didn't want an insane person at his camp and ordered me sent on the next train to Nordhausen.

I had avoided the first potential trap. I was sure there would be more, but for now, I had work to do. Mac may have been right. Perhaps Rick and I failed on our first mission, then Mac came back, and he was either the reason we failed or the reason I had to see this through. For the moment, I had to survive. First, to try to fix what Mac was doing. Second, to see if what I suspected was happening, and the Nazis were on the verge of developing the weapons of mass destruction and the delivery system. Lastly, to finish the unfinished business I had with Mac.

My charade bought me more time. It was off to the deportation center. The network of concentration camps had two purposes: to supply workers as slave laborers to work on Nazi projects and to exterminate those whom the Reich felt would not further the Aryan race. Mac had used his knowledge to help slow the pace of genocide, but only to buy time until outside forces could not stop Nazi Germany. They were well on their way to reaching a tipping point of military might, and this time the outcome would be far worse.

Inside the deportation center, the newly processed prisoners like myself lined the walls. Only the able-bodied men and women were shipped to the hard labor camp at Nordhausen. The room was filled mostly with men of all ages and just a handful of women. The women were mostly older — there were only a few who were younger. All appeared to be Jewish, or non-

German. Like me, they wore the prison uniform. It was one thing to read about it in history. It was another to be a part of it.

There was a reconciled desperation in their faces like they knew what fate awaited them. There was no anger, no rebellion, and no fight. The Germans had taken the will to live from them. Everyone kept to himself or herself. I noticed there was no socializing, no conversation. I saw a young woman in her early thirties by herself. She stood out from the rest as perhaps upper class and well educated. I slowly made my way to her section, careful not to startle the guards with my movement. Speaking German, I asked her name. She replied, "Ilse Cohen." She asked mine, and I told her. She then said, "American?" with the English pronunciation. I told her I was and asked if she spoke English. She answered, "Yes."

She was young and pretty. I feared that such a person with youth and beauty was on her way to face horrors that would forever scar her. I feared what the guards might do to rob the innocence from her face. It would turn out that we were the only two talking. I wanted to know how it was she came to be in this place. The guards did not seem to mind, but we were watchful. Her story was that she was the daughter of a German-American father and a German-Jewish mother. She was educated as an aeronautical engineer in America and returned to Germany as it began to prosper in the early days of the Nazi party. She intended to get a job helping rebuild Germany and German pride after World War I left the country in shambles. She succeeded in getting a job at the Horton Brothers Aircraft Factory in Gotha.

Slowly, she said, the Nazis began taking Jewish residents from their businesses and homes. Rumors began to circulate that they were made to work as slave laborers and their homes and belongings seized by the government and given to non-Jewish citizens. Her father and mother refused to believe it would affect them, until one day her father became caught in a Nazi roundup. Then, as she and her mother were in Berlin ready to exit for Switzerland, the Nazis confiscated their passports. Her mother taken away, and never seen again. With little concern that her words might get her singled out by the guards, she let her feeling be known.

"I am certain that have met their fate at the hands of these barbarians."

She indicated that she was brought to Sachsenhausen to be processed and sent to Nordhausen where her engineering skills could be valuable to the Reich. My heart was breaking for her, and the suffering hit home. She wanted to know my story, and I told her I was an American military pilot and also had an engineering background. Falsely accused of spying on the Nazis, I too was now ensnared in their web of terror. Even though I had only this brief exchange, I felt I could trust her. I told her I wasn't a spy, but that I was someone who was here to stop what was going to happen, and then I corrected myself to say, "What is happening." It would be a series of small victories that would win this war I was fighting, and this would be the first one. At least for now, I knew I had one ally. I would need others once we got to Nordhausen.

At 1700 hours, a train arrived at the deportation station at Sachsenhausen. These trains were nothing more than cattle cars that made this trip many times. The Nazis were indiscriminate. Males and females were loaded with as many as a car could take. We were the cattle. As I waited to climb into the car, I surveyed the train. There were five cars and a coach at the back for guards. Because the trip was short, just five hours, and stayed within the confines of German territory, the train would not be stopping along the route. There might have been an opportunity to escape if I could find a weakness in the rail car. The guards who were in the back might have been few, and perhaps I could find a way to disarm them. The loading area was within the camp border, the platform well lit. Even if I could have managed to slip away or under a train, the SS would have spotted me. It became an endless waiting game of trying to find the right opportunity. An opportunity I might never get.

I purposely made sure I stuck close to Ilse. She was now the one friend I had, and I needed to recruit others. If I couldn't make it out now and save the people in these cars, I would have to do it at Nordhausen. That would be a more difficult task and would take a coordinated effort. In the railroad car, the stench was horrendous. The smell of waste and decay permeated the nostrils. One had no choice but to try to take one's shirt and cover their mouth and nose. Some of those on the train vomited, overcome by the odors, and others were sick from what fate they knew might lie ahead. The conditions were not fit for livestock, much less human beings. The doors were closed, and the interior became dark. In the cramped quarters, you were able to sit with your legs pulled to your chest and had no room to walk to stretch. Escape from this horror was all I that was running through my mind.

The Nazis could not have planned a greater incentive to leave or a more powerful deterrent. For just a breath of fresh air, many would have given anything. The thick wood doors and floor of the car were impenetrable. The heat from so many bodies and the stagnant air only made the situation worse. As the train pulled away from the station, the lights of the camp blinked through tiny pinholes in the corners of the walls. I hoped the moving train might clear the air. If it didn't, I feared there would be many dead before we ever reached our destination. The weak and ill were finding their fate long before anyone at the death camps would get a chance to impose it on them.

As the train rolled south towards Nordhausen, there was silence. There was occasional violent coughing, sobbing, but no restlessness or talk. I was now one of the millions who might share this same fate, and I was also one against millions to stop it. I looked over at Ilse. Through the darkness, I could make out only that her head was down and face covered. The hours passed with just the thumping of the rails below until the sounds of the train's brakes

127

and the blast of steam. I had taken a detour and arrived back where I started, Nordhausen. After less than twenty-four hours here in the past, I wished I were back where it all began. Home. It was a mistake to tamper with history.

If this was indeed our final destination, we had been traveling for four or five hours. It was past midnight — probably 2 a.m. or somewhere close to that time. I may have been the only person on the train who knew what to expect, and it would not be a celebratory or welcoming party. There was commotion outside as we could hear the doors open and guards yelling for the passenger to "get up and out." When it was our turn, the door slid open, and the sudden, cold rush of air was a relief. The camp was lit up like Christmas, by no means attempting to take shelter in the darkness. Hidden deep in Germany, it was keeping many secrets from the world about what brutal atrocities were taking place here. In this place, heinous weapons were being built to steal the lives of many others. It could afford to broadcast its presence without fear of attack. Spy satellites did not exist; overflight by allied aircraft was not a threat. In plain sight, the Nazi regime might have been rewriting history or the future, and all with Mac's help.

The weakest in the boxcars were slow to move. The guards ordered prison workers from the camp into the car to beat those who did not move quickly enough to their satisfaction. Other camp workers climbed into the car to drag out the few who were dead. The guards dragged the weak and fearful off to be beaten and end their misery. These SS soldiers seemed to treat this job as if their progression through the ranks coincided with the measure of the brutality they inflicted. Mac was right about one thing: Humans are capable of unspeakable horrors against their own. Indeed, it was a fine line.

It was just a short train ride, but already some had not survived. The rest of us were lined shoulder to shoulder a few rows deep. We stood there as one by one, each prisoner on the train "checked in" with an SS officer. He asked their name and checked his list. He then told them their assignment. There were only three choices I heard him say: labor, factory, and camp. Most got assigned to labor and camp and only a handful to the factory. Labor would have been the digging of the tunnels and caves that housed the underground research and factory for the V-2. The "factory" would have been an assignment to work on the assembly and manufacturing of the V-2. "Camp" entailed routine daily maintenance of the facility. That role might have included the beating of those not executing their duties, hauling the dead, and maintaining the camp's appearance. When Ilse approached and gave her name, the guard hesitated. "You are lucky," he told her. "You are assigned to engineering as part of the re-education program."

Her skills made her too valuable to be assembling rocket parts. The re-education program was reserved for Germans whom the Nazis thought could be salvaged and turned to be supporters of the Reich. It would entail special treatment and less harsh conditions. If the Nazis deemed that re-education had failed, then the person would be shifted back to the regular camp. For most, it may not have mattered which job anyone was assigned — death came quicker for some than others, but eventually, death would try to find all.

When I approached, I stated my name and waited. The SS officer looked at the paperwork and said, "Amerikanisch?"

I replied, "Yes, amerikanisch."

He then said, "Mit Sonderbestellung der Stellvertreter des Führers Heydrich, Sie sind zu zwölf Stunden harter Arbeit und zehn Stunden Lager Wartungs jeden Tag als Strafe für Verbrechen gegen das Reich zu arbeiten." The translation, "By special order of Deputy Führer Heydrich, you are to work twelve hours of hard labor and eight hours of camp maintenance every day as punishment for crimes against the Reich."

The situation was much more desperate now. I could no longer afford to pick and choose a time for an escape. Mac certainly had it in for me, and it would be only a matter of a week or two, perhaps far sooner, that I could sustain the punishing, twenty-hour days. I needed to get out and soon, but I also wanted to free the others in the camp. I would need the help of my fellow prisoners to provide intelligence on camp activities and procedures. The element of surprise and my twenty-first-century training and tactics were the advantage that would work in my favor.

After I received my assignment, I waited in line with those who had gone before me. The process finished with a registration number tattooed on my left arm. I became number 581203. Prisoners working in the camp handed me a new uniform, and we changed on the spot, discarding the clothes assigned at Sachsenhausen. This prison uniform was no improvement. As if by design, it felt like sandpaper on the skin. There were no undergarments, underwear, or t-shirts. The camp was not in the business of doing laundry.

The standard camp uniforms issued were purposely large and loose fitting to hide the wasting of body fat and muscle from malnutrition that would affect every prisoner. The photos I had seen of these horrors in black and white that didn't seem real or were too brutal to believe. They were all too real now. It was not how I had expected my life to play out. In a way, Mac's influence had delayed what could have been more deaths. However, if I were right, he could cause more deaths than history recorded. I also had the ability to influence history. If I could stop the work here and prevent Mac from altering any more of history, I had a chance.

When the registration was complete for all of the new arrivals, we moved into a large dormitory-style barracks. From floor to ceiling were wall-to-wall racks where prisoners found a spot and crawled in to lie side by side with barely any room to turn. The conditions on the outside did not reflect the squalid conditions inside. Despite the cold temperature outside, the inside was warm, stuffy, and humid. The air was putrid from sweat, urine, and human waste.

I would get one night's rest before I would begin working. I am sure Mac intended to put me on a fast schedule to death, but also to prevent me from being out of the watchful eyes of the SS guards for too long. Those who had not just arrived were tired and dirty. All appeared to be exhausted and sound asleep. I walked down the narrow space between rows of bunks to find a group of men who were awake and talking. It took a few minutes, but I found such a group. They only spoke German. I asked if I could join them. They knew I wasn't German or Jewish. "Amerikanisch?" one asked.

I was no longer surprised by the question, only surprised that they were shocked to see an American in their prison world. They wanted to know why I was here, and I explained that they believed me to be a spy. I asked if they had thought about or tried to escape. They told me that several had tried to flee and got caught. The failed escapees returned to the camp in shackles, and the prisoners forced to watch them hanged immediately. They were left dangling for days as an example for the rest of them. Since the last attempt a few months ago, no one has tried.

I wanted to know if they observed any weaknesses in the routines and how long it took before anyone noticed someone was missing.

"The ones who tried to escape were either foolish or brave. They shared another trait in that they were all dead. They had no chance, but they would have rather died than lived one more day like this."

This prisoner said he was not as brave as they were, and as a result was here.

"At morning roll call, a headcount is taken. By then it would not matter if you were there or not, the Germans are efficient, they will find you. The fearless, or foolish that tried, were usually killed at the fence. Those men should have considered themselves lucky that they were not taken alive and brought back only to face a swift, but painful death. You cannot get out without the right equipment. The dogs will find you before you have a chance to try to dig or climb your way out."

I asked about the work routine and if there were vulnerabilities at the factory or working around the camp that we could exploit.

"Nein. In the camp, there are guards in the towers, and the lights do not provide a chance. If the guards don't see you, the dogs will find you. On the labor detail, the guards keep a distance, so there is a chance, but you will be too weak and tired after one day to even think about it."

I wanted to know what they knew about the projects inside the mountain. One of the men said they used to be on the rocket assembly detail. He said that the Nazis had made vast improvements in the rocket. A new V-4 design was in the works. He described the V-4 as a much more capable rocket with not just one engine but four engines. The rumor in the factory was that this was to be code-named the "America Rocket." The Nazis believed that the rocket could reach anywhere in America. It was another in an accumulating list of discrepancies with history. Nordhausen existed as a direct result of Allied bombers ravaging the Peenemunde V-2 site. This location was considered remote and offered protection from bombing raids. It might be that the main V-2 test and assembly at Peenemunde still existed in this relatively "peaceful" timeline, and that manufacturing of the new rocket was moved here for an extra measure of security. I had serious doubts that a Nazi rocket could reach "anywhere" in America. That would require an enormous technological leap that even with their advances I could not see coming to fruition.

There were also rumors that deep inside the mountain they were working on a giant bomb to go on top of the rocket. It was to be a bomb that could destroy a whole city.

"It was all Nazi propaganda from Goebbels. No single bomb could destroy a city," said another.

I knew better. I had guessed right that the end game was to buy time to deliver the bomb to America and Russia. Mac was as maniacal as Hitler and drunk on the possibilities of power. It made sense that the new rocket and its warhead were being built together at a secret site. They sounded close, but not quite ready. There might have still been time. If America and Russia were to be beaten before the war ever started, it would take a massive and cowardly sneak attack. It would take a nuclear Pearl Harbor. As I pieced more and more together, it sounded as if that was the plan. This change in history bore all the signs of Mac's intervention. Why he would betray his country was a mystery. If there were any signs when we were all working together on the project, I missed them. He seemed the loyal soldier, one who was willing to die for his country.

In this hellish place, this small group of frail but resilient men looked like a team I could count on if needed. I had not formulated any escape options for us just yet. More intelligence would need to be gathered before any bold actions were taken. I told them I was an American pilot and the Nazis had captured my aircraft. If I could get to the plane, I might be able to come back and take out the Nazi command structure at the camp and liberate those imprisoned here.

"The aircraft hangars are on the other side of the base. It is easier to get to them than to escape the camp, but still not easy. There is a fence separating the working camp from the base airport, but it is not a barbed-wire fence. The sentries and dogs do not patrol it regularly. However, the hangars have significant protection around the clock. They store fighters in some and research new aircraft in the others."

131

These men knew the camp and the Nazi routine and had thought about escape. Weighing all the risks, I had a hard time seeing an easy out. I had to help, for them and me. I would work tomorrow as planned. It would be a chance to get a good view of the camp in the daylight and regroup with them in the few off hours I had tomorrow night. We would have to work quickly.

The discussions with those imprisoned with me went on for a while into the night. We were all tired but gained a renewed optimism and energy from the possibility of an escape. I had been here barely twelve hours and was already planning an exit. Some of the other prisoners had already survived a year. The thoughts of what they had told me, and the things they had seen, made it difficult to sleep. It became the norm in the nightmare world in which I found myself, little time to rest, and what short time there was, I couldn't take advantage of it.

There were no clocks or watches in this dark place. One would usually find a spot and fall sleep to escape the reality of being awake. Time was inconsequential here. You woke when they told you, worked until they stopped you, and slept what time was left. My thoughts were interrupted by a sudden commotion. Guards had entered the building banging on a metal pan to wake up the prisoners. In the camp, you didn't "get ready." You were awoken, herded outside the building, counted like cattle, and fed. Each prisoner received a liquid potato soup and a piece of bread. It was a meal lacking in nutrition or calories. It was a "starvation" diet, and it showed on those who had been here more than a few weeks. With many waiting to eat, you only had a minute or so to finish and give your metal cup to next person in line.

When you finished, you stood in your formation and waited until the rest had joined. Only then did the roll call proceed. As the guard in charge barked out names, you learned to move quickly to the group with your work assignment. The labor group was the largest, followed by the factory, and then the camp. Those assigned to the camp appeared to be the weakest. They were the ones who likely started in labor and had now progressed down the line.

The SS learned to take no chances with the prisoners. There were prisoner guards recruited to help maintain order, meaning they were one of us. They were known as "Kapos" and identified by a unique armband on their work uniform. Chosen for the qualities that mimicked the SS, they were typically criminals with little regard for their fellow captives and instead only for their own survival. They supervised the work and learned that turning on their own increased their chances for survival. It also gained them favor and special privileges with the SS guards. They were more dangerous than the SS and had nothing to lose. The SS also realized that having a line of defense between the workers and them gave a buffer and time to react to revolts or escape attempts. It seemed they had worked out the perfect formula.

132

After roll call, I marched with the others outside the camp down a dirt trail towards the mountainous region. I knew from history what was achieved here. I had also been here before in my own time. The carving of a mountain to build a research and rocket assembly facility was a monumental undertaking. One facility had already been completed, and another expansion site was underway. I knew from history that there were other mountains carved to protect the V-2, but those were protective launch sites and not research or manufacturing sites. If the new V-4 were much larger, it would require a different set of logistics and would not be easy to hide. In 1945, satellites to spy on unusual activity did not exist, nor did any satellite to detect a missile launch. For the Nazis, a mass attack of rockets from the sky without warning and carrying a nuclear device would bring swift destruction and a slow reaction. Those retaliating would not know where to strike back if they even could mount a counterattack. The threat to the world from weapons of mass extinction and unfathomable destruction had to stop here and now.

It was still dark as we marched in the freezing temperatures toward the mountainside. As we approached, the mountain was illuminated for the previous shift to work through the night. I could see the brightening of the sky as dawn approached. The sun rose quickly and light fell on our work area. The scale of the mountain was imposing. The work here had just started, and not much had been accomplished. I was handed a pickaxe by a Kapo and was told to begin excavating. I was standing at the exact site where Mac, Rick, and I stood to survey what ruins were left of this some seventy years in the future. It had similarities. The massive pile of debris from the Nazis blasting in the mountain looked eerily like what I had seen. It would be my job, along with hundreds of others, to clear the rubble from the blast.

Our task was menial and dangerous. We would break the rocks in pieces, which other workers would load into carts and haul away. There was no protection as shards large and small penetrated the skin and eyes as they flew off the shattering rocks. Even with hundreds of workers, this was a task that progressed slowly. The sun was taking the edge off the chill in the air, but there was already plenty of heat. The endless swinging of the ax had most of us sweating even in the cold. The Kapos were already yelling and threatening those who were moving too slow. It seemed a futile effort. The scale of this job was enormous. It was something on the order of the pyramids, hollowing out the inside of a mountain, one rock at a time. There was so much debris that the workers were endlessly moving cart after cart of rocks away from the mountain. With all that effort, it still appeared this work was akin to spitting in the ocean. It must have been how Egyptian laborers felt building the pyramids. Only we were hollowing out the mountain to create another emperor's monument.

I used the opportunity to look for weaknesses in the operation, but like all Nazi endeavors, they had covered the weak spots. Here we were, hundreds, with a weapon in our hands, and we were powerless. It would have taken little effort to turn on the Kapos and take them out, but the second line of Nazi guards stood off with machine guns. A few us might have made to them, but at a high cost to the rest. Hundreds would die, and one way or another, all of all of us. One thing I did have from my rocky perch was a view of the camp. Now that sun was up, I got a good look at the airfield I first landed on, and its relation to the barracks. The place was sprawling, but under the right conditions, it was doable to get from the dorms to the hangar. I would need help and luck.

On a twelve-hour shift, we were given a fifteen-minute break every three hours. Allowed only enough drinking to provide a few ounces per person barely. Bathroom, water, and rest were all worked into the fifteen minutes. There was no privacy or sanitation. You relieved yourself in a designated area. Those singled out as slackers were forced to clean it up at the end of each shift. The stench and filth were bad enough that even with empty stomachs, some would vomit. Those who had collapsed or complained were first beaten and finally dragged off if they could not continue to work. Those who persevered did so only because they knew the punishment would be worse. Everyone knew that the ones who opted for brutal end of a club had given up and had decided that death was their escape. If they survived, their next assignment would be camp detail. One more rung down the ladder, and one more step closer to death. If they could not perform that work, they would be executed and sent to the crematory at the northwest corner of the camp. From where I was working, the smoke was visible from those who could not or would not fight another day.

At the end of day one, I, along with the others, found ourselves exhausted. We were dehydrated and had not eaten all day. They had been doing this much longer, and how they managed it with no food and barely enough water was a testament to their will to survive. If they had endured this, I would, but I was also afraid. I had to put on a strong front to those around me. It was a responsibility I felt owed them to lead. Inside, I knew this wasn't a game that would end, and I would return to my time. Here, it was another time, and it was real. I had looked at each turn for ways to use my knowledge to escape and found none. I could wait and wait for the right time, but I began to doubt there would ever be a right time.

When the shift ended, we marched back to the camp. This time of year, the days were getting longer, but darkness still fell early. It was easier to control the prisoners using the remaining daylight that was left to get them back inside the camp to their barracks. Despite the exhaustion, we walked at a brisk pace. Our clothes were soaked with sweat. Without a jacket, the air was rapidly evaporating the moisture on us, making us feel even colder. Once back inside the camp, we were forced to stand for another roll call. This time there were fewer of us. When no response came, the guard taking roll call would ask "disposition?" to which the usual reply from another guard was "executed" or "dead." A few had collapsed while waiting for roll call. They were the weak and ill that had made it through another day, but could not stand due to exhaustion and lack of nourishment. They, too, were beaten and dragged off. It was unlikely we would see them again.

There was a handful of us pulled from the group into a separate unit. It was what they called the "death detail." It was for the prisoners in the camp who would pull double duty and work another shift doing camp maintenance. It was known as the "death detail" because you did not get a second meal for the day. You went straight to work. There was no hiding it was intentional to work these prisoners for the short time they could tolerate it. It was a punishment for minor camp infractions and intended to send a message to other prisoners. When the final roll call finished, the regular prisoners were allowed to eat the slop the Nazis called a meal. After eating, they were then let go back to their bunks. They would get six hours of rest if they were lucky while another shift worked. The death detail would be lucky to get four, but more likely would get two or three.

The "death detail" to which I was assigned is where I spotted the first weakness in the Nazi armor. The jobs given to those on the detail were not labor intensive. The work was intended to deprive prisoners of sleep in the hope that one would collapse and warrant further punishment. The SS guards were not superhuman, and they needed their sleep. The policing of the "death detail" was left to the Kapos to supervise. They were no less brutal than the SS, but other than a club did not carry a weapon.

There were twenty of us, and only five Kapos to supervise. We were broken into groups of four with a single Kapo to watch us. It was the first sloppy mistake I had seen the Nazis make. The SS tower guards were responsible should a prisoner try to escape or attack a Kapo. Their logic was that Kapos were as expendable as prisoners. If a prisoner or prisoners turned on a Kapo, they might be successful, but the tower guards would shoot them all.

We were handed rakes and were told to line up side-by-side and rake the dirt to smooth it out. We were to pick up any trash or dog shit and put it in our pockets until we finished. I about had it and did not think that I would wait another night to take action. I could take these four Kapos before the guards ever knew what happened. I practiced restraint by telling myself their time would come. This first night, I would learn the routine and assess the opportunities, and tomorrow, plan an escape.

After eight hours in the freezing cold, walking and raking dirt across the camp following the twelve hours breaking rocks at the mountain earlier today, I felt that I could stand no more. My feet ached, and my arms and shoulders were sore, as was my back. The Kapos yelled, "Halt!" and told us to get what remained of the meal the regular prisoners had earlier, then go to the barracks. There was nothing left. They laughed at those desperately trying to get something from the metal pots. Not a drip of the watery drool they were feeding the prisoners was there for us.

Without a clock, it was impossible to tell how long we were working or how much time we had before we had to start the next day. In the barracks, there was that ever-present, stifling stench of sweat and urine. The workers were asleep from exhaustion. The only sounds were the rats scurrying across the floor. It was not difficult to find an open slot in the racks. Each day, fewer returned from the work detail. Space was available until the next shipment of workers arrived. I had formulated in my head what plan of action I would take tomorrow night. It was high risk, but I had to act soon.

KAPO

Caught between exhaustion and endless thoughts of how to outsmart the enemy, I drifted in and out of a semi-consciousness state, wondering whether I was dreaming or awake in a purgatory of the afterlife. When the Kapos came in to roust us from the bunks, it was the rude awakening I had feared, reality. With their batons, they walked down the aisle banging on the wooden supports. The Nazis had turned a prisoner against his own, and like Judas betrayed for not silver, but a few extra pieces of bread.

The Kapos were hated in the barracks. Sometimes cursed and spit on as they walked down the aisle. While they were no more than garbage to the SS, the Kapos had come to believe they were the SS. They thought they were invincible, untouchable, and above the rest. A prisoner might not assault an SS guard for fear of death, but attacking a Kapo was not the same. The guards might invoke some retaliation, but in reality, it saved them the trouble of disposing of one more body.

The Kapo who came down our aisle on my first and second morning at the camp was a real son of a bitch. He knew the weak that would not fight back, and like a bully would hit them for his own sadistic pleasure. Today he would strike no more. I knew which prisoner he seemed to make his personal punching bag. As he made his way down the aisle, I slowly made my way towards him to ensure that I got there the same time he did. He was banging on the post ordering this prisoner to get up. He was screaming. "Stehen Sie auf, Sie faule Schwein!" "Get up, you lazy pig!"

Weak and barely able to move, the prisoner climbed from his bunk and fell to the floor. The Kapo raised his baton to strike him when I grabbed his wrist with both hands. There was a stunned look on his face. I kneed him in the groin, and as he bent in pain, I delivered an uppercut to his throat to crush his larynx. Grabbing the back of his shirt, I stood him up and had two men standing by supporting him. Using the butt of his baton, I struck him dead center in his chest. He collapsed and fell to the floor. There was no question he had delivered his last blow to a defenseless human being. It was the first time I had put my SEAL training and tactics to use, and I was sure it would not be the last. If I were to go down, I would not go alone.

I propped the Kapo up against a bunk and put the baton back in his hand. His heart had stopped, and he was not breathing. I stood up and yelled, "Eilen, eilen! Das Herz dieses Mannes hat aufgehört. Holen Sie sich einen Arzt!". "Hurry, hurry! This man's heart has stopped. Get a doctor!"

Another Kapo and two SS guards came rushing in. They pushed the prisoners away from the dead Kapo. In a heightened voice on the SS guards asked, "What happened to this man?"

I told the guard, "Diese Kapo war schreien und brüllen und dann packte seine Brust und sagte, Mir das Herz.' Dann fiel er zu Boden. Wir halfen ihm, aber es war zu spät." In English, it meant "This Kapo was yelling and screaming and then grabbed his chest and said my heart. Then he fell to the floor. We helped him, but it was too late."

The SS guard paused and seemed skeptical of the story. He looked around at those standing around and looked at me. Then ordered a handful of prisoners to "get him out of here."

It was the first victory I had won. A small one, but I had taken down just one of the bad guys. It was the first time I had seen the face of a person I had killed. In my line of work, I was delivering missiles and targeted bombs to faces never seen. Faces that I had pictured in my mind would be just like this Kapo. Those whom my weapons attacked were evil henchmen who deserved the same death as did this man.

I could justify this killing as an act of war on decency and humanity, which I was defending. Had I become one of them? No. But I had developed a measure of revenge for what was occurring. In the process, I had bought at least another day for the prisoner who surely would not have survived the beating. It was one small measure of his dignity that he kept. Weak and frail, he grabbed my arm and thanked me as I helped him to the dining hall. He was spared death that morning, but he had maybe a day or two of life left in him. I would find out later that day he had died. He had gone to his grave knowing that he had outlived his captor and tormentor. Perhaps now he would join him in a place where maybe it might be his time to render justice and judgment.

There would be a new Kapo, but he did not have the same swagger. Once their invincibility was gone, they were less likely to be forceful and more likely to be fearful. They knew that their man had not had a heart attack, and they were ever suspicious that there was an enemy among them who could strike them down at will.

There should be no rejoicing or satisfaction in the taking of a life, but satisfaction is what I had felt. Through my fatigue, the adrenaline had surged, and I felt energized. I knew this feeling would be fleeting and fade quickly. Every up has its down, and every high has its low. I had gotten away with this once, and it altered my plan for this evening. Based on last night's routine, I would take down the Kapo watching us on the "death detail" and his partners if they got in my way. The element of surprise was on my side, but I may have tipped my hand with this morning's encounter. It still seemed my best option.

Once committed, there was no turning back. Under cover of darkness, I would make a break for the airfield and try to escape by stealing an aircraft. It was an audacious plan, foolish perhaps, but I was a pilot. Anyone else trying to flee had to clear the perimeter security barriers. I just needed to cross the relatively open airfield, which was inside the fence. I wasn't escaping to get away from the camp, but to fulfill the mission. With what was going on inside the mountain with the "America Bomb," the effort on the V-4, and Scheel's work on Töten Zeit, I would need to get to England or America to get reinforcements.

In just two days, I noticed a difference at the morning roll call. It was evident who was new and who had more wear on them. The decline in stamina and health would shift some of those on hard labor to less intensive camp maintenance. There appeared to be no reason or motivation to keep workers productive. There was an endless supply of laborers. Days or weeks of work from one individual were enough before moving new workers in and old workers out. It may have sounded as if that were a relief to those reassigned, but only a brief reprieve from something worse that lay ahead.

In the camp, there was one path to follow, and that was from useful to disposable. When the guard called my name, he said, "Reassignment to the factory, second detail canceled." Something had changed. Against the prevailing camp norm, I was moving up the ladder instead of down, and taken off the "death detail." It was unlikely that Mac had a hand in this or had authorized it. Working at the factory would prolong my existence, which was not what he had in mind. If the Nazis knew my background, they would not have taken such a risk. It could be related to the killing of the Kapo. Maybe it was a reward from a guard who was glad to see him get what he deserved. Even a guard was unlikely to be able to make such a move without higher approval. The change in assignment might delay my escape plans a day or two. It would give me the opportunity to get a look inside the factory complex and assess the progress firsthand.

We marched to the outskirts of the central camp compound to the factory inside the mountain. It was near the site where we were digging a new series of caves and tunnels, but this one was operational and secured. The entrance was fenced with layers of security to ensure no one entered without authorization. At this finished complex, I could visualize what the end goal was at the site I was working. The rubble that we were digging out was being used to build walls and fortifications around the site entrance. It prevented anyone from getting close to it on the ground. There was a large steel door on rails to cover the opening. It did not look like it had moved to the closed position in quite a while. I noticed thick patches of weeds growing over the tracks. That told me that the doors were likely only for an attack, and since there was no imminent threat to the German homeland at the moment, the doors remained open.

The Nazis had considered this site impenetrable. They had covered the top of the mountain with thick concrete to make it bombproof and fortified the entrance. Those fortifications might have been able to protect the inner workings of the factory from "bunker busting" bombs. However, they made several mistakes. While the inside was secure, the outside was vulnerable. Railways used to haul assembled rockets could be destroyed with ease. The test launch site on the other side of the mountain had a similar fate. It was an easy and open target. The factory could build rockets, but an Allied bombing would make it impossible for the Nazis to use them.

At the security checkpoint, the guards questioned, "Amerikanische?" He signaled another guard to get me. I was taken to a place deep inside the factory where walls and rooms had been built to house the engineering and management staff of the site. It was not a place where a camp worker would be allowed. Dusty, dirty, and smelling of sweat, I was taken to an empty room used by the German engineers. There were blueprints on the walls and spread out on drawing tables. I walked over to view them without resistance by the guard. The door opened, and in walked Ilse. To my surprise, she was wearing an SS uniform. She motioned with her head to the guard to leave the room. I asked her, "You are a Nazi SS member?

"Yes. It is complicated, but let me explain, and you will understand. When Deputy Führer Reinhard Heydrich sent you here, it caught the attention of my boss, the Obergruppenführer, Hans Kammler. Kammler is powerful and second only to Himmler in the hierarchy of the SS. Himmler and Kammler are wary of Heydrich's growing power within the Reich. Heydrich has made himself close to the Fürhrer and has threatened their influence, and that is equally as dangerous. I was put on the train to watch you and find out what I could. It was easy for me to convince them to spare your life and get you reassigned. If you are a threat to Heydrich, then they want to keep you alive, but to Heydrich, you are dead. I had word sent to Heydrich's office that you perished in an escape attempt and your body cremated. I have, and I can help you accomplish your goals."

I was startled by this change of events. I made it clear.

"I won't help the Nazis if that is what you are after. I am here to stop Heydrich. He is not who your Führer or any of you believe him to be. I also need to stop what is going on here and stop Hitler's quest to conquer Europe and beyond."

She stood there for a moment with her head bowed then looked up at me and said, "We share the same objective."

ESCAPING NORDHAUSEN

It was a reach to believe Ilse's sudden confession that she wanted Mac, now Heydrich, and Hitler stopped. She had already deceived me once, and after all, she was a member of the SS where deception was an art. I probed further. "Why should I believe you?"

"Most of what I told you was true. I was educated in America as an aerospace engineer. I was one of just a few women to complete the program. I am not Jewish; my father is German and my mother, Italian. I love America, but I also felt an affinity and obligation to my father's homeland. After World War I, they were destitute, and my father was heartbroken over what had happened to his proud country. They migrated to America to make a better life for their family, but they never really got over the defeat the shame on our country. When Hitler came to power, they believed German pride would return once again. I came back to help the military become strong, so Germany could never be defeated again. When I joined the SS, I did that for my father. What I saw was a Germany that was not just trying to protect itself from aggressors harboring a grudge from the war. It was preparing to go on the offensive again and wage all-out war. They were doing things and planning things that would not make my parents proud. It was then that I joined a resistance movement to work inside to slow and sabotage their progress."

"You expect me to believe that you are going to help me stop the madness that is going on here?"

"No," she replied. "You are going to help us."

I was skeptical but wanted to hear more. Even while we were standing here, outside in the camp, prisoners were being killed and brutalized. The longer I waited, the more carnage was occurring. "What is the plan from here on out?" I asked.

"Tomorrow night, a group of highly trained resistance fighters will conduct a raid on the camp. That operation had been planned for a while but was moved up when they heard you were here as a prisoner. Their purpose is to damage the infrastructure, the railways, and the aircraft parked on the field. They hope to slow the Nazis down. They also seem very interested in getting you out of here. When the SS respond to the attack, they will leave just a few to watch the prisoners. It will be the unarmed Kapos with a handful of trained guards who will be mainly responsible for making sure the prisoners don't join the revolt. A second group will storm the camp from the south. They will take the towers and try to get as many prisoners out as they can. The resistance fighters don't have enough men to take the camp, but they can disrupt it. Their main priority is to take out the infrastructure. Many will die, but many more will live."

It all could be a trap that was waiting to catch me. Lie after lie seemed to flow as smoothly from her mouth like water from a spigot. I was still unsure that she could be trusted. It seemed too good to be true that an insider could stand here and speak of treason against the Reich and no one was watching her. She would need to prove herself, and I would need to move cautiously. I asked her what part she needed me to play.

"I have arranged that you be given the same quarters as the high-value prisoners. You will get regular civilian clothes and a chance to shower and shave. You will work back here today and tomorrow. When the attack starts, you will go to the hangar and escape in the plane you flew here. I have looked at that plane, and it is a remarkable piece of engineering. We know that is not our plane. It is an American advancement in aviation, but still inferior to the German jets. The unique material used to build it is what interests the Nazi aviation experts. They know it was superior to their version of the old Stuka. Even if it can't match the German jets, it would still be a formidable machine against other less-advanced countries. If they can build it cheaper and export it to their Axis friends, they will do it. In a few days, they will take every piece of that plane apart and begin to reverse engineer it. If you want to steal back your aircraft and prevent any of its secrets from being used, then you need to let me help, and in turn, you help us.

"Can I ask you what your real name is?" she asked.

I had no reason to continue the charade. Maybe Ilse was just a charismatic charmer pretending to be saving me, or perhaps it was that her story was getting to me. The Nazis did not need to go through some elaborate ruse to get to me. It would have been a far-fetched hoax to want me to die then dangle an attractive SS woman to pretend to help me. There was no point other than to hope I would divulge information. Why help me to escape only to catch and kill me? They could do it now if they wanted. These murderous maniacs are the master of death and suffering. I had a fifty-fifty chance on whether I believed her or not. I wanted to test her. The price of failure for her would be fatal.

"Give me your weapon," I told her.

She hesitated and took a step back. Then she handed her Luger over to me. "Here you go. Do you plan to use me as a hostage?" I looked at her weapon, and it was loaded. It wasn't a trick. "No," I replied. "I am going to kill you right here."

With that, I walked over to her and pressed the barrel of the gun against her forehead directly between her eyes. Her eyes widened in surprise by my actions.

"Any last words before you become the next casualty of this camp?"

She stood there unflinchingly and casually replied, "No." I hesitated for a moment before I handed her the gun back. "Jake. My name is Jake Kelly."

There was a sigh of relief on her face. She smiled and thanked me.

"Well, Jake Kelly, we have work to do. Tonight, a member of the resistance group that brought a team down from Berlin will sneak into the camp tonight. It is a predictable routine the Nazis have, and he is exploiting it to hide and get on the inside. I will bring him to your barracks tonight, and you can meet him."

"Let's do that."

We could not let what was happening in this camp go on one more day. I wish we could move faster, like tonight.

If Ilse delivered as promised, I would owe her, as would everyone in this camp. She would be taking a considerable risk as an SS officer. It meant certain death if she were caught. I would proceed cautiously, but she gained a small measure of my trust for now. She had lived up to the first part of her deal. I was given the opportunity to take a shower, shave, and dress in a "valued worker" uniform. We returned to the main factory floor where Ilse walked me down the V-2 assembly line. I did not see the talked-about V-4 in this area. It was unlikely that they would let any camp prisoners near the work on the prototype. At least this confirmed that the design was not final or in production, but still in the early stages. Taking out this facility would certainly set the Nazi game plan for reliance on the "wunderwaffe," the "wonder weapons," out of the picture.

I scanned the walls of this vast, cavernous assembly area and spotted the rumored explosives meant to prevent an enemy from taking the intellectual property of the Reich. Somewhere in this complex was the mechanism to set the charges. It was likely in a secured area with one or two that were authorized to start the sequence. There were just a few guards along the line, and for that matter, inside the complex. The camp prisoners in these roles were like "white collar" criminals. Considered non-violent and educated, the Nazis deemed them a low threat. In truth, they were the highest threat. Sabotage was their greatest weapon against the Nazis.

The pace at which the V-2s were being assembled was hectic with the precision fitting of intricate piping and wiring. It moved as fast as this type of skilled work allowed, but it didn't move as quickly as I expected. I attributed some of it to the workers intentionally slowing down the assembly. It was not a smooth production line, which led me to believe that the quality was also intentionally compromised. Many V-2s failed on launch or were unable to reach their target due to worker sabotage here at the factory. Another mistake the Nazis had made, using the camp labor to assemble a critical weapon of war rather than hiring a German factory with loyal workers. Mac had apparently given them some guidance on how to advance their technology but overlooked the issues that using concentration camp workers created. I was observant and silent and didn't question Ilse about the process.

Leveraging my background in aviation and engineering, she asked me to observe and "supervise" assembly on one of the V-2s. There were other SS officers and guards around, but they seemed unfazed that she was giving "special attention" to a particular worker. Observing the assembly line, I could see the genius in the production of the V-2. The camp workers were not building the key components, just assembling the pre-built parts into a final product. It was technical, connecting the motor and fuel line to the fuel tanks and installing the gyros and guidance to the guidance fins. For its day, this was an incredible advance in technology. A more massive V-4, even with a similar crude guidance system, would be a potent delivery vehicle for a giant, non-nuclear bomb.

I had an increasing skepticism on the V-4 and the possibility of an atomic bomb. Early nuclear weapons were large and heavy. It wasn't until further advances in technology that components could be "miniaturized." The V-4 would have to have quite the lifting capability. I had my doubts that even with rocket experts like Von Braun, they could build such a destructive combination. If I was Mac and they wanted my advice, I could have offered suggestions to overcome the lift issue or maybe go the more straightforward solid rocket approach. He may have done the same, but there was no evidence of it on this assembly line. The workers on the line were focused on the V-2. It is possible that there was some truth to what one of my fellow prisoners had remarked. The V-4 could have been nothing but Nazi propaganda. As for the V-2, despite what looked chaotic, it was functioning, and V-2s were progressing along the line.

If workers were sabotaging the rockets, I didn't see any of it. When the shift ended, the workers were gathered and led out. The facility was empty; there was no second shift. I wondered how committed the SS was to this effort if they didn't work it around the clock. It could have been that they were banking on one big knockout punch. When a guard came back in and yelled for me to go with the rest, Ilse told him she would escort the prisoner and take responsibility. For her relative youth, she commanded a presence and authority. Ilse had qualities that I admired — courage and intelligence. In many ways, she reminded me of Beth. Unlike Beth, though, she was still an enigma. Masked under the beauty of her exterior, I wondered if I was dealing with Satan or a savior.

I decided to ask her about the other projects. She was hesitant.

"This is not the place. I will get you tonight and take you to meet a member of the assault team. He will be inside the camp and will hide here until the attack begins."

Returning to the barracks, I had mixed emotions my change in fortunes. These accommodations, while just a small room with a bed and sink, were like a luxury hotel by comparison to my former barracks. There were no Kapos or guards inside. There was running water and a clean bunk maintained by that lowest-tier of camp workers. Though I had only been here a short time, I shared a brotherhood with other prisoners. Even being in this "better place" did not feel right. People were dying and treated like animals. My arm bore the proof—the stamp that proved I was a number just like the rest, but also bound to those brothers. To escape and leave them behind was not an option.

We had to liberate the camp, and that would be no small feat. I didn't know how many were in this guerrilla force, but unless it was an army, it might only be a fly that the Nazis would swat. While I waited, I wrestled with the conflict of what to do if the raid was successful. Complete the mission, try to undo what Mac had done, or liberate the camp. The odds were no better for one than the other. I knew what I was sent to do, but this was the here and now. What was planned had been changed by events that were out of my control. The liberation of the camp had to come first.

I was anxious to get moving and meet this member of one of the groups sent to attack the installation and see what the plot entailed. There was much more I needed to know, not just about the plan, but also about Ilse. When she came back in to get me, others in the barracks who would see us together might cast a wary eye. Any collaboration or appearance of cooperation with the SS was cause for concern. I would have to watch my fellow prisoners. The same fate I bestowed on the Kapo could be in store for me if I wasn't careful.

She led me away from the barracks to the airfield. It was a long walk across the field from the factory barracks to the hangars. We passed several towers where guards would watch us. There was barely an inch of the camp that housed prisoners that benefited from the cover of darkness. It was as bright as daylight everywhere you looked. The only exception was that wooded area northwest of the camp and a dark area between the hard labor barracks and the airfield. This facility broadcast itself like a beacon and was a sitting duck for an airstrike.

When we finally got to the hangars, a guard was on watch standing by the entrance. As Ilse approached, he yelled, "Halt! Dieser Bereich ist verboten! Niemand darf ohne besondere Genehmigung in Kraft."

He was telling her to stop that the area was off limits without special permission. Fearless, she walked directly up to him and struck him hard across the face with an open hand. She told him. "Es gibt Ihre besondere Erlaubnis!" "There is your special permission!"

He let us pass, and we walked into a large hangar. I recognized what was in it right away. It appeared to be a working jet-powered model of the Horton brothers' "flying wing." It was different, bigger, and not painted in the standard green paint. It had a charcoal grey appearance.

"Go ahead and take a closer look. I wanted you to see this. This type of advancement in aviation is why I came back to Germany. These are the projects that put Germany's technology on top as leaders in the world. I never wanted these used as first strike weapons of attack against the people of Europe and Americans."

I touched the wing and asked about the charcoal paint scheme. I already knew what it was, and its purpose.

"It is finely powdered charcoal mixed with a special paint to absorb RADAR. The British can't see this plane when it flies. I worked on this prototype during its construction and testing. I helped to evaluate its performance and proposed changes to refine the design. When it finished and was ready to go into production, I moved to the factory to work on the new Reisenrakete, the V-4."

"So it does exist?"

"On paper, the engineers are having trouble with the new engines. There are two designs, a manned flying version that could deliver a guided bomb, and an unmanned version using the V-2's guidance system. The designers want Germany to put a man in space and show the world what Germany can do, but the Reich wants this technology to destroy, so it must be destroyed first."

"What about the uranium bomb?" I asked.

"Kurt Diebner and his team have perfected and tested it. They loaded the first bomb on an old cargo ship and sailed it to a remote area off the east coast of Greenland. They successfully detonated it. The reports were that it was devastatingly powerful. Until the V-4 is ready, the plan is to use this new class of bomber to attack London and drop the uranium bombs."

"Where is my plane?"

"It is several hangars down the line from here. They want to know the secrets of the plane and where America is with their aviation technology. Our pilot has flown it, and he says it could be effective against us. Our jets are far superior to your propeller-driven aircraft, but this could still inflict damage against us in an all-out war. In a few days, they will take it apart."

In the space of a day, I had seen the inner workings of the V-2 factory and confirmed the work on the V-4 and the readiness of the uranium bomb. I also managed to see the Nazis' version of the world's first stealth fighter. While she was being so open and apparently honest, I had one more question for her.

"There is another German scientist I am looking for and may be working on another top-secret project. His name is Josef Scheel. Is he here? Do you know if he was ever here to work on a project?"

She replied that the name sounded familiar. She had never seen or heard that a Josef Scheel was working on any of the rocket or bomb projects here or any other project for the Reich. She went to say that it didn't mean he wasn't doing something, just that she had no specific knowledge of him.

Nordhausen, as it turns out, was full of surprises. By all accounts, this was the Area 51 of Germany. It was a place where the secret weapons of the Third Reich were either developed or tested. However, the one I came for was not here. As we left, I asked her, "What do you want to accomplish from all of this?"

"Save the Fatherland and the world from a terrible fate. If I can help, and even if I don't survive, I will have at least made a difference."

There was an open-air Volkswagen utility vehicle parked near the building. We got in, and she drove to a storage facility at the far end of the row of the massive line of hangars. We parked on the side, hidden from the view of the distant guard towers. The storage depot was unlocked and dark inside. Though was light was shining through the window, I could see a shadowy figure in the corner. As Ilse flipped the light switch, I saw a familiar face. It took a moment to process and register. It was my training partner on this mission, Rick. Of all the strange things we had been through, I had to comprehend that I didn't see a ghost. I witnessed his murder from Mac's office.

"It wasn't me Mac had killed. It was a decoy to make you think I was dead. He wanted me to turn to his side and help train SS with advanced guerilla tactics. He wanted the German version of the SEAL teams, what he called the 'Wolf Team.' I refused and found an opportunity to escape and free additional prisoners suspected of being resistance fighters. I had no idea of what he had done to you, and I didn't know if you were dead. I am just as surprised to see you alive, as you are to see me. We heard that an American pilot was taken here. I knew that it had to be you. They had a raid planned already. The timing just needed to be adjusted to get to you here sooner before something terrible happened. I came here with this team to finish our mission."

After the initial shock passed, I filled him in on what I knew. Our mission had taken a different turn. Mac's presence here in the past changed things. The work on Project Töten Zeit was not here, and no one knew the whereabouts of Scheel. It was why Mac was comfortable sending me here to my death. He knew I could never find what I was looking for at Nordhausen, but he wanted to dangle his handiwork in front of me. We had to refocus on the most important thing at the moment. The secret "wonder" weapons program was further advanced than it should have been. Mac had succeeded to some degree in fulfilling Hitler's prophecy of righting the strategic decisions that cost him the war. The goal should now have been to disable communication with Berlin to buy us time, then destroy the complexes inside the mountain and the hangars, liberate this camp, and rebalance the scales of military might.

"How many men do you have?"

"Fifty. There are twenty-five outside the camp and twenty-five who will be landing in a Luftwaffe transport. There is a group of resistance fighters inside the military that will seize the plane in Berlin and bring it here. It was already scheduled to depart. Taking it won't alert the Nazis to suspect anything. When it lands tomorrow night at twenty hundred hours, we will create a diversion. It will be an explosion at the northwest corner of the camp. When the camp guards respond, the men on the transport will disembark and trap them. The team outside the camp was ready to attack the facility inside the mountain to take the documents and Scheel. If you are sure he is not here, I need to rethink that plan or abort the mission."

I weighed in on Rick's plan. Aborting the mission was not an option. We still had important work to do here. The odds of success were in the team's favor. The camp was virtually shut down by at the proposed time of the attack. The guards in the tower were the main protective force. Kapos were out with prisoners doing camp maintenance. There was no ready and prepared force at that hour protecting the camp. An explosion at the far corner of the complex would get a slow response. They would likely be caught off-guard and unprepared. By the time they did get organized, it would be too late. They would be easy targets. When I was inside the mountain factory, I saw the explosives that the Nazis were to set off in case of an emergency, like an invasion. If we could detonate those explosives, the rocket production, the work on the V-4, and development of the atomic bomb could be halted or severely crippled.

Rick asked, "Where's our plane?"

I told him that I hadn't seen it since we landed, but Ilse knew where it was. It was in a hangar waiting to be disassembled and reverse engineered.

"Can you get it out of here when we attack?" he asked.

"I might be able to get the plane out during the initial confusion, but I wanted to be a part of this battle and not cut and run."

"Look, we've got this covered. When we have done our work, we will leave on the transport that flew in with our second team and head to France where we can regroup. You need to take that plane and finish our mission, get Mac, get the document, get it delivered. I will be okay."

I turned to Ilse and asked what would happen to her.

"I will fight with the resistance and work to stop what is going on. My boss, Herr Kammler, will be blamed for the attack and the harm it did to the Reich. Himmler will order any surviving SS at the camp, and anyone who participated in the attack hung or shot. I do not fear what lies ahead."

If she was on the up and up, she was proving to be quite a remarkable woman. She exhibited inner confidence and bravery that matched her brave exterior. I had become enamored with her, her achievements, and willingness to fight for what was right at the ultimate cost to her, but all for a country she loved.

The plan was now in place. Rick would signal the team waiting outside of the new objectives. I would get to the plane and hope it was in flying condition. Then I would proceed to get to Mac in Berlin and force him to disclose the location of Scheel's work. Before we split up, I had one more thing to do. In one of the hangars, there was a Luftwaffe Flying Wing with some stealth capabilities. It had to be taken out. I would do it on my way to the plane. I shook Rick's hand and wished him good luck.

He replied, "Take care of Mac for me."

"Count on it."

With that, we left, and Ilse drove me back to the barracks. We were only gone for a short while, and nothing seemed out of the ordinary until we got closer to the barracks. Waiting, was an SS commander and four SS guards with him. Judging from the look on his face, this would not be a pleasant encounter. As we approached, he questioned her. "Ich erhielt einen Bericht von der Wache an der Flugzeughalle, dass Sie dem Gefangenen unsere geheimen Flugzeuge zeigten! Was ist der Sinn der Einnahme dieses Schwein in den Hangar und ihm die Geheimnisse des Reiches zu zeigen?" He wanted to know why she would take a prisoner, a swine, to the hangar to show the secrets of the Reich.

She was terse and formidable in her response. "Das ist kein oridnary Gefangener. Dies ist die amerikanische, die die Stuka hier flogen die wirklich eine fortschrittliche amerikanische Spionageflugzeug war. Es ist im Auftrag des Reichs Führer Himmler und Obergruppenführer Kammler, dass der Gefangene eine Sonderbehandlung erhält. Wenn er hätte alles getan, hätte ich ihn umgebracht habe mich!"

He stood stoically for a moment and backed off. Ilse had told him that by order of Himmler and Kammler that I was to receive special treatment. I had valuable information that was of great use to the Reich. She added that if I were foolish enough to do anything wrong she would kill me herself. He seemed convinced and waived his men off. We had appeared to dodge a bullet.

That night, I thought about what would transpire the next day. By late tomorrow night, we would be on a different path. There was no turning back. A new history had been charted because of Mac. We would endeavor to change the course and get it back on track. I thought back to Mac's first comments when we met him here in the past. He said that as soon as we left, nothing had changed when it should have immediately. I tried to reconcile the classic time paradox. If Mac thought we failed because nothing changed, how did he know? He would have had a new version of history that he grew up with to get him to that day. I wondered if we had failed or would fail, or if we had succeeded and he didn't know the difference. It is possible that we had failed, and with Mac's arrival, we were getting a second chance. I couldn't think about it anymore. The complexities were mind-boggling.

The next day, the rush of the prior night had given me a new optimism that we would be successful. The twists of time could still be changed. That is what I believed.

Today would be a day where I would work at the factory hand in hand with the other "high-value" workers. In a way, it was a robotic choreography, looking, acting, and working the same way as the day before. They were oblivious to what would be their eventual fate if we let this go on. There was no talking on the line — just work — and I watched as these captive prisoners built weapons intended to kill those who were still free.

I wondered how many innocent people's doorstep this rocket would bring its terror. Were they so brainwashed or beaten in spirit that they were walking about not knowing that the results of their work would someday rain death from the sky? I realized that I was like them, but playing a different role. I had seen the face of war, but also never saw the faces at the other end of my weapons. I orchestrated my part as a co-conspirator in the game of war. I never knew who worked in the factories that built the rockets I fired. I only witnessed the end result from high above my targets. I saw the massive war machine in action. If I did not stop this today, what were the names of the helpless that would be written on this rocket? The story of how this would end was now in my hands and that of a small guerilla group comprised of just fifty fighters.

As the end of the shift neared, it was twilight outside. I had not seen Ilse at the factory today. She was absent from view. I was concerned that maybe the run-in last night wasn't over and that she had been picked up for additional questioning. Workers in the factory didn't have to march back to the barracks. We just walked out of the mountain complex like it was the end of a workday at a typical factory in America. As I was walking, I scanned the camp and the towers for anything unusual. I was looking for additional security, more activity, or extra patrols. Nothing appeared out of place. Aside from Ilse's conspicuous absence, if the Germans were on to the plan, they were doing a good job hiding it. I would go back the barracks and wait the two hours before it was time to move. I wanted the time to move faster.

At nineteen thirty hours, Ilse entered the barracks. We were just thirty minutes from the first wave of the attack. She had managed to sneak in a Luftwaffe pilot's flight suit for me to wear. It would be less conspicuous and potentially avoid yesterday's run-in should we have been stopped. Changing into the uniform was reminiscent of the last time I put this on. It was the start of this journey. Walking to her car, I could see she was disheveled and rattled. It was uncharacteristic of her. I asked, "Where have you been all day?"

"I had something I needed to take care of in town. I may not be here tomorrow or the day after. It was just something I needed to do."

It was an all-too-familiar look, one I had seen before on my own face. The pain of going on a mission where there is no turning back, or going back. She was nervous, and the urgency in her voice was telling me that panic had set into this once fearless woman. She knew, like I knew, that if something went wrong, this day would end badly for us. I had let her know that before we made our way to my plane. We had to stop at the flying wing. If we couldn't steal it, we would destroy it. She was reluctant to change plans so late but finally agreed.

We drove to the hangar that housed the stealth flying wing aircraft. Once again, the guard challenged us, although this time he was more forceful, more insistent. As Ilse stepped forward, he pointed his rifle with a bayonet in front of her to stop her advance. She ordered him out of the way. He then lunged, stabbing her on her right side. As she collapsed to the ground, I grabbed his rifle, and with the butt of it, hit him in the forehead. I struck him with enough force that I believed he was dead or seriously injured. There was a chance he might still be alive. I couldn't take that chance. I took the rifle with Ilse's blood dripping from that bayonet and plunged it into his chest. He gasped and went limp. He was dead.

This was the brutality of war. Two strangers were willing to risk their lives and die for their country. Ilse was injured, but alive. The wound appeared severe, but not life threatening. I dragged the dead soldier into the hangar. Then I went back and got Ilse. I tore the dead guard's shirt and used to it to bandage the wound. She had lost some blood and would need medical attention. The injury could have been much worse. He could have killed her, but he stabbed to the right side, avoiding any vital organs. The guard's intention seemed more towards disabling her then mortally wounding her. She needed a doctor, but there was no option at the camp and no time. She was in pain, but conscious. There were less than five or ten minutes until the plane would land and the attack would start. It was time to move.

I looked at the flying wing and wondered if I could get it out and fly it. If I were flying directly to England, this would have been an option to consider. The Allies, including the Americans, would have benefited from the advanced technology, but I would have been defenseless if the Luftwaffe fighters found us. That was not to be. I needed to get to Berlin first. I wanted to find a way to get Ilse medical attention and then settle the score with Mac. Using the rifle, I shot the wing of the stealth bomber until I saw gas start to stream out. As soon as it puddled enough, I took a rag and made a trail to the door. Ilse was unable to move on her own, so I put her arm around my neck and got her to the car. As I was helping her to the car, the transport was gliding over the runway and about to touchdown. They had done it just as planned. We had just minutes before the action was ready to start.

I ran back to the hangar and glanced one last time at this beautiful aircraft. Destroying it was a difficult thing to do. While I was standing there, staring at the plane with a lit match in my hand, there was a loud explosion. The attack had begun. The resulting fireball created a brilliant glow that lit the airfield. As the sirens sounded, I tossed the match and saw the trail of fire speed towards the plane. There was no time to wait.

Ideally, the plane would have burned a while and then finally; it would explode. However, as I was driving away, there was an explosion in the hangar blowing the windows out the side. It was likely that the wing tank exploded. The Germans would now have no doubt they were under attack. We might have been too if we hadn't acted quickly. When we got to the hangar where my Stuka was kept, the sirens were still blaring, and I could see action at the main camp. I looked back at the place we had just left, and it was now fully engulfed. The Germans would be on their way to the hangar shortly.

If I couldn't get the Stuka out and off the ground, we were going to be in a firefight. The shirt I used to bandage Ilse's wound was not blood-soaked. It was a good sign that the bleeding might have been under control for the moment. Using caution, but trying to move quickly, I got her from the car to the back compartment of the Stuka and managed to get her buckled in. Gunfire was being exchanged nearby, and the sounds of shots, some distant and others nearby, were filling the air. As soon as I unlocked and pushed the hangar doors open, there was smoke drifting up the flight line. It was hard to tell how the attack was progressing, but the Germans appeared to be putting up an intense fight.

It was going to be impossible to taxi down for takeoff or to even take off from the other end of the runway. I would be heading right into the crossfire. To avoid the firefight, I would have to go across the grass and take off using a short part of the runway or just use the taxiway. There was no time to check the aircraft. I had no idea what the German engineers might have done or how much fuel it had left in the tanks. I knew they had flown it, but for how long?

Things were moving very quickly. It would not be long before forces from one side or the other made their way to the hangar. The Nazis were foolish to believe that their highly classified base was impervious to attack. The price paid for their failure to protect these assets would cost them dearly. Ilse had almost paid an equally high price for her actions.

Now, there was no time to waste. Before climbing into the cockpit, I noticed that the Germans had not offloaded the bombs on the underside of the wings. When they flew the plane, they likely wanted it fully loaded to test performance and handling. It was also a possibility that they tried to leave the entire aircraft intact until the team of engineers began work on it. That was the kind of luck I needed. These bombs could come in handy. I rechecked Ilse to make sure she was secure. I told her not to worry. I would get us out of here and make sure she would be okay. In the cockpit, I found Beth's picture on the floor. The German test pilot probably took it off the panel to get it out of his way. If I ever needed good luck, it would be now. I clipped it back where it belonged.

The Stuka fired up right without a hitch. I wished this trip would be the one back to my own time. That was not to be. Inside the hangar, the plane's powerful engine roared to life. Anyone nearby would know we were on the move. I looked ahead through the hangar doors at the thickening smoke. The fire had likely spread, and the Germans were probably too busy just understanding what was happening to try to contain it at this point. I was hoping that their ability to respond was already neutralized or greatly diminished.

Giving it throttle, I moved through the hangar doors. I turned right, but my visibility was limited. The drifting smoke was thick and choking. The pungent smell of burning fuel, rubber, and other materials made breathing difficult. I steered the plane through the drifting cloud of smoke to a clearing. It would give me a chance to assess the right spot from where I could take off. It was a beautiful thing about this sturdy World War II aircraft; it could take off and land just about anywhere.

The sound of gunfire and explosions had not subsided, but it was less frequent. The element of surprise was in favor of Rick and his team. It was the only way fifty commandos could get leverage and have the upper hand against an army SS with a thousand or more men. The further I got from the fire and smoke, the better my line of sight. I looked back and saw several hangars were now completely engulfed in flames. The fire was burning ferociously, and it did not appear there was an attempt to control it. The transport that brought in Rick's team was still on the runway. It looked ghostly shrouded in smoke and silhouetted against the searchlights. The air was the safest place for it until the attacking team had secured the camp, but there it was sitting. It looked like the strategy was to park it where it could make a quick exit if needed. If the battle prolonged, it would only be a matter of time before someone could disable the plane. That would trap the resistance fighters here. The transport was also blocking most of the runway. I had few options left.

I opted to taxi across the runway to a grassy field that separated the camp and flight line. I found a large, open spot from which to take off. On the flat level ground with a lit area ahead of me, I throttled up and started rolling. It was bouncing and a bit bumpy. The fence was rapidly approaching. I needed to get off the ground and, in the air, or risk a crash. Giving it the full throttle left, I was pushed back as the speed picked up. The bumpiness ended as the plane lifted off the ground. Keeping the throttle wide open, I climbed steeply and banked hard left. Flying back over the hangars that were ablaze would avoid the chance of gunfire from the battles near the camp. The aircraft seemed to be operating without a problem. Fortunately, it did not appear the engineers had removed anything critical or had loosened any that would prevent me from staying airborne.

I brought the plane around in a sweeping circle, banking to the left to look down and survey the action below. I wanted to see if and where I could help. From my vantage point, the drifting clouds of smoke below obscured a clear view. I could see occasional muzzle flashes. The last thing I wanted to do was risk friendly fire. Flying low over the camp, I could see machine gun rounds coming from two guard towers. I came back around and switched on my guns and took both out. There was still a way to help before I turned to fly north. The bombs I had could be used to take out the munitions bunker and the fuel depot.

Leveling off, I armed the bomb and flew straight for the bunker and dropped it on target. Seconds later, a massive explosion buffeted the plane, followed by a second detonation. Banking right, I came around to hit the fuel depot and noticed the fire getting closer to it. It would just be a matter of time before it blew. I fired a couple of rounds into it to speed up its demise. There were a few ME-262 jet fighters at the end of the flight line left unattended. I could take those out with a bomb, or I could clear the entrance to the camp for the prisoners to use to escape. I flew in low, just feet above the airfield, and strafed the fighters, hoping to do enough damage to prevent their use. I could see more muzzle flashes from inside the camp towards the attack area. It looked to be disorganized, a few lone wolves who stayed behind to guard the barracks. I came in low and fast towards the camp entrance. With the towers gone, there were a few shots, but it appeared to be nothing but a small arms fire. I dropped the bomb and blew the heavily secured front entrance clear.

My job was done. I did what I could to help. Now, it would be up to Rick and team to finish what they started. I might have never known the fate of Rick and his team, but I hoped for the best. It was now my turn to do my part. An orange glow from fires and smoke dotted the camp. Taking my last pass by the mountain factory, I could see dust, smoke, and rubble. From all indications, Rick and team had accomplished their mission, or the Nazis had detonated it. Either way, it was finished. Word would soon spread of the attack. Mac and the SS would be on alert.

CONFRONTATION IN BERLIN

Someone would pay for what happened at Dora. If Dora-Mittelbau was the Nazi equivalent of America's Area 51, it was now in shambles. If anything were salvageable from the attack, it would take a while to get it back up and running. A more likely scenario would be that the brazen and bold attack had set the Nazi's "wonder weapons" program back significantly. Some semblance of order was restored. The Allies had a chance to get back in the game, and this time, it would be a fair fight.

Mac, now going by the name Reinhard Heydrich, the great foreseer of the future, did not manage to see the attack coming. His enemies within the Nazi ranks would use this against him. Even his most ardent supporters might see him as a fraud or huckster. Mac convinced Hitler to stay patient and present a public persona of peace as he built his arsenal of advanced weapons. The attack on Nordhausen would likely unleash the underlying anger Mac had managed to temper in the Führer. Himmler and Hitler might not have cared to hear any more of his predictions. He was now on borrowed time, and his best option now would be to go on the run. The same noose he had put around so many others was now tightening around his neck. I wanted to get to him first.

It might have taken a few hours or days for what happened at the camp to filter to Berlin. It all depended on how quickly the SS managed to get a message off before communications were cut. One thing was for sure — the Nazis would want confirmation, not a chaotic or fragmented account. That might have provided me the delay I needed to get to Mac. Nordhausen was only 135 miles by air to Berlin. Cruising at 400 miles per hour, I would be in Berlin in less than twenty minutes.

Once I got to Berlin, I had other problems to solve. Ilse would need medical attention. If word of the attack had made its way to Mac, Rick or I would have been the prime suspect. Nazi and SS troops would be scouring the country looking for us. Then there was the fact that it was late in the evening. Mac might still be at the Chancellery or Wehrmacht headquarters, but at this hour, probably not. I had no idea where to start to find him or where he lived. For all I knew, he could already be on the run.

There were few options for a fugitive to land a Nazi dive-bomber in Berlin. I was going to have to be inventive with a story, and I would need luck on my side. Flying into a military base was out of the question. Even if word of the attack at Dora had not made its way through the ranks, any wounded SS officer would raise suspicions. It would be a high-profile event that would be escalated quickly up the chain of command. A better option would be to land at Tempelhof airfield in Berlin. I could hide in plain sight right under their noses. Tempelhof was not a private military airfield, but a civilian airport. The military occasionally used it for emergencies and during wartime.

There, as a Luftwaffe pilot, I could direct the civilians with minimal worry about triggering Nazi engagement. It would be a risk worth taking. If by chance, they captured me, Ilse would be safe. They would assume I her hostage and wounded her in the kidnapping. She would get the needed medical attention. I was worried about her. It was a cold night and being sheltered in the cockpit from the elements made little difference. I flew low to keep it warmer, but a matter of degrees. It was unavoidably cold.

Through this little adventure in time, she had been sent to spy on me but saved me from certain death in the camp while saving the lives of others. I had not fallen for her, but I could feel a pull towards her. My heart was seventy-one years in the future, and it still belonged to Beth. The cockpit interior was dark with only the dim lights from the gauges visible. To the left was a well-placed red panel light that cast a glow on Beth's picture. The picture appeared to be vibrating as the engine shook the airframe. I placed my fingers on the photo and pressed it to the panel to hold it steady. The unintended consequences of Project Töten Zeit changed the course of history. How much, I would have no way of knowing. The new future in which I would grow up would be different, she might be different, and we may never meet. Circumstances could be such that we were never born.

Over the nose of the aircraft, I could see Berlin directly ahead. The city lights created a glow off the bottom of the scattered cloud cover. I pulled up a bit to gain altitude to get a view of the airport's location, which should be due south of the central city. I would land there and get Ilse to a hospital, then work on a way to find Mac. I was counting that we were ahead of the communications coming from Dora. Quickly zeroing in on the airport, I raised them on the radio. My plane was in trouble, and I had a wounded SS officer who needed medical attention on board. They cleared my approach; the final chapter was about to be written.

I had seen the modern-day remnants of Tempelhof. It was a massive, sprawling complex with which Germany had a love-hate relationship after the war. In my era, Tempelhof was a park with signs of the airport still visible. As my plane touched down on the runway, this Tempelhof was a testament to its era, a modern airport wonder that rivaled any in its day. From here on out, I would be improvising. Gone was a game plan of how this would play out. What was left was a desire to get Mac at all costs. I could see an ambulance waiting as I rolled down the runway. This was going to be a dangerous game, but I pulled on a turnout, stopped the plane, and shut it down. To my surprise, German soldiers were waiting with the medical attendants.

They yelled, "What is the problem here?"

I replied in German, "My plane was having mechanical problems when I set down in a field. I heard a yell and saw two men attacking this woman. I ran to help and saw she was SS. I chased the men and flew here to get help."

"It is the work of Zionist pigs," said one of the guards.

They extracted Ilse from the plane, and as they lowered her, I reached into the cockpit and grabbed Beth's picture. I leaned over to the right and flipped the self-detonation switch. In three minutes, this plane would blow up.

I couldn't take the chance that the plane would fall into Nazi hands again. I waited a minute, maybe two, then jumped from the wing and yelled, "Zurückerhalten! Dieses Flugzeug ist auf Feuer, und es kann in die Luft zu sprengen!"

I warned them to take cover. The plane was about to blow up. Then, what seemed like an eternity had passed, and nothing happened. My first thought was that it didn't work. Perhaps the people looking at the plane in Nordhausen had disabled it. Suddenly, boom, the plane exploded with a loud thundering boom that knocked us to the ground. Debris was falling from the air like confetti. I was momentarily dazed from the concussive force of the blast. It turned out to be much more potent than I had thought. Staggering to get back on my feet, I checked on Ilse. She was safe inside the ambulance. My aircraft, on the other hand, was nothing but a fiery pile of rubble. The only recognizable parts were the prop, engine, and landing gear. Just a few pieces of the wing and tail were intact. An escape to freedom would now need to happen another way. All the intelligence that plane would have provided was gone, and with it, all the clues to the fugitives who flew it.

Other than a slight headache and some general disorientation, I was fine. I rode in the ambulance to the hospital to check on Ilse. As if Nordhausen wouldn't eventually have the Nazis looking for me, the explosion at the airfield would bring the SS and the Wehrmacht to investigate. This little event certainly wasn't the version of "hide in plain sight" that I had in mind. Himmler and Heydrich would put SS troops on alert throughout the city. They would certainly try to figure out where the plane was missing from and who the pilot and SS officer were who flew it.

Once the Nordhausen incident came to light, they would put two and two together. Ilse's injury might take days to recover in the hospital. We didn't have that amount of time. It would be hours at best before a manhunt was on for Rick and me. Rick's fate may lie in the carnage at the Mittelwork factory. Mac would take no chances and have the SS out looking for us at all costs, provided they didn't hang Mac first for what happened.

At the hospital, they wheeled Ilse to surgery to stitch up the knife wound. Thanking her for what she had done, I held her hand and kissed her forehead. It would all be okay now, I told her. Perhaps, our paths would cross again. As I left the hospital, I hoped that she would not be under suspicion for the destruction at Nordhausen. The SS could be ruthless, but maybe not to one of their own. As I said that, I remembered that the SS spared no mercy for any conspirators in the ranks. Ilse was a conspirator. Hopefully, the Nazis would not make the connection. It would all depend on whom at the camp survived and whether or not they could tie the two of us together. If Rick and the team had done the job, the answer would be no one.

Ilse would be on her own from here on out, but I was confident she could handle it. It was closing in on 0130 hours when I left the hospital in search of Mac. I had no idea where to start. My best bet would be the Reich Chancellery. There was cold and dampness in the air as I walked the few blocks to the Chancellery. It did not appear that a major storm was brewing, at least not in the sky, just dark, ominous clouds. The rain had begun to fall as I reached the entrance. It was quiet and calm with no visible activity outside. The German hierarchy had been caught sleeping while one of their critical installations burned. In the lobby, one lone SS guard was manning a desk. A single man was the extent of protection at their fortress of power on the eve of a war. I asked to see Deputy Führer Heydrich. The guard questioned why. I told him I had valuable information I was to report to him.

"For what purpose? Is this in regards to the reports of an attack tonight?

"The attack?" I asked.

"There is word coming in that an unknown enemy force attacked the installation at Nordhausen. The Reich Main Security office called earlier to see if anyone was at the Chancellery. They are calling the Reich leaders, SS command, and the Army General Staff here to meet with the Führer on the attack. Deputy Führer Heydrich is not here. The SS said they tried to reach him at home first and could not get him."

"I will personally find the Deputy Führer and bring him back here. Can you get me his home address?"

Behind his desk, he had several volumes neatly aligned side by side. He pulled one and began flipping through the pages. It appeared to be a directory of the key Nazi staff and officials.

"Here it is, 21 Schulzendorfer Street."

"How can I find it? Do you have a map you can show me?"

"Yes, here it is, northeast of the city, about two kilometers."

I thanked him and assured him I would get to the Deputy Führer. It was clear that Mac's whereabouts at the moment weren't known, but that an emergency meeting had been called. The attack would be coming as a major surprise to Himmler and to Mac. Hitler would be furious and want answers and those responsible executed. Word was spreading quickly through the ranks, and Mac probably was unaware of the attack. If the Reich Security office couldn't reach Mac, they would undoubtedly have sent a team to find him or any unaccounted-for Nazi official. I had to get there first. Two kilometers was just about a mile and a quarter from the Chancellery.

A steady rain was falling as I began running towards his house. On the empty streets of Berlin in these early morning hours, there was nothing to slow me down. It hadn't taken me more than twenty minutes to locate the house. It was a large house by German standards in a neighborhood that probably had the homes of other Nazi elite nearby. I was still wondering if I had been set up with some elaborate rouse or trap. I was cautious as I stepped onto the grounds. Who knew what security measures were in place?

As I approached the house, I could hear the phone ringing. It would ring and ring, pause, and then continue ringing. Someone was desperately trying to reach the "Deputy Führer," but no one was home. After walking the perimeter of the house and with the phone still ringing, I was convinced no one was there. Gaining access to the house was not difficult. I was able to use my shoulder to ram the rear door a few times and break it open. The rain had left me dripping wet. I stepped back outside, took off my flight suit and boots and wrung the water from them. Since Mac had so conveniently had me over as an uninvited guest, I decided I would take advantage of his hospitality.

Cautiously, I proceeded to walk through the house. There was no certainty that the house was empty. The phone was still ringing, but the breaks in between were becoming longer. As long as the phone kept ringing, it was my signal that Mac's location was still unknown. The house had all the appearances of a man who was doing well. The artwork and sculptures looked well beyond the means of an average German citizen. The Nazis had rewarded Mac well, and he took full advantage of it. It was Mac I was hoping to find, but I would be on the lookout for anything that might help, a weapon, information, maps, and contacts, anything I could use to find or fight him. I proceeded to search his bedroom and closet. Mac's wardrobe was extensive with variations of Nazi SS dress attire. I found a backpack in the closet and took one of the uniforms, including the boots and cap. It might be useful helping to get out of Berlin if all hell broke loose. There was a 9mm Luger handgun in the nightstand with a box of ammo. It was in a chest at the foot of the bed where I found a Sturmgewehr 44 assault rifle and a K98 Mauser Sniper rifle. Mac had an arsenal in his house. It was clear he was expecting the worst or lived his life in fear of the people he befriended.

In the downstairs office, there were pictures on the wall of Mac as Heydrich with Hitler, Himmler, Goering, Goebbels, Rommel, and Franz Halder. I scanned the photos looking for clues to Mac's accomplice from the future. On the front and center of desk, there was the Nazi swastika with an eagle at the top. However, it was in the bottom desk drawer where I found what I needed. I would now take my chances and wait.

It wasn't long before I heard the sound of footsteps walking to the front door. There was a chance this was not Mac, but someone sent to find him. I could hear the rattling of keys as the person was trying to find the right one to open the door. Just then, the phone began ringing again. The door opened, and a figure came into the room and fumbled in the dark for the phone. On the other end, I could hear an urgent voice, but could not make out what they were saying. The panicked figure began to yell back into the phone, "Who is responsible for this?"

The figure spoke in English. I knew it was Mac. He leaned over and opened the bottom. It was then that I pulled the chain of the light next to the chair I was sitting in. "Is this what you are looking for, Mac?"

With one hand, I held two volumes of Dr. Scheel's works up in the air for him to see.

"You bastard! I underestimated you, Captain. Were you behind the attack at Nordhausen?"

"No, Mac. I was the benefactor of your mistakes. Who will come back in time to tell you what you did wrong?" I had the Luger pointed at him. I told him to sit down. "Tell me why. What happened to you?"

"Well, Captain, the story is quite complicated. I know what you are thinking, and you have this all wrong. You may find it hard to believe, but here we are in 1945, so I suppose anything is believable.

"You and I have nothing but time, so start talking."

"You are not going to like it, Captain. As hard as you may find this to believe, I am here executing the mission I was sent to do."

"Anything may be believable, but not that–that anyone would send you to impersonate a butcher of millions and aid the Nazis to dominate the world. You must take me for a fool."

"It is true, Captain, but there is much more to the story that you don't understand."

With that, he took off his jacket. I warned him, "Don't make any sudden moves."

"I want to show you something, Captain." He rolled up sleeves. "No marks, Captain, like those on your arm. The chip is still in my arm. Unlike you, I have a chance to go home. I am going to tell you something, Captain, that will prove everything you think about me wrong."

"Go ahead. I'm listening."

"I suppose you owe me your life in a way. When you and your partner went through the portal, you failed. It didn't work. As a result, the project was abandoned and shut down. It stayed abandoned for the next twenty-two years."

My patience was running very low, and my irritation level was on the rise. I had heard enough lies for the past few days. I wanted him to get to his point quickly and end this coy guessing game he was playing.

"What are you talking about?"

"Twenty-two years, Captain. Do you get it?"

"Cut to the chase. What is your point?"

"I came from my future to your past."

"You are lying."

"It's true. In my future, the world is getting darker. Russia and China have allied against the U.S., and Europe is too weak to help us. They will be the first to fall to the Russian-China alliance. We are seventh and dropping among the most prosperous countries. Our military is no longer the powerhouse. We couldn't afford to maintain it. Only the threat of mutually assured destruction has kept them at bay over the decades. They have waged cyberwar to divide us, waged war economically against us. It worked, we were on the brink of planned and self-destruction. A limited tactical nuclear option would be the deathblow for us. It would no longer have to be a large-scale, all-out attack. We were teetering on the brink of collapse and defeat without a single shot being fired by anyone or any country. We were lulled into complacency and outsmarted.

"The Töten Zeit project was resurrected with the purpose of going back to 1941 and saving the Nazis from defeat, fulfilling the prophecy of Adolf Hitler to correct the mistakes of the war. There was just one problem. The machine limitation of seventy-seven years was never resolved. We couldn't reach 1941."

Mac's account didn't make sense. If it were true, why help the Nazis? I pressed for more details, more proof. "If what you say is true, what would be the point of coming back to help the Nazis?"

"We came back."

I interrupted him. "We?"

"Yes, Captain. I brought my own expert from the future to your time and then brought them here with me. If you are thinking of killing me, you can't. Even if by some chance you did, you would never find the other time traveler."

"Keep going. I want to hear the rest," I told him.

"As I was saying, we came back to your time to convince the government to execute the plan we had to fix the world. Our objective was to then go back to 1941 from your time, help the Nazis, make them strong and feared. They would become a military power in the heart of Europe that was unequaled in the history of the world. Once that was achieved, we would work together on an alliance with the U.S. That would allow us to take out Russia, and with Japan's help, take out China. The two countries would divide up and control the world. There would be a thousand-year peace on Earth, the likes of which it had never seen in its history."

By now, I believed his mouth only spewed the lies of a delusional madman. "That is insanity. No one would ever believe that or agree to that plan."

"Not at first, but they did eventually. When we came back, we helped fix the problems with the machine that we had resolved in our time. Despite our efforts, they wouldn't agree to the plan. Instead, they came up with the idea for your mission. It was a waste of time, all because they were hesitant to let us go. They did let me train you and get you ready. All the time, I was positioning and preparing myself to make the trip when you failed. I can't tell you how you failed, Captain. I really don't know the answer. The fact that you are here means maybe something I did changed the outcome. Maybe it was the earlier date you left. Maybe my having you intercepted at the base where you landed saved you. I can't be sure. All I know is that you did fail."

Mac's story was hard to digest, but he was right about one thing—we had a machine that could send people back into time, and here we both were in the past. It wasn't entirely out of the question that it worked. There were still holes in his story I needed to probe. "You said the project was shelved for twenty-two years. The Russians were building a similar machine. We would have never let that go on."

"We might not have, but then again, maybe we would have. The Russians didn't have the machine. They never would build one. The second volume of Scheel's work was found hidden in the steeple of a church in Nordhausen. It was discovered during a renovation of the church eleven years after your project was mothballed. Unfortunate timing, it probably would have made your project and my project unnecessary. The church turned it over to the museum curator at the Nordhausen camp who gave it to the Germans. They, in turn, shared it with the United States government. It was I who gave the Russians a copy of Scheel's information that I brought back. I wanted them to start building the machine. It was the only way to force the hand of your leaders to take action, to send me back to execute the original plan. It took a while, but it worked. They sent you back to get the document. When you failed, they sent me back to execute the plan to stop the Russians. It wasn't exactly the way I had planned it, but it worked. Here I am."

"You are insane, a treasonous murderer, and the people who sent you here are equally insane. The cost of the millions that will suffer for your vision is a price that should never be paid. You could have killed Hitler instead and stopped the bloodshed."

"Millions already died once. What difference does it make if they die again? It is for the greater good. This captain is the face of war. If you can't stomach, you are in the wrong business."

Mac's words gave me momentary pause. It was a sobering thought that Rick and I had interrupted, and now wreaked havoc, on Plan B of the operation. Who was I to judge whether my country's actions were right or wrong? I took an oath to serve, but this was different. In the vacuum of leadership, someone must step up and make the right decision. Here was a cold-blooded killer, a man who killed once and seemed unaffected by millions more that might die.

For all I knew, there was no "Plan B," as he called it. I believed he was as he said, a man from the future. It could have been that Mac's plan all along was to get himself back in time to fulfill a twisted destiny of his own. I would not stand by and let a worse future than the one Mac had described occur because we came back to rewrite history.

"Dr. Scheel is dead, isn't he?"

"I am afraid the good doctor outlived his usefulness. Those volumes you have in your hand are his works. Those documents are my insurance policy. The Nazis, Russians, and Americans don't have the technology to make it work, and they won't, for forty, maybe fifty years. If things were to turn, and somehow go wrong here, someone would want it at my price. It is what you came for, but you won't leave with it. Remember, your mission failed, Captain. As for the other book you found, let's just say that was extra insurance. You see, Captain, I was a bit of an expert on history myself, but I needed to have that reference handy. I put that military history book into the secret compartment in the storage bay of the Stuka. I never gave it to the Nazis. I just counseled them based on what I read. They were astounded. That is enough history talk. I am sorry to say, Captain, our evening must come to an end. I am needed at the Chancellery, and your time has run out."

With that, Mac opened the middle desk drawer to reach for his gun. "Aren't you going to stop me, Captain?"

"No, Mac. I am not going to stop you."

"This is why you were the wrong man for the job. Loyalty and honor only get you so far in life. In your case, it will only get you dead. I told them you weren't tough enough. You're not a killer, Kelly. Do you want to know why you were picked for this mission Captain? It had nothing to do with your skill or your background. Remember what I told you about the bloodstained

Volume II of Dr. Scheel's notes? It turned out that the blood belonged to you Captain. The DNA perfectly matched your military profile during a forensic analysis of the book. It was the only reason you were selected. Somehow, it wasn't the first time you had been here, and maybe not the last. I should have had you killed the moment you set foot here in the past. You must die, here, right now, tonight. As you are dying, I'll take your bloody hand and place it on the book. That part of history will remain true. I have to fix this once and for all. Don't you see Captain; it is you that is responsible for what happened to our future. It is you who will be responsible for many more deaths."

I dropped the gun to my side stunned by the meaning of what he was saying. It didn't make sense. Maybe he was lying to distract me and catch me off guard with another of his lies.

Then, he raised his gun at me and pulled the trigger, but it was empty. I picked up my gun and fired back. The shot hit him in the right shoulder. He dropped the gun, grabbed his shoulder and fell back into the chair.

"Bravo, Captain. You grew some guts, but you can't stop me. It is your destiny to die, not mine." Wincing in pain, he tried to reach for the dropped gun. I kicked it across the floor. "You won't kill me, Captain. You won't shoot a man in cold blood."

I pointed the gun at his left thigh and pulled the trigger. He screamed in pain as blood gushed from the wound. Words he said to me at our first meeting in Berlin came back to haunt me.

"Never underestimate the brutality and hatred that human beings have for each other. It is what makes the killing easy to take." I inflicted his pain in small measures as payback for what he had done to so many others.

"You are dying, Deputy Führer Reinhard Heydrich. It all ends here tonight."

He was pale and going into shock and rolled back in the chair. He was speaking in a low voice. "You fool! You don't realize what you have done. This isn't the way it is supposed to happen. Even if you stop me, I have changed history. It will be different this time. You won't stop the other from finishing the mission."

"I am going to do what I can to fix what you have done. I will kill Hitler next. As for you, I would suggest you bone up on your history a little better next time you travel. If you did, you would have known that a foreign spy killed Reinhard Heydrich. Here is some irony for you, Mac. I am that foreign spy. That first shot in the shoulder, that was for the shit you put me through at Dora. The thigh shot was for what you did to Charlie. This shot is for what you did to the innocent civilians you had murdered. Time is up."

I fired another shot directly into his chest. He gasped and fell from the chair to the floor. To many, he was the face of death. They could now rest knowing that with his last breath, that he saw the face of death standing right in front of him. Justice had been delivered in the name of all who suffered by his hand. A man from the future armed with the knowledge to change the world for the better instead brought only death and mass genocide. The mastermind of the concentration camps, Reinhard Heydrich, was now dead.

HIDING IN PLAIN SIGHT

Mac's death may not have gotten much reaction from the Nazis. Once they figured out what happened at Dora and Nordhausen, they likely would have killed Mac themselves. However, the incident at Dora would have probably set off a chain of events that I could not stop. It wasn't the way mission planners scripted it, but I had completed a part of my mission. I had the complete works on a workable theory of time travel that Dr. Josef Scheel had created. If I were following my instructions, I would have flown the Stuka with the documents back to England right away. My transportation was gone, and getting to London with the Nazis soon to cast a net over the city would be a challenge. I was a stranger in a strange land. No longer was this the world in my history books.

Even though I had what I came for, I had to weigh my options, taking into account all that had changed. There was no need to attempt to cover up what had happened here. Within hours the SS would be here searching for Mac. Whether they found him murdered or missing was of little consequence. By then, I would be out hiding in the shadows. What it did mean was that it was not going to be possible to hold out here for much longer. The option at the moment with the highest degree of success was still hazardous. I could take Mac's car and go as far and as fast as I could to the west. Finding my way to friendly territory and a safe haven would mean crossing a significant amount of Germany.

Killing Hitler on April 30th, as I told Mac I was going to do, would mean hiding out here in Berlin for two more months. The Nazis would have a noose around this city by then and might have even moved Hitler out to the Berghof for safety. I wanted to maintain the historical relevance of killing him on the 30th of April, as history reflected. It was my hope that somehow

168

it would fix some of the issues Mac had caused. If an opportunity presented itself to get to Hitler earlier than the 30th, I would take it.

Then there was the Ilse problem. She might be in trouble soon too. The SS would start making connections once they assembled all of the intelligence from Dora. She would either be a victim or a conspirator. I am not sure the SS cared which way it landed. Their safest bet would be to eliminate any doubt by eliminating her. Mac's parting gift to me would be his car. At least now I had transportation to get around the city. I also took the liberty of helping myself to other supplies and clothes since I would be in the city a bit longer.

After I put what I had gathered into the car, I came back into the house for a final pass. I knew Mac was dead, but I wanted to do one more check. As I was walking out of his office, I noticed something I had missed earlier. On the wall was a photograph of what looked like Mac in front of an aircraft. I took the picture from the wall and held it under the light to get a better look at it. In the photo, Mac was standing in front of the wing of a Stuka — probably the one he brought to the past from the future. There was no way for me to confirm it was the one from the picture alone. It seemed Mac had a way of not letting the Nazis in on all his secrets. If this was his aircraft, it might have been that it was parked in plain sight.

At the time the photo was taken, the plane was in front of a hangar #17. From all appearances, it was a private, non-military airport. This particular hangar looked like somewhere you would park a personal aircraft. Even though this was a warplane, it was outdated by Nazi standards. It wouldn't be all that unusual for a high-ranking member of the military to have a "vintage aircraft." Mac, as Reinhard Heydrich, could have done anything he wanted with little question from the civilian population — even hide a warplane. I surmised that this had to be at Tempelhof.

There was no way to tell when this was taken, but if the plane was still there, I might have found a way out. The fear of what the SS would do if you landed on their wrong side was well known. Just in case someone questioned me at the airport, I went back to Mac's body and took his identification papers. The shot had hit him in the center of his chest. His uniform jacket stained with a pool of blood. I reached into his pockets searching for his identification. When I found it inside his left breast pocket, blood had already stained the document. It would be useless to me.

By now, the who's who of the Reich would be convening at the Chancellery Building. Once Hitler arrived, he would be insane with fury over what had transpired. Reich security would be ordered to cordon off Berlin and check anyone coming in or going out. Lucky for me, I wasn't planning to leave the city just yet. When I did, hopefully, it would not be by car. Before any plans or actions took place, there were a few things that needed to get done. As I left Mac's house, it was early morning, around 4 am. There were no regrets that I had killed the man who had trained Rick and me on this project. Mac was no friend of humanity, and there wasn't an ounce of remorse. He was responsible for the death of tens of thousands of innocent people. He also had killed a good and decent man, Charlie. It was a fate that was intended for me.

The first thing I felt I needed to do was to get back to the hospital. As I drove south towards the center of the city, the cold rain had stopped, and a foggy mist hung thick in the air. There was nothing out of the ordinary that was visible in the city. No checkpoints, the usual SS detail stationed on random corners, but nothing out of the ordinary. When I finally got to the hospital, it was more of the same. There was no brigade of SS soldiers standing guard. I needed to be more careful here. Just because I couldn't see them didn't mean they were not here and on the lookout for visitors to Ilse. There were two women dressed like nurses at the reception desk in the hospital entrance. On the train, Ilse had told me her last name was "Cohen." That was likely a cover name since it was a Jewish surname. I had never learned her real last name. I would have to make something up quickly. Introducing myself as the brother of an SS officer who was brought in earlier today with a stab wound, I asked her condition.

"Wie heißt sie?"

"Her name is Ilse."

The woman behind the desk scanned a list moving down the page with her finger. "Ilse Schafer? Ilse Schafer? Hatte sie eine Messerwunde?"

"Yes, Ilse Schafer with the knife wound. May I see her?"

"Sie schläft und wird in dieser späten Stunde keine Besucher haben." She indicated that it was late she was sleeping, and she would not have any visitors. They did not want to disturb her recovery.

I gave it another try and played on their sympathies. "I have traveled far when I heard the news. I just got here, and I know it is late, but I want to make sure my sister is well."

"Mit Beschlüssen des Gestapo, sie darf keine Besucher haben, aber die Gestapo mich nicht erschrecken. Da Sie ihr Blutsverwandt sind, ich werde es ermöglichen. Frau Heinz werden Sie ergreifen, um sie zu sehen, aber nur für einen kurzen Besuch!" Playing to her sympathy had worked. By orders of the Gestapo, she was ordered to no let any visitors in to see Ilse. She said she was not afraid of the Gestapo. Since I was a blood relative, she would allow it. Mrs. Heinz was to take me to see her, but only for a short visit. Just the mere mention of the name "Gestapo" had struck fear into the hearts of many German citizens, but not this one.

In this early hour of the morning, the hospital was quiet. There was no sound or hustling of nurses or doctors. It appeared modern by 1945 standards, but the absence of advanced fluorescent lighting gave the halls a dim and dingy look. At Ilse's room, there was no security. That was a good sign. The events of last night and now today were too fresh for the SS or Gestapo to have digested. The absence of security was a sure sign that the Nazis had not connected Ilse and the attack on the Dora facility yet. The fact that the Gestapo had ordered no visitors was likely a routine order to protect a fellow officer.

"Danke," I said to the nurse when we arrived at Ilse's room.

"Verbringen Sie nicht zu viel Zeit. Diese Frau braucht ihren Schlaf, um eine vollständige Genesung zu machen." She cautioned me to not stay too long to give Ilse the rest she needed.

I entered the room and watched the nurse walk away down the hallway. One could not be too careful. I wanted to ensure that no one eavesdropped on our conversation. Dark inside with only outside light of the street lamps peering through the window, I could see Ilse was asleep. In the dark, I felt along the wall by the door for the light switch. When I turned it on, Ilse awoke, coming out of a deep sleep. She appeared startled and groggy at first. "You shouldn't be here. It is dangerous," she said to me.

"I was worried about you. Are you okay?"

"I am fine. My head is still groggy from the medication, but they fixed my wound."

"A lot has happened in the past few hours. The SS will either make you a hero or a villain. I can't take a chance that they will harm you. I have a feeling that sometime tomorrow if not sooner, all hell will break loose in this city. As the days go on, it will only get worse for both of us. I have to get you out of here and somewhere safe. We have to go now. The longer we wait, the riskier it is for us."

Bandaged around the waist and still under the influence of the sedation from the surgery, she was coherent, but unstable on her feet. In a perfect world, she shouldn't have been up and walking around, but the perfect world didn't exist. We had no choice but to move now.

It took some effort, but carefully and not to reopen the wounds, I helped her get dressed. She was in some pain and discomfort but could walk as long as it was at a slow pace. If we needed to run, she would not be capable. If I could get her to the car, we would be better off.

"Wait here for a minute. Let me check something out."

I walked into the hallway. No one was around, and I noticed a stairwell just a few doors down. This was our escape route. There wasn't a good way to help her walk without further aggravating the injury. I couldn't sling her arm over my shoulder for fear of pulling on the side. Carrying her would help us move faster but would cause her some pain. At the pace she could walk, it would be too slow. I had no choice but to carry her. As I picked her up, she winced. We were able to move much faster now, and I managed to get us down the stairway to the first floor. The lobby area was down to the left, but not visible. There were glass exit doors to our right. I was hoping they were not locked from the inside. As I moved towards them, the door behind us closed, and its noise echoed down the hall. I picked up the pace and got through to the outside.

The car was parked further away to avoid any detection. I carried Ilse to an area away from the building that would be safe until I could get to the car and get back to her. As I was running through the wooded area around the hospital to get the vehicle, I could see there was increasing activity at the front entrance. The Gestapo appeared in a hurry. There could have been word that a Gestapo officer was injured in a knife attack. It could also have meant that they had linked Ilse to the events earlier at Nordhausen. They would soon discover that she was missing. That would only escalate the force they would deploy in searches and at checkpoints around the city.

How much the Gestapo knew and what they wanted at the hospital would be impossible to tell. If not tonight, at some point, they would figure out that Ilse and the American fugitive were somehow involved. Ilse had said to me that Mac gave the order to have me killed at Dora, but her cover story was concocted by the men still alive and at the top of the Nazi regime. If they found Mac dead, it would have been to their delight, but also a liability. It was likely they put the finger on me at Dora and on Ilse as the person who had helped me. For them, it was perfect protection. Blame it on the dead guy and his accomplices. At the moment, it looked as if I was keeping just one step ahead of the Nazis. There was a road in a wooded area near the rear of the hospital. It hid the car while I was able to carry Ilse away from the hospital. Once in the car, I let her know that the SS or Gestapo had swarmed the hospital.

"Heydrich, the man who was a threat to Himmler and Kammler, is a threat no more. If they have found him, it will be convenient for them to put the blame on him and us. The Gestapo was probably at the hospital because your bosses have sold you out as a conspirator. We are now both fugitives."

"Where do we go from here?" Ilse asked.

There was unfinished business here in Berlin, but it would put both of our lives at high risk to stay. Each minute we remained in the city, the odds increased that the SS would find us. At the least, it would be history's equivalent of the Reichstag fire. There would be someone to blame, perhaps the Jews, the Russians, or the Americans. In the next few days, the wrath of the Nazis would reverberate throughout the city and Europe. The law of unforeseen consequences was at play. Inadvertently, a low-key war of mostly words and military poking and prodding between Germany and the British now threatened to become something much more. The two of us were cheating death by staying just one quick step ahead of it. It was the escape from Dora for me, and the escape from the hospital for Ilse.

Our transportation, Mac's car, was the standard high-ranking Nazi staff car. It would stick out among the rest of German vehicles on the streets of

Berlin, and the SS would be looking for it. Under the night and fog, we could manage our way to a nearby destination, but the car would be of limited use once morning came.

"I will find a way out of this for us," I told her.

"I am not afraid. We must do what must be done."

The "what must be done" was weighing heavily on my mind. I had the document I was sent here to find. I also had Mac's "history book" from the future. The Nazis would have likely found it a well-done piece of propaganda, but somehow Mac had used it to convince Hitler and Himmler. If I failed before getting these out of Germany, then Mac's prophecy would be correct. No matter what happened from here on out, I would not be successful. Mac was dead, and that was not in his vision of the future, so the rules had changed. I believed I would finish the mission. I had to let Ilse in on what I was thinking and give her the opportunity to take her chances elsewhere.

"The plane you saw at Dora, the one that flew us here, I believe there is another one in a hangar at the Tempelhof airport. If I am right, it won't be high on the Gestapo's list to check, even if they remember it. It is our way out. If it is there, and I can get it in the air, we can be safe. We could do that tonight. There is something else. The Germany we will leave behind will be at war soon with the world. There will be unspeakable atrocities, and many innocent people will die. Leaving now will mean years of war and bloodshed. There is only one way to stop it. I have cut the head of one snake, but the master snake's venom is the most poisonous. It is his head I must cut to end this once and for all."

It was the first time I saw her frightened. It was one thing to rebel and wreak havoc against an ideology. It was another thing to overthrow it by killing its leader. Mac's car had a radio, and I turned it on to see if there was any news or information. There was a somber funeral march playing continuously. An announcer interrupted it. "From the Reich Chancellery, Reichsleiter Josef Goebbels announced that in a cowardly and brazen attack on all of Germany, and in an attempt to starve the German people, forces from outside the country attacked a factory in Nordhausen that was providing machines and tools for farming and agriculture. Loyal German workers were killed, and the factory was destroyed. Along with this cowardly act, the same group responsible for trying to deprive the German people of the tools and machines needed to produce the food to live also took the life of a courageous and valiant Nazi leader. These enemies of the people murdered Deputy Führer Reinhard Heydrich, a leader who was committed to the Reich and its people. A search is underway for these assassins and all who helped or took part in this act of war on German soil. The Führer will make an important announcement later this morning."

Following the announcement, the music of the funeral dirges resumed. We knew now that Heydrich's body had been discovered and that the Reich hierarchy had linked the two together. It was early for them to have done that, but for the Reich, coincidence was not something the Nazi leadership would readily accept. With an attack on German soil and the murder of a high-ranking Nazi official on the same night, the Gestapo would not need evidence to link the two together. It was likely an assumption, and in this instance, they would be correct.

The cold fog and damp conditions seemed fitting for a Reich in mourning. That period of mourning would be very short-lived, and soon to be replaced with revenge. The news was just breaking, and many Germans would not be aware of what had happened until daybreak. The majority of Germans would care more about the alleged "factory" and the violation of sovereignty as spewed by Nazi propaganda than the death of a Reich leader. Josef Goebbels was the puppet master of that Nazi propaganda machine. He would ensure that the spreading of lies about what happened at Nordhausen would agitate and raise the ire of the people. As we drove, the somber music and message would continuously repeat on the radio. At this early hour, no one was listening.

The high command within the Nazi regime would want to exact a pound of flesh for Nordhausen and give the appearance of caring about the death of Heydrich. Had he lived, he may have been blamed for what happened at Dora and executed. Heydrich's death at the hands of a resistance member would seal his fate as a martyr. His death would only be an excuse to justify the roundup of "undesirables" and "enemies of the Reich."

There was no difficulty getting into the back area of the airport where the private hangars resided. It was far enough from the main airport terminal to attract any attention. The SS would concentrate on checking suspicious passengers at the terminal hoping to catch us escaping. They would have rail stations covered. Hiding here, right under their noses, was our best option. I was gambling that the picture on Mac's wall was taken here at this airport. If I were wrong, the entire plan would be at risk.

It was audacious of Mac to keep the Stuka from the future for his personal use. I wondered what his motivation was to keep it from the Nazis. He had been here a few years before I got here. The aircraft was potentially a game changer at the time if they could reverse-engineer it. Mac seemed all too keen to share other technical information to advance the Nazi military. There was that issue of Mac's companion traveling through time with him — another resource that could quickly make even this plane obsolete. There were a few possibilities as to why he had kept this hidden. He may have had reservations about the Nazis when he first arrived and needed a bargaining chip. Or maybe he needed it when the moment was right to switch allegiances and sell his services to the highest bidder. There was one last possibility, escaping to the winning side if it didn't work out for him here with the Nazis.

Still groggy, Ilse had fallen back asleep when I finally reached the private side of the airport. There were numerous hangars used for private planes lined up along a taxiway. Each had a light hanging over the front doors, which lit up the hangar number. Seventeen was the last hangar. It was slightly larger and isolated from the others — a good sign that this was indeed the place I could find Mac's aircraft.

The car's headlights were pointed at the hangar doors as I walked to see if we could get in. The two thick hangar doors were on a rail. One would have opened to the left and one to the right. However, two steel poles ran vertically on each, and there was a thick chain wrapped around them with a lock. No windows were visible anywhere on the building. I had no way to see what was inside. There was another steel door on the side, but it was also locked. It was readily apparent that this was a place where Mac did not want prying eyes. My best shot to get in might have been the door, but I would eventually have to get the aircraft out. I also had to hide the car. Provided this hangar didn't have three planes inside, that wouldn't be a problem. I could have tried to shoot the lock, but the gunshot might have drawn unwanted attention.

As I came back around to the front, I looked again at the lock. Perhaps Mac had put the lock key on the same set as his car keys. There were only ten keys on the chain. I sized up the lock and then looked at the candidate keys. It appeared there was only one possible match of the ten. I inserted the key and crossed my fingers. Sure enough, it was a match. Anxious to see if I gambled correctly I unwound the chain and pushed open the hangar doors.

The lights from the car beamed through the foggy mist. It cast a dim, eerie glow on the aircraft. No question, there was a plane in the hangar, and just one. It was parked to the right and left plenty of room for the car to pull in. There was something different about it, but in the darkness, it was hard to tell exactly what those differences were. It did not appear to be the same type of Stuka that I flew. Just in case we needed a quick exit, I backed the car into the hangar. With the car still running, I closed the doors. The headlights provided enough light for me to find the main light switch. When I turned them on, it gave me my first good look at the aircraft parked here. Indeed, it was different.

There was no doubt that this was a Stuka, but with some modifications. After a closer inspection, it was Mac's Stuka. It had the right design but was sporting a new paint scheme. The fuselage was red and the wings black. Painted in black with an outline in white on the rear of the fuselage was the German Iron Cross. The rear-mounted gun was gone and the gunner's compartment modified to have a passenger facing forward, not towards the rear. There were no under-wing armaments, like bombs or a drop tank. Mac might have had this aircraft equipped like mine when he left the future, but this one was different.

After looking over the aircraft, there were a few things that had crossed my mind. Mac might have had the plane modified for his personal use. It could have been modified before he left, or maybe this wasn't the same plane. Perhaps this was a copy built from Mac's original. My imagination was running wild with speculation. It might also have been possible that my and Rick's presence here in the past changed just the slightest thing in the future. This could have been the right plane from that altered future. I wasn't overly concerned with any of it at this point. I needed to make sure this thing could fly, whatever the story was behind it. It was evident that this plane hadn't been flown in a while; the wings had a visible buildup of dust on them. This plane would need a good going over. If I had to guess, I would say this plane hadn't moved in at least a year. There was a chance it wouldn't fly.

Ilse was out of the car and began looking at the plane. "Will it fly?" she asked.

"I'm not sure. Let's keep our fingers crossed."

I walked over to the back of the car and grabbed some of the clothes and supplies I had taken from Mac's house. I asked Ilse if she was well enough to stow them in the plane. She said she was and proceeded to take the clothes around to the other side of the aircraft. Waiting a few minutes, I took another item around to Ilse — a gun. I had the Luger that I took from Mac's house pointed at her.

"When did you know?" she asked.

"I wasn't a hundred percent sure until this moment. When I was in Mac's house tonight, I saw a picture of you and him on his wall. The picture was of the two of you standing next to this plane. Roll up your sleeves and let me see your arm."

She rolled her sleeves only to reveal no markings. Mac had no markings on his arm. If she was Mac's other traveler, that meant she was from the same future as Mac.

"You might have known from my plane where the storage compartment was located, but you shouldn't have known that this plane had the same thing. My plane was the only Stuka with a storage compartment. It wasn't something you would have thought of unless you had seen it before. Of course, when you asked, it only confirmed it for me. You were the second person to come back with Mac."

I didn't know what exactly I would do with her. Her involvement with me from the train at Sachsenhausen, the camp at Nordhausen, and the escape left me wondering. The more I knew about her, the greater the enigma she appeared to be.

"As easily as water flows from a spigot, so are the lies that have come from your mouth," I said.

"Let me explain."

"More lies? I don't want to hear it. Mac was dangerous, and you are dangerous. I've heard Mac's version of the story. Go ahead. Let's hear your version. I'm warning you now, if they don't match, you and Mac will share the same fate. How about we start with your real name?"

"Jennifer Davis. Yes, I came back with Mac. I'm sure Mac told you that we both came from your future to our past and your present. We came from a bad place with good intentions to make our world better. It was misguided, but we were desperate. Mac was misguided and would stop at nothing to complete the mission. Whatever you think of Mac, he was a patriot. His means didn't always justify the ends, but in his eyes, the means were necessary."

"Mac was a murderer. My America would never agree to murder the innocent when there were other options."

"Your America was different. There are countless examples in history, yours and mine, where America murdered the innocent in the interest of security or the greater good. My America mismanaged our promise and our dreams. We are on the verge of irrelevancy on the world stage with no way back. Only our nuclear arsenal keeps us in the game. After what has happened, the future here is now as uncertain as the future there."

As she spoke, I realized how quickly killing came in the name of peace or justice, or that somehow taking a life today would pay dividends tomorrow. In less than forty-eight hours, I had killed three men: the Kapo at the camp, the guard at the hangar, and Mac. All were done in the name of preventing more cruelty and bloodshed. Still, I could not let those who should protect the innocent kill the innocent as a means to an end that for which there was no guarantee. How did it ever come to this, I wondered? What once seemed a risky plan, to alter only a minor thread of the future had somehow become twisted and perverse. Ilse, now Jennifer, seemed remorseful and seemed to believe in what she had done, but seemed to be pained by the events. I wanted to give her more time to explain how this horrific plan was originally put into motion.

"We planned to do exactly what Mac and I did — get back to your time and use it to transit back to pre-war Germany. We believed we had the power and knowledge to gain the Nazis' confidence and trust. We would prove it and accelerate their technological development."

"Wait why not just come back to my time and help steer us away from that dark future? Get us on track to avoid it. Why back to 1945? Why not give it to the Americans in 1945? Why leave so much history in between that would be altered in ways no one could foresee?"

"It is easy to second-guess. Changing things in your time would not have made a difference. The people in my time believed in this plan. The people in your time did not. For decades, this capability went unused after the first mission failed. It worked, something just went wrong. We came back to tell them you would fail. Shelving the program and mothballing the technology for twenty-years was too long to wait. They did not listen. In essence, you have gone back twice. The first time that failed in my history books, and here you are the second time around. Maybe there will be a third or fourth. Who knows how history will play this one out?

"As for going back to give it to America first, let them dominate the world with advanced technology. It wouldn't work. The scenarios our people modeled came out worse. This path backward was the only way forward for us. All the problems in your world and in my time started here, right after the war. They took a long time to develop, but they eventually manifested themselves. Once the Russians had missile technology and the atomic bomb, there was a stalemate. This information is nothing new to you. That part of our history is the same. That stalemate would go on and on for decades after the war. It would only be broken when a way was found to cripple the other without destroying themselves and the planet. Truth be told, we were our own worst enemy. We put ourselves on that road."

"But it didn't go as planned did it."

"No, it didn't."

She stopped. Her appearance became more somber as she reflected on what to say next. Her tone got softer and shallower while her eyes began to well up.

"I knew Mac. That's how I got on the program. He could trust me. Mac only ever trusted those he knew or were close to him. I was the engineer who was to help their rocket team. Time was running out. The machine limit of seventy-seven years was never resolved. We needed to get to your time, the time of the first operational use of the portal to get to 1941. We had only a year to spare before it would be too late. When we finally went back, Mac in 1941 had no trouble getting to the Nazi hierarchy. He had no trouble convincing Hitler and Himmler. He would prove it to them by making them the dominant European and Asian power, unrivaled and unmatched."

"What went wrong?" I asked.

"We were separated. Mac was given an identity and worked in Hitler's inner circle. He became indispensable to Hitler. I, on the other hand, was sent to Himmler." Tears were now streaming down her cheeks.

"Did something happen there? Were you hurt?"

"It was one thing to see photographs from this time or read about these people you only knew from the pages of history books. It was another thing to be standing in front of them. These people were monsters. Whether Himmler actually believed Mac, I wasn't sure. He certainly seemed to believe him, especially since Hitler believed him. Himmler was also jealous of this newfound savior of the Reich and his close relationship with Hitler."

She stopped again, sobbing more, her hands covering her face. I realized that this wasn't a charade or an act. There was a genuine pain inside of this woman. I put the gun away and walked to hug her. She pulled me tight against her. This woman with steel nerves I had only just come to know was breaking down under the weight of what she was carrying inside. She let go, took a step back and said, "Thank you. Let me finish the rest of the story."

I told her there was no need to explain anything further, but she insisted. "I need to finish the story."

We sat down on the floor next to the plane. I reached over and held her hand.

"My first meeting with Himmler. Here was a man who changed the pitch in his voice from calm to high-pitch elevated to irate often in the same sentence. He told me I was in the employ of the SS. I was to report to him once a month. Insecure, he wanted me to keep him apprised of any conversations I had with Mac. He then…"

Stopping to catch her breath, she continued.

"He complimented me on my appearance, then proceeded to make advances on me. I pushed him off. "I see," he said. Then he told me that I would report in the morning to meet with Albert Speer and Hans Kammler. Then he told me to get out. The Nazis provided me with a place to stay until I was reassigned. Later that night, while I was sleeping, a man in the apartment awakened me—a brutish man in an SS uniform. He pulled out a dagger and raped me. When he finished, he said, "The next time the Reichfürher asks you to do something, you do it." Then he left. The next time I saw Mac, he told me he heard I got promoted to 'Himmler's whore'. I made up my mind then that I would stop them. I wanted to bring them down."

"I'm so sorry," I told her.

She continued with her story. "I was put on that train by Himmler to keep an eye on you and report back to him on your activities. When he heard that two Americans were captured and that Mac took a special interest in them, he was suspicious and wanted to keep tabs on you, especially when he heard that Mac wanted you brutalized and dead within a week. I was to make sure you stayed alive, even if it meant lying to Mac. He wanted to know what secrets you might know that would get Mac out of favor with Hitler, and him back in. I was to report you dead to Mac, and Himmler would get you back out of the camp to meet with him. I suspected that would have been quite an unpleasant thing."

She had been through quite an ordeal at the hands of the Nazis. It wasn't that I just felt sorry for her. I felt deep compassion. I put my arm around her and pulled her close to me. I wanted so badly to make her pain go away. That would be a tall task. Perhaps the best thing I could do would be to continue with my mission, but also to do what I could do to finish her personal objective.

ROGGENTIN

The fact that a second team was sent and was here made me wonder about the future. Would there be others? The first mission apparently failed. I didn't know about the second mission, but the future already knew. The radio was still playing in the car when the continuous funeral march music was interrupted again. The announcer came on "From the Reich Chancellery, the Führer Adolf Hitler."

"Letzte Nacht, in einem unprovozierten Angriff auf das deutsche Volk und die deutsche Heimat, die amerikanischen Streitkräfte zerstört eine civilan Fabrik und töteten unschuldige deutsche Arbeitnehmer. Diese amerikanischen Streitkräfte auch brutal ermordet Stellvertreter des Führers Reinhard Heydrich in seinem Haus ohne Gnade. Ich will nicht schlafen, noch werde ich mein Soldat Uniform ausziehen, bis die Feiglinge, die angegriffen und getötet unschuldigen Deutschen vor Gericht gestellt werden. Ab sofort, Deutschland, Facist Italien, und das Reich von Japan haben gemeinsam den Krieg erklärt Amerika. Die SS wird die amerikanische Verbrecher zu finden und hängen sie in der Straßen von Berlin für die Welt zu sehen. Ich bitte alle Deutschen auf der Suche für diese Feiglinge sein. Mein Freund und Gönner des Reich, Reinhard Heydrich, wird mit einem Staatsbegräbnis geehrt. Das deutsche Volk kann nicht und wird nicht angehalten werden, bis die Gerechtigkeit gemacht wird!"

History has repeated itself. In Mac's death, the mistakes of the Second World War were back on. The Führer had rightly blamed the attack on Americans, but also implicated the entire United States as a co-conspirator. America was not to blame, but we, Rick and I, definitely were. Germany, Italy, and Japan were now at war with the United States. From the moment the words came out of his mouth, Germany was doomed again to defeat.

Hitler had no way of attacking the mainland of the United States. The weapons he had so counted on would now be delayed due to the attack at Nordhausen. His best option was to disrupt commerce with U-boats along the coast. It was an advantage he wouldn't have for long. Germany would be formidable but would have to play a defensive war to protect its homeland from American might. There was little doubt America would eventually win, but at what price? If it prolonged, it would be costly for both sides. A costly war had to be avoided. He also vowed to bring the perpetrators of the events to justice and hang them in the streets of Berlin. The SS would be scouring every corner of the city and the country looking for anyone associated directly or indirectly. How safe were we here in plain sight? I wasn't sure.

"What should I call you?" I asked Ilse.

"Jen. Call me Jen."

"Well, Jen, they have a price on my head, and probably on your pretty head too. This country is at war with our homeland, and we must protect it. I am going to start this thing and if it runs. Let's get everything loaded from the car to the plane."

As she headed back to the car, I stopped her. I turned to her and said, "I will protect you. I will get us out of here."

She smiled, as she walked to the car to gather the remaining gear while I looked over the plane. There was no question in my mind that I could fly this thing. The unanswered question remained whether it would fly us. It would depend on how long this plane had sitting here. The battery could be dead, the fuel could be bad, but I had a good feeling about it. I put Jen behind the car for safety and fired the plane up. The prop sputtered around a few times as if gasping for air. At least the battery was working. That was a good sign. Adding more choke and giving it a bit of a richer fuel mixture, I fired it up again. It sprung to life as smoke filled the hangar from the exhaust. It was running, albeit a bit rough. Keeping hard on the brakes, I brought it up to speed. With the hangar doors closed, the air was getting as bad as the noise was loud. If we were trying to hide our activity, we weren't doing a good job. The roar of the engine was probably being heard across the airport. Glancing at the cockpit panel all seemed to be within limits. It had fuel, and the oil pressure was a bit low, but within limits. As I backed off the throttle, it began to run rough. This baby needed to fly.

There was no choice but to shut it down. If we needed to get out of here, I was not convinced this would work. Just because the engine ran didn't necessarily mean it was airworthy. Mac would have had no way of knowing we would be here. I didn't give any thought that he might have sabotaged the plane like he did Charlie's. We needed to ventilate the hangar, or the exhaust would have choked us. With the lights off, I pushed open the large hangar doors. Jen and I sat outside with our backs to the wall relieved to have fresh air.

"Jake, what's our next move?"

"I am going to kill Hitler and his henchmen, but first I am going to get you out of here. The last place they would be looking for us is in the air, but this paint scheme will stand out. If it had been the Stuka standard, we would be better off. With this one, I think we will be an attention-getter if we are spotted. It is also going to be a bit harder to hide."

"You may kill Hitler, but you will be killed in the process. Don't do it. There has to be another way," she said to me.

"I don't intend to die, but this must be done. If I don't stop this, millions will die in a war over the next few years, and millions will die in concentration camps."

We were both exhausted, but sleep was not an option. The last thing we needed was to be caught sleeping by the SS. The fog and mist still shrouded the airport. There was no way for me to get the plane out until at least it was closer to dawn, and I had some light. Just in case we had a problem, I would want some daylight to put it down. The weather was going to be the biggest foe, but it would also give us much needed cover.

What was left in the car, we loaded into the plane's storage, including the rifle and Mac's SS attire. As soon as the Stuka was packed, I said to Jen, "Let's get out of here."

She was still in rough shape from the stabbing. I helped her up onto the wing and into the rear compartment. It was a place she was familiar with, but this time it would be me, not Mac, in the pilot's seat. I walked back out to the front of the hangar and looked to where the sky was beginning to brighten to the east. The clouds and fog weren't helping, but it was close enough. It was time to go. There were no parachutes this time. We would live and die on the fortunes of this plane's wings to get us up and back down again safely.

There was no doubt we were getting out of here right now. Staying at the hangar any longer was pressing our luck. I felt we were on already getting by on borrowed time. We had already been here longer than I had wanted. Maybe it was safe, maybe it wasn't, but staying here wasn't worth the risk. It was chilly on the ground, and it would be colder in the air, but at least we weren't in an open cockpit.

In the cockpit, I followed my tradition and kissed Beth's picture and secured it on the panel. My preflight was done, and all appeared to be in good, working order. With the hangar doors open and the canopy closed, I fired up the Stuka. There was no problem at all this time.

Taking my foot off the brakes, it began to roll forward through the hangar doors slowly. The fog was thick enough that I wouldn't have seen anyone if they were right on top of us. I taxied to the airstrip keeping off the radio. Once I was positioned at the end of the taxiway, I did a quick run up on the engine. I turned onto the runway and cut it loose at full throttle. They probably heard us in the tower but couldn't see us. The weather was a perfect cover for us. I'm sure they were shocked that any plane had taken off in these conditions.

The power of this bird as it throttled down the runway pushed us back into our seats. I pulled back on the stick it made the all-too-familiar whine as we soared over the end of the field. Keeping the nose up, I did a sharp, steady climb, looking to get above the clouds and fog. Fortunately, it didn't take long. At just about six thousand feet, I broke through into blue skies and a sun peeking above the eastern horizon. Looking for a break in the clouds, I climbed higher to get a better view of the situation.

To conserve fuel, I leaned the mixture and throttled back to keep it at around two hundred miles per hour. I planned to get a little way out from Berlin and put us down on a farm or field. We would need a place where we could hide the plane and get to a nearby town. A place where we could take refuge until a better plan emerged. There, we could scout out anti-Nazi resistance members who might want to help us. It didn't take us long to clear the cloudbank. I began to scout for a suitable landing location. At our speed, we were rapidly moving further away from Berlin. Finding the perfect spot was proving to be a challenge. What I needed would be an open field with a few strategically placed trees under which I could park the plane.

Finally, I spotted a small town with a quite a few flat fields surrounded by rolling hills. "This might be as good as it gets," I thought to myself. It was still early, and our plane would wake the residents if we made too many low passes. To keep the noise down, I made an extended, sweeping circle and came in from the northwest to avoid crossing over the town. The sturdy Stuka could land anywhere. I brought it down in an open field. The field was a bit bumpier than it looked. On touchdown, the Stuka bounced off the grass and down again before stopping.

A beautiful line of tall pine trees sprouted in a line along the edge of this field. Behind the trees was a protective hill that would serve as a backdrop. It was not dense or a long stretch of trees, but it had enough room for me to squeeze the plane under its canopy for cover. This time of year, there were no leaves, but this was a strip of pines that would give me just what I needed. Making sure we could get out quickly if needed, I swung the nose around and pointed it away from the woods. I figured we were anywhere from forty to sixty miles northwest of Berlin. Jen was aching from the bumpy landings' effect on her wounds. Although Jen was moving slowly and in quite a bit of pain, she wanted to tough it out. I had my doubts as to whether she could or should do it, but this was one tough lady.

I had taken money from Mac's house for food and supplies anticipating it might come in handy along the way. The town we overflew appeared to be our best bet for a place to stay and to get rest and food. In this low-lying field, there was that distinct chill of winter in the air. It was the one thing we didn't account for in our haste, warmer clothes. It was quiet out here in the country away from the city. No birds were singing or the hustle of life, just a cold sky, and dampness in the air. As we were walking, I spotted a sign that said "Roggentin 2km." That must have been the name of the town we had flown over. It was just a little over a mile and a half away in this isolated small hamlet with trees, hills, and fields.

I felt the plane was safe, but just in case, I disabled it to prevent anyone from going for a joyride. I carried with me the books I took from Mac's house. It was something I felt I needed to keep with me at all times and defend it at all costs. There was another small we problem we needed to resolve. While I had taken civilian clothes from Mac's house, Jen still had on her SS uniform. That would cause an alarm if we went strolling into town. I would need to go first and get us a room and then get her a change of clothes or sneak her into the village at nightfall.

It was becoming increasingly evident as we walked that the stab wound was bothering her, but she didn't complain. We took it very slowly and tried to avoid anything too strenuous. Twenty-four hours ago, we had awakened knowing a plan was in place, but not understanding the full ramifications of our actions. Now, here we were cold, exhausted, and fugitives on the run from what had transpired in that short time.

As we made our way closer to town, there was an abandoned old barn. It looked like a safe and comfortable place for Jen to wait while I did a little bit of reconnaissance on the town. I was a bit hesitant to leave her there alone, but I felt we were safe and undetected for now. The trauma from the wound and the day had taken a toll on her. The old barn had a hayloft that was the perfect place to hide. I helped her up, and she found a comfortable spot to lay her head. Her eyes were fading as I stroked her hair. She would be okay here for a little while.

I walked the rest of the way to the town. From a spot on the road atop a hill overlooking the village, it reminded me a bit of America. This town could have just an easily been a quaint New England town. It was a typical, tree-lined Main Street with small shops, a restaurant, an inn, and a church. All of it compacted into an area of about six or seven blocks. In all the confusion, I had lost track of what day of the week it was. The town was quiet as if it might be a Sunday morning, but it was still early. It might have been Saturday. I wasn't sure. I wondered what the reaction would be when this sleepy town awoke to the news that it was at war with America. This rural village seemed the unlikeliest of places anyone would be looking for us.

The appearance of strangers in town might raise some level of suspicion and alert. That would be especially true if a bulletin were broadcast over the radio. Certainly, if anyone had spotted Jen in her SS uniform, we would have been in trouble no matter which way anyone felt about the Nazis. As I continued to walk down the streets of the town, I could hear loud talking and then a woman yelling, "Dieser dumme Hitler hat Amerika den Krieg erklärt!

Gott schütze Deutschland!" A translator would not be needed to understand her frustration and anger. "That stupid Hitler declared war on America! God save Germany!"

The citizens of Germany were now waking up to a new reality. It was no longer a war of words and skirmishes between England and Germany. A global war with America was underway. The Axis powers had united, and America had yet to ramp up its war machine. Several of the residents of this town began to come out and gather. The effects of World War I were still fresh in everyone's minds. This small hamlet knew what was in their future. They did not appear to have the confidence in Hitler's military genius as others across Germany. From the onset of Hitler's rise to power, Germans were divided between the restoration of German pride and avenging the humiliation bestowed upon the country by the Treaty of Versailles. My destination was the inn but walking within earshot of the group was unavoidable. A woman who was engaged in the discussion shouted over to me, "Haben Sie heute Morgen die Nachrichten gehört, dass wir uns im Krieg mit Amerika sind?"

Before I could answer the question, a man next to her weighed in with his view. "Nein! Amerika befindet sich im Krieg mit uns! Sie griffen das Vaterland und unser Führer hat getan, was notwendig ist, um uns zu schützen!"

This sleepy little town's politics might be more divided than I thought, or maybe the country's loyalties were also. The woman stated that Germany was at war with America, while the man corrected her and said that America was at was with Germany. I chimed in with my two cents. "Die Amerikaner würden einen Krieg mit Deutschland nicht starten. Das ist alles Nazi Propaganda. Die Führer will einen Krieg, und das ist, wie er kann man beginnen!" I let them know that America would not start a war, and that this was all Nazi propaganda so that the Führer could start a war.

"Vielleicht sollten wir die amerikanische Frau fragen, die das Gasthaus betreibt, was sie von dieser Sache hält!" The man in the group said we should ask the American woman who runs the inn what she thinks of all of this.

"Ich werde sie fragen! Ich brauche einen Ort, um für ein paar Tage zu bleiben. Ich hoffe, sie hat ein Zimmer." I let them know that I would ask her since I was looking for a place to stay for a few days.

They resumed their debate while I walked towards the inn. It was not a typical hotel from my era but reminded me of a boarding house from an old movie. It was then that I realized that I was primarily an actor in the rerun of an act that ran long ago.

A bit musty was my first impression of the smell when I walked into the foyer of the inn. It had that classic odor of old rugs and damp air that felt as if were standing in wet leaves. By all standards, this was a large house. While it seemed a bit out of place, this was likely a bustling place in the summer, as residents of Berlin took advantage of the lakes and forests in the area. There was no front desk, just a bell, and a note. "Ring dieser Glocke, um ein Zimmer zu bekommen." "Ring the bell to get a room" is what it said, and that is what I did. While I was waiting for a response, I noticed something strange on the wall. Side by side were pictures of an American and German flag. It wasn't the Nazi flag, but the pre-Nazi tricolor flag with the black, red, and gold horizontal bars. It was then that I heard the sound of a door closing followed by footsteps. An older woman appeared at the top of the steps.

"Wer ist da? Was wollen Sie? Who is there? What do you want?" she asked in German and repeated in English.

I replied in English, "I am a traveler looking for a room for my wife and me. Do you have a room?"

"Amerikaner?" she asked in surprised, higher-pitched voice.

"Yes, American."

There was little doubt that she had not seen an American in a quite a while. Her mood changed, and she became exuberant as she hurried down the stairs. It seemed a comfort to her to be in the company of a fellow American.

"Did you say you had a wife with you? Where is she?"

"We were hiking across Germany on our way to Berlin. She was injured in a fall and wasn't feeling well. It was her idea that I scout ahead and find a place for us to rest. She also needs to get some new clothes. Do you know of a shop here in town to buy some?

"On a Sunday morning in Germany! Nothing is open! I have a closet full of clothes that people have left here over the years. Maybe there is something in there that might work. You can help yourself to whatever you want."

"I am sorry, I didn't catch your name."

"Anna Kruger, of Raleigh, North Carolina. Before that, I was Anna Winters, still of Raleigh, North Carolina."

"Frau Kruger, it is a pleasure to me you. I am Jake Kelly, of Baltimore, Maryland."

In her kitchen, she had a little desk where she kept track of guests.

"How long will you be staying?"

"A few nights, maybe three or four," I told her.

"That will be five Reichsmarks a night, and you get three meals a day."

"That will be fine. By the way, have you heard the news this morning this Hitler has declared war on America?"

"What?" she exclaimed. "That fool! I thought for sure that little tramp had better sense than to drag this country into another defeat! He will ruin this beautiful country! It will take time, but eventually, they will come looking for the Americans living in Germany as they have done with the Jewish people. It won't be a good thing for anyone."

Even this little idyllic village nestled away from the heart of Berlin had heard or been touched by what the Nazis had done. We might have only had days before the SS could start sweeping the countryside as they cast a wider net searching for Mac's killer.

"Could I possibly borrow your car to get my wife for an extra five Reichsmarks?" I asked her.

"Why certainly!" she exclaimed. "I hardly ever drive it anymore. It would be good for someone to take it out and use it for a change!"

As it turned out, she had married a German businessman who had passed away many years ago. She stayed in Germany and cherished the safety and security of this quiet little town. It reminded her of home. There was nowhere for her to go now that the Third Reich had America in its sights.

Americans would now join the list of enemies of the Reich and would be sent along with Jews to concentrations camps. The turn of events made her nervous, but she realized they might never track her down. Still, after she showed me the room and helped with clothes for Jen, she sat in the living room listening to the events unfold on the radio. Her nervousness would be a good gauge for me. If she worried about the townspeople turning her in, I would need to have it on my radar also.

The car turned out to be a two-door Mercedes coupe from 1937. Though eight years old, it still looked sharp and drove smoothly. It had the look of something that a German officer might drive. It could come in handy when I needed to enter Berlin. At the barn, Jen was still sleeping in the loft where I left her. It was cold in the barn, and she was curled up to conserve heat. As she sat up, I hugged her to warm her up. She held me tightly, placing her head on my shoulder. It was a feeling that neither of us had felt in a while. Her head rocked back, and she kissed me.

"You and I are alone here in this time. All we have are each other," she said to me.

"I know, I know."

Tears were streaming down her cheeks. We both knew what needed to be done. The outcome would leave one of us truly alone in this foreign land in an unknown time. I tried not to show it, but I was feeling the same emotions of duty, loneliness, attraction, and a fear of what lay ahead.

"Hey there, no more tears. Let's get out of here and get to someplace warm. It will all work out." I told her.

I tossed her the clothes and let her know I had found a place where we could settle in for a few days. After changing, she looked like she could easily play the part of a wife. Gone was the rough and tough SS officer she had to portray. Standing here was another girl-next-door type for which I always had a weakness. I had to remind myself of where we were and why we were here. It was a moment where we felt like real honeymooners on a sightseeing tour around Europe. Romanticizing a different time and place may have been the lack of sleep and the fury of the last twenty-four hours. After her confession at the plane, we had developed a bond. It was something that was unique to us and difficult to describe. We were strangers who didn't belong in this time and place. The intense feeling of loneliness seemed to be pulling us closer together as the moments passed. As the world around us was falling apart, I, too, was falling in a different way.

I loaded the trunk of the car was with the supplies from the plane, but I left the rifles hidden in the abandoned barn for safekeeping. Only a single loaded handgun in the backpack was our insurance in case there was any trouble. Out of the corner of my eye, I could see her occasionally wipe tears from her eyes.

"It will be okay," I said her in a low soft tone.

"No, it won't be okay. You are going on a suicide mission. I don't want you to do it. All it will achieve is getting you killed. There has to be another way. Let's take the plane and go to London. Let's go now. We can give them what they need to win. They will believe us."

"They might believe us, but we know the fight, the time needed to scale up American muscle. By the time it is done, millions will lose their lives. We can't take that chance when we can end this here and now."

"I am not going to let you go. You are all I have. Please, let's go back to the plane and leave this place."

"Let's talk about this after we have had some rest. We are both tired and not thinking clearly."

At the boarding house, I introduced Jen to Frau Kruger.

"So this is your wife! She is beautiful. How long have you been married?"

"In a way, we are sort of on our honeymoon. A case of bad or maybe good timing."

"Honeymooners! I will cook a special dinner for you both tonight!"

In the room, I picked the discussion back up with Jen. "That nice woman is why I need to do what must be done. If I don't, eventually the Allies or the Nazis will lay waste to this town, Germany, and Europe. These innocent people and many other innocent people, are the ones we need to save."

Jen walked to the window. By now, residents of the small town were walking the streets to church. We had taken some small measure of refuge here in this little town, but we could not let our guard down. I feared what was happening in Berlin might somehow be traced here to us. Still looking out the window and with her back to me, Jen said, "Something's wrong with me."

"What's the matter? Is the wound bothering you? Lie down for a while."

"Maybe it is the life I left behind. Being here in a time and place that is a nightmare and knowing there is no hope for me. I don't know what I was going through my head when I signed up for this."

"Talk to me."

She turned and faced me. "Seriously. You don't know? I have fallen in love with you."

There was little doubt about the mutual attraction between us. I had not gotten all the way to that place, but I was heading there. I was still feeling the pull of Beth on my heart. We were both lost souls, and neither of us was thinking with a clear head. She was right about us being alone in this together. The morning sunshine had backlit her as she stood there facing me. It provided an angelic glow around her. An old dress and tear-swollen eyes did not tarnish her beauty. I walked over to her and took her hand. Looking into her eyes, I said, "You know—it goes without saying that this is going to be complicated, very complicated."

"What's one more complication at this point?" she replied.

Taking her hand, I pulled her onto the bed. This was going to change things. How they would change, I didn't know, but from here on out, it would be different.

A late morning of lovemaking became a long afternoon of a relaxed sleep as I held her body close to mine. We were oblivious to the world around us. I had awoken first and admired her softness and beauty. The room was dark, and I could see the sun making its way to the horizon. It was already early evening. As I lay there, I had time to start thinking with a clear head for the first time since we got here. There was an element of guilt over Beth. I also felt a bit of relief that we were now both locked in this together. It was an emotional tug of war inside of me. I wondered what happened to Rick—whether he made it and could he keep the resistance going. There was no way to find or reach him. If he did survive, he was out there somewhere. Our paths would likely never cross again. If he had survived the siege on Dora, then we both were probably thinking about the next move. Tap, tap, and tap. There were three soft knocks on the door.

"Suppertime, you two. Come down when you are ready."

"Give us a few minutes, Frau Kruger, and we will gladly join you."

I could hear her footsteps go down the hallway as she left.

"Time for dinner," I whispered in Jen's ear.

"Oh, thank God, I am starved!

She was infused with energy and joy that I hadn't seen from her. She hugged me tightly as we kissed. The afternoon had turned her spirits. I was all too aware of the unlikely prospect of a fairytale ending to this story. This was a different Jen than the one I had first seen on the train and at Dora. Her guard was down. She was no longer fronting the tough exterior but was now a soft and vulnerable person who needed my care.

189

Frau Kruger had prepared a hearty, warm dinner with fresh chicken and vegetables from local farmers. It looked more like a typical American meal. I asked if she had listened to the radio and kept up on the war news today. In a skeptical voice, she brought us up to speed on what she had heard. "It is all Nazi propaganda. Goebbels was on ranting about an American attack and how German Jews hid the Americans and helped them plan the attack. He said that the Reich was now going to accelerate plans to resettle Germans Jews and rid the country of these treasonous vermin, but did not say where or when. He said silence from the Americans to the declaration of war on the U.S. by Germany shows those cowards are afraid of the German people's will to defend their homeland."

In the version of history I knew, the Japanese attack on Pearl Harbor and the declaration of war on the United States by Germany brought us reluctantly into the conflict. Might it be possible that Roosevelt did not respond, I wondered. By this time, Franklin Roosevelt had weeks to live, and his health had been in a steady decline. Roosevelt may not have had the appetite or the strength to wage an all-out war. I suspected that left unchecked; history would once again repeat itself. Hitler would likely succeed in overpowering his European neighbors and eventually run into the American and Russian buzz saws, but only after much bloodshed. The news just strengthened my resolve to do what was needed. It was not something that Jen would be on board with, but I didn't plan on a suicide mission. I planned for success.

In the sitting room of Frau Kruger's boarding house, we gathered by the fire to listen to the radio for any additional news. The ongoing playing of funeral dirges was interrupted only by the details of Heydrich's funeral arrangements. "On the day after tomorrow, the Reich will hold a state funeral open to the public to honor Reinhard Heydrich, a man so valuable to the German people," The voice on the radio announced.

That announcement gave just one day to plan for what would be a pivotal moment in this new timeline of history. I would assassinate Adolf Hitler, and if I were able to get to them, Himmler and Eichmann.

THE FINAL SOLUTION

It was just thirty-six hours from my first, and perhaps last opportunity to take down the Third Reich and prevent an all-out war. A lot of thought went into what I wanted to do, but little thinking to this point as to how I would do it. We paid our respects to Frau Kruger and retired for the evening. At the room, I knew what Jen was thinking, and she didn't wait long to confirm my suspicions. With a disappointment in her voice, she spoke what was on her mind. "Despite all that has happened between us, you are still going to do it, aren't you? You are going to try to kill them, but it will only result in you being killed."

"I don't know what the future holds. I don't know if we will grow old together or something else. Perhaps raise our families and make the world a better place the next time around, but that would be my plan. I will do this job, but I also will succeed, and then we are going to get out of here and chart a new course in our lives."

She stated with resolve in her voice that I knew I could not shake from her, "If this ends badly or happily ever after, I won't let you go alone. I won't let you die alone. I am going with you".

A plan would be needed to increase our odds of success. I couldn't just go waltzing into Berlin to attend the services. Even though the funeral was open to the public, it didn't mean that anyone outside verifiable Nazi party members would be allowed anywhere close to the main ceremony, especially after what had transpired at Nordhausen.

The Nazi propaganda machine would be in full overdrive for this spectacle. Security would be tight inside, but they would want thousands in the streets paying homage to the "fallen hero." It was not out of the question that to capture and show this spectacle on film to the German people that Hitler would make a high-risk appearance in the open. It was Hitler's own belief that it was Divine Providence that spared his life. Time after time he dodged assassin's attempt to take his life so that he could rule Germany, and eventually the world. His hubris could be his downfall.

I lapsed into a moment of reflection contemplating what Mac had said and what lay ahead. Both missions were a failure, and a new script for the future was being rewritten each day. The more I planned, the more impact I would have on the future I left behind. My momentary trance-like state was broken by Jen's voice asking me a question. I turned and looked at her. She was smiling but holding back the tears. Then she spoke. "Hey, hey, that grow old together stuff, if that was some flyboy way of proposing, don't you think you should buy a girl dinner and take her on a date first?"

"I promise you that date and dinner when we get out of here. It won't be long now."

Part of me believed what I told her, and part of me knew the odds were not in our favor. I could very well accomplish the mission and be killed or fail the mission and also be killed. Being killed was not high on my list of things I wanted to have happen to me. At the moment, it seemed the one outcome that had any degree of certainty. One thing I might not be able to do is letting her go on without a watchful eye. It would be tough, but that would be another decision I would have to make—take her with me and risk our capture, or ensure that she would not go on to change the future more than we already had done. The easiest course of action would have been just to take the plane and leave now. It was a shot in the dark that we would be welcomed when we made it to London. Mac convinced the Germans he was a man from the future. Convincing the Americans and Brits might be a tougher sell. If we failed, it would mean the war and the atrocities would go on.

There were other things to consider. Before World War II, America was not the leading military power—not even close. It was the war that propelled us to the front of the pack. Stopping the war here before it started was a choice between saving lives now and risking a different world order. A world order with a less dominant United States that might cost more lives down the road. Of course, there was a sliver of hope that somehow the world would come to its senses and war would be avoided this time around. However, given the human history of conflict that did not seem a likely outcome. You could drive yourself crazy thinking about all the potential what ifs and possibilities. I had to park any ideas about what the new future would hold, for it had already changed.

The here and now was what was front and center for me. The greater risk was here in Germany, and that Hitler would go unchecked for years if I did not act swiftly. The fact was that America did not start the war with Germany, but an unauthorized American, not directed by the government, did start this fight. It could also change the focus and dynamics of the coming conflict. It might have explained the reason behind the lack of response from the president. Roosevelt did not know the mission or us. That much was true, and Roosevelt had deniability. He could rightfully claim that the revolt was the work of foreign renegades and internal insurgents. That would also explain the hesitancy to engage. They wanted to continue looking for a diplomatic solution to avoid further escalation of this crisis. It would likely have crossed their mind that this could be a trap. Much like the Reichstag fire that Hitler had used as a ruse to seize additional powers, this was also a Nazi inside job to escalate a war. While the powers that be in America were planning their next move, I had my own to execute. I had one last night of rest, but with so much to think about it, there would be no sleep.

The break of dawn had come. The plan was to kill Hitler today. Everything between now and the end game would be ad hoc. It was an awful thing to wake up and have to prepare oneself to kill or be killed today. Jen was already awake and getting ready. We couldn't walk out of here dressed as Nazis. We would have to appear as normal as possible. The smell of Frau Kruger's breakfast filled the air like a whiff of perfume. I had been through this "last supper" routine before. The last one did not, but I wondered if this would be the one that lived up to its name.

Our long journey was reaching its climax. Breakfast seemed a bit of a waste of time and energy. It was akin to feeding a death row inmate his last meal. What was the point? The road ahead would be long and tiresome, but we would need the energy. In what was becoming the norm, Frau Kruger had a prepared a breakfast that was more than anyone could eat. She could have fed an army, an army I wished we had had behind us in this battle. In the past few days, we had lucked out in this little town. It was a safe haven with friendly hosts. It had given Jen and me a bit of normalcy, albeit for a short time.

"Frau Kruger, might we borrow your car today?"

This time she was more cautious.

"Germany is much more dangerous now for all of us. I doubt the Germans will come looking for anyone just yet, but if you ran into the Gestapo, it would be bad. Be careful."

I assured her we would take precautions and just needed to look around and get a sense of the activity. Of course, nothing could have been further from the truth. I thanked her for her hospitality. It did not appear she suspected anything, but we exchanged looks that seemed to say this might be goodbye. In the room, I left Frau Kruger the remaining money we had taken from Mac. I left her a note thanking her for her kindness and hospitality. I told her to take care of herself and stay safe.

Frau Kruger would likely have noticed that we didn't eat much. We gave the illusion that we did by pushing the food around on our plates and nibbling on the fresh fruit. We were running on a full tank of adrenaline, and it remained to be seen if it would be enough to see us through.

As we drove away, Jen asked, "So, what's the plan?"

"I'm thinking," I told her.

It was the truth. I had been visualizing how this would play out. There was no nervousness or fear of what might happen. It was just that I needed to formulate what would give us the best odds of success. I wasn't sent to here to "try my best". I was sent to achieve success no matter the cost and exhaust every option at my disposal to see that the mission was accomplished. The thoughts were traversing back and forth across my mind that Mac and Jen came back because Rick and I had apparently failed. I couldn't second-guess every decision as the one that might be the wrong one. I just had to get it done.

It weighed on me which option I would choose and as a result what future for the human race would be created from my decision. What I didn't know was if Jen's and Mac's presence changed the outcome or if it was preordained that we failed. I believed that I could change it even if once we had been here before and failed. I also had the documents that many had already paid a hefty price. It was a price that allowed me to complete at least one part of the mission. Getting caught would put that information back in play. At some point during or after the war, either friend or enemy might find it. I couldn't let that occur. I would have to protect it or destroy it if it came down to the end.

I began driving, staring at the road straight ahead as the world around me was going by quickly. The more I thought about the plans; the less any of the ideas appealed to me. Getting into Berlin undetected by the Gestapo, pulling off the assassination, and escaping seemed quite foolish. Hitler survived many an assassination attempt when security was lax. There would be a ring layered of protection the likes of which those just outside the inner circle of the Führer could not penetrate. From seemingly out of the blue, I had a hunch. If my suspicions were correct, it would be a game changer, maybe.

"Hey, what are you doing?" Jen asked.

She was reacting to an abrupt stop and U-turn I had made. I was racing back north towards the town we just left.

"Why are we going back?" she asked with a sense of urgency.

I replied, "I have a hunch about something. It is a bit of a long shot, but if I am right, we might have a better plan."

I continued through the town and back towards the plane. There it was, untouched. I was pleased to see that it had not been discovered. I jammed my foot on the brakes and brought the Mercedes to a skidding halt. I leaped from the car and ran towards the plane. Curious, Jen raced to see what had me so preoccupied. At just about a quarter-way down the leading edge of the wing away, I pulled off a small cover. Then, I climbed under plane near the landing gear and unlocked a door, and let it swing open.

"What is it?" Jen asked.

"It is what I hoped to find. I suspected that Mac was always hedging his bets and ready to take services to the highest bidder. He retooled and repainted this plane, but kept it armed in case he needed to make a quick exit. What you see here, this is our plan."

She looked puzzled by my response.

"This is how we will kill Hitler. The funeral is out in the open at the Olympic Stadium. That is their best bet to control security and get the maximum propaganda effect. It will be their vanity that will lead to their downfall. The one threat they can't stop is the one from above. They might have fighters patrolling the skies, but I highly doubt it. That is something we would do in our time. Even though they are at war, there is no threat yet from above. If we time this right, we can swoop in, strafe the podium, and topple the Third Reich in one swift move. They have been uncharacteristically complacent and sloppy as of late. In their haste to arrange this funeral, they may not even have anti-aircraft batteries installed around the stadium. This is our best chance, and it may be our only viable option.

"You make it sound so easy. Then what?"

"I think we will catch them off guard. No way they are expecting this. They might be prepared for a rogue assassin on the ground, but not from the air. If we hit this right, we can turn west and hightail it out of there before they even know what happened."

It would now all come down to timing. The element of surprise was ours, but we would just get one shot at it. By the time they reacted to what had transpired, we would be gone. I started to move the gear we had stowed in the car back to the plane. This "stuff," the weapons and uniforms I had not planned on ever needing again. However, one could never be too cautious. I kept a Luger on me and stashed another in the cockpit. If I had to use them, it would mean we were on the ground in a firefight for our lives. After this mission, I had planned on making a straight run for the English coast. Fuel was the unknown. Maybe we had enough, or perhaps we would end up in the English Channel.

We had time before we needed to take off. I used it to check the plane out and make sure everything was good to go. There was no way to test the guns here on the ground without firing up the engine. Besides, I didn't want to waste one round. I hoped all was in good, working order. If something went wrong, I did have a Plan B. With the plane ready to go and the gear secured, I started looking over a map I found in Frau Kruger's car. It would help me find the stadium and the best escape route. The weather was good. It was a lucky break that would keep the outdoor funeral plans on and my best view of the target in clear sight. The next few hours would pass by painstakingly slowly. It was more about the anticipation to bring this to a close and end this nightmare for all of us. I sat under a tree near the plane with Jen sitting next to me. There wasn't much either of us had to say. For all that she had been through, it seemed that at this last hour she was the most frightened. She would be along for the ride with little that she could control. Finally, I said, "It's time to go."

I looked across the field to size up area I had to take off. It seemed good. Jen climbed up, and I secured her in her seat. I kissed her on the forehead and told her I would see her soon on the ground in friendly territory. Through this entire ordeal, Beth's picture that was in the Stuka we flew to Berlin had survived. I looked at it for a moment wondering what she was doing and thinking as if she were somewhere here in this time. Keeping with tradition, I stuck it on the panel in a small gap between gauges. Taking two fingers on my left hand, I touched them to my lips and then to Beth's picture, perhaps for the last time.

The powerful engine of this Stuka from another time roared to life. There wasn't much need to pre-check anything. We were going no matter what might be wrong. Easing off the brake, she started to roll out to the field. Wasting no time, I pushed the throttle forward. In an instant, the Stuka thundered across the field, rapidly picking up speed. Pulling back on the stick, the nose of the aircraft came off the ground, and we were airborne. Banking steep to the right, I turned the plane 180 degrees and headed back to Roggentin to make a final pass. If I came in too low, the town might be spooked, so I took it up and throttled back a bit and took a last look down as it passed to my left. I leaned the fuel mixture to conserve as much as possible and set a heading for Berlin.

Our cruising time would not be long, even at this slower speed. My plan of attack was to come in high and well off the stadium to survey the activity. Once I thought the events were underway, I would take a wide approach, come in at treetop level, and take out the podium. It would be a tricky maneuver. At this speed, I would need to pop up and down and back up to clear the arena. There wasn't much of a choice. The higher I came in, the more time they had to react and take cover. Off in the distance, I could see the city approaching just ahead of us. Scanning the skies left to right, there was no air traffic or patrols that I could see. It was a good sign. So far, all was going smoothly. The weather was perfect with clear skies and no haze. I could easily see for miles.

As I approached the stadium from a distance, I could see the crowds in the stands, but not much detail on any activities on the field. I would need to get much closer and higher to get a look inside. Banking to the right, I headed away from the stadium to throttle up and climb without too much attention before heading back towards the stadium. Out of the corner of my eye, I spotted what appeared to be a long line of black cars headed down the main drive leading up to the stadium. Even at this distance, it looked like the funeral procession. The red Nazi flags were unmistakable. Our timing was off, or maybe they were late. I was going to have to make a closer approach to see if my hunch was right. I would bet the farm that Hitler's car was in that procession. It was a gamble I had to take. We couldn't hang around too much longer without drawing suspicion. I knocked on the cockpit glass to get Jen's attention and pointed in the direction of the suspected motorcade. It was now or never.

There wasn't much time to take action. The motorcade was moving towards the stadium at a slow but steady pace. There was going to be no escape for them. Crowds lined the streets, and they had nowhere to hide. Unfortunately, avoiding any collateral damage was not an option. To ensure total success, some of the general staff that was against Hitler would probably be killed along with some civilian casualties. I rationalized that a few would die so that millions would live. Ironically, it was the same argument Mac had used on me to justify his actions. Time was running out. I pushed the throttle forward and banked to come around to align dead on to the motorcade. The guns had to work. Plan B was not going to be a good outcome for any of us. It would mean a kamikaze mission to take out what I could. It was all for the greater good. The documents would be destroyed, and the mission, of sorts, would be accomplished.

The sands of time were running fast through the hourglass. The killing time had arrived. I knew that if I came over the stadium and dipped, they would be out of sight for a few moments. I had to come in to their right, bank steeply, and come right down the line. I would take out as many cars in the motorcade as I could on this pass. They had to hear this coming, but there was little reaction until I got closer. Suddenly, the crowd started running, I pulled the trigger, and the guns fired, strafing and hitting the line of cars. In their panic, it was perhaps their greatest fear coming to fruition, or maybe the inevitable day of liberation they had hoped would arrive.

There was a cloud of debris and smoke from the rounds hitting glass and concrete, and yes, bodies that had fallen. The sacrifice of the innocent bystanders was necessary for a better world if I succeeded. If I failed, they would become propaganda martyrs. I had one more chance to finish off what was left. I banked hard left and came in perpendicular to the motorcade, which had now stopped. The crowd had scattered, and there was concentrated activity around one of the vehicles. I surmised that had to be my target. There was no way for me to know what wounds I may have inflicted on Hitler and his staff or if they were fatal. Now that I had a target, I came in slower and more deliberately. My focus was on taking out that one vehicle. As I approached, the remaining SS guards and what appeared to be some regular army had their rifles and handguns pointed at me. They were firing in futility. I opened up and strafed the vehicle, taking out most of the men protecting it. The job was done, at least I had hoped.

The attack was a total surprise. I had caught Hitler's elite protection team flat-footed and unprepared. A response of scrambling fighters might occur, but by the time the message got relayed, we would be on our way. I turned the aircraft to head west and headed for a new home. The remnants of the motorcade were to my left. There were flames and coming from the line of cars in the procession. The results of my actions would not be known until we reached our next destination in England. We might have been welcomed, or we might have been fugitives, arrested and extradited. It would have been the ultimate irony that we might have saved the death of millions at the hands of a sadistic dictator, and then somehow, we would be the war criminals.

THE WHITE CLIFFS OF DOVER

As we headed east on our escape route, the weather had deteriorated. The sunny skies we encountered in Berlin had now turned more ominous and dark. This looked more like the typical German weather one could expect this time of year. As far as I could see, there were clouds, drizzle, and fog. It was the perfect cover for our escape, but lousy for navigating. The cloud deck was too low to duck under and too thick to soar above. It would have been the equivalent of flying blind. The mind can play tricks on a pilot in these types of conditions. Keeping it at eight thousand feet and four hundred knots we should cross the channel and see the coast of England within ninety minutes.

Jen shouted over the whine of the engines, "Good shooting! I think you got them."

"I hope so. Keep scanning the sky for any aircraft. We are not in the clear yet."

The worst might have been over for the people below and us. The billowing smoke and dust from the carnage of our attack was behind us. A loud hum and vibration could be felt through the aircraft as I throttled forward and increased the distance between the past, and headed towards our future. Our version of "shock and awe" left us in a position where I did not expect we would encounter any resistance from here to the English coast. The personal war we were fighting was over. It remained to be seen if the world would still be at war.

History had changed, not because of Rick's and my involvement, but because of Mac's as Reinhard Heydrich. I was still processing how the vision of a madman to send a message back in time to himself to avoid the mistakes he made had in a way failed in his time, and somehow managed to succeed to some extent in another. Somewhere, there was a message for future generations in what transpired here. Mac had been the message and the messenger. There was no conceivable way that Hitler could have imagined that failure in his time would lead to the effort working in another. I realized what a terrible weapon this might have been in the hands of the wrong people. What would the future hold where history had been rewritten? Would this version of history be better, worse, or maybe somehow the same? Perhaps this was not the first time or the last that someone had tinkered with time. I had nothing but time to ponder the possibilities. Soon, I would know. As the skies cleared to a broken cloud cover, I could see a coastline off in the distance and a large body of water.

We had encountered no resistance, and we were nearing friendly territory. I made a quick scan of the skies and spotting nothing I slowed the aircraft down. Banking left, I made a small circle hoping to get a better bearing on where we might be. There was no question that that was the English Channel. By my dead reckoning, that should have been the Netherlands below, maybe just the northern border of Belgium. If I crossed the channel and headed on a slight southwest direction, we should have sight of London shortly. I could continue straight and look for the famous White Cliffs of Dover, a landmark I could use to get my bearing, but one that had British radar installations and was fraught with risk and reward. At this point, I just wanted to get us on the ground anywhere in friendly territory and in one piece. I decided to make a run for London or somewhere thereabouts.

The total time elapsed had been less than two hours. By now the news had spread around the globe that Hitler and at least some of the high command had perished with him. I hoped that I had done the job. If Hitler were to survive another assassination attempt, it would have secured his messiah complex and embolden him to take greater risks.

The aircraft banked slightly left as I headed across the open channel. Freedom and a lot of explaining to do were just minutes away. I throttled the plane back up and raced towards London. Fuel was running precariously low, and I wanted to ensure that we at least made some headway to get as close to London as we could. Just then, out of the corner of my eye, I saw approaching from the left a squadron of fighters. They were probably British Spitfires who got wind of us from radar installations on the English coast. I had no intention of engaging them. We were on the same team. The problem was that they did not know it.

I could have played this a few ways: outrun them and risk running out of fuel and be a sitting duck ripe for the plucking, or extend the olive branch and hope they would escort me down safely. I could outrun them for a little bit, but with the low fuel, it was questionable how long. These Spitfires were fast, not as fast as this bird, but good enough to keep me in their sights. Outrunning them would also bring their ire and give the impression that I was a rogue warrior mounting a lone wolf attack. They would try to stop me at all costs.

The choices were limited but clear: I would extend the olive branch. As soon as I crossed land and with British soil beneath me, I slowed the plane down. The British fighters were closing fast. I began to dip and raise the wings in a continuous motion to signal my friendly intentions. It would only take one overzealous pilot looking to be a hero to take us out. As they drew nearer, I had a bad feeling that they were not interested in my extended hand of peace. Before I could rev up and take evasive action, they opened fire. We appeared okay, and I tried to get us out of there when they hit with another round. This time, they found their mark. The close-range fire penetrated the fuselage. My right arm was numb, and I could feel the warm flow of blood down my side. I was struggling to stay conscious. This was Mac's modified plane, and it was not equipped with parachutes or a way to eject.

Unfortunately, we would have to ride this down and pray they did not want to finish us off. It was getting harder to control the plane. I couldn't focus on what might be wrong. Instead, I had to just fly with my instincts. I mustered the strength to yell back to Jen, "Keep your head down, this is going to be a rough landing."

There was no response. Our situation was bad. Some of the control surfaces must have been damaged in the attack. The long trek through time appeared to be coming to an end on the British coast unless we pulled off another miracle. I scanned the skies and could see the Spitfires around us in formation. They appeared to be waiting for us to fall from the sky to know their work was done. I knew I was hurt badly with maybe minutes to get this plane down before I was out. The Stuka was sputtering, and we were falling fast. It seemed sluggish to respond. Pulling the stick back hard, it was ever so gradually coming out of the descent. This was it. It started to level, but not fast enough. I could see open fields ahead. We were going to hit hard. Just then, we slammed into the ground. It was the last thing I remembered.

When I regained consciousness, I realized we had made it. I was thrown from the aircraft and lying face down, but alive. The air was rancid with the smell of burning fuel and rubber. It was already difficult to breathe. The smoke was choking and blinding me. As I looked up, all I could see was the plane strewn in pieces across the field. It had cracked behind my seat with the nose pointed down. The canopy had blown off, accounting for how I was ejected. The rear of the plane was lying flat. Jen was still strapped in her seat with her head slumped forward.

Debris littered the area. I was still dazed and did not realize the extent of my injuries as I crawled towards Jen. There were muffled and low voices in the distance that were getting louder. Perhaps it was the Spitfire pilots who landed in the field to check us out, or maybe it was residents from a nearby village who heard the commotion and came to help. As I struggled to get to

Jen, I found in the debris the objective of our mission. The wreck had thrown the volumes of Dr. Scheel's work on Töten Zeit along with Mac's history book clear of the plane. As the blood ran down my arm to my hands, I clutched Scheel's book and pulled it close to my side. This book was what this mission had been all about, and now, in what I thought were final moments of my life, I had achieved what I set out to do, but at a high cost.

Weak, I closed my eyes and put my head down on the grass. I could feel the heat from the fire on my face. It gave me moments to think about what had been accomplished. The portal was a hideous tool, a weapon that could be used to go back in time by anyone to alter history. Mac tried it and failed. I could not let it happen again. Preventing anyone from ever getting their hands on this or having any knowledge of this project would be my greatest service to the country and the world. With my last bit of strength, I pushed myself up and threw one of the volumes into the flames and watched it start to burn. I grabbed Mac's history book and tossed it towards the fire. I watched as it slowly started to burn. I began to reach for the last volume of Scheel's work. As soon as my hand touched it, someone kicked it away from my reach. As I began to slip away, I could hear the voices yelling at me.

"Who are you? What is your name?" The British accents were unmistakable.

"American, American," I whispered in a faint voice.

"Did he say American?" I heard one of those gathered around shout out.

I was hanging on, just barely, when I thought I heard another voice. "I think the other one might be dead."

It would be the last thing I would hear. I had collapsed and become unconscious.

LONDON

For all I knew, I had died that day on a cold and barren field somewhere on the northern outskirts of London. What I remembered about the crash was gone, and suddenly there was a warm feeling of sunlight on my face. I felt stiff, achy, and sore. It was difficult to move. I had that same feeling one has a day or two after a car wreck, but I was not in serious pain. As the fog began to clear from my head, I started to remember a plane crash and crawling in a field. Was it a dream or was it real? As I opened my eyes, the bright room made it painful to see. It was akin to leaving a tunnel of darkness into the bright light of day.

I wondered if this could be the afterlife. Maybe death had found me. Was the light I was seeing in front of me, the same light that those who passed on and came back spoke of so vividly? I squinted to slowly let my eyes adjust. This was no vision of the afterlife, but an infirmary or a rehabilitation center. A drab tan and gray paint scheme with none of the amenities of a modern hospital could only mean one thing, a military facility.

I tried to get up but was handcuffed to the bed. Hopefully, this was for my own health and not because they believed I was the enemy. The sudden movement made my head hurt. It felt like a bad hangover. I relaxed back to the bed and started thinking what the last thing I remembered was. Piecing together what had transpired was key to my understanding where I was and what happened to me. Parts were coming back to me. My memories appeared like puzzle pieces scattered on a floor—fragments that eventually would paint a picture, but at the moment, made little sense to me. If there was any good news, I appeared to be in one piece and in relatively good health. There was no telling how long I had been here — hours, days, or weeks?

A nurse entered the room. She was an older woman with a stern look and an unmistakable English accent. "And how might we be feeling today, young man?" she asked.

"Where am I?" I replied.

"You are at Debden Station, His Majesty's Royal Air Force."

She grabbed my handcuffed hand to take my pulse. Staring at her watch and counting the beats of my heart I asked more questions.

"There was a woman with me. Is she okay?"

With that, she finished up.

"The doctor will be making his rounds this morning to check up on you. I will let them know you are well enough to answer their questions."

Ironic. Answer their questions? What about getting answers to mine? The nurse was obviously dodging a response to my questions, but I wasn't surprised. What was more intriguing was the "they" she mentioned. As she left, through the opening of the door, I could see an armed detail standing watch over my room. I began to fiddle with the handcuffs. I was becoming acutely more alert and energized. It was not my intent to get up and escape, but just to get up, look out the window, and see the sun shining on friendly territory. I had hoped this was a sign of a new dawn in this new time.

It was a cliché, but it is true that minutes pass like hours when you are frustrated, angry, and anxious. Getting up to shower, shave, get dressed in something other than hospital garb, and getting answers was quickly climbing on my list of things to do. I no sooner finished my internal rant than two officers entered the room, one American and one British. The British officer walked directly to my bed and reached for my free right arm. He shook it with vigor and gratitude. The American officer stood off looking much less enthused.

"You have been through quite an ordeal, and you are fortunate to be alive. How are you feeling?" the American officer asked.

"Considering I am cuffed to a bed and can't seem to get any answers, not bad."

His head tilted down. He mildly chuckled to himself before raising his head back up.

"You think you are looking for answers? We have plenty we need to get from you. Let's start with who you are, a name."

"Before we play Q&A, the woman in the plane with me, I'd like to see her first", I said it in a way that I hope conveyed that I wasn't willing to compromise. The British officer stepped back. Neither had taken the time to identify themselves.

"When you crossed the channel, we picked you up on our radar installation. Our patrol aircraft identified the plane as German, with unusual markings, but unmistakably a German fighter. For all we knew, and for all we still know at this point, you were a spy, double agent, or rogue pilot looking to inflict one last blow after the war ended. If you were escaping, we didn't know. One of the pilots spotted your signal of non-aggression, but another thought it was a ruse, even though you essentially made yourself an easy target. He made the call to shoot you down."

"The woman, I asked, where is the woman?" I asked.

"She suffered a concussion and is otherwise in good health except for the serious stab wound injury which we are treating. We expect that she will make a full recovery."

"I want to see her."

"Very well, but first some answers." Words finally from the American officer. "Your name and what you were doing in that plane?"

I had no intention of lying or deception, but I wasn't crazy enough to tell the whole truth at the moment.

"Jake Kelly, American, operating under the express orders of the President of the United States, Franklin Delano Roosevelt."

There was a look of anger on the face of the American officer. "Impossible! You are a liar. An assassin killed Franklin Roosevelt in 1933, after just months in office. Vice President John Garner finished his term and was reelected to finish a second term. Roosevelt's assassin was a coward that took his own life rather than face justice. Perhaps you are a member of that same treacherous spy ring that has now murdered two national leaders!"

"What! That's impossible!" I exclaimed.

It had dawned on me the magnitude of Mac's influence on the past. His plan was more extensive, deeper, and more heinous that I had thought. I could only surmise that in his plan to ensure Nazi domination of Europe and Asia that he would be willing to kill the President of the United States.

As I was pondering the implications of a vastly different world from what I had already witnessed, the British Officer spoke.

"Irrespective of who you are, we know that you are the one that ended the tyranny the world was facing. It was a brave thing to take on the Third Reich almost single-handedly. You will be revered by many and reviled by few for your actions. Some will see Hitler as a great statesman driven to hostility in response to a hostile world around him. We know he was a monster in waiting.

"You will be a welcome guest of the British people for as long as you would like to stay. We are prepared to offer you political asylum should you wish. At some point, we would like to hear more about what transpired and how you came to be in a position to topple Hitler and his henchman, but for the moment, get rest."

Over the objections of the American officer, he ordered my cuffs be removed. "You will need time to heal and recover. I would expect a week or so here under our care. After that, we will get you situated here on base until we can get all of this sorted out."

The American officer demanded that after my co-conspirator and I recovered, we be moved to a brig. There, we would be kept under constant guard until more details could be had through an interrogation. The British officer would have no part of it.

"This man is in the custody of the British Empire and on British soil. We will handle him as we determine appropriate. At the moment, he is confined to the base, but otherwise, he will have no restrictions. Surely a man who risked so much is no threat to England or America. We are prepared if necessary to offer him sanctuary, which will prevent further involvement with America or any other interested government. I would hope that it would not be necessary and that we can work together."

Before they departed, I had one request. "Would it be possible to get the daily newspaper and a radio to listen to the news? If possible, provide any current reading material, magazines, and books? Lastly, a change of clothes."

"Consider it done," said the British officer.

With that, they left the room. The conversation had further crystallized the fragments of my memory. but that it had all just seemed to come together magically. I felt the weight of what transpired and the disbelief that I was a stranger in a world I no longer knew, a past I was now a part of, but a history that was not mine. President John Garner? It would be a different world and a different future, and of that, I was certain.

I let out an exasperated deep sigh as I lay my head back and stared at the ceiling. Political asylum? I had options now, but America is where I belonged. I had been so focused on everything that in this moment of solace and reflection, I wanted to be home. Call it remorse, regret, or second thoughts, but I wished that it had been someone else in my shoes. The price paid for a remote chance of securing the future was high, and I struggled to understand if the risk was worth the reward. For the millions who would not die in concentration camps and on battlefields, there was little doubt, but would millions more die in this new future of uncertainty? I wondered if the universe would seek to rebalance history in another way.

The Brits had made good on my request. They brought clothes and a wealth of magazines and books along with a radio to listen to news from the BBC. As I skimmed through the material, it was much like reading a reimagined history of the world. The names of the key players in world politics, the prominent issues of the day, were now foreign to me. I wondered what this world would be like and if I could still make a difference here. Putting aside the material and relishing the solitude of not having to answer questions or battle the demons of history, I tried to wrap my head around what had really happened here. I wasn't sure that it had all sunk in yet. The stress and weight of everything had created a mental block in my head that would not let me piece it all together. It would have to wait for another time when my head was clear, and I could focus.

Tomorrow, I would meet with the Brits and hopefully decide my next move. I was interested in going home to a strange and new America. For now, I managed to get up from the bed and tried to loosen up the aches and pains permeating through my body. I changed into the civilian clothes to take advantage of the freedom offered by my British hosts. No longer were guards stationed outside my room. I could walk about unrestrained. I walked to the nurse's desk and asked about the American girl who was brought in with me. She came out from around the counter and directed me to a room down the hall and on the left. I was praying that I would find her as they indicated, alive, well, and recovering. I pried her door open just enough to be able to see through. She was awake and sitting up. I opened the door and walked in. Her face lit up.

"Oh, thank God you are okay. I was so worried about you."

"I'm fine. How are you feeling?" I asked her.

"Nice landing, I thought we were goners. I'm just a little sore, but I'll be fine."

"That's good news. I think we are going to both be okay. I am meeting with representatives from the Brits and the Americans in the morning. So far, the Brits seem a bit more welcoming than our home team. We'll see how it goes tomorrow." I hugged and kissed her. "Get some sleep and rest. I'll stop by later. I'm hoping that in the next few days we can get out of this place."

With that, I left her to rest and myself to catch up on what I had missed. When the sun rose again, I would likely be grilled on things I did not know and share information no one would believe.

AN APPOINTMENT WITH DESTINY

The dawn came, and sunlight peered through the gap in the curtains into my room. The ray of light lit the dusty air like a beam from a floodlight. It was early, but I knew this day would bring more intrigue with a meeting of the leaders of the British command. Hopefully, a deal had been worked out to settle all of this uncertainty around my status. At this point, they knew very little about me other than a name they would have no record of anywhere. I had not yet told them the truth of our mission from the future to the past.

I expected that would be a tall tale they would not believe. The sooner we were able to get this over, the sooner I hoped I would take Jen and go home to America. Under our original orders, we were supposed to sacrifice our own lives to minimize our impact on the future. That day had come and gone. We might be of more help in the days, months, and decades ahead to right the wrongs of what Mac had done. Partly out of my own curiosity, I wanted to see how this all worked out. Did all the interference of the past make this a better world, or were we destined to make the same mistakes?

The news on the radio was positive. BBC reported that there was no declaration of war still standing. Peace negotiations were underway with the acting head of the German state. It was now confirmed that the attack on the funeral procession resulted in the deaths of Adolf Hitler, Hermann Goering, Heinrich Himmler, Joseph Goebbels, Joachim von Ribbentrop, and Adolf Eichmann, along with the top members of the German military. In a single blow, the architects of a mass genocide and rampant bloodshed were gone. It was only through the death of Reinhard Heydrich that they all came to be in the same place and vulnerable. In death, Mac may have done more to create a better world than the warped plan he had to reshape the future.

As more days passed, the horrors of the Nazi regime were coming to light. There was little chance now that I had created a martyr with my actions, but instead exposed a monster. Still, this might not have been as much about the "what" as the "how." The Brits had done an excellent job of keeping the fact that they had Hitler's assassin in custody, and that he was an American.

However, rumors were beginning to circulate that indeed that assassin had fled Germany and was in the custody of the British military. It might just be a matter of time before this broke wide open. I wasn't too worried about it. The Brits and the Americans had more to lose. It was in their best interest to keep a lid on this and see if it the focus could be shifted to make it appear to be an inside job. It was, after all, a German fighter plane that inflicted the carnage, and there was no proof that it wasn't a disgruntled Luftwaffe pilot. Implicating one country would, by default, implicate the other in a conspiracy that would have far-reaching and long-lasting impacts. I would know more shortly.

As for now, with a clear head, I once again focused on the infamous paradox of time to see if I could make sense of the things that had happened. It was mind-boggling to try to think about it, but I took some pen and paper and began to sketch a timeline. There might have been some things I would never have an answer to and may have never been able to reconcile. For example, Mac said that after Rick and I left, they knew right away that we had failed. That triggered the second attempt with Mac and Jen going back earlier to complete the mission by being there to help us. I had made this trip twice, but of course, I never knew. I wasn't sure what it all meant or how the fabric of time was woven into our lives.

There were so many questions and few answers. If I told this story to the Brits and Americans, they would undoubtedly struggle with the same problems to which I had no clue. As I sketched it all out, I wasn't sure I believed it. I couldn't get past the fact that they knew Rick and I failed. If we didn't make it on the "first pass," but did on the second, then what happened to us? The only way they would know that Rick and I failed is if nothing had changed. How would they know? Any change in history would become part of their history. In their mind there was no difference between the old from the new because to them, it was the one in the same. Their memories would change as they experienced a different history.

It is possible that it didn't work, that nothing changed. There would only be two scenarios that would make that possible. The first, that the transfer never worked, and we never made it back in time and were lost somewhere along the way. The second, that we died in the transfer process or killed upon arrival by the enemy. In any other scenario, our actions would become their history. They would have no recollection of a "before" and "after" history to compare. There would always only be "one history."

So then it must have been Mac's interaction on his return to my time or his return to the past that altered what happened. That must have been the factor that changed the fate of Rick's and my efforts. I wondered if there wasn't a third possibility. Maybe this was the most likely of all. Could it be that you could create a new history, but never change it in the future you left? What I surmised was that the reason Mac thought we failed was that nothing we did in the past could change that instance of the future. It only appeared that we failed when in fact; a whole new separate timeline of events was created. That would mean that somewhere out there, my world existed, and here, there would be a distinct new future.

Of course, that would mean that in the history I left behind, there was a failed effort. Families, and friends, and Beth would wonder whatever happened to us. It might have also meant a more dangerous world where two superpowers had a weapon that they believe could wreak havoc on the other. If I were right, no matter what they did would or could make a difference. I supposed it didn't matter at this point. I remembered what Mac said about the calibration of the time machine. They knew how to pinpoint a time by sending objects back and locating them in current recordings of history. That alone would lead me to believe that there was only one timeline in history. The less-than-perfect world I left behind might now have been on a course to be even less perfect. There was nothing I could do to get back to fix what had been done. Maybe fate had brought me here to help the world get a do-over of its history.

The time to resolve my present and my future had arrived. It was an atypical London morning with a sky filled with lots of blue and with just a few scattered clouds. The lack of fog and rain was perhaps a harbinger of better things to come. There was a waning moon setting in the east. In this time, it was a moon where a man had yet to set foot. There must have been a time where someone before stood here and gazed at the same sky. Could they ever have imagined that in less than thirty years from the spoils of war, a human would set foot on the moon? I wondered if it would happen here. The true spoils of war and what I knew painted an uncertain future. I would hope that a brighter future might lie ahead for the world and myself. I was still a bit slow on my feet, aching from the injuries from the crash. It did feel good to be out and walking in a free society without fear and the duties of the mission hanging on me.

The next few days moved more slowly than I would have liked. Both Jen and I were released from the hospital. The Brits lived up to their word and assigned us a temporary house on the base where we could begin to wind down and recover. For a few days, we were left alone. It was beautiful and quiet here, but both Jen and I were homesick for a place that didn't exist here in this time. There was no surveillance on us. We were free to walk about the base unrestricted. I appreciated that from the Brits. They believed they owed us a debt. I wondered how they would feel when and if the whole story came to light.

While I had the time, I spent those few days feverishly writing notes on all that had happened. I wanted to capture them while it was all still fresh in my mind. Jen was bored and wanted to get out. She wanted to be isolated from the world. Her idea was to get back to America and be anonymous. Take refuge in a small, remote coastal town where no one knew us or bothered us. A place where there would be solitude from the clamor and clatter of the alien world around us. It would be a place where we could be alone and live out the rest of our lives and not worry about the past or the future. It had an appealing sound to it, but I suspected our lives would never be that simple.

I was becoming absorbed with understanding the extent of the changes in history we had brought about by using the time portal. There was a library here on the base where I spent hours each day pouring through books, mostly history, to understand the new reality of which I was now a part. Everything was the same right up until the assassination of Franklin Roosevelt. From there on out, everything was different. A portion of the history I knew was the same, and the present was different. Was it possible, I wondered, to have this anomalous part of history be just a blip? Could I get the future I knew back on track? From my current vantage point, it seemed unlikely.

There had been no Second World War, no battlefield heroes like Eisenhower. The U.S. had not built a massive military in the World War II ramp up. We might not have been the dominant force as we were post-war. So much was changed. The world ahead was uncertain on many fronts. Germany, while now brokering for peace, was still a formidable technological and military power, even though we had hampered their "wonder weapons" program. They were the dominant player not only in Europe but also in the world. World War II might again happen if tensions rose between rival powers around the globe.

There was something else bothering me. The chip had malfunctioned in my arm and Rick's but was still working in Jen's. Mac once said that within a few days of completing the mission, we would know if it changed the ability to bring us back. It seemed far-fetched, but I could I wake up one day only to find Jen had disappeared back to a future. A future that could be as strange as the past she would leave behind.

It hadn't happened and seemed unlikely to happen. If it did, Jen could go back and perhaps fix the mistakes once again. I wondered how many times someone might have tried, only to make it worse. I wanted to believe that just maybe this timeline did turn out better, and there was no longer a need to fix the past. I knew the uncontrollable temptation that a capability like this in the hands of the military would be. Like a drug, or an addiction, once they had a taste of it, their thirst to use it would be insatiable.

There was a knock on the door. I opened to find a lone British soldier.

"Mr. Kelly, I have been asked to escort you to a meeting this morning with The Right Honourable Anthony Eden and a Special Envoy from the President of the United States, the Honourable Henry Stimson, Secretary of War."

I asked if they wanted Jen to come along.

"Sir, not at this time," he replied.

I walked over to kiss and hug Jen. "I'll be back soon," I told her.

With a tone of frustration in her voice, she replied, "I'm not going anywhere."

With that, we proceeded to walk over to the headquarters building on base. There, in a conference room, were two men. Henry Stimson was the President's Secretary of War, and Anthony Eden was a special advisor and close confidant of British Prime Minister Winston Churchill. I knew both these men, but only from what I had read. Stimson was older than I had expected. He appeared vigorous for a man in his early seventies. In a way, he was the architect of the American military buildup. Eden repeatedly argued against appeasement of Hitler during the pre-war expansion by the Nazis. He also disagreed with his British bosses on the close ties with America. There was a streak of American resentment hiding within him. Here were two men whose careers hinged on an all-out war with Germany. It remained to be seen if they would be pleased that I put an end to the conflict so quickly.

As I entered the room and we greeted each other, they were polite but formal. I don't know what I had expected, but it reminded of the interviews back at the Pentagon that secured my fate on this project. They wanted to start at the beginning with name, date and place of birth, and background. I told them the truth and went on to detail my involvement in Project Töten Zeit.

"What proof do you have for these claims?" Stimson asked.

I merely replied, "Manhattan Project."

Stimson went silent. He turned to Eden and asked if he may have a moment alone with me. Eden obliged and left the two of us in the room. As the door closed, Stimson asked, "What does Manhattan Project mean to you?"

I explained in detail what I knew it meant. "You are working on a highly classified and secret effort to build the first atomic bomb. A General Leslie Groves is leading the project for the Army and Physicist Robert Oppenheimer at the Los Alamos laboratory. You will or may have already planned to test the device in the New Mexico desert at the Alamogordo Gunnery and Test Range. The code name for the test is Trinity. Your test was scheduled to occur on July 16, 1945. At least that is when I knew it was tested."

"How do you know this? You must be a spy," he said with force in his response.

"Trust me. I am no spy. I am a colonel in the United States Air Force, sent here on a mission that went terribly wrong. I did what I thought was right to fix the damage that had been done."

"It is too fantastic a story to believe."

In his shoes, I would have the same reaction. I don't know that I would believe me. He had a few more questions to ask.

"The British pilots who shot you down. When they approached your aircraft, they saw you deliberately throw information into the fire caused by the crash. What you see here is what survived."

He pushed across the table the remains of three books. The first was Volume II of Dr. Josef Scheel's notes on Project Töten Zeit. It was intact with very little damage. Just as Mac said, it was stained with blood, my blood. Volume I was burned three-quarters through and had heavy charring to what was left. It was unlikely any of it was readable or of any use. The last book was Mac's insurance policy that he brought back from the future. It was a history book from his time that encompassed the twenty-two years of the future I had yet to experience. It had not caught fire and burned, but suffered severe heat damage. It was fragile, and its pages charred dark brown and black. Only if you looked hard could you make out the ghostly images in its soot-covered photographs.

I had never looked at the contents of the history book to see if it reflected what happened to our world. If the pages contained information about a future that no longer existed, then it was of no value to anyone as a roadmap. If it somehow updated to reflect the timeline as it changed, then it was in itself a weapon, much like the time portal.

Know the future and by changing just one thing now could have a ripple and magnifying effect further down that timeline. Knowing the mistakes that were made by trying to tamper with history left me little doubt that anything, any information would be militarized. Regardless of its contents, it likely contained information that could be used preemptively against countries, leaders, and people. It would be better now if the world found its own way rather than having the knowledge contained in these books fall into the wrong hands.

I let Stimson know that I had indeed fulfilled my mission as ordered. I had retrieved both volumes of Dr. Scheel's works and returned them to the hands of the Allies. Stimson indicated that the British agreed that the documents would be sent back to the U.S. along with the wreckage of the plane for further examination. Stimson asked Eden to return to the room and join us. I asked them what would become of Jen and me.

Stimson answered first.

"I'm not sure. The President has granted me wide discretion. I'm just not sure. I think it will all depend on the analysis of the documents and the plane. If what you say is true, you provoked war acting as a de facto agent of the United States government, then proceeded to assassinate the leaders of Germany on your own accord. By your own account, none of those events correspond to the direct orders you were given in the past, present, or future. You are either insane or if you are telling the truth, your knowledge may make you the most dangerous man in the world and maybe the most hunted if this ever gets out. You are welcome back in America contingent on us getting some validation of your story."

Eden then spoke with Britain's offer. "The British people owe you a debt of gratitude. Though they may never know your name or know what you did, we will know. You spared the lives of millions and perhaps saved the British Empire from a long and costly war and possibly defeat. In our eyes, you prevented a great war. We are willing to provide you with living accommodations wherever you choose in our territory and a new identity. You will be provided for as long as you live."

There they were, two offers for our future. One of those was pretty firm from the British, the other one not so firm from my home country. I kindly thanked Mr. Eden for his gracious offer and hospitality but said that I thought I needed to take my chances with my own country. With that, we had adjourned. Stimson was flying back to Washington in the morning and would have liked to have Jen and me on that flight with him. I agreed and would let Jen know we were going home. Our fate would now lie in the hands of our own countrymen.

ON TO WASHINGTON

Barely two weeks after the end of the Third Reich and the assassination of Adolf Hitler and his high command, Jen and I were headed to America. We left London with the clothes we had on our backs. I had kept the newspapers and the books the British had provided and stowed them in a backpack. It was as if we were immigrants headed to a new country. In a way, that was true. We had no place to live, no money, no identity, and no means to get any of those things. As tempting as the British's offer to give us safe harbor was, we placed our bets on America.

Jen and I, along with Secretary of War Henry Stimson and a few military members, boarded a plane headed for Washington. The flight would be long, with stops in Ireland and Newfoundland to refuel before landing at the Camp Springs Army Airfield in Maryland. It was what I knew would become Andrews Air Force Base. There was little privacy in the cabin. It was noisy with the whine of the props. Occasionally, I would glance up and catch one of the military brass staring at us. It gave me pause. I was a member of the military, and I felt more as if I were a prisoner being transported. Only once during the flight did the Secretary come back to talk to us. He informed us that upon arrival in Maryland, we would be staying at the base overnight and meet with the president in the morning. It had an all too familiar feel to it.

As we journeyed across the Atlantic, Jen and I had time to talk about our plans. She was worried about life in 1945. She and Mac had already been here since 1941. The prospect of a lifetime in the past seemed to bother her.

"I think I understand why they told us when the mission was complete to terminate our own lives. It wasn't as much about keeping secrets as much as they knew we might not be able to adjust," she said.

"I don't think they were smart enough to think that through. We'll be just fine," I replied.

She had a valid point. I had studied this era, watched movies and documentaries, and had a longing to be a part of this time. I falsely romanticized a horrible chapter in world history. How it would play out from here, I didn't know. There were second thoughts I was having about adjusting to a world that had yet to discover the progress that was already a part of my everyday life. It all looked good in the movies, but those were make-believe snapshots. This would be forty or fifty years of living it day after day.

I put my arm around Jen and rested her head on my shoulder. I whispered in her ear, "I'm going to spend the rest of my life with you. I'll protect you and take care of you. No matter what happens, we are always going to have each other".

She looked up, and for the first time on the flight, smiled.

"I told you, no proposals until you buy me dinner first!"

It was evening when we touched down at the airfield in Camp Springs. It was the middle of March, but there was a light dusting of fresh snow on the grass. The air was clear and crisp. Winter appeared to be hanging on with one last gasp. The chill in the air only fitted for what I thought might be a frosty reception back here at home in America. There was a car waiting to take us to accommodations on the base. We would be guests of the airfield commander, Captain Andrew Salter. We would stay at his residence on the grounds of the airfield. For the first time since either of us left through the time portal, we were back on our home soil. Secretary Stimson let us know that a car would be here in the early evening tomorrow for dinner at the White House with the president. That would give us time in the morning to get the proper attire and prepare to meet the president. After that meeting, we would get direction on what our next steps would be and where we would go.

We arrived at the base commander's residence. It was a beautiful, two-story home estate named "Belle Chance" within the base perimeter. The house was built in 1912 and was acquired when the War Department decided to create a base and airfield here in 1942. Waiting on the steps to greet us was the captain and his wife. I saluted the captain, and he returned my salute. He was warm and welcoming. His wife offered Jen coffee, and they proceeded into the kitchen while Captain Salter invited me into his den. After sitting in the belly of the cold transport, the fire going in his fireplace felt warm and inviting. I walked over and placed my hands in front of it to feel the heat.

"A lot of rumors going around this base. Word on the street is you are the guy that took out Hitler. You don't need to tell me anything. I just want you to know that military and secret are two words that as of late don't belong together."

I let him know that I appreciated his hospitality and that more might come out tomorrow. He continued.

"I've got some folks coming over early in the morning to take your measurements. We'll get you a suit, shirt, and tie for you to wear to the dinner tomorrow night. I figure that might take an hour. They will have something back to you by early afternoon. My wife will take Jennifer into town to get her something to wear. After we finish here tomorrow, what would you say to getting up in the air? I know you've probably had enough flying for now, but if it helps I have a few P-47 Thunderbolts here that we could hop in and take a ride."

I walked around his den, admiring his pictures of various aircraft and places he had been on tours of duty.

"I would never say no to doing some flying," I replied.

"Good. Let's plan that. The lady, Jennifer, what is your relationship to her?"

"We have been through a lot together in short period of time. It has created a strong bond between us. However we can serve, I hope we can do it together."

"I'm sure it will all work the way you want it."

We continued to chat. I was impressed with him. He was relaxed, informal, and friendly. It was different from the tepid response I had received from those in the political arena. As I sat in a chair watching the fire in the fireplace, it felt like home.

It wouldn't be long before Mrs. Salter came in with Jen and was going to escort her to her room. I let Andrew, Captain Salter, know that I would also like to get a good night's sleep and retire for the evening.

"Is that by chance the evening paper?" I asked him pointing to the newspaper on his desk.

"Yes, you are welcome to it. I'm sure you want to catch up on the news of the day."

With paper in hand, I retired to my room for the evening. I did want to catch up on the news, but I also hoped to get the answer to another question. Who was president? I found the answer on the front page with a photo of President James Farley with Secretary of State Cordell Hull. James Farley?

It took me a moment to get my head wrapped around how this might have come to pass. If John Nance Garner completed FDR's first term and was reelected, he would not have opted for a third term. He adamantly opposed FDR's third term and challenged him in the 1940 election. That year, Garner Nance finished third behind James Farley. Farley was a political force who was an immense help to FDR. I can only assume that he did the same for John Nance Garner, positioning himself for the 1940 election.

I noticed another front-page article below the fold in the right corner. It read, "Who was behind the overthrow of The Third Reich?" It denounced speculation that it was British commandos on a covert mission or an American plot to prevent a war in Europe. It pointed the blame at internal members of a resistance movement inside the German army as the likely source. The article was most likely the result of American and British propaganda meant to reassure their people that they had no involvement. It was essentially correct.

Out of respect for our guest and in keeping with the period, Jen and I stayed in our separate rooms. It was our first night apart since the ordeal began, and hopefully the last. The next morning, I was up early. I used the time to pull the books that I received in London from my backpack. Before I met the president tonight, I wanted to brush up on my history.

Captain Salters knocked on the door and cracked it open. "I brought you something."

He came in with a selection of flight suits and shoes along with a much-needed razor and a tube of a brushless shaving cream called Burma-Shave. "I wasn't sure of your size, so I had my men bring over a few sets this morning. You should be more comfortable wearing this around today." He said.

"Thanks for that, I will be much more comfortable in this uniform."

"I have some additional information on your dinner tonight. A car will be here around seventeen-thirty. Dinner is at nineteen hundred, but this will give you some extra time to get to the White House and socialize with the guests before dinner. The women got an early start and went out to breakfast and shopping. Let's take care of this measurement for your suit tonight and then let's get in the air."

It didn't take long to get the measurements done. It felt a lot like getting ready for the prom. On our way over to the airfield, Captain Salter struck up the conversation.

"You're getting a VIP treatment I've rarely seen for a mystery pilot. I'm going to level with you. The general asked me to check you out. Why we're going up today."

"The general?" I asked.

"The general. It was none other than Hap Arnold himself. I'm supposed to call him later this afternoon after we're done. He's a good man. After what the Germans did with their advances in aircraft, we dodged a bullet. The Luftwaffe would have had the best of us, for now. Hap believes the future of warfare will be fought in the air, not on the ground. If we can get our hands on those German planes, I know we will get them built here."

We arrived on the flight line to a line of P-47 Republic Thunderbolts.

"They tell me you're an experienced fighter pilot. Must be a Navy boy. You ever flew one of these P-47s?" he asked

"Can't say that I have."

"You think you can fly one of these?"

218

"Oh, I think I can handle it."

"I don't know that I'm supposed to do this, but instead of one, let's take two. I might be putting my ass on the line here, but I am the commander of this airfield. That should give me the authority to make the call on it."

"Where do you want to head to?" I asked.

"How about we head due east out towards the ocean. These things are gassed up, so we'll have about eight hundred miles or so to cruise around. Once we get out over the water, we'll hug the coast south to Assateague Island, turn west to Pax River, and then head for home. That should get us a few hours up in the air."

"Definitely."

The irony of this flight plan and what would follow did not escape me. The last time I arrived at this same airfield, the first thing I did was take a plane out for a run over the ocean followed by a dinner and meeting at the White House. It wasn't history that was repeating itself. It was the future. It was a déjà vu in another era. Salter walked around the plane with me to get me familiar with it.

"Go ahead and get in. I'll give you a quick rundown of the cockpit."

I hopped up onto the wing and got situated in the cockpit. Following my routine, I pulled Beth's picture from my chest pocket. Miraculously, it had survived the crash. While I was recovering, I asked the British if they could locate it in the wreckage, it was important to me. They gladly obliged and returned it to me.

As I was putting it in place, Salters popped his head into the cockpit. "Somebody special?" he asked.

"A good luck charm."

"I got one of those too." He reached in his flight suit and pulled out a picture of his wife and kids. "They always fly with me."

"Lucky you," I told him.

After our quick rundown, Salters situated himself in the other P-47, and we fired up the engines. We rolled out in tandem to runway one right. We held short for a moment while an inbound Douglas C-54 Skymaster touched down ahead of us. As soon as it cleared the runway, Salters radioed, "Let's roll."

As soon as we made the turn onto 1L, I throttled the engine up to full power. It was thundering loud and powerful, but the heavy aircraft lumbered slowly before gaining speed. We banked right on a northeast heading towards the Chesapeake Bay. Except for a scattered cloud here and there, it was clear all the way out as we climbed to ten thousand feet. Getting right back on the horse and being in the air was good therapy for me. I was doing what I love, and I was high above the unsettled world below. Despite having a wingman alongside me, it was the solitude needed and appreciated at this moment. After tonight, I wasn't sure I would get much more of it.

MR. PRESIDENT

It wasn't long before we crossed the Delaware coast to the open waters of the Atlantic. The town of Rehoboth Beach was just off my right wing as we banked right and headed south following the coastline. As we headed down to the Maryland shoreline, I looked at the small seaside towns dotted along the sandy beaches. I was familiar with this area. These ocean retreats were a modern-day collection of bustling resort towns that stretched from New Jersey to Maryland. This time it was different. As we passed by Ocean City, Maryland on my right, gone were the high-rise condominiums and commercial buildup that I knew. In this era, this tiny spit of sand resembled a sleepy little seaside hamlet. Its most prominent feature was a large, rocket-shaped water tower perched on four legs. It resembled a spacecraft from a 1950s sci-fi film. I had never seen it before. Horses were running in groups of four or five on the isolated dunes of Assateague Island. No showboating, this flight was a peaceful sightseeing tour. Looking out the cockpit window was like looking at a scrapbook of old photographs. I was mesmerized by what I was seeing.

"Take the lead. Let's set a course due west that should take us over Pax River, then we'll turn northwest to the field," Salters said over the radio.

"Roger," I replied.

I turned the Thunderbolt on a due west heading as Captain Salters slid behind me off of my left wing. We headed back over the Chesapeake and the Patuxent Naval Air Station.

"Isn't that beautiful," he said.

Salters was referencing the fact that the Pax River Naval Air Station was nearly brand new. It was a sign of the American navy's rising air power. Just this year, 1945, it would be graduating its first class of Navy test pilots. All seven of the first Mercury astronauts would go through training at that base on their way to space. I was envious as we flew over. It was a goal that seemed out of reach for me. Over the nose of the aircraft, the Potomac River came into view, and in the distance, I could see the Washington Monument and the dome of the U.S. Capitol. It was time once again to get ready for a date with the president.

Runway 1R was in sight, and I throttled back the engine to glide in and touch down. The P-47 was not the Stuka, but it was a fun ride and a tank of an aircraft. The descendant of this plane was one I would be more familiar with, the A-10 Thunderbolt, known by its more frequently used nickname, the "Warthog."

After we parked the planes and walked to the car, I let Captain Salters know what I thought. "Thank you for that, Captain. I can't tell you how good that felt to get up and fly."

"No trouble at all. I know the feeling. I can't tell you how many times I just got up to clear my head. I often fly that long loop. It's relaxing up there."

We drove the short distance from the hangar back to Belle Chance. As we pulled in front of the house, it appeared the ladies were back. Coming out on the walkway was Anna, the Captain's wife. She hugged her husband and looked over at me.

"I worry about him every time he flies," Anna said.

"Did you get much done today?" he asked her.

"Oh, I think the two of you will be very pleased."

As we walked into the foyer, I turned to the left to the Captain's den. Jen was standing there.

"You look..." I paused. "You look absolutely amazing."

The day had done her well. Jen was wearing a slim, knee-length yellow dress with sleeves about halfway down her forearm. She looked ahead of her time and very Jackie-esque.

"Mr. Kelly, they delivered your attire just as we got home. You'll find it on your bed," Anna said. "Let's leave them alone," She whispered to Captain Salters.

"Mr. Kelly, you better go get shined up. You are going to be on stage tonight," Jen said softly to me, mimicking a sultry Marilyn Monroe.

"Do you think I am the kind of girl you can spend the rest of your life with?"

"Yes, I do, and my dear, I am afraid no one is going to upstage you tonight."

The fact of the matter was that we would both be on stage tonight. Our fate might lie in how well our performance was received. Here at the airfield, we were embraced and welcomed. It seemed we had turned a corner, and perhaps as crazy as our story sounded, someone believed it.

It was a bit of a miracle, but somehow, they pulled together a suit, shirt, tie, shoes, socks, and the other necessary items appropriate for a dinner at the White House. I had showered and quickly got dressed in a dark blue suit, white shirt, and a red tie. We hardly looked like the old black-and-white throwback images of cigar-smoking politicians from the 1940s. Jen looked striking for any era. Brains, guts, and beauty — she had it all.

Together, Jen and I might have looked like a modern-era Camelot couple when we appeared at the White House tonight. We were both interested to see if this dinner was the fattening of the calf before slaughter or something else.

The car arrived as scheduled, and we made our way to the White House. As we left Belle Chance, I took Jen's hand and grasped it firmly.

"I don't know what the outcome will be from tonight. While I was up flying today, I had time to think. We've known each other for a few weeks. So much has gone on that I have lost track of time. I was alone in that cockpit today, and I feel alone in this world, but I don't feel that way when I am with you. I want us to be together, not because of the circumstances that put us here or because of the situation we find ourselves in right now. I want this to be real."

She looked at me with a bit of twitch to her lip as if holding back a tear. Then she leaned in and put her head on my shoulder, taking her other hand and placing it on mine. No words were necessary.

Dinner was scheduled for 1900 hours. We had arrived at the White House about thirty minutes early as instructed. In the space of a few months, at least by how I counted days, I had been in this building twice. It was two different buildings under two different presidents. This one was the historic original White House that every president since John Adams has walked in these halls and slept in these beds. The White House in my era was gutted and rebuilt. It was, for the most part, a replica. I was walking here in the footsteps of Jefferson, Lincoln, and Teddy Roosevelt. It was as if I were treading on sacred ground. I couldn't help but look around and listen to the creaking floors and notice the water stains in ceiling corners. This place must have been a sight for visitors when it opened in 1800, but one hundred and forty-five years later, it was showing its age.

Upon entering, an attendant escorted us to the Breakfast Room. The "Breakfast Room" was just a smaller dining room located off the larger State Dining Room. Waiting for us there was Secretary of War Henry Stimson, a man he introduced as the Vice President, Cordell Hull, and the U.S. Ambassador to Great Britain, Claude Bowers.

"So, you are the man who singlehandedly started and ended the shortest war in American history," Hull said.

"I'd like to think we prevented a much larger global outbreak of war that was in the Hitler playbook," I replied.

"Well, I think the only thing that saved us from another great war was the uncovering of what was really going on in those camps of Hitler's."

"Trust me, Mr. Vice President, it could have been much worse," I said.

"I suppose you're right. We are walking a diplomatic tightrope with our Allies. They don't believe this was a rogue German assassin, but a planned overthrow by the United States. Fortunately, they have no proof. Given what was going on under the Nazis, even if they did, they likely wouldn't press the issue."

As we were talking, a man appeared in the doorway.

"Mr. President," said Cordell Hull.

He walked into the room and acknowledged the presence of the three men by their first names. "So, these are the two who caused all of our trouble. Be seated, please." the president said.

The images of James Farley and FDR had escaped much notice in my readings of history, even though he was a pivotal figure behind FDR's legislative and campaign successes. What I knew of him was that he objected to Franklin Roosevelt's third term and sought the nomination against FDR and lost. Before that, he was the Postmaster General, but more importantly, he was a powerbroker in the Democratic Party. The falling out that the two had over the third term cooled their relationship, and Farley left public service. His quest to become president had been realized thanks to Mac's intervention. This man who was the president was imposing, a balding man with grey hair and a stern face. He seemed atypical to the jovial Franklin Roosevelt who was part of my history.

"Henry has briefed Claude and me on your story. It is difficult for me to believe. I am not sure I can believe it," he said.

"Mr. President, I have a difficult time believing it myself."

"I guess there are only two possibilities. All of this is a well-orchestrated hoax of some sort, or you are telling the truth. If you are lying, this is the greatest fraud ever perpetrated. I am not sure why you would go to such a risk and extent to pull it off. If you are telling the truth, well, we'll see. Tell me, if you are from the future, what does history say of my presidency?"

"Mr. President, my history is much different. In the world I come from, you were never president. Franklin Roosevelt was elected four times and died of heart failure not long into his fourth term."

"Four terms? I don't believe it," the president said emphatically.

"It was a difficult period. First, there was the Great Depression, then the World War in Europe. To many people, he was revered as the man who saved America from the depths of the depression and then rallied to win the war."

"And what became of me?" he asked.

"Take no offense at this, Mr. President, but I don't have much information on you. I know you objected to the third term and ran against FDR, finishing a distant second. From there, I think you left public service."

223

"That sounds like me. I would be opposed to any president's third term and would be stomping in anger at the mere idea of a fourth term!"

He leaned back a little in his chair and let out a deeper breath, an exasperated sigh. Then he leaned in and spoke. "I received some information this afternoon from the British. They are shipping the wreckage of your plane and its contents here. Before they packed it up, they did their own assessment. Harry and Cordell haven't even seen this yet. The plane is made of something they haven't seen before, a strong, lighter material. The engine is different also. The Germans had advanced from pistons and propellers to jet engine technology. We were trying to catch up, but this plane seemed to have an advantage over anything we have currently have in our inventory. Any comments from our guests?"

"Mr. President, the plane is not German. It was built in America, a future America. It was meant to look like the German plane to blend in, but had technology superior to the day, but not so much to be too obvious."

"And the explosive device in the plane?"

"It was meant to prevent the plane from falling into enemy hands. The plane that I came back with, I destroyed using the device at an airfield in Berlin."

The back-and-forth questioning continued. It was quite apparent that the president and the men around the table were having difficulty understanding how this all came to be. I was finding it equally difficult to explain.

Dinner was served, but it didn't slow down the conversation. As the president paused to eat his meal, Stimson and Hull picked up the questioning. "How exactly did you fly a plane from the future to the present, Mr. Kelly?" asked Cordell Hull.

"I don't know exactly how it all worked. I wasn't a scientist, just a mission specialist. I guess you could say we did fly back, but that's not exactly how it worked. The plane was just added as a tool to help us," I replied.

The president put down his fork and took a sip from his glass, then spoke up.

"There was more to the British investigation. They reported that the pilots who came upon you and the lady saw you deliberately attempting to throw documents into the fire caused by the crash. Why would try to destroy the very thing you said you were sent to retrieve?"

"Mr. President, it is an incredibly complicated story. I think explaining it would make you think that I am not of my right mind."

"I want to hear it from you," he stated.

"Mr. President, I want sent to execute a mission that the people in my time believed would make the world a safer place. We were to retrieve those documents and get them into the hands of the United States. Something went wrong. The people in my time believed I failed and sent another team with a different mission. That mission required a direct intervention of history. It involved giving knowledge to a government that would surely misuse it. All in the name of hoping that Germany and America would unite to destroy Russia and China. They believed those two countries were the true future enemies of freedom and prosperity in the distant future. I am not sure as I sit here that Reinhard Heydrich, a man from my time, wasn't executing his mission orders as his President gave them to him. It was wrong, and it was dangerous. The Nazis killed millions upon millions in my history books. It was brutal and senseless. It went unchecked for so long, and no one stepped in to stop it until it was too late. I ignored my orders, because I could not let history repeat itself. What we did was terrible. The machine that was created to come back in time and change history is a capability no country should ever possess. I tried to destroy the documents to prevent the information from ever being used."

"If you were in my shoes, would you believe me if I were telling you this story?" Farley asked.

"I don't think I would, Mr. President."

"There's more to that report from the Brits. Those documents you tried to destroy — one was burned pretty badly, another damaged heavily, and the last was undamaged. The undamaged book seems to corroborate your story. It appears to be the notes of a German scientist, a Dr. Josef Scheel. It appears he was trying to do something similar to what you described. The second book of his notes was heavily damaged. The third book appeared to be a history book of some sort, and although slightly damaged, it was readable. The Brits were of the same opinion that I said earlier—that it was either the real thing or the greatest forgery and hoax of all time. They believed it to be true. As incredible as it sounds, I tend to agree."

There was little reaction from Stimson, Hull, or Bowers. I took it as a sign of the regard they had for the president and his strength as a leader. The president didn't quiz me on the "Manhattan Project." I suspected that perhaps Hull and Bowers weren't privy to the project, and he didn't want bring up the topic in front of them. The conversation then turned a bit lighter for the remainder of the evening.

"We haven't heard from the young lady all evening. I understand you worked more closely with the Nazi leaders. Did you ever meet Adolf Hitler?" the president asked.

Poised and confident as usual, Jen responded, "First, Mr. President, let me vouch for everything Captain Kelly stated. What he says is absolutely true. The mission that we were part of was ill conceived. We followed our orders, and in the end, we did what was right for the people of Germany, and for our country. As for the Nazis, yes, I met Hitler and Himmler and many others. These men were ideological savages who cared nothing about people.

Only power. If this had been allowed to go on, it would have brought the world to the brink of destruction."

Much to the dismay of Stimson and Hull, the president seemed intrigued with us. He seemed to take a particular interest in Jen.

"I'm impressed with the two of you. From what I understand, you are a rocket scientist, and you are a pilot, and a historian I suppose?" the president stated.

We both answered the same. "That's correct, Mr. President."

The president leaned forward in his chair. His elbows rested on each arm and his hands together against his mouth. He paused like that for just a few moments, and then spoke.

"Here's what I want to do. You, young lady, I would like to go to Alamogordo, New Mexico. We have a test range there, and under a peace agreement with the Germans, they are sharing they technology with us. They are sending some of their team and rockets to New Mexico to teach us how to build and operate them. I'd like you to be there on the ground and work with them as my representative."

Before anyone spoke or answered, it had become clear to me that Mac and Jen's original mission plan was being fulfilled. The Germans and Americans had worked out a technology-sharing arrangement, and that could only mean one thing. The Germans, fearing war with the Russians, were aligning themselves with the United States. There were other possibilities. The Germans knew of Mac's plan all along and only triggered it when the tide had turned against them. Perhaps someone who had seen the document in the British government tipped the Germans off and convinced them to cooperate. Whichever scenario was the case, the alliance appeared to be on as planned.

The president continued on with what he had in mind for me.

"For you, Captain, I would like you to go to Langley Field in Virginia. We're shipping several of the advanced German fighters and bombers over. It is their best and most advanced weaponry. A technical team from Wright is going to test and dissect them. I'd like you, as our expert and my envoy, to be there to work on that project."

Before I could get in a word, Jen responded, "Mr. President, I would be glad to serve and help the country. I can be of great assistance with the rocket program, but…" She paused.

The president asked, "But what? Speak what's on your mind, young lady."

"With all due respects, Mr. President, I was hoping that the captain and myself could be a team and work together."

"I see. Yes, I see. I really could use you both on those projects, dedicated to these projects, but I think I understand. Okay. You'll work as a team and split time between the two locations. Something like two or three weeks at one, then go to the other. That should be fine. At least for the first few weeks, I would like you to initially each be at your site just to get things started."

We both thanked the president. He then gave directions to Claude Bowers regarding the logistics of explaining two people without a past.

"Claude, we are going to need new identities for these two. Work with Hoover and see what we do for things like witness protection. We'll need it all, education, certifications. Get the captain a military background and pilot's license. Just tell him we have two federal witnesses related to the Nazis whom we want to protect. Avoid giving him any details. That's a headache we don't need. There must be some reward money we keep around here somewhere. Let's get them something to get started. Get them on the federal payroll as advisors or consultants. Now, I want you two to take a week or so and go somewhere to unwind. Claude will stay in touch and get you squared away with the details for Alamogordo and Langley once the German equipment and team get here."

There was one final question I felt compelled to ask the President. "Mr. President, what will become of the documents that were found in the wreckage?"

"If they are as dangerous as you say then we will archive them. I will order all of it placed where it will be safe from prying eyes and prying spies."

The president laughed heartily at his comments. Hull, Bowers, and Stimson followed his lead. They just were not quite as enthusiastic as the president.

The remainder of the evening at the White House became filled with light chatter about the Washington Senators upcoming baseball season and the president joking about throwing out the first pitch at the home opener. There was no further discussion on the events that had taken place. President James Farley seemed every bit the person you would want to lead. He wasn't curious about the future. He probably wanted to know but preferred to pave the way on his own rather than plan his actions around a lot of what-if scenarios.

The president guided us through the White House on a personal tour to close out the evening. We thanked him for his hospitality and for taking a leap of faith with us. He closed by saying this shouldn't be the last time we meet.

"Stay in touch, and come back and see me with your thoughts after a few months on the job," he said.

The President turned and walked up the staircase to the residence. We had a new path to follow.

OUTER BANKS

We walked out the front of the White House to a waiting car. It was the second time I left the White House with a direction that could change the future. The opportunity was exciting for both of us, but I had mixed feelings about what we were doing. Regardless of how we might have felt, we were here to serve our country.

In the ride back to the airfield Jen was quiet, distracted. "I didn't want us to be apart," she just blurted out as if she had done something wrong.

"I didn't want that either. I would have been okay if we both just walked away. I felt we had an obligation to try to make this right. We were, after all, partly to blame, but I didn't want us to be apart."

She seemed comforted and reassured. Much like on the ride over, she leaned in with her head on my shoulder and wrapped her arm around my arm.

"I'm tired and exhausted. It's the up and down ride we've been on, and I'm feeling the lull of not having, or having, that adrenaline constantly coursing through my veins. I want to get away and relax. Let's take their advice and go hide for a week or two, just us."

There was no question the toll this had taken on both of us, physically and mentally. As if the events of the past few weeks weren't enough, I was still somewhat in awe that I was standing here in 1945. I tried not to think too much about it, but it was inescapable. The adrenaline of the mission had worn off, and reality was beginning to set in.

"I'll talk to Bowers tomorrow. See how quickly we can make plans. It is still too cold to head north, but not warm enough yet to hit the coast here. Maybe we head south to the Carolina coast," I said.

"Anywhere, cold, warm. Cold is fine. I'm okay just staying inside."

"You do realize we are not going to have cable, Internet, computers. Not for quite a while," I said with a smile.

"I know. I was counting on not having those things!"

Back at Belle Chance, Captain Salters was still awake. "How did it go with the president?" he asked.

"We had a great discussion. He told us to take a two-week vacation."

"It sounds very productive. Maybe I need to go meet with him!"

"It's been a good night. I think we are going to stay up a while and decompress if that's okay."

"Sure," he said. "The fireplace in the study is still going strong. There's brandy on the table. I'll see you in the morning."

With that, Salters went upstairs to bed, and we retired to the study. The battle had been won. Our mission had been accomplished, and here we were, stuck in the past, with an uncertain knowledge of the future. What was the right thing to do? I wish I could have answered that by saying to wait it out sixty or seventy years until we caught back up. That was not going to be an option.

There were a lot of clichés that came to mind — fish out of water, caught between a rock and a hard place. They all seemed appropriate. I don't know that I can adequately describe what it was like to live in one time and go back to another, a more primitive time. I don't mean to demean it. Maybe a simpler time is the right term. The two of us had the knowledge to make a game-changing difference, to stand on center stage and do for our country what few could do. Yet here we sat, feeling more alone than anyone could handle, more disconnected than anyone had ever felt. I was sure she felt it too. I know now what it is like to share a world with billions of people and not know a single person. Not one, not even this woman sitting next to me asleep with her head resting on my arm. We'd make friends, and we'd become a part of this society, but nothing would ever fully take away that feeling of loneliness that I was feeling now.

There, I sat for about an hour watching the fire with Jen asleep next to me. I pondered all the possibilities. The two of us pick up and leave and be anonymous somewhere. Decline the president's request and go about getting a regular life with a 9-5 job. Yes, I even thought about if we should the final step of our mission. Was this time better or worse with us here? In the end, I took an oath to serve, and country meant everything to me. I felt compelled to honor the president's wishes and help however we could. The next day would bring more time to think about it.

The night had come and gone quickly. We had awoken to find just a few glowing embers left in the fireplace. The sun was up, and we had slept all night in the captain's den. I would be counting on Claude Bowers to come through and get us started with enough identification to allow us to get out and move around. This wasn't a time where people left their identity footprints all over the place. A simple paper driver's license and birth certificate would pass.

As Jen rubbed the sleep from her eyes, she too was hoping for a chance to get out.

"Where are we headed to get away?" she asked.

"I had three places in mind. Three extremes. Florida for sun and warmth, the Outer Banks as the middle ground, and Maine to just get snowed in and do nothing. Pick one."

"Being snowed in sounds tempting, but I have had enough of the cold weather for now. I don't feel like being in a crowd at the moment, so Florida is out. That leaves just the Outer Banks."

"You got it. Outer Banks it is."

Anne Salters was already up cooking breakfast when there was knock on the door. Our new best friend, Claude Bowers, was also an early bird.

"I have some documents for both of you," he said.

"So soon? You must have been up all night."

"When the boss wants something done, nobody sleeps until it's done."

He handed me two Virginia driver's licenses and an envelope. I glanced at the simple paper licenses with names and addresses — our real names. "These were easy to get. We have people who surprisingly can get these done as quickly as we need them."

"The addresses?" I asked.

"Probably made up. No one will know."

I peered into the envelope, and there was a lot of money. It was a mixture of ten and twenty-dollar bills. In 1945, this was a windfall. The average annual pay was $2,500. A house might rent for $65 a month, and a car might only cost a $1000. We appeared to at least have $500. This amount of money would get us clothes, food, and a place to stay for the next two weeks.

"Did you rob a bank this morning?" I jokingly said to Bowers.

"In a manner of speaking. The president called the Treasury Department and had this brought over. He wasn't finished. There's a car outside that's yours to use. He made calls last night to his friends and got one of them to provide this. Few people are as connected and as well respected as the president. As you would expect, when he calls, things happen."

"Please convey our appreciation and thanks to the president, will you?" I said.

"One more thing. Here's a number where you can reach me. If anything goes wrong or you need something, call me. By the time you are back in Washington, I should have more permanent documentation for you." Bowers handed the keys to a 1944 Nash Ambassador. It was a behemoth of a car with large whitewall tires. "Any chance you can give me a lift back to D.C.?" Bowers asked.

"Definitely."

I felt terrible that Bowers and the president had worked through the night to make things happen quickly. I wasn't sure how our new team would feel about us after that chilly reception in London. For now, the highest-ranking member of the government and his closest allies appeared to be 100% in our corner.

Jen stayed behind while I drove Bowers into D.C. It was the first time I had gotten a good look at it in the daylight. It was different. It was quaint and cleaner, with old cars by my standards and men walking the streets with hats on every head—something I had only seen in old photographs and movies. It was an odd sensation to see the familiar surrounded by the not so familiar.

I pulled up to the White House to let Bowers out. He had some parting words. "He's taken a shine to the both of you. The president has good instincts about people. He respects what you did. I'm not sure where he is on the whole story, but he likes you. Don't let him down."

"I can assure you we won't."

We shook hands, and Bowers walked through the gates to the White House. I sat there for a minute and just looked at the building. The streets were busy with people going about their business. In my time, this area was secured and blocked off. Here, it was still the people's house, not a bunker. The thought of terrorism and mad bombers had yet to destroy their innocence. I hoped it would stay that way.

As I pulled away from the White House, I glanced in the rearview mirror. Usually, I might say it was time to put the past behind me, but this was really about putting the future behind me. A new future was ahead of us, different from the one we knew. The rising sun brought with it a new chapter in my life, and it started with just some time to get away and clear my head. There were exciting things ahead for the two of us, along with some dangerous ones. None of it would likely equal what we had been through so far. It was time to move on.

I arrived back at Belle Chance to find Captain Salters dressed in uniform. It was a back-to-work day for him. I was still wearing the same clothes from the dinner last night.

"Did you go out and buy a car this morning?" Salters said jokingly.

"It's a loaner from the White House," I replied.

I told Salters we would be heading out this morning for a two-week retreat. The destination was unknown, but probably the Outer Banks.

"Will we see you two again?" he asked.

"I'm not sure. The president had some things in mind for us to get started on when we get back."

"It was a pleasure to meet both of you, and you are welcome here anytime. Let's fly again sometime when you are back in the area."

"Deal."

As Salters left, I turned to find Jen already dressed and ready to get started. Throughout our adventure, I had tried to put out of my mind the ordeal and pain she must have gone through at the hands of Himmler and his henchmen. Jen was smiling and excited to go on our mini vacation. I knew that much of her excitement was driven by the need to escape and be in a place where she might begin to heal. "Alright, let's go." She had an excitement I had rarely seen. Assaulted, stabbed, shot down, she was ever resilient.

We bade our farewell to Mrs. Salters and left the Camp Springs Airfield. Destination, the Outer Banks of North Carolina. It was just months ago in another time that I had driven the back roads of North Carolina and Virginia to get to Andrews. Now I was going back, and I wasn't exactly sure the same routes would get me there.

"Do we know where we are going? Do we know how to get there?" Jen asked somewhat sarcastically.

"Well, I was a Boy Scout, and I am a pilot, and I did get us from Berlin to London without a map."

"Yes, but we also got shot down."

"You are a smartass. Let me do the driving, and you keep your comments stowed." I smiled at that last statement I had made. Finding our way through back roads to a beach was the least complicated thing we had done.

During our drive through the rural Virginia country roads and small towns, I was getting a taste of American life in 1945. Jen had fallen asleep and was oblivious to the sights and sounds of a bygone world through which were passing. I wasn't quite sure what to make of it. The America I knew during World War II and immediately after was portrayed on the screen in movies. It was often a romanticized version that depicted more love and bravery than it did brutality and loss. Its simplicity about life, the lack of distractions, and the crystal-clear focus on objectives is what made it appealing.

It wasn't what I had imagined. I was feeling that sense of withdrawing from the world I knew. This is what the movies don't tell you or show you about picking up someone and placing them in a different era. For the first time, I understood how difficult this would be. I knew what lay ahead, but it was out of reach for me. It sounded somewhat selfish, but the creature comforts of mobile devices, digital music, internet, computers, and cable TV were absent from this world. The act of getting information from books and communicating with people by the spoken word, and by a telegram was a lost art in my time.

As we drew closer to the Outer Banks, I started to tune the radio, looking for a station. I was particularly interested in news updates. I picked up a strong signal out of New Bern, North Carolina. The call sign was WHIT, and the announcer added: "Where Hospitality Is Traditional." The news led with word of flooding along the Ohio River due to persistent and unusually heavy rainfall. It was compared to the Great Flood of 1937. From the flood, they transitioned to what seemed more optimistic words that a new round of peace talks in Europe would be scheduled with the German military. The remaining hierarchy of Hitler's generals was still leading the country after his death. They likely would stay in charge until democratic elections could be held, if they would be held.

While the alliance between Germany and Italy brokered peace in Europe, a third member of the Axis powers was not so accommodating. The Japanese in the Asian theatre were not ready to roll over and relinquish their opportunity to gain a dominant foothold in the region. With the issue of Germany and Europe apparently settled, nobody appeared to have the appetite to go after Japan. The new world order still had wrinkles and threats before a permanent peace could be established. For now, that was neither of our immediate concerns. This slight respite from reality was what we needed.

Jen was waking as we drove down the Outer Banks of North Carolina. She looked out the window and asked, "Where are we?"

I jokingly replied, "Far from anywhere."

In truth, we were making our way far down the coastal area of North Carolina. I figured somewhere past Kill Devil Hills and around Nags Head, we would stop. As we passed Kill Devil Hills, it dawned on me that somewhere still alive was Orville Wright. It was just one more hard-to-fathom moment in what had transpired.

It was desolate here in March. The tourists had yet to arrive, and year-round residents were sparse. I found what appeared to be the center of activity along the main coastal road in Nags Head. A combination grocery store, restaurant, and five-and-dime that was open year-round. This was as good a place as any to get out and stretch our legs and inquire for a place to stay. As Jen and I stepped inside, the first noticeable thing was the creaky wooden floor. They moaned and strained as we walked across. The store was empty of customers. It was an unusual place with a variety of souvenirs, largely seashells and homemade nautical memorabilia along with the usual consumer staples.

We walked over and sat down at the lunch counter — a small one with only six stools. An older man walked over and introduced himself as Dave, the owner. "You folks just passing through?" he asked.

"We're on a bit of a vacation, down from Washington," I replied.

"You government people or something?"

"As a matter of fact, we are," I said to him somewhat cautiously.

"I figured you for government people. Now that there's not going to be another war, I guess everyone is going on vacation. I'm afraid there isn't much to see or do down here this time of year. It doesn't start getting busy around here until early May, but really in June," he said.

"We were looking for a place to relax for about ten days or so. Do you know anyone who might have a place to rent?"

"We have cottages we rent right on the beach. They're all boarded up for the season, but I could let you have one of those for a few dollars a night if you board it all back up when you're done. You have to pay now and bring the keys back here when you leave."

"I appreciate your hospitality. That would be perfect for us. Thank you."

We had a place to relax and unwind for the next week and a half. I think we both needed the time to be away from people and news and decompress. It would also give me a chance to probe the mind of my patriot in arms.

THE PROGNOSTICATORS

There was little trouble finding the cottage along what was known as "cottage row." One might describe these as boxes with windows on stilts. They were bare bones buildings and meant to serve the purpose of accommodating tourists for short stays with front door access to the ocean. I wondered if, at high tide, I could step right off the porch into the surf. It had been a long night, followed by a long drive, but I was getting a bit of a second wind. It was just midday, and the sun had warmed the chilly air. The ocean temps were likely in the 60s at best. There would be only watching the sea on this trip. The inside of the cottage was vintage, even for this era. It had the smell of trapped salty brine that washed underneath the building and permeated through the floor. It would need a good airing out.

We got about as settled as we could. I had removed the boarding on the windows and placed the rockers on the porch. This respite from the world was indeed roughing it with just the basic necessities, but it offered a peaceful solitude. As we settled into the rockers with blankets to stay warm, the only sound was the crashing of the waves.

Jen broke the silence. "It's peaceful here. I could stay here forever, just like this."

It was a topic I had avoided, and this seemed like an inopportune time to bring it up, but I wanted to know. "Jen, tell me about the twenty-two years of the future, what happened?"

She was visibly uncomfortable about the subject and seemed hesitant, but she knew this topic would come up sooner or later. She paused, put her feet on the chair, and pulled her knees close to her chest. "I don't know where to start," she said.

"Take your time," I replied.

"Well. The safest the world will ever be is today. Tomorrow and each day thereafter is one day closer to a global apocalypse. Not a war, an apocalypse. A war has its losses and horrors. In time the wounds heal, but scars remain. In an apocalypse, the wounds may not be fatal, but they never heal. That was my world. You may not see or feel it now. You may not have thought it in your era. It is cunning and stealthy. Security lulls you into complacency. Complacency and tolerance are the enemies of freedom and democracy. Imagine a battle where we helped the enemy defeat us. Not consciously, but still we were complicit. Let me tell you about Mac. I didn't like his means, but he was a warrior and patriot. You see him differently, but his goal always was the greater good. I just couldn't get there. That is why I helped you. He would stop at nothing to prevent what became of our world. If you were in his shoes, I believe you would have done the same."

She paused as if she knew I would take issue with those statements. They were puzzling, and I wasn't sure what she or Mac was advocating was a better system. I wanted to let her go on, but I took the bait on her comments. "I find it difficult to believe I would ever go there. I could not place millions of lives at a mythical sacrificial altar of peace and justify it."

She continued, "You wouldn't risk thousands, maybe hundreds of thousands, a million, to save billions? What about to save everyone on the planet? Would you take that gamble?"

"No. I couldn't. I value each life equally. Even if I went along with your hypothesis, this would be a bet with no guarantee," I replied.

"You didn't live to know what happened, but you knew your world was dangerous and getting more precarious by the day. The time portal was a ruse. It was a means to an end. Mac was right, though. Your mission failed, and the project was shut down," she stated.

"If my mission failed, why was Mac intent on killing me by sabotaging the plane."

"He couldn't and didn't want to take the chance that our presence would change something and make the project a success. That would end any chance to go back and make a case for a second trip."

"What does this have to do with that apocalypse?" I asked.

"It was a long time coming, but during the Cold War, there were only two superpowers. Each knew the price of conflict. What no one saw coming was the power that smaller countries would gain by acquiring nuclear weapons. Countries like India and Pakistan, which always slept with their finger on the button. Israel and Iran, both harboring weapons of annihilation ready to go down in flames taking each other out. Then there was North Korea. It was a powder keg looking for a spark and had been for a long time. As much as the Middle East was full of religious zealots believing that they were acting on God's behalf, North Korea was dealing with its own messiah complex. Leader after leader who was willing to risk the lives of everyone in his country and beyond just to say he landed a devastating blow to the evil western giant, the United States."

"Who started it?" I asked.

"It's a matter of debate when it started. You could argue that we were laying the seeds of our demise by running up huge deficits and trade imbalances, slowly strangling the lifeblood from the weakest of our nation, and like a disease progressed upward into the middle class, sowing doubt and unrest in our people. It could have been the dwindling of our ability to defend the free world by outspending every nation. We were battle fatigued and broke. Then there was the impact of climate change eroding our last national strength, the ability to feed our people. Water shortages and heat were decimating our agriculture. Technology and the use of artificial intelligence created new ways to attack countries and made new weapons that no one would have dreamed of possible. Those were the contributing factors, the spark to what became that global apocalypse from a match we lit."

Seeing that Jen was about to reach the pivotal climax of what I thought might be the story of how the world would end, I didn't respond. I gave her pause to compose herself and go on.

"Wars of your not-too-distant future were less about soldiers on battlefields. The enemy had patience and was more strategic. There were more ways to sink a country and have it turn against itself than bullets and bombs. Those who wanted to see the United States fall saw this and used it. We were failing economically, politically, socially, and militarily. Our time was rapidly running out. The great experiment that was America was coming to an end. We had mortgaged all of our tomorrows to live it up today, and there were no more tomorrows left to trade off. In the mind of politicians, nothing cures or unites a country like a war. Only this was no ordinary war. It started as a cyberwar. First, we detonated a series of nuclear missiles on North Korean launch pads by hacking them and using an artificial intelligence virus to do the work for us. Using AI viruses was becoming commonplace. You didn't need hackers per se. You could just create the AI worm and get it inside. It would then figure out how to grow and execute its mission. I'm not sure we believed it would work, but it did, all too well. It was deemed another failure of the North Koreans to responsibly handle nuclear weaponry.

By this time, nuclear proliferation had spread around the globe. The responsible countries knew better of the dangers, but those smaller rogue countries, not so much. When the North Korean blast occurred, no one knew we were behind it, although the North Koreans blamed us. Thousands died, and tens of thousands were sickened from the fallout, including many in China and South Korea. The goal was to eliminate one problem and then move to the next. What we didn't know was we were being played. Behind the scenes, there was a mass global conspiracy mounting against us. It was a pre-ordained alliance that dwarfed the Axis powers of World War II."

I stopped her. "You are telling me all this, this wild plan to go back to World War II Germany, was all part of a plan to stop this world-ending cataclysm? What was the conspiracy? Wouldn't it have made more sense to go back to right before the start and figure out a way to prevent it?" I was puzzled that the rationale for what seemed to be a cataclysmic event didn't have an immediate solution, but instead this long, concocted plan that was high risk. Attacking the known and immediate threats seemed the obvious approach.

She tried to explain. "It was an option, but it was decided that that would only be a stopgap that would make things even worse."

"What could be worse?" I replied

"You would be talking about a preemptive strike on a threat we weren't supposed to know existed. It would have started a global war. That would have been a war that annihilated the planet all at once and ended life, as we knew it. Hence, Plan B. Everyone was of the belief that time existed only in the present. Once the past was changed, the present would change. All the changes would accumulate and roll to the present. No one believed that the present and the future would go on unchanged while a new timeline was created. They all believed that changing the past meant changing the future for us. Somewhere out there right now, your future and my future should already have been changed. You and I will never know. Everyone thought your mission failed. Maybe it didn't. Maybe it succeeded in creating a new future in that time, but left the other time unchanged."

"So then it was the hope that the events of seventy years would instantly change history for the better at the hands of Mac and you? There are so many questions and issues with that thinking that I don't even know where to begin," I said.

"For decades, we ruled the planet. Everyone feared our might. Even when we were weak politically or militarily, we still packed a punch. Sometime, giants are even easier to topple. Just like we were caught sleeping on 9/11. We were caught sleeping again, and our biggest vulnerabilities were left unguarded. It didn't take long, maybe a week after the North Korean accident, for two simultaneous events to happen. It was the middle of the night when a small nuclear explosion happened underwater off the coast of Miami. It might have been planted there a long time ago in a cargo container waiting for a signal. It could have come from the most heinous weapons humans had created. Those terrorizing weapons were unmanned, nuclear-powered drone subs. Small, silent, and virtually undetectable, they could roam endlessly at depths far beyond normal subs. Their intent was to explode and dump waste to ruin fishing grounds and waterways. Some carried a single nuclear missile that could be launched undetected from close to a coastline.

Most carried torpedoes that could sink targeted ships. Like a silencer on a gun, no one would see them coming. Those drone subs were expendable, the damage everlasting.

That particular blast wasn't likely meant to kill people. It was meant to spread its radioactive poison along the Gulf Stream, crippling fishing and rendering coast areas uninhabitable. At the same time, a satellite, likely North Korean, passed over the Midwest and detonated a nuclear bomb high in the atmosphere. The electromagnetic pulse fried nearly everything from Wichita to Atlanta to Chicago to Boston. Cars, planes, trains, power stations, and hospitals were down. There were blackouts as night fell and widespread panic that only grew in the darkness, as no one was equipped to respond or mobilize. There were very limited communications. No one knew what was going on. The densest part of the country feared the end was near. It nearly was. The country was in shock, and so were our leaders. While we focused immediately on recovery and secondly on retaliation, a number of things occurred. By no coincidence, Russia moved to seize parts of Eastern Europe and regain their old Soviet empire while China seized Taiwan and North and South Korea, along with the Philippines. They also had Japan's back to the wall. In the Middle East, Iran seized Iraq, Kuwait, and Yemen. Syria, and with the help of the Russians, decimated Israel. Israel did not go down without a fight and managed to hit Tehran with several nuclear attacks. They both paid a price and both fell.

Russia stepped in to fill the gaps, taking effective control of Syria and claiming Iran and its captured states were now under its control. By the time we had formulated a response, it was too late. The world's political map had changed irrevocably. It was a perfectly executed conspiracy by those we trusted and by those we didn't. No one might have believed it possible. We had one last card to play, and the time portal was it. It was a desperate act by desperate people. I hope you can see that Mac was doing what he believed was right. He saw the horrors of our world, and what happened here in this time paled in comparison. It was the best option on a list that did not have any good alternatives. We would rewrite history from 1936 on and ensure the dominance and survival of the United States. Here we are."

"Yes, here we are, two prognosticators of the future with a world to reshape," I said.

I looked back to the peaceful calm around us. This was a simpler world in a simpler time. This world might have been different in the long term from Jen's nightmarish landscape. However, I suspected that the nature of human beings would not support a world at peace for very long. When we finished our mini-vacation, our orders from the president were to continue building out those weapons to secure the very future Mac and Jen hoped to achieve on behalf of their president. I had become more pessimistic that no matter what we did, the world could not have peace as a result of being held hostage by the threat of war. It didn't work once. I doubted it would work again.

The next two weeks, we both put this behind us. Over that time, we continued to grow closer and closer to each other. Here in the desolate late winter on the Outer Banks of North Carolina, we found each other in new ways. I still wrestled with my feelings of guilt and betrayal. I was reconciling the compassion and intense emotional connection I felt towards Jen with the hard reality of what her mission was and the deception when I first encountered her. Here, I began to understand that whatever misleading or transgressions she may have had, we were now on the same team. Alone, isolated, we were, for better or worse, the only hope for a better future. It was unknown if we would ever be able to adequately adapt or fit in. We were looking to cement our own "pact of steel". An alliance that would make us inseparable through whatever remaining time we had in this life.

As our time here closed, and it was time to take on our new assignments, we pondered how we could impact the world for the better. There were so many options to do greater good for the world with our knowledge. Peace through strength seemed well down the list.

A DANGEROUS COURSE

We made our way back to Washington. With only the exception of what little radio we had listened to, we were oblivious to what was going on in the world. In our time of instant communication and breaking news updates, the world seemed to stay at status quo for the past two weeks. After arriving in Washington, I met again with Claude Bowers to return the president's "loaner car."

"The president said to keep it. You will need to get around and get settled here before you leave on your new assignment. There won't be much time. You will be leaving in a week."

Bowers then handed me a set of keys and a note.

"What's this?" I asked.

"We knew you wouldn't have the time or means to get a place and get secured. At the direction of the president, we found you a place. It is a few blocks from the White House. It will be convenient when you are back in town."

I was taken aback that we were provided such hospitality. I wasn't sure in this era I would have believed our story. I wanted Bowers' honest take on it. "Do you believe us?" I asked him point blank.

"It's a fantastic story and hard to believe. I can't grasp the things you have said and the place and things you described that lie ahead for all of us. Yet, all the evidence supports your story. The proof, I suppose, is if you can help us here and now. The president believes you can. Right now, I just hope you will."

I asked him if it would be possible to get time again with the president to talk about a new course we might want to pursue.

"Now is not the time. The president sees this as a once-in-a-lifetime opportunity to secure peace and prosperity for the world. He is a man of peace but believes a strong America is the heart of that peace. Before I forget, while you were gone, we secured new identities for you and your companion."

I knew it was a long shot at this moment to get another meeting. The timing just wasn't right, but I felt we had time to sort this out in the coming weeks or months. The urgency to the president did not appear to be that critical at this moment. The immediate task at hand was to secure a strong Europe and a strong European alliance with America. It would hold the Russians at bay for quite a while. If the Germans had nearly defeated the Russians single-handedly in my time, surely a much better alliance could keep the peace. It was peace I hoped we were aiming for in the short term while we came up with a better strategic plan for the future. Whatever plan was devised; it was my hope that it would be more realistic than the one Mac had sought to achieve. Somehow, all indications were pointing towards the pieces of his puzzle fitting into place.

Bowers handed me a large envelope. I glanced inside and saw about thirty to forty typed pages and several official documents. I carefully pulled the papers out. "This is your life. Your new history," Bowers said. He went on, "We have a pretty good process for this. In special cases, we have created new identities with thorough backgrounds. You'll need to get familiar with this, and at some point, visit the areas we utilized, just in case you get questions. I was hoping your new identity would have you local to Washington, but it might be too risky. So you end up getting places that are medium sized where we have people in place to set this sort of thing up."

As I glanced at the documents, I first saw the new birth certificates. Mine said "John Thomas Behrens," born in December 1916 at the Charlotte Memorial Hospital in Charlotte, North Carolina. Jen's document indicated she was born in January 1913 at the Durham Regional Hospital in Durham, North Carolina under the name Maria Lucia Mueller. There was a driver's license for each of us, military papers for photos, and various old black-and-white photos.

"Photos?" I asked.

"The family you never had, in a manner of speaking. Everybody has photos from their childhood. These are yours. You were both born to German immigrants. It is a familiar story, one of immigrants who came to America fleeing the specter of the Great War, the war to end all wars. It was convenient for many reasons, most of all because it is easy to hide their history," he said.

"I'm impressed with your thoroughness. It is quite amazing that government moved so quickly in this time. It only got slower from here on out," I said to Bowers with a smile.

242

"You're on the government payroll now. The president wants frequent updates from the both of you. We'll probably arrange another meeting here in DC in a month or two, but keep him in the loop on what you see. His name will open doors and clear a path for you. If you have any problems, let me know."

I paused for a moment. "I'll do my very best for the country and to serve the president. I fear that we don't have much time no matter what route we take. Whatever course we pursue, history, and in this case, the future shows that inevitably, the world drifts on a dangerous course. The Russians are a capable people, much more capable than we have ever given them their due credit. Together, we can find common ground and work for peace. Military action would only serve to simmer the boil of discontent and revolt for the blink of an eye. It would fail in ways we might only begin to imagine."

"I understand, and the president understands. The forces are strong within the military and with those who build the arms. They are fervent in their belief that an imperialistic America that controls our enemies can control the world's destiny. The president is not with them, but they are strong and persuasive. I will share your thoughts with the president. You can take it up with him next time."

With that, we said our farewells. We now had names and a make-believe history to match our make-believe world.

The two weeks at the Outer Banks had tamed the constant adrenaline surges and the emotional swings we had been on since Nordhausen. A state of recovery and normalcy had set in, although I believed that normalcy would never be the appropriate description of our lives. Not then, not now, never. In hindsight, we probably should have spent the time acclimating to life here in 1946 America. I assumed there would be plenty of time for that. How much time we had, one could never be sure.

I had a strange feeling. It was something akin to déjà vu. It was a foreboding feeling that either I had missed something or that something ominous was going to happen. It was back to Belle Chance to pick up Jen and share the news that we had a place to call home for the next few days. On the way back into downtown Washington, Jen had something on her mind.

"Do you want to go back?" she asked.

Not understanding what "back" she was talking about, I assumed it was the Outer Banks. "Back to North Carolina?" I asked.

"No, no, back home, home to our time, your time."

"I don't know that we should think about or dwell on that time and place. It is something that is unattainable."

"I don't want to go back, but I am not sure I want to be here either. It is by far the better of the two choices. Witness a world torn apart by misguided beliefs and ambitions, or stay here and watch it slowly die all over again," she said.

"The difference this time is that we are here, and maybe we can be the catalyst for change," I replied.

Truth be told, she was probably right. The problem was in the DNA of a human being. The gene to dominate as a means of survival was strong. There was a sliver of hope for the future, albeit slim. Here was a world that avoided unfathomable evil, yet was much like a ball of clay. It could be shaped and molded and changed. The original mission might still have been accomplished, just in a different way.

I didn't share my true feelings with her. There was a part of me that did want to go back. It was torturous to think about it. There was no hope that anyone would come for us. By my own hands, I had accomplished that by destroying what I could of Scheel's notes. I thought about what Mac said about my blood on the book. Was he lying, or had I been here before? Would I be here again, and again? It seemed a vicious cycle that could not be broken unless I could be the difference maker. Maybe I had tried and failed to prevent another attempt in the future. Perhaps, no matter what I did, this was an endless loop. A series of efforts to travel back that would never end unless somehow I broke the chain of events once and for all. The original project wanted to send a message to the past. Being in the past, I had the easier task, and advantage, of sending or leaving a message for the future.

I had to keep focused on what I could do in the here and now. As far as any of us knew, there was only one Dr. Scheel. Someday, there might be another who comes up with the workable way to move through time. For now, the technology didn't exist, even if the method did. I felt compelled to stop it right here and now. It was the worst of all possible weapons that we saw misused firsthand.

Stability was something we longed for, but knew would be short-lived. That first-week planting roots in our new home went by quickly. The house was furnished and comfortable. Those creature comforts of television and internet were sorely missed. I used the downtime to walk around Washington. I watched and listened to people go about their lives. Each day I read as much as I could and spent time at the library understanding the real impact Mac and Jen role in the course of events.

Mac's influence was stark. The assassination of Roosevelt occurred as his motorcade traveled from Annapolis to the White House on July 4, 1933. The perpetrator was a lone sniper perched on an overpass. That sniper, a Russian national, was found dead at the scene of a self-inflicted gunshot to the head. It was presumed that the sniper took his own life after successfully killing the President. This heinous act had to be the direct result of Mac's interference. He had managed to hold off World War II at the expense of killing a President and by risking building a Germany that would never be defeated if a global war started. I was reminded, though, of what we stood for during a visit to the National Archives. It was there that I was able to view the original Constitution of the United States. It was a sobering moment. The pillars of our democracy and freedom contained on this parchment are what I swore to defend and uphold in any time.

As I walked back to the rowhouse, I had that recurring feeling of mixed emotions about what I was being asked to do and what I felt should be done. It was an all too familiar struggle between competing versions of what was right. I supposed they were both right for differing reasons. It was all a matter of perspective. For now, following orders seemed to be the best course, although it would only serve to keep the world moving again on that dangerous course. If I were going to change anything and have influence, I would need to establish my credibility.

The time had finally arrived for Jen and me to part ways for just a little while. In a strange way, it was like a kid leaving home to go away to camp for the first time. In spite of the fact that both of us had only here a short while, we were like vines clinging, and holding tightly to what was within our reach. Washington felt like home. It wasn't the first time we would leave the familiar for the unfamiliar, but the first time we would leave each other. I was worried about her and her safety away from the protective watch I had over her.

I drove Jen to Union Station and watched her board the train for New Mexico. Her next stop would take her to the forefront of what I had once dreamed about, working on getting humans to space. It would all start there for the U.S. space program. While the seed of human spaceflight was born there, the task would be to enhance the weapons of war. Her emotional state was teetering back and forth between a melancholy homesick feeling and the trauma she endured in what she thought would be a better place. I wasn't sure she would open up or that her interactions again with the Germans might stir the anger inside of her. We would only have occasional phone calls and telegrams to keep in touch. My concern for her would be a distraction from the job I had to do.

My trip would be much shorter. I was bound for Langley Field in Hampton and Newport News, Virginia. I would be acting as a special consultant to the president on the inspection of German aircraft technology. I expected to find the advancements that Germany led during World War II, but I was prepared to find the advantages Mac had provided. I had witnessed some of that in the hangars at Nordhausen. What I had seen was likely just the tip of the iceberg of what I would find at Langley. I suspected Jen was in for a few surprises of her own when the next generation of German rocketry arrived.

SECRETS

I watched as the train pulled away from the station in downtown Washington. There was a feeling of finality that I couldn't quite explain. We were both drained, and hit bottom physically, and mentally. The two weeks at the Outer Banks started a slow rebound, but we had not entirely come back to our peak capabilities. While everyone was so accepting of our story, and of us, no one else could understand what was going on inside our heads. To the outside world, we had put on a mask that hid our internal struggles with living in a page out of a history book. Aside from the obvious impact on history, maybe the mission planners knew how difficult it would be to adjust and live in a time so different from our own. I was only fooling myself if I thought this would all just work itself out.

The weather had taken a turn for the worse as I left the station. There was a torrent of water falling from the sky and dark, and ominous clouds were overhead. I wasn't the superstitious type, but it gave me a momentary pause. It was an eerie feeling that maybe something was going to happen to Jen or me. I brushed it off and made my way down to the field to get to Langley.

The flight was short and uneventful. We had waited for the storm to subside before taking off. The weather had improved in southern Virginia, and that unsettled feeling I had had was gone for now. The plane was crowded with an assortment of military and civilian personnel. I was dressed and was playing the role of a civilian. It would have been difficult to pass me off as an officer assigned to this project. Even with the new identities, the higher-ranking military brass might have started asking questions and poking around into my history. I was sure there were names of the notable and famous on this flight, but I couldn't place any of them.

It was down to business right away. Greeting us was a small team of high-ranking officers that escorted the group to an empty hangar. It was there that we each gave brief introductions then received a briefing on what we could expect and our obligations to keep secret the information we were given access to over the course of our stay. During the briefing, we were told that as part of the agreement with Germany, we would be provided access to the latest in German aviation advancements. I was eager to see up close what they had produced. What I saw would then give me a better read on the depth of technology transfer Mac had given to the Nazi regime.

Just before we headed to the hangar, the highest-ranking officer pulled me aside. "I hear you may have some deeper level of expertise on this subject matter. It is my understanding that you are here on behalf of the president and that you did intelligence gathering for us on the ground in Germany," he said.

"That's correct General. I am quite familiar with advanced aviation technology, and I am also a pilot."

"I doubt you have seen anything like this," he stated.

We progressed with the rest of the group to another hangar. The hangar was guarded, and as I looked down the line, several others appeared to have armed sentries protecting them. The massive hangar doors were closed, and we entered through another entryway. The general was right and wrong about a few things. I hadn't seen anything like this here in this time, but it did look strikingly familiar. It was a flying wing, but unlike the one I had found at Nordhausen, this seemed more advanced. It had the distinct lines of a B-2 stealth bomber. Looks might have been deceiving. This aircraft had the look of the B-2, but I doubted that its electronics were advanced beyond the primitive technology in any other fighter of the time. As I walked around, I saw that this undoubtedly was the handiwork and influence of Mac.

"This is incredible. Does it actually fly?" asked one of the fellow group members.

"Not only does it fly, but it is invisible," remarked the general.

"Invisible? What do you mean?" asked another member of the group. "Once this is airborne, it is impervious to detection by RADAR."

Upon closer inspection, my suspicions were correct. I noticed that there were odd things about this aircraft. Unlike the Horton Flying Wing I had seen and destroyed, this was far more advanced. The intake cowlings were above the wing with the engines embedded inside. The back of the engine exhaust had a ceramic nozzle intended to absorb heat. This would be effective against "heat-seeking" missiles, but those did not exist. The paint was also different. It had a dull, chalky appearance. It was a dark charcoal color with a tint of gray. My best guess was that this paint had a substantial amount of charcoal dust mixed in to absorb the RADAR waves. It would offer some protection, but not provide 100% of the stealth capability.

This beautiful plane was a marvel for this era. It was puzzling that with Mac's knowledge of aviation, decades ahead of mine, there wasn't anything significantly different or advanced beyond what I knew about aircraft technology. I surmised that it was likely just the level of technology the Germans could absorb, but it was an intriguing oddity.

"Follow me. There's more I want you to see," said the general.

We moved to another adjacent hangar, and this turned out to be a bigger surprise. There, was what appeared to be a modern-day fighter jet. Modern, that is, for my time. It had the lines of a Russian fighter with elements of the American F-15 and F-18 — twin engines, twin tails, and engines mounted internally adjacent to the fuselage. If this was for real, it was a game changer. If this was Mac's handiwork, he likely threw everything he knew into one hybrid design.

The general addressed us. "What you see is one of only four like it. The Germans were testing these and were just about ready to mass-produce them when circumstances prompted a change in plans. We have two of the four here. This assembled, ready-to-fly version, and one partially assembled. The bomber next door is only one of two. It was still in testing. Your mission is to help us determine the capabilities and usage of these formidable weapons. This fighter beats anything we have in our inventory hands down, but the Germans believe it is underpowered and can do more. They focused their time and energy on building more powerful jet engines. These aircraft, along with the brainpower in this room, will provide us a force the likes of which the world has never seen before in its history."

I climbed the small ladder next to the cockpit. The internal workings looked standard for the era. This might have been just little more than a pretty face on the same old base technology as previous prop-driven fighters. It reminded me of the Russian MIG 25 ruse that led to the American response of the F-15. We believed the Russians had created a game-changing high-performance aircraft. When in reality, it was just big engines on old technology. It could go fast but lacked agility. It wasn't nearly as capable as it appeared. Don't get me wrong on the where this was heading. If these aircraft were just half of what they seemed to be, it would be a revolutionary design advancement. The next giant evolutionary step would occur when microchips replaced transistors and transistors replaced the tube-based electronics in this aircraft. We were still some ways off from technology driving the machines of war.

There was an energy and enthusiasm in the hangar for what lay before us. It was a sense of domination rather than defense. The vision that Mac and the leaders of his era had for the future was on the cusp of coming to fruition. Oddly, what I had done to stop his intervention may have in the end only served to accelerate it.

It could have been that here in this hangar on the southeastern tip of Virginia that history would write that the seeds of a more devastating war started here. I was by no means a pacifist. I loved a strong military and believed it was a necessity. Here, when peace had its best chance, the first thoughts were strength now, then peace later. It was easy to see how civilizations started and endured wars since humans first picked up a club. Peace was, in reality, never a mutual concept based on trust, but rather one where the bigger club only created the illusion of peace.

There was one man who stood out in the crowd. He was a man not too much older than I. He was quite enamored with the aircraft and studied its lines and movable surfaces. I walked up and introduced myself. His name was Kelly Johnson. It gave me momentary pause. I shook his hand, and we talked extensively about the plane as we combed through its secrets. Kelly Johnson was an aviation legend. Only he didn't know it yet. From his designs and management would come the U-2, the SR-71, and many other famed aircraft of the Cold War.

Over the next few weeks, I developed a close working relationship with Kelly. We shared the same interests but came from differing backgrounds. His résumé for aviation engineering placed him or would put him, among the elite in developing breakthrough aircraft that would play a significant role in the decades ahead. I brought the pilot's perspective, and of course, my knowledge of aviation's role in future conflicts. On more than one occasion, I let slip some of that knowledge. The first time caught his attention. While looking over the German fighter, I made remarks about its design.

"The profile of this aircraft is very stealthy. It would have a small RADAR cross-section," I said.

"What did you say? Stealthy? Are you an engineer?" he asked.

I let him know that I was a pilot who had an interest in aviation design. This plane had more of a story to tell. Johnson was focused on the exhaust.

"This is by far the most unique aircraft I have ever seen," said Johnson. He went on.

"You see this? What do you suppose this is?

Johnson was pointing to the unique exhaust nozzles on the aircraft. I gave it a close look and recognized it immediately.

"This is a ceramic lining inside these nozzles. The intent is to absorb and reduce the heat or infrared signature of the plane. These movable nozzle flaps look like thrust vectoring capabilities to increase maneuverability," I remarked to Johnson.

"I'd like to meet the man who designed this. He has a brilliant mind. We've been working on a jet engine since 1938. This aircraft is years ahead of where we are today."

"Well," I said. "Perhaps the creator just had an active imagination or could see the future, much like Jules Verne. The big question, I suppose, is can it fly?"

It was the right question to ask. It would take a pilot with daring and skill to operate the thrust vectoring all manually. The wrong move would be akin to jamming the rudder pedals at high speed. It would rip this airframe apart.

"You're a pilot. Would you take this thing up?"

"Without question," I replied.

"Maybe you'll get a chance."

I wanted that chance. It was an unlikely scenario. The Army would bring in the best they had to test it. There would be only one person who had even flown a sophisticated fighter, and I was right here.

This man, Kelly Johnson, was the real genius in the room today. If only he knew that the design for this plane was an offspring of the pioneering work he would do decades ahead. At the end of day one, I kept my word to update the president. I typed a letter and proceeded to locate a mail pouch headed to DC. It would take a few days to get to the president's desk. I hoped he would read it and listen to my recommendation. The next few days were spent reviewing the unassembled plane. I asked Johnson what he thought of the structural integrity of the airframe. "Could it take the stress of supersonic speeds?"

"Most definitely. This material looks to be Pantal, the standard German metal comprised of aluminum with titanium used to harden it. It's strong. The Germans were adept at engineering tough and durable aircraft. This airframe appears up to the task of whatever stress is put on it. I bet this thing is not only fast but also highly maneuverable. There are already rumors that the Germans may have broken the sound barrier in a jet aircraft flying in a straight line, not a dive."

It hadn't flown yet, but if it checked out to be the real deal. It made me realize how close Mac had come to fulfilling his mission. In my version of World War II, the German Me-262 jet fighter was a game changer. It just came too late and too little to turn the tide of the war. If it had been produced earlier in mass numbers, it most likely would have spelled defeat for the Allies. Even lacking the computer technology, this fighter easily advanced the current state of aviation technology twenty, maybe thirty years ahead. We needed to get it in the air.

No sooner than Johnson and I finished going through the cabling to control the movable services did the general came in. "I just got word from the White House. The President wants you, Behrens, to take this plane up and test it out. I strongly recommended against it and wanted one of our men to fly it first. He's the chief, and those are his orders. You'll take it up in the morning. Don't make this one of those 'I told him so' moments. I hope you prove me wrong and him right."

"Congratulations! Better you than me!" exclaimed Johnson.

There was a bit of irony. Before this mission, I was headed to Edwards to be a test pilot for an advanced aircraft, and here I was fulfilling that dream. I was looking forward to getting back up in the air tomorrow. I knew nothing about its handling characteristics, but one thing I had over everyone else was a benchmark to compare to, my own experience in advanced jet fighters.

While most of the team focused their work on the unassembled plane, Johnson and I moved over to the test fighter. I climbed into the cockpit and familiarized myself with the layout and controls. It was different, but not by much. It was an odd mix of the old and new. I tested the flaps and moveable surfaces. Johnson and I looked extensively at how the thrust vectoring was designed on the other plane. For the first flight, I didn't plan to try it. We wanted to get the baseline performance and maneuvers down first, then stretch this bird and see what it could do.

As dawn broke the next day, the weather was perfect for flying. Skies were clear with the usual marine layer of condensation visible on the eastern horizon out over the ocean. There was no fear or trepidation about flying a new aircraft today. It was a certainty that the brass in charge of this program were nervous about the president's order to let a stranger fly the plane. If I was feeling just a little pressure, it was more about not letting him down.

At the hangar, the plane had already been rolled out. We spent an hour going over what was expected on this first flight. The orders were to go up and around a few times at slow speed, perform a few touch-and-go landings, and then slowly increase the speed and maneuvering. All in, I would be in the air for about ninety-minutes on this flight. I felt emboldened by the president's confidence and ready for this challenge. Of course, it helped that for all of its advancements, that it was still far inferior to the aircraft I was used to flying.

As I left the briefing, I walked over to Johnson. "Wish me luck," I said. "You got it!" replied Johnson.

With that, I proceeded to climb into the cockpit. Through all I had been through, I still had Beth's picture with me. I was alive, and in a way, she was with me every step of the way. Using what looked like a small notebook clip holder on the right side of the cockpit, I secured her photo. In one of the many paradoxes of time, I wondered if somewhere out there she was going about her life. I refocused back on the task at hand and looked over at the ground crew. I got the all clear to fire up the engines. As if test flying wasn't already dangerous, this would be the maiden flight of this aircraft. The design of this plane had to be an awe-inspiring sight for those on the ground, but it had to be the roar of those twin jet engines that sounded the arrival of the future of warfare.

For this first flight, we were relying on solid German engineering and their attention to detail. All was going smoothly as I taxied to the end of the runway. There was a steady, strong vibration running through the plane as those engines idled. I could feel the enormous power difference from the advanced Stuka I had brought back with me. As I received the all clear, I pushed the throttle forward, and the g-force of the thrust pushed me back in my seat. In just seconds, I hit takeoff velocity and pulled back on the stick. I kept the angle of attack at about forty-five degrees and held a steady climb out to ten thousand feet.

Once I hit altitude, I made a slow, sweeping turn back over the airfield. I made a few small maneuvers to check the aircraft's handling. It was responsive and crisp. It closely matched the modern fighters I was accustomed to flying. As requested, I made a few slow approaches to the runway, briefly touched down and powered back up. Each time I increased the power and angle of attack, I was getting more confident in the plane's abilities. On the last pass down the runway, I retracted the gear and flew low and fast down the runway. I pulled the throttle back to the max. The engines were thundering, and I soared at 300 knots over the airfield. It was increasing to 400, then 500 knots, about 575 miles per hour. Faster than the ME-262s reported top speed. I pulled back sharply on the joystick, and she climbed vertically, shooting up to twenty thousand feet in an instant, but I wasn't finished yet. If we wanted to test this bird, we would have to know what she truly was capable of achieving.

I made another wide turn and climbed an additional ten thousand feet. I positioned the aircraft to fly a straight heading that would cross the airfield and head out over the ocean. Once again, maxing the throttle, I was looking to hit the magic triple sixes on the airspeed. Six hundred and sixty-six knots was enough to break the sound barrier. Keeping it true and on course, I watched as the airspeed rapidly climbed, five hundred, and then six hundred. I felt the stick shaking, and the plane began to shudder a bit, and then I glanced down at the gauges. We hit seven hundred knots before topping out at just over eight hundred knots. This remarkable aircraft had a top-end of nine hundred miles per hour. Through all of this, I had burned a significant amount of fuel and set a course back to the field.

I came in for a soft landing, touching down gently about a third of the way down the runway. On the way back to the hangar, I was beaming at the flight. For a moment, I had the sensation of being back in my time. There was no doubt that this felt like an aircraft from my era. I also realized that what I was sitting in would change aviation's part in the next conflict. There would be an all-out arms race to dominate the skies. Historians from my day might argue that the Luftwaffe dominated the skies early in World War II, but ended up losing the war. As crucial as airpower was, it was the strategy, overwhelming brute force, and the side that made the fewest mistakes that eventually won out.

I taxied back to the hangar where everyone was waiting and brought the aircraft to a stop. I shut down the plane, unclipped Beth's picture, and put it back in my flight suit. There was a definite level of excitement and high energy from those who had witnessed the plane's performance.

"My God, that was unbelievable. I had my doubts, but this is for real!" exclaimed the general.

"That was the boom heard 'round the world. The opening shot in a new era of airpower," said Kelly Johnson.

"What was your top speed?" asked the general.

"I topped out at about nine hundred miles an hour. It might have been able to do just a little bit more, but I felt it was getting close to its limit," I replied.

"You did it. You proved that we could go faster than the speed of sound without damaging the aircraft or the pilot. More importantly, you proved that this thing could fly. You handled it like a pro up there. I will have the team go over the aircraft and check it out to make sure everything is intact. No structural defects or anomalies. If it looks good, we'll schedule more test flights with different mission profiles."

We did schedule more flights, each more ambitious with different configurations. Some with simulated bomb loads on the underwing pylons, some with external fuel tanks to increase the range. While I was focused on the fighter, now known officially as the FA-1, codename "Eagle," another team got the flying wing bomber in the air. I sat in as the copilot on the first three flights to get a feel for its performance. It would become the B-1, codename "Bear." After a month of rigorous testing, we regrouped to review and assess the findings. It was no surprise that there was unanimous consensus to start a program to build the aircraft here in America.

"We have two choices, as I see it," said the general. "We can buy these from the Germans, or we can build these here. I say we build them here. Johnson, do you think Lockheed can tackle this and replicate this plane?"

"Yes, General," Johnson replied. "Not only can we build this, but we can also make it even better!"

I found it ironic that Mac's mission to advance German military technology and eventually broker an alliance with the United States had come to pass. Inadvertently, I played a significant role bringing the two together, perhaps faster than with Mac's plan. Did I wonder if somehow that was part of the project all along? Could I be the pawn that finished what Mac had started? Was everything a lie from the beginning, and somehow Mac knew he had to die for me to carry out the rest of the mission? Eerily, it was his plan that seemed on track, not mine. It would just be a matter of time before this new alliance would create a pair of world powers unlike anything history had ever witnessed.

As much as I wanted to stay on and keep flying, I had to get back to Washington to meet with the president. After that meeting, I would be headed to New Mexico to join Jen. Before I left Langley, we had a group photo taken with the team in front of each aircraft and with both parked together. As I stood next to Kelly Johnson while the pictures were being shot, he asked me to join him in California. "We're going to build these things, and I would love to have you join our team. I'll build them, you test fly them!" he said.

"Let me give it some thought. I have a significant other who is a rocket engineer working out in New Mexico. We were hoping to get settled and lead a normal life at some point. We hoped that point would be sooner rather than later."

"Bring her with you. We'll hire her for the rocket program we are working on."

"I'll talk it over with her, and I have to see what the president might want me to do. I'm not an engineer, but I do have some keen insight that could make this aircraft even better."

"Fair enough," said Johnson. "It is a standing offer."

Johnson's offer was tempting. I wasn't sure where we fit in this new world. Were we destined to be "fortune tellers" for the government? Perhaps we would serve in roles that amounted to being endless nomads that functioned as the extended eyes and ears of the president. The world's destiny was its own to choose and not for any prognosticator to decide for it. In any era, I felt duty-bound to serve. It would be up to the president to determine which path I would follow.

EQUILIBRIUM

April showers may have been the rule, but in the time I was at Langley, our weather held out. We managed to accomplish quite a bit in our task to analyze the German fighter and bomber prototypes. By the time I arrived back in Washington, it was already early May of 1945. It was well into spring, and the air was fresh and the sky bright. I felt the energy brought on by the vibrant colors and smells of nature's annual renewal cycle. It was invigorating. Back at the house, I opened the windows to let the spring air clear the musty smell that had accumulated while I was gone. I sat down to catch my breath and relax. The only piece of mail in our box was a telegram from Jen. "Made it to New Mexico. All is well. There is lots of excitement here. Hope all is well with your trip to Langley. Hurry over. Missing you lots. Love, Jen."

There was a measure of guilt I felt in reading her note. Here I was carrying through time and tribulation a picture of my soulmate, a woman I would eternally long for, but would never be able to see again. Then there was Jen, a remarkable woman who had suffered hardships that would have broken anyone. Yet, she survived. My feelings were torn between the two. One woman, I knew well for a long time, the other I had barely scratched the surface. Jen was remarkable in her own way. She was smart, intelligent, and surprisingly, a lot like Beth. On my way over to meet the president to give him my report, I stopped at the Western Union office and sent Jen a telegram. "Glad you made it OK. Langley was interesting, to say the least. Got some flying in while I was down there. There's much more to tell. Headed your way in a few days. Looking forward to seeing you. Miss you too. Love, Jake."

There were no lies, no stretching of the truth for convenience in my note. I had come to the fork in the road and needed to reconcile those feelings. I determined that right here and right now, I had fallen for Jen. It didn't mean I loved Beth any less, and just like many lost loves, it was time to let go as best I could. There was more to sort out, but time would take care of that for us.

I arrived at the White House and waited just a few minutes to see the president. When it was time, I was in his office, and he got from behind his desk to greet me. "I read the report from Langley. You really put on a show. For that group of warmongers to be impressed, I know it must have been something. I want to hear your thoughts. You know more than anyone the real story. Tell me what you are thinking," said the president.

"It's hard to gauge. It's not supposed to be this advanced for this time. It is capable, and I believe it will only get more and more capable as we continue to refine it. In my era, these things usually work out to have one country take the lead and another quickly catch up. The equilibrium and balance of power are never as far off as it seems. This aircraft's design and thought process is twenty-five years ahead of its time. However, as slick as it is on the outside, the internal workings are about right for the time, maybe just slightly ahead. Don't get me wrong, against prop-driven fighter and bombers it would have a decisive advantage."

"I see. There are those who see us, our country, as imperialists, keeping the peace by dominating the world to make sure it lasts. They see those German wonder weapons as the road to that peace. They believe that if we mass produce these weapons and build the rockets and bombs, they are testing in New Mexico, we will be ready to take out Russia and China. Do you believe that?"

"I know someone who did believe that was in the best interest of future generations. These things never last. Adolf Hitler's thousand-year Reich is no more. The Roman Empire came as close as any country in history to rule the world. Where are they today? Even our country will be tested and pushed to the brink of extinction despite having the best and brightest."

"Do you have a suggestion?" asked the president.

"The answer is not to lay down our weapons and carry the olive branch of peace in extended arms waiting to be slaughtered. I think we prepare for equilibrium between the world's great powers. It's my guess that at any time, it will be the norm. As long as there are men and power, there will be proxy wars that are fronts for conflict between the larger rivals. It is unavoidable and inevitable. We must be strong and prepared, but as a defensive measure, and go on the offensive when needed to protect the helpless who can't help or defend themselves. Those who try to overplay their hand are the ones who that usually end up getting more than they bargained for."

"All of this will be work for the next president. I have decided I will not run in '48. I plan to go back to New York City. I will remain active in politics, but I feel my work here will be done when this term ends. There is still much time and much to do before then. I received a call the other day from Bob Gross, the President of Lockheed. He said he wants you to join his team. His people were impressed with you at Langley. Is that something that might interest you?"

"It might. Jen and I are looking to get back to a normal life," I said.

"Me too. I've been in this game too long, and it's time to get my own normal life too. If you decide to take it, I would like you to do one more task for me. Go to New Mexico and check on the rocket work. There is a test of a new device planned for July I would like you to witness. Send me your thoughts on what you think. Then go lead that normal life. The country has to chart our own course from here on out, and you must do the same."

"Thank you, Mr. President. I will certainly do that."

"Before you go. I have some of the world's leading scientists meeting in the other room to talk about the special project going on out in New Mexico. One of them I asked to look over the notes of Dr. Scheel and give his opinion. He's waiting to come in and talk to us. His name is Albert Einstein, a scientist."

"I am quite familiar with the works of Einstein. He is a man famous in any time."

If anyone could understand the secrets of Dr. Scheel's work on time travel, it would be Albert Einstein. Scheel's work is likely an expansion of Einstein's work. Confirmation from him would undoubtedly validate our presence here, but also may shed light on could we find a way home, back to our time.

The president left the Oval Office to get the esteemed Professor Einstein. It gave me a moment to look around and wonder about the men in this time that would be next to lead the country. So much in history seemed to have changed, and yet so many things remained very familiar. When the president returned, I was in awe. Standing there was the iconic professor with his distinct hair and mustache. We sat in the center of the office. The president sat in the lead chair and the professor and I opposite each other.

The president spoke first. "Professor Einstein, I was wondering if you could share your insight on the papers I asked you to review on time travel by Dr. Scheel."

Einstein replied in English but with an unmistakable German accent.

"I have read the works of Dr. Scheel and find his theories on how to time travel quite thought-provoking. It is consistent with what I believe and what I have previously written. It is possible that one-day people might be able to travel back and forth between the future and the past. While it is possible in theory and on paper, it would take an enormous amount of energy to execute."

I already knew that time travel was possible; I was the proof of Scheel's theories. What I really wanted to know was could you go from the past to the future. "Professor Einstein, if someone were able to travel in time to the past, could they get back to the future?" I asked.

"I want to make something clear that is a common misperception in your thinking. There is no such thing as time. It is a mirage, an illusion that we humans have created. Space and time exist as one and the same. To answer your question, yes, you could go from the past to the future and from the future to the past. The method to do this does not, and likely will not exist, but it is theoretically possible.

"It is a hard thing to understand but let me try with this simple example. Think of space and time like this. Each moment is like a frame on a strip of film. As everything in the universe moves through space, it leaves behind those frames and adds more as it continues to move. If there were a man standing over there, and I dropped a pen on the floor, all four of us would see it happen at the exact same moment. If that man were walking away from us looking back, he would think he is seeing the pen drop at the same time, but it is not. There is the slightest change in space and time. He can't detect it, and neither can we. It is so minuscule as to be imperceptible. However, keep moving that man further and further away, far away in the galaxy. As he looks back, he doesn't see the pen dropping on the floor, he starts seeing the frames on these filmstrips in the past. The farther he gets away, the farther back he is able to see into the past. To travel there, he would just need a method to locate the frame he wanted and go there. We experience what we call time continuing to move forward. The man in the distance does not. If he were to turn around and head back towards us he would start seeing the frames move forward. At some point, he would pass where we dropped the pen and start seeing a future he had yet to experience. To him, it would be the future."

Professor Einstein's description of how space and time were linked was elegant but left me with little prospect that I would ever be able to return home. The president seemed intrigued but was lost in the far-reaching theories of Einstein. If I read his analogy correctly, traveling from a far sophisticated future with the technology to develop time travel could send people back to an era where the technology did not exist to send them back. To go back and forth in time meant you needed the technology to be in both places. You could not reach from the future to the past to pull someone forward. Such was the circumstance I found myself. It was of small comfort that the malfunctioning tracking chip placed in my arm would have been of little use anyway. Einstein continued to talk throughout the evening. I found it fascinating, but President Farley seemed to tire of Einstein's continuous dialogue on how the universe worked. When he finished, the president and I thanked him for his time. I spent a few more minutes speaking with the president.

"You did a courageous thing back in Berlin. The world owes you a debt that you were never given credit for doing. You might have saved the free countries of the world from a maniacal dictator, or at the least, another Great War. We can't repay your service, but we can let you go and enjoy the freedom you fought to preserve. Please let me know what I can do for you. Don't forget to send me your thoughts on what is happening down in New Mexico. I want your perspective on it. I could use your advice."

I left the White House wondering if I would ever return again or ever see the president again.

I took what little we had and boarded the train for New Mexico. Our vagabond existence might have finally been coming to an end. Within the space of a few months, we had rolled across Europe to England to Washington, and now to New Mexico. I was longing for that quiet time we experienced on the Outer Banks of North Carolina. The isolation there gave us time to decompress, but only briefly. As the president remarked, it was getting to the time where we needed to leave the future in the hands of those who would shape it, not us who would rightly or wrongly influence it.

The train rolled across what seemed like a vast empty space of the American Midwest. Nothing but fields of grain as far as one could see occupied a landscape that appeared to be devoid of people. The only exception was the small towns and cities we stopped at along the way. I wondered how the absence of the war and the missing baby boom generation would affect the transformation of the country. I guessed it would somehow slow it down, which might not be a bad thing. After a long trek across America, the train finally arrived at Albuquerque, New Mexico. It was hot, dry, and dusty when I stepped off the train onto the platform. It was a small inconvenience of the era. No rental cars or instant communication. I had hoped Jen had received my telegram. If not, I would be taking a bus down to Alamogordo. It was then that I thought I heard my name being called. No sooner than I turned around was Jen on me. She hugged me with both her arms around my neck as she kissed me.

"I missed you so much," she said. She went on to say, "I have got a lot to catch you up on. What is going on down here is quite amazing, and quite frightening."

"I've got a few stories to tell you also," I said.

"I've got a car I borrowed from the facility. Catch me up on the way back down to the range."

I was quite interested in what Jen had found out about the advancing missile technology. I'm guessing she wasn't too surprised since she might have had a hand in the designs back in Germany. I laid out my encounter with the advanced German fighter designs at Langley. While still underpowered and lacking advanced avionics by my era standards, it was formidable, and only improving. I also let her know that we had a standing job offer to go to California and work at Lockheed. It was a chance to settle down and get out lives on track. She seemed mildly interested, perhaps torn between the opportunity here and the one out at Lockheed. It was then her turn to describe what she saw at the missile test range. She confirmed that the rumored V-4 was not a myth but was indeed being tested. She had already known of the design, but they had kept her sheltered from anything more advanced on the drawing board.

It was then that she told of something new that she had not even heard rumored before seeing it at Alamogordo. "I saw something being assembled for a test. It was an enormous rocket by V-2 standards. The V-4 with its four engines had increased the rocket's range to twelve hundred miles. It was a gargantuan leap in the targets it could reach. This new rocket I saw had two stages with two solid rockets attached to the side. It looked like the V-4 as the first stage and an improved V-2 type for the second stage. That V-2-looking stage on top might even have been something with a solid rocket motor. I'm guessing if it worked, it would easily reach a sub-orbital height. I would say the range would be two thousand to twenty-five hundred miles. The other thing is that it could be a test to lift a heavy payload, say a nuclear warhead, maybe more."

"What is the word on the nuclear bomb test?" I asked.

"From what I heard, they are close. There is a team working out at a site about thirty miles from where we are testing the rockets."

"The timing fits. If they stay on track for history, it will happen next month, but everything we have seen so far is well ahead of schedule."

The next day, I went with Jen to the missile work site. I was introduced as an observer sent by the president. Jen pulled me over to meet the man in charge of the rocket design work. I approached from the back, and as he turned, I recognized him immediately.

"Dr. von Braun, I would like you to meet someone," she said.

"It's a pleasure to meet you, Dr. von Braun," I said as I shook his hand.

"Isn't this magnificent?" he said, pointing to the rocket. "One day, this will carry men to the moon and stars."

"What are you calling this one?" I asked.

"This is the A-6, for the six motors it will use to liftoff," replied von Braun.

I was certainly no rocket engineer, but I knew enough to recognize what I was seeing. Much like the F-1 fighter at Langley, this rocket technology had advanced beyond its years, and like the F-1, was capable, but still lacking modern, sophisticated electronics. It was an impressive rocket. Mac was no rocket engineer, and the design was not of his or Jen's making. It got here more quickly because Mac's contribution was that he was capable of was focusing the Nazis in the right direction. By not letting them get distracted with ground wars, he managed to channel their enormous talents and engineering skills on advancing the weapons of mass destruction. I wasn't capable of making a judgment of which was the worse option. Mac's intervention and escalation of the global war machine or if the war itself had it come to pass.

It seemed saving the millions of innocent lives was the price to be paid for letting these machines of war advance. Perhaps they would keep the peace and act as a deterrent, as they had done in my time. However, it remained to be seen if they were a deterrent or if they would be used as offensive weapons as Mac had planned. Time would tell.

It had only been a week that I had been observing the missile work. Jen was right. Even I could recognize the capabilities of these rockets. The goal seemed obvious: Build something that could carry an atomic bomb to a distant location. I was not sure they had enough range or precision yet to make it all work, but as the Germans had shown us, there were ways to get around that. There were loose lips all over this project. I heard mention of launching them from ships. Another mentioned putting it on the back of a submarine. There seemed no shortage of ideas to get this weapon deployed.

As another day on the missile work came to a close, the word came that those working on the rockets we were invited to witness the test of a new weapon early the next morning. Jen and I knew what was coming. It was 2:30 am when the bus picked us up at our dorm. We rode the bus for only a short while before coming to a stop. As we disembarked, we were handed a set of goggles. As I held them to the headlights of the bus, I could see they were very dark glass, welder's glass. Speakers were hanging from hastily erected poles. A voice came over the loudspeaker saying that the test would be conducted at 4 am. The winds were calm, and the skies were clear. There were a million stars visible in this dark desert sky.

While we were waiting for the test, the man leading the missile program came by and introduced two men responsible for designing the weapon we were about to witness. "I would like you to meet Maria Behrens and her husband John Behrens. Maria is an engineer working on the rocket program, and John is a special envoy from the president." It was the first time we had been introduced as husband and wife, although we were not married yet. "This is J. Robert Oppenheimer and Richard Feynman. Mr. Oppenheimer is the genius behind what we will see tonight," he said.

"It is a pleasure to meet you, Mr. and Mrs. Behrens. You must be one smart lady to be working on the rocket program!" said Oppenheimer.

He seemed quite smitten with her. It might have been unusual for him to shake hands with such a capable woman in this time. As they moved on, I whispered in Jen's ear. "How did that Mr. and Mrs. Behrens sound?"

"I think it had a nice ring to it," she said.

The 4am time had come and gone without further announcement. Finally, at 4:35am, we were told to take our positions. The test would be conducted in fifteen minutes. We had positioned ourselves at a spot along the row of four-foot sandbags. In all, there were hundreds of people here, and most were packed several deep behind the sandbags. Some were seated on bleachers, and others were just standing in open areas. I doubted any of these witnesses were expecting what would happen next — not even Oppenheimer and Feynman.

At 4:45, the announcer came on again asking everyone to put their goggles on. The test would proceed in five minutes. A few minutes later, the one-minute warning, then thirty-seconds, then fifteen, then five, four, three, two, one. On cue, there was a brilliant flash as if the midday sun were above; the air was quiet and dead silent. Through the dark glasses, it was apparent that this was something extraordinary. The flash faded quickly, and there in the distance was the rising column of what appeared to be fire. Then, there it was, the familiar mushroom-shaped cloud. As I stared at the developing and growing aftereffects of the explosion, there came what at first sounded like a distant rumbling. It grew louder and louder. The ground shook. Many of those viewing the blast were trembling with fear. I lifted my goggles and looked at the terrified faces in the crowd. They had just gotten another physics lesson: first, the effects of splitting the atom and second, how much faster light travels then sound. They seemed more frightened of the second, and most probably did not understand the ramifications of the first. In the bright light of the world's first nuclear test, Jen and I had witnessed the dawn of a new era. The world would never be the same.

It would turn out that the bomb was three times more potent than predicted. As the bomb's effects had grown in size, many had wondered when it would stop. Had America created a single weapon that could destroy the world? Well, not entirely, but my prediction would be that soon there would be enough of these to accomplish just that purpose. Barely a week had gone by when news came that the Russians had successfully tested their atomic bomb. As fate would have it, the best-kept secret in America turned out to be the worst kept secret in the rest of the world.

It was likely a combination of leaks from German defectors combined with espionage that led to the Russians' rapid development of their atomic bomb. Leveraging the atom to create a weapon was not the big secret anyone thought it to be. In my era, it was only the German invasion of Russia that was responsible for delaying the Soviet atom bomb project. As that invasion did not materialize in this timeline, Soviet work on the bomb progressed rapidly and undeterred. I suspected I would see more and more of the unforeseen consequences of good intentions.

It was with some hesitancy that I convinced Jen to leave the rocket work behind and chart a new course in our lives. The world had reached a strange equilibrium like it had seen many times before in its history. Each side would play a leapfrog-and-catch-up game from here on out. The world would teeter on the brink of a nuclear trigger for the rest of this planet's existence. Nature and nations were all fighting for balance. It seemed a universal law that imbalance would not be sustained for long without dire consequences. For all the twists and turns of time and all the plans to change the future by altering the past, it seemed history would only bend and flex, but not succumb so easily to change.

DAYS GONE BY

I wrote my last letter to the president before leaving New Mexico for California. The game had changed, and all the best-laid plans were now obsolete. The world may never see a direct conflict between the nuclear superpowers, but rather a series of conventional wars fronted by other actors. I stressed the importance of not letting an arms race bankrupt our country in pursuit of peace through domination. Instead, take care of the people, the economy, and always be prepared, but do not be the aggressor. Lastly, I thanked him for his belief in us. For as fantastic as our story sounded, we were grateful for all he had done for us. It was thanks to his faith that we had any future at all.

Jen seemed in her element working on the rockets here in the New Mexico desert. Von Braun must have thought he had come across the smartest woman on the planet. Her knowledge of advanced rocketry, thanks to seventy-plus years of future rocket technology knowledge, far eclipsed his background.

We could have stayed here in the hot and dusty southwest, but we would have just had the rocket program. Heading out west, we would have choices and things we both wanted to achieve waiting for us. It was undoubtedly one of the advantages of our lives since Jen, and I had come back. We were nomads with maximum mobility in search of a place to put down roots. We had no real belongings and could move freely around the country to wherever we wanted to go. It was both a blessing and a burden. The longest we had been together in one place was the two weeks at the Outer Banks. For us, taking up Kelly Johnson on his offer to work on his new advanced projects research team was the right option. We boarded the train that would take us west to Los Angeles.

When we stepped off the train in L.A., Johnson was there to meet us. I had telegrammed him to let him know we would be happy to join his team. He vigorously shook my hand and gave us a warm welcome.

"I'm glad you decided to come out here and join us. We are going to be working on some exciting things, and you will get to fly them. This must be the little lady. I have heard some great things about you from the team at Alamogordo. We are so glad you came along for the ride, too!"

It took about two hours to make the drive from the train station in Los Angeles to the site at Palmdale. It was a warm August day in L.A. that got hotter as we worked our way towards the dry lakebeds of California. The location of Lockheed's advanced weapons was a place that looked very much like the desert of New Mexico we had just left behind. Johnson then took us on a tour of the operations, paying particular attention to several huge hangars. Inside the first were several jet fighters. "This is the P-80 Shooting Star I designed," said Johnson.

It was a straight-wing fighter with engines along each side of the fuselage. I knew from the moment I saw it that even if time had never been altered, this aircraft was already obsolete. Johnson went on to say.

"I thought I had something here until I saw those German fighters. I am going to design and build a whole new fighter from the ground up. This thing has barely flown, and it looks outdated and obsolete. I talked to those government people at Langley before I left. The Germans have agreed to ship a few more of those fighters to the U.S., and we are going to get a complete one. I'll start by fine-tuning one of those. We've got a few new British-supplied jet engines that should be more powerful. I'd like to fit those in and have you give them a run. I lost a pilot last year testing those new General Electric I-40 jet engines when the blades on the turbine came apart and destroyed the aircraft. He complained those engines couldn't match those of the Brits. It looks like we have some catching up to do to perfect what the Germans developed. Maybe you want to take this up later and give me your thoughts compared to this fighter you flew at Langley."

"Absolutely. I'm looking forward to helping you with this effort and testing these aircraft. You know, this might still be used as a trainer. Or perhaps if it were redesigned with swept delta-type wings," I replied.

"I think you're right. I'll try that."

I looked over at Jen. I knew what she was probably thinking, that she would be the first person to become a widow before she ever officially got married. These first-generation jet aircraft were dangerous, but I had a bit more experience flying jet fighters than anyone else on the planet at the moment. I felt pretty confident I could handle anything that came along.

The next day, we found a house in nearby Palmdale and settled in for what would be a long trek to the future. That day and the days that followed started a long and fulfilling chapter in our lives that would last the next twenty years here in California. I had told Kelly Johnson that I would need a week before I started. I put that week to good use. Jen and made the two-hour drive to Santa Barbara, and as the sun set over the Pacific, we were married on the beach.

Something that had started as an encounter on a train headed for a German concentration camp became a love affair. I truly loved her, and her spirit. There were only two great loves in my life, one separated by fate and another born of destiny. We spent the week just being alone, enjoying sunsets on the beach and afternoon rides along the Pacific coast. Over the days, we reflected momentarily on the past we knew, to guide us on how we should approach our future. This was our time now, and our life. We wanted to raise a family and build on the original promise of Project Töten Zeit, to fix the mistakes of the past and make the future a better place.

When we returned to Palmdale, Kelly Johnson was already hard at work. It seemed that the Germans had ignited the creative genius we all knew he had buried somewhere. He had sketched new designs and was working with General Electric on requirements for new engines. He and I collaborated closely over the next few years. He would design them, and I would fly them. We made a great team. I sparingly used my knowledge to improve his designs, but I was always careful not to tip the balance too far. Jen began her work on the missile design and rocket development. She was passionate about rocketry and space travel. It was another thing we had in common, a desire to reach space.

Her career would be temporarily cut short. On January of 1948, our first son James was born. Jen wanted to stay home and raise him. She relished the chance to spend time with our son. I think it was the softer side of her that was finally able to let go and come out. Gone was the hard-driving woman with nerves built of steel, and here was the doting mom content in this world. I kept on flying, and Jen would occasionally make visits to the rocket program where her insights were always welcomed.

President Farley stayed true to his word and did not seek reelection, but instead supported an old friend of his, Harry Truman, a senator from Missouri. Truman would pull an upset victory to become the nation's 35th president. It was the first time I had seen history, as I knew it, try to pull itself back in line. I recognized that this close to the impact of the changes in time brought on by Project Töten Zeit, while substantial, had little effect on the familiar political players of the time. They were already in place when the changes began. However, I knew a multiplier effect was coming. The fifty to sixty million people who would have lost their lives in World War II were now alive. Their impact, as well as that of their children and their children's children, would only increase exponentially as time went on.

The world around was also changing in ways we could have, and in some could not have, foreseen. There was no "Iron Curtain," no Berlin Wall, but

Germany was feared among its fellow European neighbors as well as those countries to the east, like Russia. While Hitler's death led to the uncovering of several atrocities, none reached the level of what would have occurred had Hitler lived. This freak twist of fate allowed the Nazi party to weather the storm and remain in control minus Hitler.

The new Nazi regime was led by a predominantly military contingent that didn't necessarily support the Nazi ideology of an Aryan race. However, they continued to promote the image of strength and fear that Germany now projected around the world. The fact that following the death of Hitler, Germany quickly aligned with the United States on a military and technology sharing alliance only led to more unease and tension in the region. Battle-tested leaders forged in war would not exist outside of Germany. The Eisenhowers, Pattons, Bradleys, McArthurs, and their kind who honed their skills on the beaches of Normandy, in the seas of the South Pacific, or in the trenches of Germany would only lead paper armies and navies in mythological "what if" war exercises.

Power imbalances in geographic regions, along with differences between political and religious philosophies, had always caused tensions to rise in areas around the globe. In one of his frequent letters, former President Farley remarked that he was concerned that the "arbiters of peace were no more than wolves carrying an olive branch in one hand and a knife in the other." He believed that even his handpicked successor, current President Harry Truman, could be persuaded to wage peace through war with quick, decisive blows at the enemy.

It was a strategy reminiscent of Hitler's blitzkrieg approach. Peace, it seems, was an ever-elusive mirage. The closer you got to it, the further away in the distance it appeared to move. My greatest fear was that the next war might be worse than the one we had avoided. This next battle would have more frightening weapons with more destructive power than all the conventional bombs in anyone's inventory. In the years that followed, the former president was a frequent letter writer and would on occasion pick up the phone and call, just to talk about the current state of affairs or check on the family. I had made a lifelong friend without ever realizing the connection and belief he had in me.

There was irony and a ring of truth that the famous quote regarding history repeating itself was truer than it was false. The sparing of millions of Russian lives, the lives of the Jews in Europe, the countless millions who would live and bear children, they would now live in a world where a second global war was never fought. It was a world where sixty million living human beings that would have died as a heinous byproduct of war were now alive. I wrestled with the dynamics of this new world and felt the pangs of guilt over my contributions to it. I never believed I made a mistake in what I had done to end Mac's absurd plan. However, as I watched events unfold, I couldn't help but wonder if his strategy wasn't as irrational as I had first thought. I couldn't have let millions die, but stopping Mac's plan at its midway point could have led to the death of millions more in future conflicts. Like Jen and I, it was now up to the world to decide what course it would take. Still, it haunted me.

Harry Truman, while revered later in the history I knew, this time around had an uneventful four years in office. Midway through his term in 1950, our second son Matthew was born. In the absence of World War II, Truman lacked the credit for its final victory. In a way, it would be his good fortune. He would not have to carry the angst and notoriety of being the first leader of a nation to use an atomic weapon in war. Challenged by his peers in the Democratic Party, he sensed defeat and withdrew from running in 1952. He slipped quietly from view.

The split left the party fragmented and cleared the way for a Republican victory. Thomas Dewey, who lost in his previous attempt at the presidency, won this time. That year would see the birth of our last child, a daughter named Leigh Anne. Three years into Dewey's term as President in 1955, former Vice President Cordell Hull died of sarcoidosis at the age of 84. Sarcoidosis was an incurable ailment that caused a series of growths in his lungs, which eventually led to his death. Just another three years after Hull's death came news that Claude Bowers had died from leukemia at the age of 79. In the short span of twelve years, two of the three key players who knew our secret were now gone.

Throughout Dewey's term, he proved an honest and effectual leader, but his ideology served only to escalate the "Cold War." His tone was fervently anti-communist. He was a believer in the "domino effect." If one country fell to communism, others would follow. It would be that approach that would lead America into wars that I hoped could be avoided this time around, first Korea, and then Vietnam. It would be up to the next president to see if the repeating cycle of history could be stopped.

Jen and I were often bewildered at the changes in history that were so strange to us, but also so familiar. I was not anywhere near Einstein's level of insight into the underpinnings of our world, but I often thought of what he said in that meeting in the Oval Office. The universe was indeed a strange place, and I wondered if there was some pre-planned destiny awaiting all of us that we had little chance of changing. Yet, I had done it. I had changed the fate of millions, but would time try to fix it? In very odd ways it seemed to be doing just that very thing. While Dewey was not Eisenhower, he was a two-term Republican. For history to right itself, a Kennedy would need to follow a two-term Republican. Here again, it happened. A senator from Massachusetts, Joseph Kennedy Jr., successfully won the Presidency and appointed his younger brother Jack as attorney general. The avoidance of

World War II spared the life of the oldest Kennedy son and allowed his father's destiny to be fulfilled.

The 1960 election marked a changing tone in the country. Even though I knew it was coming, it still surprised me. Maybe it wasn't so much the end of the war in the 40s or the baby boom that followed. Perhaps it was just time for a transition in history. It was an evolution of the mind and the progression of new ideas that was fostering change. In 1960, I was now 44 and Jen 47. Our children were now 13, 11, and 9. Time had passed so quickly. With the blessing of Kelly Johnson, I left Lockheed to form my own company. I thought for a fleeting moment of entering politics to further foster change but considered it too much of a risk. There were still those who might recognize us from Germany, England, or Washington, and who might raise questions about our past. Lurking somewhere could be government insiders who knew who we were and could try to harm the children or us. It was a chance we could not take at the moment.

My company was called Behrens Aerospace, and with the help of Kelly Johnson, we became a supplier of parts and technology to Lockheed. As we grew, we expanded our reach to other aerospace companies. The kids were well on their way through school, which provided Jen time to spend at the company. She was an enormous asset. She spent time consulting with Lockheed engineers on rocket development and helped us create our company's rocket parts and engines. Our firm specialized in design work along with the building of airframes, composites, and rockets. In just a short time, we had built a successful company with a growing employee base. It was providing Jen and me with more and more time to spend with the kids on long summer vacations. It was my hope that one day they would run the company while Jen and I found a quiet place to retire and finally watch the world go by.

As time went on, we needed that place. The 60s were as turbulent here as they were the first time around. The "red scare" dragged the country into endless wars. The technology had changed, which only served to make each conflict deadlier. Fortunately, the use of a nuclear solution was withheld, but many lives were still lost. As the middle 60s approached, our children were coming of age. In 1965, our oldest James entered the Air Force Academy. His brother Matthew followed him in 1967. Our youngest daughter took a different path and followed in her mother's footsteps, studying as an aerospace engineer. At the same time, the civil rights work that James Farley and his predecessors had worked so hard for had stalled in the 50s and early 60s, but had finally gotten on track as another decade turned.

The space race turned out to be more of a crawl. It was the Russians' "October surprise," first with Sputnik and then with the first man in space, which led to the American charge to the moon, culminating in those first historic steps by Neil Armstrong on July 20, 1969. Here, even with better technology, the focus was on the militarization of space. The moon was not seen as an object of exploration, but of conquest. Americans would finally reach the moon first, but only to find out that economic and political issues here at home would place conquest of the heavens on the back burner, at least for now.

At the midpoint of the 70s, our children were all married. Jen and I sold the company we had founded to Lockheed. It would operate as a wholly owned subsidiary, and we remained engaged as consultants, but only part-time. We retired back east and bought a sprawling summer compound on the coast of Maine, and a winter retreat in North Carolina. The beautiful Maine house was perched on a rocky cliff where we watched the sunrise each morning over the ocean. We named it "Belle Futuro." It meant "Beautiful Future." It was a partly a tribute to the time we spent at "Belle Chance" at Camp Springs Field, and to the original mission in which we both played a part.

Jen loved the peaceful and soothing sounds of the ocean crashing against the rocks below. She cherished the crisp changing of the seasons. The sudden arrival of the fall and winter seasons was a stark departure from our years in California. The house was an annual summer and sometimes Christmas retreat where we all gathered. It would become the pseudo-headquarters for the family. A place that was a sanctuary for the children and grandchildren to come whenever they wanted. That same year, our first grandchild Andrew arrived, followed in 1980 by Scott. Those were James' and his wife Mary's children. Our son Matthew and his wife Marsha had three children: Kyle, Anne, and John, born in '80, '82, and '85. Our daughter Leigh would bear one child, Mark born in 1986.

The year 1986 was a bit strange for me. It was the year I was born in another time and another place. Somewhere, I believed, the two of us now existed at the same time. In another year, if all held true, Beth would be born. I was both curious to know how it would all work out, but the days were growing shorter. The twenty years we spent relaxing here in Maine were not enough to slow the march of time. Einstein remarked that time did not really exist, but as the years went by I could attest that it was no mirage. We were both now in our seventies. Jen was 73, and I was 70. I slowly began to notice a change in her, as she seemed to turn frailer. The vigor and vitality of youth was escaping her. I, too, was tired, but brushed it off to normal aging. The years, I feared, had finally caught up to us. On a beautiful fall September morning in 1986, she went out to the front yard and watched the sunrise as she had done on so many mornings for one last time. That night, she passed away peacefully in her sleep. I was heartbroken and devastated. This remarkable woman, one of only two I had ever loved, was now gone. We had spent forty wonderful years together trying to make a difference in the world. We ended up making a difference for each other.

All the children and grandchildren came in for her service. She loved that the grandkids got to spend their summers and the holidays here on the coast. She loved Maine and cherished its beauty and its privacy. In accordance with her wishes, her ashes were scattered near the cliff at the back of the house. There were many tears shed that day. Three of the four of us responsible for changing time as we knew it were now gone. I was the only survivor still who knew all of the secrets.

The grandkids ranged from nine to fourteen when Jen passed away. The younger ones would likely only have faint memories of her as they grew. Everyone stayed on for a few days and then departed. It would be the first time I would be alone, truly alone, since we came back to this era. I filled my days writing the true story of what happened with "Project Töten Zeit." I enjoyed spending time writing and reading. At night, I would spend as much time as I could to use the small observatory I had built on the grounds of the compound. The dark skies made for perfect viewing. I loved observing the night sky and still dreamed of space, but it was not to be.

Our boys were pilots in the Air Force, and their work scattered them and their children around the globe. As their children grew, they looked to be on the same path of entering the academy and joining the service. Leigh's son Mark, much like his mother, was more interested in blazing a trail rather than following one. He spent as much time as he could up here at the house while his mother and father worked at NASA in Washington, D.C. He loved to talk about history and science, and his goal was to be an astrophysicist or astronomer. I could see in his eyes how much he loved the stars and space, much as I did. When he graduated high school, he could have gone anywhere to study astronomy, but he opted for the University of Maine to be able to stay here at the house. Those few years I got to spend with him, I will cherish. We were always tinkering with something or working on capturing photographs of the planets and stars. I saw so much of me in him. Born in the same year as I, but here we were seventy years apart. Perhaps he was meant to be a better version of myself. He graduated college early but opted to stay and complete his masters and Doctorate in physics and continue to live at the house.

The early arrival of the Maine winter in 2010 was symbolic. The season had changed, but I felt its chill cast an impending shadow over me. I would need Mark to lean on and help me accomplish one last thing.

LAST WILL AND TESTAMENT

It had now been twenty years since Jen passed away. I sensed there were few sunsets left for me to see. As much as had changed in history, the names, and the faces, so much had stayed the same. The world today resembled much of the world I had left behind. I knew that it was only a matter of time before someone would once again try to right the wrongs of history and use the work of Dr. Scheel to go back into the past. Tried, as I had to destroy the materials, some of it survived, and there were people in the right places who knew about it, and possibly figured out how to make it work. One of those was now deceased, but Einstein could have very well finished or wrote the working theory based on what he was given by then-President Farley.

If history held its course, I knew I would not make it to that day to be able to stop it. I was now 94, and I had developed a persistent cough that I couldn't shake. I spent the days getting my affairs in order and my nights huddled by the fire trying to stay warm. Jen and I had the good fortune to manage our business and finances well through the years. We were able to leave enough money to the children that they would be comfortable for the rest of their lives. The grandkids all had substantial trust funds. Along with his fund, Mark was to get the house in Maine. I knew he loved it so much and would care for it. It was my gift for the time he spent with me. There was one last request, which a woman named Elizabeth Rosa Milano, "Beth," would receive an amount of $100,000 to spend fulfilling whatever her life's dream would be.

My oldest son, James, now in his early 60s, had been working at the Pentagon and just retired from the Air Force. He and his wife stayed living in the D.C area. I called and asked him if he could make it up to Maine for the weekend. There was no good way to let on what the topic was that I wanted to discuss with him. It was a snowy Saturday morning at the house. I asked Mark to make the trek into Bangor to pick up James. I stood by the window watching it fall as it glistened on the trees. As I saw my reflection in the glass, I didn't recognize the face of the old, dying man staring back at me. Time, the eternal enemy of life, had taken those closest to me away. The Grim Reaper, the symbol of Projekt Töten Zeit, was looking to collect on a long overdue debt.

The weather had delayed flights into the airport, and with the terrible road conditions, it was late afternoon by the time everyone got back to the house. Mark helped James get settled while I sat by the fire in the study. I spent a lot of time in this study. It had pictures on the wall of everything, from the planes I flew to the presidents and dignitaries we hosted and met. I had thirty years of memories accumulated before I accepted the mission that would change my life and the lives of so many others. I had the good fortune to spend sixty-four watching a new world take shape. Perhaps it was no less frightening than it had before, but to the lives of the millions who were spared a fate they never knew, I had hoped it made all the difference.

It was then that James and Mark entered the study. I stood up and hugged James. "It's good to see you son. I am so glad you could come up in this terrible storm. Pull up a chair and enjoy this warm fire," I said.

"Dad, Matthew, Leigh, Mary, and the rest of us, have been talking through this, and we think you should sell the house and move down south with us. You'll be much more comfortable, and the weather isn't nearly this harsh," James said.

"Oh, no, no, no," I said. "I have no intention of leaving this place, but let's talk about why I asked you here." The years had slowed my speech, but I was still mentally sharp. I just couldn't get the words to flow quite as eloquently or with the same expediency as before.

"There is only one thing in the universe that remains undefeated. That thing is time. We can try to slow it, but usually, we just waste it but never beat it. It always wins in the end. I've beaten it for about as long as I can, but it will defeat me also like it has done to so many others before. I have updated my will and filed it with the county clerk's office."

I handed James a copy of the will and expressed that everyone would be the benefactor. I had a few notable standouts in the will that I wanted him to be clear on and understand my intentions.

"First, Mark will take ownership of "Belle Futuro." Your mother and I loved this place, and we would want to see it go on for generation after generation. More than anyone, Mark loves this place, and if he were willing, I would love for him to continue its legacy. There may be things here of significance that some of the family may want, and that is okay, but I want the house to remain in the family. All I ask is that this study stays as it is today, at least for a little while longer. It will always be the family's summer and Christmas retreat, and I hope that will go on. Mark, this is a big house, but I know one day you will fill it with a family of your own. Second, James, you are to be the executor of the estate. The most important thing that you will inherit is the title of the patriarch of the family. Please see that my wishes are followed and keep the family and its generations alive with the same drive and spirit!"

"Dad, you'll probably outlive us all," he said.

It was then I asked Mark if he could excuse us for a few moments. I had something I needed to share with James in private. "I need you to do me a favor," I said.

"Sure, Dad. Name it, and it's done," he replied.

I pulled open the lower right desk drawer and pulled out a brown envelope. It was sealed with shipping tape as to be very secure. I handed it to James. He paused a moment and looked at the package.

"I need you to hang on to that until September 2016. At that time, deliver it to the name on the envelope. He'll be an Air Force officer. I need you to promise to make that happen. If something happens to you, I need Matthew to make sure it gets delivered."

"Can we get it to him now. Is this Jake Kelly expecting it?" James asked.

"No. It's a long story, but it has to be done at that time. It can't be any earlier or any later. It must be delivered at that specific time. Write it on a calendar, set a reminder, but don't let it slip. I know it is years away. Put it on your desk and look at it every day. Don't forget it. It is critically important."

"Okay, I promise I will make that happen. You can count on it."

I knew I could count on James. He had worn a uniform that had three stars on it. The chain of command and following orders was nothing new to him. There was no doubt that my request would be executed. I got up from the desk, and we moved to the family room, where Mark was stoking the fire.

James picked up a picture of his mother from the mantle. "This place has so many good memories," he said. He walked to the expansive floor-to-ceiling windows with a wide view of the ocean. "I never got tired of this view. Mom loved to sit out there and listen to the sounds of the ocean."

"Her spirit lives on and is still there listening to the waves. She cherished the times we all had here, and she never wanted to leave any of that behind. She never wanted to let that go. Right up to the end."

We spent the next few days snowed in and catching up. When the skies cleared on James' last night, Mark and I took him out to the observatory to view the stars. The bitter cold was not helping that deep, painful cough I couldn't shake. I was used to the winter here in Maine, but it felt different now. It was as if I was just a skeleton, and the cold was encasing my very bones. They probably knew, but I didn't let on that my time was growing increasingly short. I wondered what it would be like to die. Now though, I knew what it was like to be dying. It was a terrible thing to finally understand that the last sands of time were now waiting to fall through the hourglass of my life.

We had a great time that night searching the heavens. It might be the last time we have these moments together. As much as Jen loved the sea and sun, I loved the stars and night. Mark gave James quite the lesson in astronomy.

The next day, Mark drove James back to the airport. When he returned, I asked him to come into the study. From the same drawer from which I pulled the envelope I gave James, I reached in for another and gave it to Mark. It was sealed. "I need you to deliver this to the name on the envelope, but it needs to be done in March of 2017. It also can't any sooner or any later. It is imperative. Promise me you'll take care of this."

"Absolutely Grandfather. I will make sure it happens," he said. He looked at the envelope. "Elizabeth Rosa Milano," he said.

"Yes. It may take some detective work to find her. When the time comes, you can start by looking in New York or Maryland." I reached my hand back out to take the envelope back. "I'm not quite finished with this one yet. When I am, I'll seal it up and leave it here on the desk. Seven years is a long time. It will collect a lot of dust sitting here, but you need to make sure it goes where it is supposed to when the time finally arrives."

"I'll make sure it is done," replied Mark.

I came back from around the desk and hugged Mark. "You've been like a son to me. I look at you, and I saw myself so many years ago. You have heart and a sense for what is right. I love that you have that insatiable curiosity about the world, history, and how things work. Thank you for all you've done and for the time you spent here. You'll never know how much that has meant to me to have you here. I hope you will find love and happiness here in this house. "Belle Futuro" means "Beautiful Future." This place could be your beautiful future, but I won't hold you to stay here. You have so many opportunities waiting for you out there. Go where the spirit in your heart leads you."

"I plan to stay here and do my research. I'll teach part-time at the university and take a few research assignments now and then, but this will always be my home base."

Tears were streaming down my cheeks. My long journey was finally coming to an end. Time was proving once again that it would be the victor.

THE FINAL ENTRY:
TUESDAY NOVEMBER 9TH, 2010

My Dearest Beth, I hope this note finds you well. If you have gotten this far, you now are just one of a handful of people who knows of Project Töten Zeit.

It is not a fabrication or a work of fiction, but a real account of what happened. In another time and place, you were the love of my life. Fate called me to a destiny that would forever separate us. Know that I never forgot, nor did I ever stop loving you. By now, I will have long since passed. I realize that the events in this story may never make sense or add up the way I described. The fact that history has changed might mean we never crossed paths. Jake Kelly may be a total stranger to you. That would be the second tragedy of this ill-fated love affair. Perhaps, it was just not meant to be.

Somewhere out there, a Jake Kelly exists. He and I are bonded by blood. It is a trait, which will doom him to the same fate as I. Time has separated the paths of destiny and created new ones. At about the time you are reading this, history will likely repeat itself. Project Töten Zeit will try once again to right the wrongs of the past. This time, it will be different. This time, I will ensure that a Jake Kelly understands what is being asked of him and he will do the right thing. He knows what I know. In his heart and mind, we are alike. We are the same person. The pillars we are built of, honor and sacrifice are the same.

Please know that there was no greater sacrifice than to be apart from you. The original Töten Zeit failed in many respects but succeeded in making this future just a little better. It is my hope that it will continue to be made better. The risk of playing with time was all too evident. When they try again, he will bring an end to this most dangerous of weapons, the means to change history. I believe he will do the right thing. After all, I know him as well as he knows himself.

I asked him to sacrifice his own life so that others may live. The aircraft contains a self-destruct device. If it is activated, within three minutes, the plane will explode, destroying the complex, its secrets, and the opportunity for anyone to ever alter time. This is the price, and the pain, of love. If by chance, he is not on that aircraft, find him. He will be looking for you also. You belong together.

He now has in his possession my most prized possession. It is the proof that what I have said is true. The picture that you had once given me with the note "I will always love you." You have no idea how much that meant to me. It survived many an ordeal. It kept me going when the odds were against me. The only journey it didn't make was this one. I have lived a good, long life, but one with many regrets. If I could give one piece of advice to you, it would be to never look back at the past. Always look ahead to the future. When the end comes, leave no regrets behind. My heart was broken only twice, once in leaving you, and again at the loss of my wife, Jennifer, the two great loves of my life.

The man who delivered this to you is my grandson. He knows nothing about this memoir and nothing about my past. No one does. No proof survives that anyone would acknowledge. All of the answers are in this document. All of the unanswered questions you may have, you must seek out and find those answers. I always let my brain lead, and my heart follow. Always follow your heart.

You may have noticed that there was a check enclosed with this document. Besides an undying love that I will take to my grave, I have nothing else to give. Please use this to follow your dreams and pursue happiness. I want so much for your life to be filled with joy and happiness. Focus on your love of photography, the music you play on the piano. Follow your dreams, Beth, and live a beautiful future.

There may never be a Jake Kelly and Beth Milano, who will live with eternal happiness, but once there was, and I will carry that memory through the end of time with me.

Love Always,
Jake Kelly / John Behrens

EPILOGUE: THE JOURNAL OF BETH MILANO

It was the strangest of things. I was sitting in my apartment in Brooklyn when the buzzer went off indicating that someone was at the main front entrance. I wasn't expecting anyone or a delivery. I walked to the intercom and said, "Hello, can I help you?"

The voice on the other end asked if I was Elizabeth Rosa Milano, born on January 10th, 1987.

I answered, "Yes."

He indicated that he had a package for me that he was asked to deliver in person. I asked him his name.

He replied, "Mark Anderson."

"Who is the package from?" I asked.

The reply came that it was from "John Behrens."

"I don't know any John Behrens," I replied.

"Miss Milano, I made a promise to my grandfather to deliver this package to you. I will write my information on the package and lean it against the door and walk across the street. Please just come down and get the package. I will leave you alone."

As polite as the voice was, I couldn't be too careful. I agreed and walked down to the front door. As the man had stated, there was a thick, 8x10-size envelope leaning up against the door. I opened the door slightly until I could reach the package and pulled it inside. It had my name on it. I looked through the glass at the man standing across the street as he had promised. It was still daylight, but a cold rain was beginning to fall. From what I could see, he was a young, clean-cut man, well dressed. He gave a slight wave and started to walk away. I felt the package, and it seemed to be a thick set of documents.

It was all a bit of a mystery that intrigued me, and I wanted to know more about it.

I stepped out onto the front porch into the rain and yelled for the man to come back. I stepped back in and closed the door, waiting to see him up close. When he arrived at the door, I saw he was a handsome man, about my age.

"Do you have any identification?" I asked.

"Would a driver's license and work ID be okay?" the man replied.

"Yes. Anything to tell me who you are."

He reached into his pocket and pulled out his wallet. His first pressed his driver's license to the glass. "Mark Anderson, Bar Harbor, Maine." I nodded. He pulled out an ID card that showed he was a professor at the University of Maine. "That's fine," I said and opened the door.

"What is this?" I asked.

"I don't know," the man said.

"Why is this for me, and who is John Behrens?"

"I don't know why this is for you, and I have no idea what is in the package. John Behrens, he was my grandfather. He was a great man who accomplished many things in his life and raised a great family. You might know him as the founder of Behrens Aerospace, or a pioneer in aviation. Does any of that ring a bell of how you might know him?" he asked.

"No. I think I've heard the name mentioned before in the news or something, but I don't personally know him if that's what you mean."

"Seven years ago, right before he passed away, he made me promise to deliver this envelope to you this month in this year. I don't have any idea what is in it or why now. By the way, thank you for answering the buzzer. It was nice of you to trust me under these circumstances. I've left my information on the package. If there is anything I can answer or that you may need don't hesitate to call me."

I hesitated for a few moments. My curiosity had the best of me. "Is there a place in town I can reach you?" I asked.

"I'm afraid not. I'm planning to start driving back to Bar Harbor tonight. I was down in DC visiting my parents and aunt and uncle, and this was the right time on my way back to keep my commitment to deliver this package."

"Bar Harbor? What is that, like a ten-hour drive?

"About eight and a half," he said.

"Look, I don't want to hold you up, but my curiosity is eating away at me to see what is inside this package. I don't normally invite a stranger into my house, but would you like to come inside while I look at this?"

I know that was pretty dumb of me, but I was so caught off-guard that I probably wasn't thinking straight. This guy seemed well mannered and very polite. It could have been the most elaborate rouse ever to commit a robbery, but I didn't get that feeling. From what I could tell this looked like a nice, regular guy. We walked up the stairs to the apartment, and I sat on the sofa while he sat opposite me in a chair. There was no question that it was meant to protect it from damage and curious prying eyes. It was clearly meant to protect it from damage or prying eyes. I finally resorted to using scissors to cut it open. When I finally freed the contents, I slid them out of the package and onto the coffee table in front of the sofa. It appeared to be a book of some type, about 400 printed pages, bound with a metal strip through the three punch holes.

"It's a book, I think," I said to the man.

"Can I see it?" he asked.

He carefully looked it over. "This was definitely written by my grandfather. There is a note tucked inside the front page," he said as he handed the book back to me. The note said, "My dearest Beth. The answers to your questions will be found in this book. Please take the time to read this story."

As I flipped through the pages, a check fell out of the book. I picked it up and must have had a look of shock come over me. "There's a check here made out to me for $100,000. It is dated March 1, 2017 and signed by John Behrens. When did you say he died?"

"Seven years ago, at the age of 94. This package has sat sealed and unopened since then."

"I think this is a case of mistaken identity," I said.

"How many Elizabeth Rosa Milano's born on January 10, 1987, to Angelo and Luisa Milano could there possibly be in Brooklyn? I think you are the right person," he said.

I handed him the handwritten note. He looked at it and gave it back to me. "That's my grandfather's handwriting. I would do as it says, read the book and find the answers, and go cash the check. You may not have known my grandfather, but somehow, he knew you. However that occurred, you left a big impression on him. He was quite generous like that."

He got up and headed for the door.

"Wait, don't you want to know what this is about?" I asked.

"I know all about the man. I worshiped him for who he was. It is your turn to get to know him. Don't worry. I am certain it is all good."

With that, he left and disappeared into the cold night. I put the book on the table and went to get ready for bed. It was driving me crazy, the connection of how this man knew me or cared enough about me to remember who I was. I wondered if I had helped him somehow and didn't realize it. I was racking my brain trying to make sense of it. Then I remembered what the note said. The answers are in the book.

I changed into my pajamas, wrapped myself in a warm blanket, and put a cup of hot coffee on the end table. I was ready to tackle and solve this mystery. The book appeared to be written much like a novel. The title, "Killing Time: The Story of Project Töten Zeit" sounded rather ominous and nothing like what I would have expected. If I could manage to stay awake, it would take me hours to get through it.

I began to read through the book. The first thing that struck me was that this was some sort of science fiction novel. I was puzzled why this person would weave this fantasy of me into the story. Certain elements were right and many other items that were wrong about me and about history. It took two more cups of coffee and another four hours, but I finally got to the end. The last entry was a personal love letter to me from a man, an old man, whom I never knew. I suppose stranger things have happened in this world. Everyone knows that the government works on clandestine and secret projects the public never sees, but this was too fantastic a story to believe.

It was 2 am by the time I crawled into bed to get sleep. I lay there and thought about what I read. I wasn't believing the story, but rather thinking of ways to disprove it. I also wanted to know why of all the people, this love story selected me. The thought still crossed my mind that this was just the imagination of a senile old man who somehow crossed paths with me and decided I would make a good character for his book. I feel asleep pondering the possibilities of why me.

I tossed and turned throughout the night. It was the mystery, and the need to solve it, that was bugging me. When I finally got up, I rushed to the computer to search for answers. Who were John Behrens and Jake Kelly? There was a wealth of information on John Behrens, but surprisingly, I was unable to find any good photos of him beyond the last few years. He was quite accomplished, not known as an eccentric, but was mostly a recluse for the past thirty or forty years of his life. The man who was at my door, Mark Anderson, was indeed his grandson and a professor at the University of Maine, just as he had said.

As for Jake Kelly and John Behrens, according to the document, they were one and the same, but two different people, or the same person in two different times, something like that. The only information I could find on an Air Force captain named Jake Kelly was that he was recently killed along with twenty-six airmen when a munitions storage depot exploded at Minot Air Force Base in North Dakota. It was another odd coincidence in the book.

If this book had been sealed for six years, how did John Behrens know a Jake Kelly would be at that location? I found another odd coincidence in the story. While researching the pilot who assassinated Hitler and his high-ranking staff, I came across a rumored conspiracy theory. In what were supposed to have been eyewitness accounts by RAF pilots who landed near the downed plane, they recalled that the pilot and rear passenger in the aircraft were Americans. The rear passenger was German, German-American, or American, but definitely a female. This story went against the documented history that said that a lone rogue German pilot was the assassin who escaped and provided asylum along with a new identity in the UK. To this day his name has never been revealed. There seemed to be only one-way to solve this mystery, and that was to follow the trail to see where it led. I needed to go to Maine.

I called my boss and told him I had an emergency and needed some personal time off. I booked a spur-of-the-moment flight to Bar Harbor. There were no direct flights. I would have to stop in Boston and hop a small plane from there to Maine. The mystery man who delivered the package was my best lead. I felt like a detective on the hunt and about to crack the case wide open. It would turn out that the difference between flying and driving wasn't much at all. By the time I changed planes, waited for my flight, and landed in Bar Harbor, about six hours had elapsed.

Bar Harbor was just to the north along the eastern coast of Maine. It was a large island close to the coastline that was home to the well-known Acadia National Park. I had never been here before. Given my spur-of-the-moment impulse to make this trip, it was fortunate that I was able to rent a car at the small airport. It was something I hadn't thought to do in advance, and this tiny airport did not appear to be a bustling hub of activity. As I drove through the small town, it was Main Street America. Main Street that is, for a waterfront town in New England.

It was small, appeared affluent, and had a touristy feel, but was mostly quiet in the early days of spring. I had not given notice to Mark Anderson that I would be coming into town. This visit would be a surprise to the man who was nothing but polite and courteous in brief encounter, but still a stranger. I felt it best as part of my sleuthing to catch him off-guard, just in case this was some elaborate rouse. Why? I still had no idea.

The house was quite a ways around the island from downtown. It was on the eastern-facing side, on the other side of the national park. I was quite stunned as I approached the house. It was a sprawling, two-story, white house on a large property overlooking the ocean. There was an American flag on a tall flagpole. The flag appeared extended and taut, thanks to a stiff ocean breeze. Given the size of this house, I was expecting a large family to live here, and I assumed that someone would be home. I rang the doorbell and waited. There was the loud bark of a dog. Standing there waiting, it was colder here with nothing to block the air coming across the frigid ocean waters. The door opened, and it was Mark Anderson. He opened the door and hurried me in from the cold. "Ms. Milano, what are you doing here?"

"Beth, please. I couldn't sleep after you left, and I need to get answers."

"So you felt compelled to drive the 9 hours from New York to Bar Harbor? You know, you could have called also," he said as he mildly chuckled. He then went on.

"I was going to call you in a few days to find out what that document my grandfather left you was all about, but I'm glad you came," he stated.

I quickly apologized. "I'm sorry if I am intruding. I didn't mean to pop in unannounced and disrupt your family."

"No need to apologize, I live here alone. I spent as much time here as I could when I was growing up just to be close to him. When he passed away, he left me this house that he and my grandmother cherished. I am its resident caretaker. Well, me and my dog Comet."

"It must get lonely here," I remarked.

"At times, but it is peaceful, and it is beautiful. We have a large family, and this house belongs to all of us. During the summer months, this house comes alive with my aunts and uncles and my nieces and nephews. Something tells me you didn't come all this way to hear about the house. What information can I help you with?"

"Well, it's a long story. Would you by chance have the time to read the document that was in the package? As you go through, it I can fill you in on the details. It took me about four hours or so to get through it."

"Sure, come on in and make yourself comfortable. Let me get another log or two on the fire, and I'll start tackling it."

We walked in the large family room. The ceiling was at least fifteen feet high with floor-to-ceiling glass windows that had an expansive view of the ocean. This house probably had as many stories to tell as the book. I wanted to stay but didn't want to be forward, and I was hoping he would ask. "I better head back into town. Why don't you look that over, and I'll come back in the morning," I said.

"Wait a minute. What? Drive back into town? You just got here. No way. You are welcome to stay here tonight. I have all this room, and you couldn't get a better view of the sunrise anywhere on the island. Make yourself comfortable over there, and I'll whip us up some dinner and get you a glass of wine. When we are done, you can sit here by the fire and watch TV while I'll go in the study after dinner and start reading."

I'd be lying if I said I didn't feel some attraction to this man. I wasn't sure what it was: the good looks, the combination of somewhat rugged and all nerd at the same time. For now, I needed to get myself in check and work on the mystery.

The dinner was delicious, and we spent more time than we should have at the kitchen table talking and getting to know each other a little better. There was awkwardness at first, given how all this had arisen, but that seemed to disappear quickly. Suddenly, this looked like someone I had known all my life. I think a large part of that was just the calm, make-you-feel-at-home manner he had. He was apparently brought up well by his parents and grandparents.

"Well, I better get cracking on this. There is a remote on the table. The TV has satellite, so that means about 400 stations and nothing to watch," he said.

"Could you possibly sit here and read it, or would that be too much of a distraction?"

"No, I would love to sit here by the fire and read. It is something I do a lot of," he replied.

His dog Comet, a beautiful German Shepherd, lay on the rug next to his chair. Looking at him with the fire in the fireplace and the whole décor of the room was something itself out of time. It was a scene that belonged in a painting. He would stop occasionally and look up at me, seemingly puzzled by what he was reading.

"I would see this on his desk now and then. He would work on it and then stop for a while. I never knew what this was, but I assumed it was some military history or military strategy book he was writing. I had no idea why he would send it to you, but it seems you are a central figure in this story. Is it possible that your mother or your grandmother knew my grandfather and he just used your name?"

"It crossed my mind, but I called my mother, and she had no recollection of meeting or ever hearing of the name John Behrens or Jake Kelly."

"Okay, let me keep going. A lot of this story is unfamiliar to me as well. I've never heard any of this before, and I don't think my mom or my uncles would know of this either."

My eyes were getting heavy, and the crackling of the fire was soothing. It had been a long night and a long day. I quickly fell asleep on the sofa.

It must have been something about the Maine air or maybe just being away from the hustle and bustle of the city. I was in a deep sleep until I felt a gentle rustling of my arm. "Time for you to get some sleep," Mark said.

"How long have I been asleep? Did you finish it?" I asked.

"About three hours, and yes, I got through it all."

"Fact or fiction?" I asked.

"I'm not sure. I think the most reasonable conclusion would be fiction, but I knew this man. He would have no reason to make up this story and go through this elaborate exercise with you. Especially seven years after he passed away. I don't know if we could ever prove it."

"I was afraid that would be the answer."

"You know, maybe this is something else we can do. The book speaks about my grandfather providing the information to Jake Kelly and asking him to end the cycle by destroying that time portal device. I watched my grandfather seal this envelope over seven years ago. If he was right, that explosion in Minot might hold the proof we are looking for, if we could see it."

"Let's go!" I said.

"Hang on. I've got other ideas, and second, they are not going to let us walk onto a military base and snoop around, secret project or not. Let me make some calls in the morning and see what I can find out. Right now, you get some sleep. Let me take Comet out, and I'll get you settled."

He took his dog out in the backyard. There was what looked like a near-full moon rising above the ocean. It cast a long, white trail across the black expanse of the sea and then across the snow, right up to the porch. The wind had stopped, and the air was cold, but still.

This was a good man, and these looked like good people. What all this was about was another story. They say you can tell the heart of a man by how he treats his dog. You could see the bond between these two. They were like kids staying out late and playing in the snow when school was closed. My eyes were watery, and I didn't know why.

When he came back in, Comet shook side to side, like dogs always do, to shake the water or snow off of his fur. Mark was running his hand through the hair on the dog's head saying, "Good boy, good boy."

"I need to go," I blurted out.

I was holding it together, but sniffling to prevent from sobbing. It was a thundering wave of emotion that had come over me without warning.

"What prompted this?" he asked.

"I don't know. I just need to go."

"It's late. There's nowhere to go. Nothing is open, and it's too far anyway to go back into town. What's wrong?"

I wished I could have given him an answer, but I didn't know myself what was wrong. He stepped forward to hug me and placed my head on his shoulder. "Whatever it is, it will be okay. I promise."

"Nothing is what I expected. These past two days, my world had been turned upside down. You show up out of the blue and give me a book about a guy who traveled in time and changed history but never forgot the woman he left behind. That guy who I never met could be dead or alive. It is a sad enough story without everything else. Can you see why I'm going crazy?"

"I am so sorry," he said. "I was just fulfilling the last wishes of a dying man. I had no idea this would upset anyone."

"It's this house too," I said.

"Oh, well let me drive into town, and we'll see if we can find someplace."

"No, no, it's not that. I love this place. I feel a strange connection here, even though it doesn't show at the moment, an inner peace. I'm a bit overwhelmed, in case you didn't notice."

"I hardly noticed it," he said with a smile.

"Let's put you to bed, and a good night's sleep will help. We'll figure this out in the morning."

For as old as this house seemed to be on the outside, the inside was quite modern and well appointed. The sleeping quarters were large and warm, and the bed was inviting and comfortable. I sank in, crawled under the blankets, and fell right asleep to beams of moonlight filtering through the blinds.

When morning came, the sun was up and shining through the window. I opened the blinds and gazed at the sun rising over the ocean. The sea was sparkling as the sun reflected off the waves. The smell of breakfast permeated the air. Bacon and eggs, I think. I put on a guest robe and walked downstairs. Mark and Comet were in the kitchen.

"We're usually up late or early around here. I'm glad you got to sleep in late. Are you feeling better this morning?"

"I think so. At least I am not quite the mess I was last night."

"The morning does you good. You look bright and refreshed!" he said.

I was trying to get back on point with why I came here. It was all starting to seem a blur. I felt like someone on vacation rather than a detective out to solve a mystery.

"In the light of a new day, what are you thinking are our next steps?" I asked.

"I gave it some thought overnight. I am at a bit of a loss. I want to believe the story, but it is hard to do that. What I thought I might do is call my uncle down in DC. He just retired from the Air Force as a lieutenant general. I can ask him to make some calls about "Project Töten Zeit." It is a bit of a risk. If the story is a fictional fabrication, I don't want him to look bad. He might also be able to get us on the base at Minot. I have another uncle and two cousins who are also in the Air Force and can help. Let's have breakfast, and I'll make the call.

As we sat down for breakfast, I wanted to change the conversation. I started poking around about his personal life. Inquiring about girlfriends, things he liked to do. It was part curiosity and part something else.

When we finished breakfast, he excused himself and headed to the study to call his uncle. I heard him on the phone. "Hey, Uncle Jim. How is everything going with retirement?" They chitchatted for a few minutes before he got down to the point of the call.

"Did you ever hear Granddad talk about a Project Töten Zeit? How about an Air Force captain named Jake Kelly?"

There were pauses as he listened. Ever curious, I walked into the study. Mark was behind this gorgeous wooden desk. The room had bookcases along the wall and old pictures neatly framed. I walked along the wall studying the photographs. Suddenly, I yelled out, "I know this guy!"

I was pointing to an old black-and-white photo of a man standing next to a fighter jet. Mark put his hand over the phone and said, "That's my grandfather."

"No, this guy," I said pointing to the man in the photo.

"Uncle Jim, can I call you back in a few minutes?"

He hung up the phone and walked over to the photo. "That is my grandfather, John Behrens. He was much younger in this photo. This was probably taken in 1947, maybe 1948. Do you think you met him sometime before he passed in 2010?"

"It was this guy, this exact guy, the guy in this picture. I was in a bar in Brooklyn with friends after work. It was October or November. When I went to order another drink, the bartender said it had been taken care of. We didn't think much about it. Those things happen occasionally. Later on, a man came up to me, a young man, my age, and asked if I could join him for a few minutes. He was polite and nice, but I said no. I lost track of him, then about thirty minutes later, he showed up again and said he had to go. He gave me a piece of paper. I put it in my purse thinking it was a phone number. When he left, I felt really bad about it. He seemed nice. I never saw him again. I'm telling you, it was this guy." I started looking at more of the photos. There was one of John Behrens with President Farley. There was no mistaking it; this was the guy who came up to me. "I might still have that piece of paper in my purse."

I ran out of the room and up the stairs to find my purse. Like a crazed person, I went rambling through it looking for that small piece of folded paper. When I finally located it, I opened it and read what it said. "Live a beautiful future." It was how the note ended in the book. I was frightened and confused. I ran back downstairs to show Mark. His uncle had called back. He motioned to me to hang on a second.

When he hung up the phone, I showed him the note. "I am beginning to believe."

"I am too. We're going to Minot. My uncle made a few calls and will get us to the site where the explosion took place. They assured him it was nothing but a pile of rubble. He indicated that you had someone close to you who was killed and you wanted to visit the site as a memorial tribute. He will fly up and meet us there. They want him to escort us personally."

I was shaking. The adrenaline was surging through my body. I wanted to go out on the deck and scream to release the pent-up energy.

"When do we go?"

"Tomorrow. I need to make our flight arrangements and get a sitter in for Comet. Go into the family room and relax. It is early. We have the whole day to kill and things to do to get ready."

I was too hyped up. I went back into the study and looked at the pictures on the wall. I browsed through the books on the shelf. Most were about history or the military. I noticed in the hallway that there was a collage of family photos hanging on the wall. John Behrens and his wife, their kids, and the generations after were here on this wall.

"Where are John and Maria's parents?" I asked.

"I don't know. I'm not sure we had any pictures of them, or ever saw any. My grandfather loved these photos of the family. He would always say that it was our parents and grandparents who built our families. We shouldn't lose sight of that or their memories. We should always have the whole family on this wall and the generations that come after so we never forget them."

"And yet there is there nothing here about his parents or grandparents. Don't you find that odd?"

"I'm finding a lot of things odd today," he said. "After you take a shower and get changed, we'll head into town for lunch and run some errands."

The adrenaline was coursing through my veins. For the first time in my life, I could feel it running through my body like an unstoppable force. My heart was beating faster and faster. I knew the reason why I was feeling this way. I was going to Minot, North Dakota to solve this mystery, and I was scared of what I would find.

I had gotten ready, but before we headed into town, Mark said he wanted to show me something. We walked to the backyard, and near the cliff, he bent down and brushed the light snow from two stone markers in the ground. One said John Behrens, 2010, and the other Maria Behrens, 1988. "I was only three when she passed away. My only memories of her are the photos."

"Is this where they are buried?" I asked.

"Their ashes were scattered here and along the cliff. They never wanted to leave here. He said that she loved to sit here and watch the sunrise. Now, they watch it together."

I knelt down beside him and instinctively just held his hand.

"I miss him every day. Someday, my children and their children will spend their days here, and I hope they love it as much as she did, as he did, as I do."

"I am sure they will. I've only been here for a day, and I love everything about this house."

We spent the afternoon in town after I dropped the rental back at the airport. We grabbed lunch at a local place and ate it in the car with Comet getting his fair share of our meal. The drive back had a calming effect on me. My head was still spinning, but I was feeling better.

"What will we find tomorrow?" I asked.

"Have you already found all the answers you need?" he asked.

"Perhaps I have, but there are more questions. I want to tell you something. I trust you. The last few years have been unsettling for me, and this is unsettling, but I feel different here with you."

"I want you to feel comfortable. After all the trouble I've caused you, I'm glad you feel that way."

It had totally gone over his head. I was coming on to him, and he missed the signal. He was just too good to be true! He had let me know that there would be a slight adjustment in the itinerary for tomorrow. Since it would take so long to get to Minot and there wasn't an easy way to get from here to there, we would have to spend the night in Minneapolis and leave the following day for Minot. If we tried to go straight through, we wouldn't get there until dark. This way, we might be able to get in and out of Minot the same day and maybe make it back to Boston. We'd be stuck there until the next day. Then he asked me a question. "I'm guessing you want me to book your return flight back to New York?"

Yikes. It made sense. Why would I go back to Maine when I had everything with me? It was time to let the cat out of the bag. "I want to come back to Maine. Look, all this happened so fast, but I want to get to know you better before I go back. Is that okay?" He was silent. A bit stunned, perhaps. I think it finally started to sink in. Maybe all of this was our destiny. "Sure. You're welcome to stay as long as you like. Won't someone miss you in New York? Like your employer?"

"Yes. I'll take a bit more vacation. I hope my boss will understand."

The next morning, we dropped Comet off at a neighbor friend of Mark's on the way to the airport. Then we were off to bring what I hoped would be a close to this mystery, first on a small plane to Boston, later on a bigger plane to Minneapolis. Between layovers and stops, by the time we got to Minneapolis, seven hours of travel had passed. Mark's uncle had arrived before us and was waiting in one of the large lounge areas. They hugged, and Mark introduced me. His uncle Jim was much older than I had expected. He appeared to be in about his late 60s, but healthy and vigorous.

Before we shuttled to the hotel, his uncle wanted to take a few minutes and talk about what we were after.

"A trip to Minot was the last thing I was expecting. I was a little surprised when they asked me to be your chaperone. I talked to the base commander, and he reiterated that there wasn't much to see. The explosion obliterated the site, and because it is still dangerous, they haven't begun recovery operations. The Air Force wanted me, as a friend of the family of an officer killed in the line of duty at the site, to offer my condolences on your loss."

He looked over at me.

"You knew one of the airmen who was killed at the site?"

I was caught off guard and didn't know exactly what to say. I fumbled the words a bit.

"He was a friend of the family," I said.

"I'm very sorry for your loss," he responded.

"We will have limited time at the site tomorrow, about thirty minutes. That will be just enough time to pay our respects. It is still hazardous. It will be cold, windy, and somewhat desolate there. In the morning, we'll meet with the commander. He's an old friend who used to work for me."

We headed out to dinner, where the conversation was warm and friendly. Mark and his uncle were making plans for the whole family to spend time up in Maine. It was an idyllic American family. As the evening wound down, Mark tried to open the door a little and asked a few questions about his grandfather. "Do you know if Granddad was ever here at this base?" he asked.

"I never heard him mention it, but he was quite involved with so many things with Lockheed and the Air Force that it wouldn't surprise me at all."

"Do you know what he was doing before he worked at Lockheed?"

"I don't know a whole lot. He didn't talk much about that, but you know how connected he was. He was doing work for the president, and your grandmother was doing work in New Mexico. When you think about it, they witnessed some of the key events in history. From the atom bomb to the development of rocketry, to advances in aviation, they had quite the ride through life."

The dinner ended, and we made our way to the hotel. Mark had booked us all in separate rooms. It was okay. I didn't want to push anything, and this wasn't the right time or place anyway.

Morning came, and we took off for Minot. The flight was only about an hour and a half. We had been traveling so much the past few days that I was feeling the jet lag. It wasn't like I was having second thoughts about being here, I just wanted to end the mystery and get back to regular life again. At the airport, there was a black SUV waiting for us. A man hopped out from the passenger side. He was dressed in a blue military uniform. "General, how the heck are you?" he said to Mark's uncle.

"Steve, it's good to see you. It has been a long time."

"Too long!" he said.

Jim introduced us, and the commander offered me his condolences on my loss. The charade had me feeling a bit uneasy that we weren't truthful and upfront. As we drove off, the commander made small talk. "Did you have a good flight in? Where are you from?" He then turned a bit more serious. "We are going to head right to the site. It is in a fairly remote part of the base. As I told the general, there isn't much to see, but I understand the need for closure. I ask that you stay outside the fenced area. I can't allow anyone inside the perimeter of the site, and please, no photos of the site."

We went through the gates to the base and passed the buildings that housed the personnel. I could see bombers out on the runway as we drove past the airfield.

"This spot is in a northern field. It is off the beaten path, but not too much further. I have to warn you, with these open fields, the wind is howling, and the cold can cut through you like a knife," said the commander.

The SUV came to a stop, and the commander said, "This is it." We left the SUV, and he was right. The wind must have been blowing at a stiff twenty miles an hour. There wasn't much to see. The area had a large, chain-link fence surrounding it. It was at least eight feet in height with barbed wire at the top. The fenced perimeter was enormous. As I stood with my face against the fence, it was my guess is that it was at least a half-mile to the center. I noticed the MP who was driving was armed and left the vehicle to stand watch over us.

"You are welcome to walk around the fence. It is a large area, but as long as you stay on this side, you're okay."

"How many were lost here?" Jim asked the commander.

"Twenty-six. We're not sure what went wrong or when we will be able to begin work on recovery."

While Jim, the commander, and the MP stayed near the SUV, Mark and I began to walk the perimeter of the fence. You could quickly tell which way the steady winds here would blow. Anything that didn't have substantial weight to it was piled up along an area halfway down one fence and halfway up another. It was trash, torn and weathered papers, drywall, ceiling tiles, fixtures, fabric from carpets, tiles, anything you could imagine was piling up pushed by the winds. I grabbed the fence with both hands and pressed my face to the chain link to peer just a little closer.

"Did we find the answers?" I asked Mark.

"Well, something happened here, something big. This mess could be what the military says it is. It's just that more pieces tend to fit the story in the book than the stories the real world is telling us."

I grabbed his hand. "Let's go home."

I looked through the fence across the way at our escorts. They were standing there casually watching us, but we had walked for quite a while around the perimeter. As we walked back, I kept my head down, shielding it from the cold. It was unusually noisy. There was a constant rustling of debris against the fence. I was scanning the debris when something caught my eye. The first thought I had deep inside of me was that I had found a needle in a haystack of debris. By all appearances, it looked about the size of two business cards placed side by side.

Something was caught on the fence, and it was fluttering in the breeze like a deck of cards being shuffled. It was tinted brown with soot and charred. Presumably, that damage came from heat and smoke of the explosion. It had a clip attached to it that was stuck on the fence. It was the only thing that kept it from making it through and across the empty plain and into oblivion. Without looking at it, I put it in my pocket and kept walking. I knew what it was.

"Did you find something?" Mark asked.

"I think I did," I replied.

"Let me have a look at it?"

"Let's wait until we get back. I'm afraid of what it might be."

When we returned to the vehicles, I noticed another black SUV off in the distance. A man and woman were standing near it watching us. They were too far away to make out any specific details.

"More security?" I asked the commander.

"Those two are special investigators that were sent by the President. They arrived here the day after the accident."

I stared at them for just a few seconds and wondered. I thanked the commander for his hospitality and for allowing us the opportunity to see the site.

"I hope this helped you heal and bring closure to this tragedy," he said.

"I believe it has. Thank you."

We were driven to the airport where we bid our farewell to Mark's uncle and headed back to Boston, and then on to Maine. All the while, tucked in the jacket might be the answer to the question of whether this was real or the imagination of John Behrens. It could have turned out to be another piece of debris that meant nothing. What were the odds? It was more out of fear and that I might be right that I didn't want to look. After two days, and hours and hours on planes, we arrived back in Bar Harbor. On the way to the house, we stopped to pick up Comet. He was so excited to see his master.

When we walked in the door, I felt at home. I was a stranger in his life, but he found his way into mine, and into my heart. This home felt like where I needed to be.

"Alright, I guess we better take a look at what you've found," Mark said.

"Do we really want to? Or just end the story here?"

"I don't know that the story has an ending."

I reached into my pocket and handed him what I found. He looked at it carefully. It is badly damaged.

"Maybe we should try to have it professionally cleaned to see if it can be recovered."

"No, let me see what can be done." He took a soft cloth and began to wipe the article.

"This is on thick. I may need to moisten the cloth and try again." As he slowly and carefully cleaned the item, the writing on the back became clearer until I could finally make it out. "Some things never change. I meant what I said the first time."

"The front. Clean the front," I said.

Slowly, the thick char and soot on the front of the picture came off. I was staring at my own image.

"It was true! Oh my God, it was true!" I picked up the photo and looked it over. "It's me. It is my handwriting. I never had a picture like this taken."

Mark looked at the front of the photo and then flipped it to see the back.

"There's no doubt about it. This is you in this photo. The name of the place where the photo was taken is listed here on the back. "Allison Roberts Portraits – Owings Mills Maryland"

I was stuttering and somewhat frantic. "I've never been, I've never had that photo taken. The story, the story was true. He hugged me and tried to calm me down. I was coming off of the emotional cliff I was on and getting a handle on myself.

"I believe it myself, and there is nothing we can do about it. What's important is what is here, now. Not something where the people involved are no longer around. My grandfather never let go of what happened. Do him a favor and let go for him. Bring closure to it."

He was right. I walked to the fireplace and picked up the canister of matches. I walked to the door and looked out at the ocean. Suddenly, I started running for the cliff. Mark and Comet were in pursuit. "Wait!" he yelled. I stopped. I looked down, and I was right at the markers for his grandfather and grandmother. I knelt to the ground and placed the picture on his grave. Taking a match, I lit the photo on fire.

"What are you doing? I thought you were going to jump off the cliff."

"I'm making this right."

It had taken just a few seconds for the picture to burn completely. I picked up what was left and crumbled it in my hand as I watched the ash fall to the ground.

"They are together now. Mystery solved. Case closed. That person in the book, in that photo, whom your grandfather loved, it wasn't me. It was a real person but from another time and place. The person in that picture is with him now. I don't know about a John Behrens or a Jake Kelly, but I know about you. Your grandfather said in his book you were a better version of him. If the book is true, he wanted the best for me, and he loved you and wanted the best for you. I think he loved us both. This thing I feel between us is the redemption of what transpired and what tortured his soul. It is now our chapter to write, our destiny, and this is what would make the future right. Come, come with me."

I grabbed his hand and ran back to the house. The nervous energy had me shaking. I rambled through my purse and pulled out a business card that had my picture on it. I flipped it over and wrote on the back and handed it to him. He looked at it, and his eyes welled. He hugged me tightly.

"It's all I got," I said.

"It will do," he said.

I had written the words, "Let's make a beautiful future together. Love, Beth."

This brings about the end of one chapter in a story and the beginning of another. The mysteries, facts, or fiction of Project Töten Zeit lie buried in a field in North Dakota and among the ashes along a cliff in Maine. As a remembrance of John and Maria Behrens, Jake Kelly, and the original Beth Milano, we changed the names and some facts and published their document as a book. The book became somewhat of a "cult favorite" spawning conspiracy theories about time travel and alternate history.

While it was just another "science fiction" story, we knew better. We knew it was non-fiction. It was a tale that no one would believe, but we wanted and needed it to be told. It was the story of life, love, loss, sacrifice, and redemption by those who gave so much to try to make the world a better place. The story of Project Töten Zeit is a warning of the dangers that come about when political and military leaders join forces to harness science as a weapon. Peace through strength has only resulted in the continuing escalation of more and more destructive weapons by each side. Where does it ever end? I wasn't sure it would end with the sacrifice of Jake Kelly, and the innocent men and women that died with him on that fateful day in a barren field at Minot. Only time will tell.

The next few months, Mark and I spent our precious time looking ahead to the future and forgetting the past. When summer came, and the whole family arrived for vacation, this house became a beehive of activity. This time, it was slightly more active. Mark and I got married on the lawn near the cliff overlooking the ocean with the entire family and Comet there to witness it. Mark continued to teach part-time. I taught piano and sold photos I had taken of the sights along the Maine coast in galleries from Boston to St. John's. It wasn't long before our family grew and we had the privilege to raise them in this house, a place where we created our own beautiful future. A future I hope would remain unchanged.

-- The End --

THE ASSASSINATION OF
FRANKLIN DELANO ROOSEVELT

A Short Story Prequel

to

Killing Time:
The Story of Projekt Töten Zeit

Michael Patrick O'Hara

ASCENSION TO THE THRONE

The difference between life and death, of success and failure, is often separated by moments in time. Perhaps, it was a last minute phone call that delayed your departure and prevented you from being in an accident. Maybe it was a chance encounter with a stranger that changed the course of your life. Such are the ways of the universe. The past and the present are intertwined. Each event has a cascading ripple effect downstream. This is one such story. A chance set of circumstances that placed two people in the right place at the right time to change the course of a country. It is only by sheer luck that fate would intervene. Months later, a more deliberate attempt to once again change the world's destiny would occur. Only this time, it would place one of those people in the right place at the wrong time.

It would not be a ripple from the past that would alter what was written as history, but a messenger from the future. This time, divine providence would not intervene. An assassin would succeed in killing the 32nd President of the United States, Franklin D. Roosevelt. It would be the fourth time a President had been assassinated in office.

Since the beginning of the Great Depression, even the summer months seemed dark and cold in America. Americans were jobless, hope for a brighter future for the country was dimming. In the years that followed the crash of 1929, it seemed a foregone conclusion that President Herbert Hoover's bid for reelection in the 1932 election would fail. Hoover promised a return to prosperity if he was reelected, but Americans had little faith in his leadership. The only question that remained was who would win the nomination at the Democratic Party's national convention. The victor would most assuredly be the next President of the United States.

The battle for the presidency came down to three candidates. Franklin Delano Roosevelt, John Nance Garner, and Alfred Smith. One would be

President and the other Vice President. The third, also a former Governor and businessman, would go on to build and operate the Empire State Building. In the shadows of the race for the presidency was a little-known figure by the name of James Farley. James Farley was a master strategist. If Roosevelt was the cheery, optimistic face of the campaign, Farley was the puppet master that pulled the strings. It would be Farley's interaction that would seal the deal for Roosevelt as his party's nominee.

Roosevelt and Farley had orchestrated a winning campaign strategy from the outset, and it looked like clear sailing to the nomination. There was just one obstacle, the Democratic nominating process. By their own rules, a nominee for president had to gain a two-thirds majority. As strong as Roosevelt was as a candidate, he successfully obtained a majority but fell short of the two-thirds. His opponents, Speaker of the House John Nance Garner, and Former New York Governor Al Smith saw this as a strategy to secure their nomination or that of another outside candidate, anyone but Roosevelt.

Their strategy appeared to be working. After several ballots, Roosevelt failed to hit the magic mark. Campaign manager James Farley negotiated a deal with Nance Garner to drop his bid and join Roosevelt on the ticket as his Vice President. With an agreement in hand, Roosevelt easily won the nomination.

On Tuesday, November 8, 1932, the country's optimism lifted to new heights. Franklin Delano Roosevelt was elected President of the United States in an overwhelming landslide. His victory was by a margin the likes of which the country had never witnessed. The election ushered in sweeping changes for the country. Gone was the twelve-year Republican control of both Houses of Congress. In was a new era of leadership and a new deal for the country.

By the numbers, the country was still heading downward, but the bottom was in sight. The election would mark the beginning of the end of the Great Depression and set America on another collision course with history, or so it was thought.

It would be five long months before Roosevelt would be sworn into office. He wasted no time planning his future and pitching his vision for America's future, "The New Deal." The President-elect believed that optimism was a strong a cure as government intervention. Until he officially assumed office, it was the only card he had to play.

On February 15, 1932, just seventeen days before officially becoming the 32nd President of the United States, Franklin Roosevelt was finishing a vacation in Miami. He used the time there to put the final pieces in place for his administration. As his prepared to leave the city, his car made its way through the crowds lining the streets of Bayfront Park. A special ramp had been built for the vehicle to roll up and elevate it above the crowd.

Seeing hope in the eyes of those gathered to hear him speak, Roosevelt sensed a moment to rally the crowd with his rhetoric. The car stopped at the summit of the ramp with all eyes fixed on the soon to be Commander-in-Chief. Roosevelt carefully propped himself up against the back seat of the open touring car. It was a choreographed charade to hide his polio affliction from the public. With the crowd cheering, Roosevelt gave a speech to inspire those seeking a turn in their fortunes. As he concluded, in his unmistakable New York accent, he vowed, "he'd be back". Before he finished his remarks, a voice yelled from the back of the crowd.

"Too many people are starving!"

The voice came from a diminutive man named Guiseppe Zangara, who stood only five feet tall. His small stature made him barely visible over those standing in front of him. Suddenly, he raised his .32 caliber handgun and fired a shot towards the President-elect. The crowd startled, began to scream in horror. His first shot missed. He raised his gun again and took aim at Roosevelt. It was then that fate intervened. A woman standing in front of Zangara, a doctor's wife grabbed his arm. Shots flew at random striking several and wounding Anton Cermak, the Mayor of Chicago. At the time the bullet struck Cermak, he was standing less than a foot, maybe two from Roosevelt. It was perhaps a sign of divine intervention that the proclaimed "Savior of America" would be spared.

It did not take long before an angry mob stormed the would-be assassin. As the crowd knocked Zangara to the ground, they began to kick and relentlessly pummel him with punches. As if God-like, Roosevelt commanded his supporters to cease its attack and exclaimed, "Let justice judge this man." It was then Roosevelt slid back into his seat and cradled the dying Mayor in his arms as the car sped away towards the hospital. Mayor Anton Cermak would later die at Miami's Jackson Memorial Hospital from a bullet fired from an eight-dollar handgun.

Perhaps it was not the hand of fate this time that spared Roosevelt, but the quick reaction of a bystander. Roosevelt's would be assassin Guiseppe Zangara, would die in the electric chair thirteen months later. He would outlive the man he sought to kill.

THE ASSASSIN

It sent a shudder through the psyche of Americans as they read the headlines in the morning paper that the President-elect had barely escaped assassination in Florida. A sense of hopelessness could be felt that morning. Perhaps, "this endless depression is our fate," remarked one man after hearing the news. All hope was not lost, Roosevelt had survived, but it was feared that the struggles of the unemployed and working poor would continue without an end in sight.

Meanwhile, eleven hundred miles to the north in downtown Philadelphia, a mysterious man, and a woman waited in a crowded train station. They appeared out of place. Standing out in the crowd by being obvious about not trying to stand out. A nosey woman seated in the station near the couple became alarmed when she thought she heard the man mention the English words "kill" and "President" interspersed in the German, or perhaps Russian they were speaking. At first, she thought they were referring to the events in Florida. As she watched them more carefully, she became suspicious of their behavior. Fearing the couple was up to no good, she decided to play it safe and alert the police.

By the time she found a policeman in the station and returned, the couple was gone. The policeman thanked her for her diligence and assured her.

"We're all on pins and needles ma'am. I'm sure they were just as shocked by today's news as we were."

As he glanced at the schedule posted on the wall, the cop remarked.

"They probably caught that last train to Baltimore or the one to New York."

"That same Baltimore train also goes to Washington!" She exclaimed.

"And Richmond, Raleigh, Atlanta - That train goes a lot of places ma'am. I'm sure it was nothing. If it makes you feel better, I'll call the police

299

in Baltimore and tell them to be on the lookout for the couple. Can you give me a description?"

"The man was older than the woman. Maybe in his 50's, she was much younger, maybe 25-30 years old. They were speaking German back and forth, or maybe it was Russian. No, I think they were both Germans, but they could have been Russians I suppose. The age difference will give them away. I think they were those German Nazis we keep hearing about!" She said. Her loud tone drew curious attention from onlookers in the station.

Though Hitler had just come to power two weeks earlier, word had spread quickly around the world of a new and dynamic Chancellor of Germany, who was also the leader of the Nazi party. Images of Hitler standing on the balcony of the Reich Chancellery to the cheers of thousands painted the portrait of the arrival of two new leaders on the world stage. In both countries, America and Germany they were seen as saviors sent to rescue their people from the depths of depression.

"What makes you think that they were Nazis ma'am?" Asked the Policeman with a slightly hidden laugh in his voice.

"He had a confidence and swagger, and a typical German brash attitude. He looked military to me by the way he walked and by the tone of his voice."

True to his word, the cop did tell his desk sergeant who in turn did notify the police at Penn Station in Baltimore. Since there was no credible threat, only the hunch of an eavesdropping woman, the police in Baltimore passively kept watch. When the train stopped at Penn Station, the police on the platform watched those departing and then walked through the train. No couple matching the description was found.

Of course, they wouldn't find a couple. Indeed, this mysterious man is a would-be assassin. He and his companion were traveling together until they reached Philadelphia. Further confusing the search, they were not German or Russian at all, but Americans, speaking in a foreign language to disguise the context of their conversation.

Unbeknownst to anyone, the suspects had caught separate trains. The woman boarded a train to New York's Grand Central Station, while the man headed to Baltimore where he disembarked. While the police were looking for a German or Russian speaking couple, he slipped by unnoticed. The event was chalked up to the overactive imagination of a nervous bystander. Little did anyone know that FDR's assassin was now in the clear and one step closer to his target.

Renting a room in downtown Baltimore was convenient for this mysterious figure. He was close enough to Washington to scout his victim, but out of the glare of the activities, and scrutiny around the upcoming inauguration. By all accounts, he seemed to be just another average citizen. What stood out to his neighbors was not that he appeared unemployed, although many were, but that he didn't have money problems. They also found it odd that he never went anywhere without his briefcase. However, these oddities were never enough to reach the threshold beyond "just strange" to "worrisome."

In the would-be assassin's room, he laid out papers and maps detailing where the President-elect would be over the next five months. By some strange manner, he had gained access to information that the President-elect himself did not have or know. On the counter was the newspaper with the headline about the attempted assassination of FDR. The man did not seem fazed by the news that an unemployed malcontent had sought to steal his prize. It was almost as if didn't care or wasn't surprised by the failure. "It what was to be expected of an amateur," he said to himself.

Meanwhile, aboard a friend's yacht in the Caribbean, Franklin Roosevelt continued his vacation before sailing up to Washington for the inauguration. Roosevelt's ample weeks on the sea after the election, and before assuming the presidency, provided plenty of opportunities for an experienced sailor to plot an attempt to kill him. Sinking the President-elect's yacht, especially at night, would likely have presented the disabled Roosevelt with limited ability to escape from below deck. Little did Roosevelt know that as he soaked up the sun and the salt air he loved so much, that his days were numbered.

In a rented room in the city of Baltimore, a stranger circled on a map, a small Canadian island named Campobello on the southern side of New Brunswick. He carefully drew a line through the waters down the Atlantic, up the Chesapeake Bay, and to the Severn River. There, he circled the city of Annapolis and wrote the date, July 4, 1933.

AMERICA RISES

It was to be the dawn of a new era for America. Finally, after nearly four years of struggling through an economic downturn, which Americans had never seen in their lifetime or their parent's lifetime, hope had emerged. It was March, just another late winter day typical for the metro Washington area. Skies were cloudy, and the temperature was in the low 40's. Too warm for snow, too cold to be comfortable outside. It had been a long few months of waiting since Election Day, but coronation day was here. America would get a would-be King.

To his credit, Roosevelt had a plan in place to revive America. The challenge would be that just taking the oath of office and sitting behind a desk in the Oval Office on the first day was not going to make a difference. Franklin Roosevelt had one great advantage; he was already a master of illusion. Throughout his candidacy, he had hidden from the American public the severity of his polio affliction for fear of not looking fit for the job.

On this day, with the heavy steel braces supporting his legs and his remarkable upper body strength, he walked to the podium. The crowd had no idea what an incredible feat this was for the President-elect. It was only by clinging to his son, and carefully swinging his legs that he gave the appearance of walking.

As Roosevelt finished the oath and approached the podium, the audience in attendance was silent. Security was tight, and the crowd of two hundred and fifty thousand focused intently on the new President. Positioned near the front on the east side of the Capitol stood the mysterious figure from the train station in Philadelphia. He surveyed the sea of people gathered as they salivated like hungry animals waiting for their master's table scraps. He then turned his attention back to the platform and focused on Roosevelt's every move. He appeared more interested in the mechanics of how Roosevelt maneuvered. The man was dressed for the weather in an overcoat and hat.

Missing was the briefcase that always seemed in his possession. As Roosevelt started to speak, he focused intently on him as if he were watching prey through the scope of a rifle. The opening words of the inaugural speech would be the most memorable.

"So, first of all, let me assert my firm belief that the only thing we have to fear is fear itself. Nameless, unreasoning, unjustified terror, which paralyzes needed efforts to convert retreat into advance. In every dark hour of our national life, a leadership of frankness and of vigor has met with that understanding and support of the people themselves, which is essential to victory. And I am convinced that you will again give that support to leadership in these critical days."

Continuing for another twenty minutes Roosevelt's message was targeted at those most affected by the Great Depression. He railed against the bankers and businessman whose greed was the spark that ignited the economic downturn. He offered hope for those unemployed by promising not to talk about the problem, but act. The man in the crowd was unimpressed. If only Roosevelt knew what I knew, he thought. Then, he would have greater fear. For this mysterious man knew the future. He knew what the next few months would bring.

Roosevelt wasted no time getting to work and would not attend any of the inaugural balls. Instead, he would acclimate himself and his staff to the White House. Within hours, he convened his new cabinet and had them all sworn in at once. Like shots fired from a cannon, the new team landed new ideas, and program after program in the halls of Congress. The Hoover mantra of small government was laid to waste as Roosevelt brought the heavy hand of federal intervention to bear with an avalanche of programs and subsidies. Within days, Roosevelt had a banking relief act drafted and through Congress. In just over a week, the Treasury Department had banks open again for business. The onslaught of government integration into the fabric of America's economic engine slowly began to take hold. America was like a giant ship. Roosevelt's inauguration did little to stop the downward slide, but gradually the boat started to turn.

The first hundred days of Roosevelt's presidency defined all future administrations with its audacious goals and ambitious agenda. As the summer of 1933 approached, storm clouds were forming on the horizon. A dark, ominous cloud was about to appear and signal the return of dark days to Washington.

CAMPOBELLO

It was the evening of June 16th, 1933. A car left the White House with the President. The presidential motorcade was headed to Washington's Union Station. At 8:30 pm, the President boarded a private train headed for Boston. Earlier in the day in Baltimore, at the front desk of the apartment building where he was staying, the mysterious man received a cryptic telegram. It contained only the words "The seas are calm, and the sands are cooler at night in Bethany." Upon receipt of the message, the man hurriedly left in his car. Driving for hours, he finally arrived at Bethany Beach in Delaware. The long summer days meant daylight lingered well into the evening. He drove down the road into Maryland where he dined at a local seafood restaurant. Even in this time where families struggled, the town was visibly more crowded with renewed optimism and summer vacationers trying to escape the problems back home.

As the evening grew late, the man drove his car to a secluded spot just south of Bethany Beach. The beach was deserted. This desolate stretch of sand was a protected seashore with no homes or cottages anywhere in sight. He waited, and waited, scanning the vast ocean. It was after midnight when the moon appeared on the horizon. It was less than a half-full waning crescent moon that cast a dim white streak across the ocean to the shore. Only the repetitive sounds of waves crashing on the beach broke the strange silence that was in the air. Finally, off in the distance, he spotted a blinking light. Using a flashlight he had brought along, he sent a message back. It was confirmed that the vessel offshore was his intended contact. Occasionally, he would signal the ship to provide a bearing. An hour had passed when a large raft with four men rowing reached the breakers and then the shore.

"Is this what I asked for?" the man said.

"Yah" replied one of the men.

From the raft, the men removed two wooden boxes. Each box was about three feet long and a foot wide. Without further conversation, the men climbed back into the raft and headed back out to sea. The man watched for a few minutes as they disappeared into the darkness of the night. Where they came from was just one more part of the mystery.

He unlatched the boxes one at a time and inspected the contents. It brought a smile to his face. This was exactly what he wanted. Despite their length, the boxes were not too heavy. He was able to carry them both to his car where he carefully placed them in the trunk. It was far too late to drive back to Baltimore. He had already been up all night and into the wee hours of the morning. He managed to find a vacancy at a local "mom and pop" motel in Bethany and stayed the night. The room was not up to his standards, but he was looking past the sparse accommodations. There was no rush now, in just sixteen days, this would all be over.

At 7:30 am, the train carrying the President arrived in Boston. The busy first hundred days had kept the President away from his real passion, the sea. His upbringing prepared him for greatness, but it was the simple things like sailing the seas were perhaps his true calling. The President's agenda that first day called for a stop in Groton, home of the exclusive prep school he attended, and then off Marion to depart for eleven days at sea. The selection of Marion as a launching point was no surprise. The place where Roosevelt's boat was docked belonged to a doctor, Dr. William McDonald. McDonald was well known for his therapy treatments for polio patients. One of those patients was Roosevelt. This stop on the president's itinerary was a check-up with the doctor before casting off. Unlike when Roosevelt sailed the waters of the Atlantic before taking office, this time the seas would not be empty.

The vessel that Roosevelt would be sailing was the Amberjack II, an impressive forty-foot yacht leased for the President's voyage. From the time the President left the train and made his way to Marion, security was visible and tight. The last thing anyone wanted was a reoccurrence of what took place in Miami. When Roosevelt finally left the dock, a Navy destroyer and a flotilla of vessels were in his fleet. The forty-foot schooner, flying the President's flag at its stern was on its way.

"We're going to give these boys a grand time! Let's see if they can keep pace." Roosevelt laughed out loud to the crew. Nothing it seemed was going penetrate the screen around Roosevelt's ship, but this wasn't going to be a direct route to Campobello. His boat would zigzag the coast darting in and out of coves and making numerous stops along the way including Woods Hole, Portland, and up along the Maine coast before crossing the Bay of Fundy to Campobello Island on June 30th. The thick summer fog that shrouded the cold waters of the North Atlantic delayed his progress. By the time he reached Campobello, the President had been at sea for eleven days.

The President's time at Campobello was short-lived. The Roosevelt's had owned a house and property here since the late 1800's. Campobello was in Canadian territory just barely across the border from Maine. This island was a quiet and remote place, whose isolation was its biggest draw. It was only ten miles long, irregular in shape, and just a few miles wide.

"I have so many fond memories here, and just one bad one." He told the staff that was with him.

"I have a sense I shall never set foot here again."

Indeed, Campobello was a place that Roosevelt loved dearly, but it also harbored painful memories. It was August of 1921, when here on Campobello Island that Roosevelt first felt ill. It was here that his polio was first diagnosed, forever robbing him of the ability to walk on his own. Before polio, Campobello saw the athletic and vibrant Roosevelt, hiking, boating, swimming, and partaking in the entire offerings of this small Canadian island. Now, with just a day and night spent here, he was ready to go back to the sea.

Back in Baltimore, the man's time was running out. He was becoming more of a curiosity to his neighbors, and it was making him uncomfortable. He was getting a reputation with those he encountered for being abrupt and rude. The fact that he was always well groomed and well dressed with no visible means of support drew the ire of some in these tough times. All it would take was one bent out of shape neighbor to call the cops, and his plan might be exposed. It was July 1st. He just needed three more days.

As evening arrived, the President bid farewell to Campobello. A launch had come from the USS Ellis to take the President to the Navy destroyer. Arriving at the ship and unable to walk the ramp, Roosevelt was hoisted to the deck. A sailor raised the Presidential Flag on the main mast of the vessel. Ship's Commander Leland Lampman saluted the Commander in Chief as he reached the deck. His aide helped Roosevelt to his feet.

"Permission to come aboard Commander," said the President.

"It is an honor to have you onboard Mr. President." Replied Lampman.

"I'm glad to be aboard such a fine ship with such a fine crew."

"Thank you, Mr. President. We are just about ready to get you on your way to the Indianapolis."

"Commander, You've heard of a slow boat to China?"

"Yes, Mr. President."

"Well, I'm interested in a slow boat to Annapolis!"

The President laughed heartily at his own pun. Roosevelt was at home on a warship. If he could be commanding a ship instead of a country, he would do it in a minute. Fate had dealt the President a hand he didn't want to play. First, it was his father refusing to let him attend the Naval Academy, and then the onset of polio. It was a lesson in time and destiny. Was it these events that put the man in this position to lead the country at this critical time, or did it prevent him or someone else from a leading a different cause? In just a few days the co-conspirators of fate, time, and destiny would meet to intervene once again in Roosevelt's life.

It had been a short cruise on the Ellis when it came alongside the USS Indianapolis at midnight and transferred the President to the nearly new flagship Portland-class cruiser. Being a flagship, it had the accommodations for a flag officer and his staff. As Commander in Chief, it was only fitting that the President would occupy that space, a moment he relished. Captain John M. Smeallie welcomed the President to the Navy's state of the art vessel and then ordered her to sail at full speed to Annapolis with the Ellis trailing behind. As the Indianapolis came up to full speed, the eight boilers were consuming a thousand gallons of fuel every hour, twenty-five gallons for every mile of ocean she sailed. Those boilers were powering the four steam turbines, which in turn drove the ship's four screws. Churning through the water, the Indianapolis reached her top speed of thirty-two knots. The President was just two days from reaching his destination, the Naval Academy.

They were not alone on the seas. Sitting off in the distance, undetected, and carefully watching the event was a submarine. Was it a friend or foe? It sat stationary at periscope depth. An enemy of the United States would have had the perfect opportunity to sink the ship, but the U.S. was not at war with anyone. Such an act would have started another World War, but against who? Only when the Indianapolis and Ellis cleared sight, did the sub break the surface and headed east into the open waters of the Atlantic.

ANNAPOLIS

As the Indianapolis continued to steam south from Maine, preparations were already underway in Maryland's capital city. It was already Sunday, July 2st. Further down the Atlantic, it was a typical hot and humid summer day in Annapolis. The town was full of flags and banners celebrating the upcoming 4th of July. With such proximity to the holiday, it was hard to know if the patriotic displays were for the President, the holiday, or both. The mood was noticeably different for this year's Independence Day celebration.

An enlightened mood in the country made for a more festive atmosphere than in past years. It was unlikely that the people celebrating in the streets at the Annapolis City Dock were aware that the President was on his way there. In the crowd was the man who sought to change the mood and the course of history. He had no reservations about his task. For him, this was all about country, but whose country? Was this man of mystery a foreign agent or a domestic terrorist? No one would believe his story if he were caught, and if he got away with it, no one would understand the greater good he sought to achieve.

This was not a mission for personal fame or notoriety. For the man had no qualms with the President and no anti-government ideology. His part was just one piece of a larger puzzle, not a pawn, but a chess master, making one calculated move after another. This was the first piece of that puzzle, and it remained to be seen if the larger picture would come into focus. If it didn't work as planned, he would be the architect of perhaps one of the greatest tragedies in American history.

In the flag officer's conference room, the President met with his closest friends and advisors that were traveling with him, Henry Morgenthau, who was in line to be a future Secretary of the Treasury, and Colonel Louis Howe, the President's Secretary. Louis Howe was a long time friend and Roosevelt's closest confidant. His title was "secretary", but his functioning role was as Chief of the White House staff.

Howe wasn't actually a colonel in the military sense, but rather a "Kentucky Colonel". It was an honorary title bestowed on him by the Kentucky Governor, at Howe's persistent urging. Howe was thin, and had a gaunt appearance with sunken cheeks and darkened skin under his eyes. At just sixty-three, he looked much older than his age. While Roosevelt was also a chain smoker, Howe spent almost every waking moment with a cigarette in his mouth. He had known to be sickly for most of his life, and the smoking only aggravated his condition. The room was filled with enough smoke that it would have choked the average person. Morgenthau, a non-smoker seemed particularly bothered by the stagnant air. After reviewing the country's economic progress and the status of further economic reforms still pending in Congress, the conversation began to wind down. The restless President had enough of the stuffy room.

"Gentlemen, you are keeping me from the fresh sea air topside," said the President.

"Mr. President, are we planning any response to what is happening in Germany?" said Morgenthau.

"We need to fix America and not worry about Europe." Said Howe.

"Now, now fellas, I'm with Louis on this one. Germany is digging out of the same hole we are, and this Hitler chap is feeding propaganda to the masses. It is all talk to get German people's mind away from the despair they are in, not unlike what we are doing. I've read Mein Kampf, and its translation it abhorrent to me. I suspect the translators took some liberty with the words to incite us into another war. The Brits and the French are feeding this hysteria."

Morgenthau was insistent.

"Mr. President, there's word that Hitler is about to enact a law that bars all Jews from holding public office. Shouldn't we have a response?"

"We'll stay out of it for now. Hitler and Germany are Europe's problem, America is ours." Said Roosevelt.

The President, helped by his son, FDR, JR., who was also onboard, made his way back to the deck.

"We have big oceans on each side of this country. Therefore, the White House would have been much better suited if it were a ship!" Remarked the President.

"Commander, when do you expect us to dock in Annapolis?"

"Tomorrow morning Mr. President." Said Captain Smeallie.

"Splendid! Another day at sea!" replied Roosevelt.

Unlike the fresh sea breeze created by the Indianapolis cruising over the cold waters of the North Atlantic, in an apartment room in Baltimore, it was sweltering. The man arrived back from Annapolis and began to clear out his temporary home. The notes, maps, papers detailing his plan had all been removed from the walls. The risk was increasing daily for him, as the time grew shorter and shorter. He was sitting on a pile of incriminating evidence that at the moment would be difficult to explain and equally difficult to discard. Between the two large boxes in his car and this information about the president's itinerary, a stop, a search by the police would not be a good thing.

It wasn't his first choice, but he opted to stay in the apartment another day until late afternoon on Tuesday, the 4th. Just sitting and waiting for his time. Prohibition was still in effect, but he had managed to get his hands on a bootleg bottle of whiskey from a neighborhood speakeasy. He drank just a few small shots. The intent of the shots was not to take the edge off his nerves but to sharpen them. After those first few shots, he indulged himself with a few more but was careful not to impair his senses.

He had an enormous task ahead of him. Out on the road, he ran the risk of innocently being caught for a traffic violation that might grow into something more. He knew where he had to be and when. Sitting tight, staying out of the way of everyone was his best chance at success.

It was 2 am in the early morning hours on Monday, July 3rd when the Indianapolis left the Atlantic Ocean and turned into the Chesapeake Bay. She was now heading north again up the bay toward Annapolis. She had slowed to 15 knots and was just 90 miles from her destination. By 8:30 am she dropped anchor just outside the area where the Severn River met the bay. The United States Naval Academy was visible from the ship's port side. In the morning briefing by Howe, the President was given the news that Morgenthau's warning had come to pass. Hitler had enacted a law that barred Jews from holding office.

"Put this on the agenda. We'll discuss this if we have time with the cabinet when they get here tomorrow." He told Howe.

The President was home but wasn't ready to leave the comfortable confines of the ship just yet. This ship was only a year old compared to the one hundred and thirty-three-year-old White House. The contrast was stark. The White House seemed in disrepair and was showing its age. Though he had only been in office for four months, Roosevelt either cared little or didn't notice the deteriorating condition of the building.

It was strange since Roosevelt was used to a somewhat higher standard of living. Perhaps, he saw the executive mansion not as a luxury for the President, but as the "people's house", and like the people, it had fallen on hard times. It perfectly matched the depressing mood the country had just suffered. However, this ship was brand-new, and the sea air was invigorating the spirit of the President and the new course he set for America.

The President's son, FDR, Jr. departed the ship early to head back to the White House where his mother, Eleanor, had already returned by train from New England. The President stayed on board for his meetings with military leaders as an excuse to remain at sea. It had been almost 157 years to the day since America declared its independence from the British. If they had to fight a war today, the military, much like the people it protected, had also fallen on hard times. The United States once mighty army had slipped quite far since World War I. The blessing of vast oceans separating the country from potential enemies gave Americans peace of mind. The navy was the one bright spot. Overall, the U.S. ranked somewhere around the 17th or 18th in total military power. It's army, somewhere between the Belgians and Portuguese in troop strength. The mighty United States was hardly a country with a battle-ready force. If a war were to break out in Europe suddenly, or on the homeland, the U.S. was not ready to fight.

In Congress, the appetite was not on battles and future wars, but on isolationism. "Fix America before we try to fix the world" was the mantra heard through the halls of Congress. Franklin Roosevelt seemed in agreement for the moment. The French and the British were sounding the alarms of another resurgent Germany, but he wanted no part of it at the moment. Any military budget increases or buildup would have to wait.

As the sun set over the bay, Roosevelt stayed on board the Indianapolis for one more night. From the deck, he watched the fireworks up river towards Annapolis. He could hear the sound of revelers celebrating the holiday.

"Listen to them." He said to Louis Howe.

"We've made a difference in their lives, whether real or imagined, and we did it in just four months. They feel like celebrating again. Look at what we can do in the next four years!"

"Mr. President, after what Herbert Hoover did to this country, you are a miracle worker, a God in their eyes." Responded Howe.

"Herbert is a good man, a victim of circumstance more than anything. It could have happened to anyone, even a democrat! As for this idol worshipping of politicians. A President is a man, not a God. I am a mortal. The hand of God can take me at any moment, but the spirit of the American people can never be taken."

Howe wheeled the President to his room where he retired for the evening. He had a book that he was reading, "Down and Out in London and Paris" by George Orwell. The semi-fictional work was a half-truth account of life in those two cities. It was meant to be a thought provoking look at society and poverty. A man who was born with so much pondered the meaning of the words from those that had so little.

The President read a few chapters while drinking a martini and smoking his cigarettes. The former, he didn't want to indulge in on the deck in front of the troops. Eventually, he fell asleep. The partying and reveling continued in the city of Annapolis well into the night. It was akin to a lullaby that was music to the President's ears. It was a joyous celebration of a country on the mend.

A DAY OF INFAMY

The President slept in later than usual on Tuesday morning July 4, 1933. Perhaps it was the late-night revelers, the second martini, or the prospect of having to leave the ship that evening and head back to the White House that had the President wanting to stay in bed. At 9 am, Louis Howe knocked on the President's door and entered the cabin. The President was sitting up in bed.

"Perhaps I put a bit too much gin in that last martini." He said as he laughed.

"What time are they getting here?" Roosevelt asked, referring to the cabinet members.

"They should be here around 1pm Mr. President. You are scheduled to meet until 5 pm, then a celebration on deck for the 4th. Finally, we'll depart for the White House around 8 pm.

"We're going to miss the fireworks! Rockets' red glare from aboard a ship!"

"I can delay our departure, Mr. President." Said Howe.

"No need for that, I doubt I could top Francis Scott Key when it comes to reflecting on our great country. Although, the irony of putting the words to British music. Those Brits must get a kick out of that each time they hear it!" The President then began to cite a verse.

"O thus be it ever, when freemen shall stand
Between their loved homes and the war's desolation.
Blessed with victory and peace, may the Heaven-rescued land
Praise the Power that hath made and preserved us a nation!
Then conquer we must, when our cause it is just,
And this be our motto: In God We Trust.
And the star-spangled banner in triumph shall wave
Over the land of the free and the home of the brave."

"Those are powerful words. We must never seek to conquer, but seek to bring peace wherever the whisper of war is spoken." Said Roosevelt.

"Yes, Mr. President. Do you think there will be another war?"

"I pray not. War is terrible, a scourge put upon a land that leaves scars that never quite heal, and for many, the harm is much greater. Those Germans seemed destined to want to rule the world, and the Soviet Union isn't far behind in their ambition. What is it about that people? Time after time they try and try. I will give them credit. They take a punch and get right back on their feet and are ready to go again. I feel the next war will be one that will end all wars, but at a terrible price."

It was just after 11 am when Lowe wheeled the President to the deck. There was a mild breeze, but it was warm and humid. This was after all Maryland in July. Captain Smeallie came by to check on the President.

"Is there anything I can get you, Mr. President?" Said the captain.

"Take us back out to the Atlantic captain." Replied Roosevelt.

"Is that an order sir?"

"No, no, captain, I wish we could, but I suppose it is time for me to get back to work!"

Roosevelt sat on the deck for an hour, enjoying the sea air and the occasional sound of water lapping up against the hull of the ship. He was busy writing personal letters and notes. One letter was to his mistress, Lucy Mercer Rutherfurd.

My Dearest Lucy,

I have just had the most wonderful few weeks at sea. First as captain of my own vessel, and now as Commander-in-Chief aboard this tremendous naval vessel. Oh, how I love the sea. I only wish that you could be here with me. Once we get the country back on its feet, I will find more time for us. I promise.

All my love,
Franklin

He had carefully chosen his words. Stepping over the line, but not so far as to be divulging any more incriminating details beyond what was needed. Mercer might have been the love of his life, but it was difficult to ascertain. He had a mesmerizing pull on the fairer sex. There were others that seemed to be in love with him at any given time. Most enjoyed the flirtatious banter and dancing on the ever-dangerous line of being involved with a married man, especially this married man, the president.

314

Roosevelt sealed the letter and handed it to Howe asking him to see to it that the message reached Lucy Mercer personally. Howe glanced at the envelope and nodded to the President. The ship was still at anchor on the mouth of the Severn when a launch carrying the highest-ranking members of his cabinet arrived.

The country was not at war, but warmongering by the new German leader had brought the specter of another world conflict to the forefront. This meeting was to bring the President up to speed on the latest saber-rattling by the Germans. Roosevelt had no interest in getting America in the middle of a British, French, and German squabble.

Present at the meeting were the Secretary of State, Cordell Hull, Secretary of War, George Dern, Secretary of the Navy, Frank Knox, and the current and future Secretary of the Treasury, William Woodin, and Henry Morgenthau.

Dern led the briefing by saying that "war in Europe was inevitable." Woodin apologized for what he was about to say, and then proceeded to speak "a war where we are the supplier to the Brits would give the economy here a significant shot in the arm." Perturbed, Morgenthau stated, "only if the Brits paid us for what we provided, otherwise we would only make matters here worse." Roosevelt interrupted the skirmish.

"Gentlemen, we are not supplying materials for war, nor are we going to war. We are not going to fix our country by supplying the means for others to destroy theirs".

The squabbling continued, but the President was firm. The focus was on America.

Roosevelt might have had a change of heart had he known the real motivation behind Germany's bluster. The Germans had a chip on their shoulder, namely the war reparations and the humiliation put upon them by the Treaty of Versailles after the First World War. Their end game was to build an empire strong enough to punish those that placed impossible post-war demands on Germany and to defeat the Soviet Union. Hitler from the outset dreamed of an alliance between America, and a Europe he controlled to defeat the Soviets.

For the moment, FDR was too focused on America's woes. That opened the door for Hitler's only other recourse, build a war machine that would conquer Europe, and then bring America to the table later to jointly finish off Russia. It was a fool's dream. America would not likely let a free Europe fall to Germany. It would take an extraordinary set of circumstances to convince FDR and the American people to back Germany against Russia. Little did anyone know, but just such an event was about to appear on the horizon.

The meeting adjourned after a few hours, and the Fourth of July celebration began on deck. The crew of the Indianapolis had the chance to mingle with the upper echelon of the government. There was laughter and the telling of long tales, mainly by the President himself.

In Baltimore, the time had arrived. The man did one last sweep of his apartment to ensure nothing had been left behind. Convinced it was clean, he took a handful of papers and tossed them above his head. They fluttered into the air, then scattered, making a mess on the clean apartment floor. He surveyed the papers strewn on the floor and then left abruptly. Acknowledging no one on his way out, he got to his car and opened the trunk. The boxes were there. He slammed the trunk lid and hurriedly sped away. It was the first sign of nervousness he had shown.

It was early evening on a day of joyous celebration, America's independence from Great Britain one hundred and fifty-seven years earlier. It also marked the beginning of a resurgent United States. It was hot and humid, but the typical summer thunderstorm appeared to be building off to the west. The threatening storms were a welcome sight for the mysterious stranger. Overcast skies would aid in bringing darkness a little bit sooner, and the impending rain would keep revelers off the roads. He had made his way towards Annapolis, pulling off and parking near an overpass on Route 50. There he waited patiently in his car until 7:30 pm when another vehicle pulled up alongside him. He left his car and got into the passenger side of this new stranger's vehicle that just arrived.

"Do you have the information about your government you promised?" The driver asked in a thick foreign accent.

"Yes, I do." The passenger responded.

With that exchange, the man pulled a weapon from his side and shot the driver in the head killing him instantly. He then put his gloves on the lifeless driver to ensure that the gunshot residue would give the appearance of a suicide. Before he left the car, he placed an envelope under the passenger seat. It was then that he transferred the box in his trunk to the vehicle of the dead man. The mysterious stranger then removed the contents of the boxes he had just placed in the trunk of the dead man's car. Carrying two weapons he made his way to the overpass. It was now almost 8:30 pm. It had started to rain and the extended evening light of summer had been chased away by the storm clouds. In the rain, he watched light traffic below on Route 50 as it headed from Annapolis to Washington, D.C.

Finally, he spotted what he had been waiting for, a police car escorting the President's car, one in the front and one in the rear. A few vehicles were trailing, likely the Secret Service. The rain it appeared had scuttled the typical motorcycle escort, and in a stroke of luck had limited the protection detail around the President's vehicle.

The man on the overpass had his weapons of choice, an early version of the German Panzerfaust, a rocket-propelled grenade launcher. It would come to be known as the "Iron Fist" during World War II. However, this weapon should not exist yet. It was ahead of its time by at least ten years. The grenade launcher was German, but the markings on the weapon were Russian. It translated to "Devil's Spear." He would get only two shots, one with each weapon. A steady hand and luck would be what he needed.

As the vehicles approached, he placed one of the grenade launchers on his shoulder and aimed at the first police car. It was just sixty feet from passing beneath the overpass when he fired. Boom! It struck the police vehicle directly on the front causing a thunderous explosion and fire. The car stopped and momentarily blocked the president's car. As the president's car tried to back up and navigate around the debris and evade the sniper, a second shot was fired. It was a direct hit through the windshield of the car and into the main compartment.

The explosion blew the car apart and rained pieces of debris on the highway. A cloud of smoke had engulfed the lanes limiting visibility. It was evident there would be no survivors in the president's car. The police in the following vehicles were unscathed but were unsure where the shots originated. They radioed for help and began a search for the assassin focusing on the overpass.

THE PRESIDENT IS DEAD

A large picture of Franklin Delano Roosevelt covered the front page of every paper. The words "President is Dead" in big bold letters appeared above the portrait. In smaller print below the headline appeared "Suspected murderer takes his own life after killing Roosevelt." The citizens of the United States had awakened to their worst nightmare, a gunman taking the life of their savior, along with the hopes and dreams of the nation. In one swift moment on a rainy night in Maryland, it was all gone. Roosevelt's sudden death at the hands of an assassin sent shockwaves throughout the country.

John Nance Garner, known by many as "Cactus Jack" was now the 33rd President of the United States. At the urging of Treasury Secretary William Woodin, Garner ordered the stock market and banks closed until Monday, July 10th in honor of the fallen president. In truth, they thought the fragile American psyche would be so spooked by Roosevelt's death that another market crash and run on the banks would occur.

An event like the crash of 1929 would reverse all the gains Roosevelt's administration had made to put the country and the economy back on track. Flags were ordered at half-staff, and while the preparations for Roosevelt's funeral had begun, the investigation into his assassination was already underway.

The new President ordered the Bureau of Investigation, the predecessor to the FBI, to take jurisdiction over the case. J. Edgar Hoover, in charge of the division, assigned his top field agents to look into what happened that night on Route 50 in Maryland. Quickly, they identified the dead man in the car as a Soviet national, Viktor Polechenko. Items found in the vehicle included a newspaper with an article about the president's arrival in Annapolis on the USS Indianapolis, along with a document that contained the names and contact numbers of six of Polechenko's fellow Soviet spies in the United States. The weapons used in the assassination and their containers were also recovered at the scene.

Meanwhile, in New York, the mysterious man boarded the flagship of the Nord German Lloyd line, the Bremen. Upon boarding, he checked in under the name "T. McCarthy." The attendant checked the manifest and immediately changed the tone in his voice.

"Mr. McCarthy, welcome aboard the Bremen. You are in the First Class Cabin, #1419. Your traveling companion, Miss Jennifer Davis has already checked in. The captain would like the two of you to be his guests at dinner tonight."

"Please inform the captain that my companion and I would be honored to join him." Said the mysterious man, whose identity was now known as Thomas William McCarthy.

When McCarthy entered his cabin, he found the young woman waiting. She held the paper with Roosevelt's picture on the front.

"Mac, this has your handiwork all over it." She said.

"Shut up. It had to be done this way. Would a bullet to his head have been a method that was more to your liking? He replied.

"Did you have to kill him in such a manner?"

"As a matter of fact, I did. In the end, it doesn't matter what measure of violence you use to kill someone. Murder is murder. Roosevelt was about to do more harm to the country than any spy or spies could ever do. In November, he was going to reinstate and normalize relations with the Soviet Union. That day would be the true start of the Cold War. After that date, Soviet spies would flood into the country stealing our military and industrial secrets for their benefit, and to use against us. Roosevelt may not have known it, but he was a traitor-in-chief to the country. He had to be stopped, and I had to stop the Soviets from gaining the knowledge to level the playing field with us, and with Germany. The Soviets would steal everything that wasn't nailed to the floor, including the atomic bomb secrets. Yes, it was brutal, but I had to be sure. Never underestimate the brutality and hatred that human beings have for each other or what they will do when it is necessary to act. You may not have liked my tactics, but I did the country and the world a favor. Framing the Soviets only serves to put the Nazi regime at the top of the desired European allies list. Especially, when Hitler sweetens the pot with an offer to help fight Soviet aggression by offering a mutual defense pact."

Back in Washington, J. Edgar Hoover reported to the President that the evidence was "clear, compelling, and overwhelming" that Polechenko killed Roosevelt, and was alone on the overpass that fateful night. Out of respect for the Roosevelt family, Garner told Hoover to withhold releasing any report to Congress or the public until after the funeral on Thursday.

On Wednesday morning, the remains of Franklin Roosevelt lie in repose in the East Room of the White House. President for just four months, grieving citizens waited outside the building but were not allowed inside to view the casket. It was 8 am on Thursday morning July 6th when former President Herbert Hoover accompanied by Eleanor Roosevelt paid his respects to her fallen husband. Large crowds had gathered along Pennsylvania Avenue, clinging to the cast iron fence along the front perimeter of the White House.

Mrs. Roosevelt, dressed in black with a veil covering her face, knelt before her husband's coffin with former President Hoover. After ten minutes, she left, but noticed her husband's long-time secretary Marguerite 'Missy' LeHand sitting in a chair against the wall in the hallway outside the East Room. She had been there the entire time Roosevelt was lying in repose. She walked over to Lehand, who was openly weeping, and said, "Perhaps you loved him more," then turned and left the White House. She would never return.

Immediately following her visit, Roosevelt's body was moved to the Capitol Rotunda. A horse drawn caisson would bring the slain president's casket in a procession down Pennsylvania Avenue. Roosevelt's remains would lie in state, as did the three assassinated presidents before him, Lincoln, Garfield, and McKinley.

After a just a few hours, enough to give members of Congress time to pass by the casket, a brief service was held. President John Nance Garner, Congressional leaders, along with members and friends of the family paid their last respects. The body was taken to Union Station where it was placed on a train bound for New York. A crowd of two hundred thousand people or more lined the streets of downtown Washington as the casket had made its way to the train station. The era of the New Deal had lived only as long as it architect. The next day, a political bombshell would be dropped on Washington.

At 10 am on Friday morning July 7th, Bureau of Investigations Director J. Edgar Hoover appeared before a joint committee of the House and Senate. He was there to brief the members on the preliminary findings of the investigation into Roosevelt's assassination. By any standards, the conclusion was quick, perhaps too quick. The nation was anxious for answers, and Hoover appeared to have them all.

He identified the assassin as Viktor Polechenko, a Soviet agent operating in the United States. Evidence found in Polechenko's possession included a list of six Soviet agents working in the United States. The list also included the names of nine American's with knowledge of military intelligence and industrial trade secrets. Those nine American were collaborating with the Soviets in an espionage ring to betray their country. The Soviet agents were arrested, and classified information was found in their possession.

The American spies' homes were raided, and top-secret documents were also found along with a significant amount of cash. Hoover told the committee "while tragic, the president's death uncovered an equally tragic breach of our national security."

Josiah W. Bailey, the senior senator from North Carolina, questioned if the assassin's motivation was known and why would he leave such incriminating information behind?
Hoover replied.

"We traced information we found on the body to an apartment in Baltimore. People we interviewed recalled the man in the apartment, Polechenko, as rude with no means of support, but also with no apparent need for money. In his apartment, we found a map tracing the President's trip from Campobello. The President's itinerary was likely leaked to him. We found anti-Nazi propaganda in the room. We surmised that he, or the Soviets, believed that Roosevelt was going to form an alliance with the Nazi regime against the Soviet Union. This barbaric act was seen as a means to stop that work."

Senator Bailey went on, "why didn't he escape, why did he kill himself"?

Hoover responded, "The car wasn't running. We found a loose wire under the hood of the car. By a twist of fate, he couldn't get away, and likely thought the officers from the car behind the president would quickly find him. Rather, then be taken alive, and face a hostile America, and a public trial that would end with an equally public execution, he took the easy way out."

The briefing lasted another hour. When it ended, all were satisfied that Polechenko was indeed the lone killer of Roosevelt. Others may have been involved in the conspiracy, but Polechenko alone pulled the trigger. Following the briefing, Hoover released the report to the press.

Anti-Soviet sentiment took on a new fervor. Four of the six Soviet spies were found guilty and executed over the objection, and threats, from Joseph Stalin, General Secretary of the Communist Party of the Soviet Union. Two other Soviets we sentenced to life in prison. The American spies fared equally as poor, with six of the nine found guilty and executed, and two sentenced to life in prison.

There would be no talk of a sinister conspiracy theory behind the murder of the President. The American people believed the Soviets were to blame. President Garner announced that negotiations were broken off regarding the normalizing of relations with the Soviet Union that Roosevelt had started.

In Britain, the failing health of Prime Minister Ramsay MacDonald created instability and inconsistency in the British reaction to what was transpiring in the United States, Germany, and the Soviet Union. MacDonald appeared at times to ramble nonsensical thoughts. Winston Churchill, an outspoken former First Lord of the Admiralty during World War I, and more recently the Chancellor of the Exchequer, sounded alarm bells about Hitler and German Rearmament. Across the Atlantic, there was no appetite from the American government to wage war in Europe and potentially destabilize the continent and leave it wide open for the Soviets to pounce. A strong Germany was seen as a definite deterrent to Soviet aggression in the region.

The drumbeat of war was being heard loud and clear across the English Channel and on to the streets of London. On the shores of America, the Cold War had already begun.

BIRTH OF THE HANGMAN

On Monday, July 10th, the steamer Bremen finished its transatlantic crossing from New York to Bremerhaven, Germany. It had taken just a little over five days for Roosevelt's true assassin to land on the shores of his new country. Arriving at port in midday, the skies were clear, the air brisk, but the minds of those disembarking were full of uncertainty. Emerging from cabin 1419 was the assassin, a man who boarded as Thomas McCarthy, was now in full Nazi military uniform. Accompanied by his beautiful American companion, McCarthy also had a new name and title, Brigadeführer Reinhard Heydrich, a Major General in the SS.

The look of fear was on the crew and the passengers as he made his way from the ship to the shore. A car was waiting to take him to the train station where he had an appointment in Berlin with the Chancellor of Germany, Adolf Hitler, and with the Reichsführer of the SS, Henrich Himmler.

Heydrich and his companion took a space in the more luxurious section of the rail car. She stared out the window while he was consumed with writing notes in preparation for his meeting with Hitler. The mood was quiet. Surrounding passengers tried to avoid direct eye contact with the couple, but couldn't help looking at the pretty American woman with a high-ranking Nazi officer.

It would take four hours for the train to arrive in Berlin. Upon arrival at the train station, Heydrich's companion made her way directly to their Berlin apartment while Reinhard Heydrich made his way to the Reich Chancellery.

There, he found an ecstatic Adolf Hitler.

"You have done what you said brilliantly! The Soviets are blamed for Roosevelt's death, and the communists here have been swept out of power and into prisons. The rest sent to their death thanks in part to framing them as the ones behind the Reichstag fire. It is all coming together. That cripple Roosevelt is dead, the Americans hate the Soviets, and that feeble-minded MacDonald in Britain doesn't know what day it is. Soon, that old fool Hindenburg will be taking his last breath, and mentally isn't much better off than MacDonald. When he dies, I will take unchallenged authority over Germany. I will take that Treaty of Versailles and personally shove it down the throats of those behind it. I will stand there and watch them choke on it as they beg for mercy. Germany will dominate in ways the world has never seen before."

Heydrich was cautious. "We must follow the plan I have laid out. Hindenburg will be dead in less than a year. You will have full control of the government. We must proceed methodically, and the pieces will come together. You must focus on building the machines of war, train and build strength in our military men, and do what I have outlined on progressing rockets and jet engines. You will be able to seize Austria and Czechoslovakia without resistance. Poland, we must wait. It will raise issues with the Brits, and to take Poland without starting a war now with the Soviets before we are fully militarized will mean splitting the spoils with them. Have patience Mein Führer. Don't worry, your conquest of Europe, and eventually, the Soviet Union will come to pass. Your destiny is written."

The ordinarily mystical Himmler was growing increasingly wary of the hold Heydrich had over Hitler.

"How do we know this so-called messenger from the future isn't just an American ploy or a trick? Said Himmler directly addressing Hitler.
Hitler replied.

"Roosevelt is dead by this man's hands. He knows what I think, what I plan, what I dream! He will help us crush our enemies and fulfill the prophecy of a thousand-year Reich!"

"What of your partner that you say came with you from the future Herr Heydrich? What knowledge does she have that would be of use to the Reich? Asked Himmler.
Heydrich responded.

"She can be of great use to you. I won't need her services any longer. In my time she was part of the spying arm of the American government, we called it the Central Intelligence Agency. I was a member of the same group. Her focus was to analyze the enemy's armaments and advanced technologies of war. She is brilliant and understands how to build weapons, and where to guide your resources. You already have brilliant people with the knowledge in their heads to build these weapons. She can identify them and get them to where you need them to be faster, and with improvements to their ideas. Put her in the weapons design, or factories, or war planning. I guarantee she will make a difference."

Himmler sensed the opening he was looking for, "Very well, I will take her under the arm of the SS and have her work to advance our weapons. I will take a personal interest in her to see what value she has to the Reich."

Heydrich, the American outsider from the future, was not about to get into a pissing match with Himmler.

"You will find her skilled in any number of positions," Heydrich said as he smiled.

"One more question for your Herr Heydrich. If you are from the future, why is there not more of your kind coming here?"
Heydrich responded.

"There will be at least two more like me that will arrive in early 1946. They will be expecting to find a Germany in ruins, but I will have a surprise for them."

"And how do you know this?" Asked Himmler.

"Because I trained them." Replied Heydrich.

EPILOGUE

It was on that day in the Reich Chancellery that the man who would come to be known as "The Hangman," and "The Butcher of Prague", and by many other sinister names was born. While America vacillated on who was the true threat in the world, it became an isolated country with John Nance Garner as President. A withdrawn and stationary America was precisely what Heydrich had planned and hoped would occur. As America mourned and focused inward, the pieces of Hitler's master plan to build an unstoppable and unprecedented German military power was now falling into place. Guided by Heydrich's hand, the small country of Germany was destined to become the world's preeminent military power.

Over the next few weeks Heydrich worked closely with Adolf Hitler to refine the vision and course Germany would take to conquer Europe, and eventually the Soviet Union. Heydrich knew the mistakes Hitler and the Third Reich made, but he also knew that he could not stray too far from their original playbook. He would need to temper their ambition, accelerate their technology, and keep them on a steady course.

"It will take just ten years to build this country into a world power," Heydrich told Hitler.

Hitler seemed slightly impatient and ready to demand faster progress. Before he could speak, Heydrich took an approach that would temper Hitler's aggressive goals. Showing the deference he knew Hitler craved.

"Mein Führer, what is a mere ten years in a thousand-year reign for the Third Reich?"

Hitler was beyond impressed with his gift from God in the form of the American that was Thomas "Mac" McCarthy, who now would become the infamous Reinhard Heydrich. Heydrich was also impressed with Hitler. He quickly fell under his spell, and like so many others became mesmerized and fooled by the allure of Hitler's personality. In his early stages of power, Hitler was driven, imposing, and was less erratic than the maniacal caricatures which he was often portrayed as in print. It was a question of who the puppet was and who was the puppet master. The answer would be Adolf Hitler. Reinhard Heydrich would become just another pawn that came under the spell of the monster that was Adolf Hitler.

Much to Himmler's chagrin, Hitler gave Heydrich a senior role in war planning and oversight of Reich security. It was an influential role that gave him the freedom to meddle and dictate the use of Germany's resources by invoking Hitler's direct authority. Heydrich's new role stepped on what Himmler thought was his responsibility, and he was not pleased. It would force Himmler to find other ways to satisfy the Führer's appetite for depravity. One such method was to ramp up his efforts on one of Hitler's pet projects, what Himmler called "the final solution." Himmler also knew that Hermann Göring would also not look kindly on this so-called "meddler from the future" telling him how to dominate the skies.

Empowered and emboldened by the trust placed in him by Hitler, Heydrich cared less about Himmler's "final solution" and its tactics. As long as Himmler provided the forced labor to build the Reich's new weapons facility at Peenemünde and Nordhausen, he would turn a blind eye to the means, and the human price that was paid. Heydrich found the taste of blood in his mouth far better than the feel of blood on his hands. Himmler and Hitler could handle the real dirty work, while he made sure the most critical aspects of the war plan were executed rather than the cultural purification agenda with which they seemed so obsessed.

Heydrich now had thirteen years to transform Germany into a world power. No one, no country, was going to stand in Germany's way. The only thing that could remotely interfere would be if the two visitors from the future did arrive in February of 1946. He wasn't sure they would show up and couldn't be sure that his arrival did not change their fate.

Perhaps, it was a new future where they would not be sent back in time, but he remembered a theory he had heard about just such a scenario. It seemed it might be possible that if you left after another time traveler, you could not impact their journey no matter how you changed the past and their future. It was complicated, but it was the belief that at the moment they left, they were somewhere between their present and the past, in a separate instance of time. In that nowhere land, they would be unaffected by any changes to the past, present, or future.

It was mind-boggling. All he knew was that technically they left before he did and maybe somehow, they might still be transiting in time towards a fateful rendezvous with him. Would they show up as planned? If they did, he would be waiting.

-- The End --

ABOUT THE AUTHOR

Mike is a native of Baltimore, Maryland and currently resides in his adopted hometown of Charlotte, North Carolina. Mike's professional career spans thirty years in the financial services industry.

While Mike has spent a career in banking, his true passion lies in reading the early works of science fiction pioneers, studying the golden era of space exploration, and analyzing the history and events of World War II. Killing Time The Story of Projekt Töten Zeit is his first novel. Mike has written several short stories that can be found on his Amazon Author Page.

amazon.com/author/oharaauthor

www.michaelpatrickohara.com

www.ingramcontent.com/pod-product-compliance
Lightning Source LLC
Chambersburg PA
CBHW030413180626
46812CB00005B/1994